STORM OF SECRETS

ALSO AVAILABLE BY LORETTA MARION

House of Ashes

The Fool's Truth

STORM OF SECRETS

A Haunted Bluffs Mystery

Loretta Marion

CROOKED
LANE

NEW YORK

Copyright © 2019 by Loretta Marion

Published in the United States by Crooked Lane Books, an imprint of The Quick Brown Fox & Company LLC.

Crooked Lane Books and its logo are trademarks of The Quick Brown Fox & Company LLC.

Library of Congress Catalog-in-Publication data available upon request.

ISBN (hardcover): 978-1-64385-175-4
ISBN (ebook): 978-1-64385-176-1

Cover design by Erin Seaward-Hiatt
Book design by Jennifer Canzone

Printed in the United States.

www.crookedlanebooks.com

Crooked Lane Books
34 West 27th St., 10th Floor
New York, NY 10001

First Edition: November 2019

10 9 8 7 6 5 4 3 2 1

You do not become an author until someone believes in you.
This book is dedicated to all those who believed.

Especially for Henrietta Haskett, who always believed in me.
I miss you every day, Mom.

There are some things you learn best in calm, and some in storm.
—Willa Cather

PROLOGUE

Cape Cod Bay

"The wind is with us today." The skipper took the red bandana from his neck to wipe his weathered face as a stiff breeze whipped up, though it did nothing to relieve the stickiness of the heavy August air. His love of sailing had cost him his youthful looks, but he thought it a fair trade. "We're making good time."

"I don't like the look of those clouds." His mate gulped from the water jug and jutted his chin toward the darkening westward sky.

The man at the helm frowned. Though the forecast hadn't called for rain, it wasn't unusual for a storm to pop up in the heat of the summer. Checking their position, he did a rough calculation of the distance to shore before calling out, "Reef the sails."

"Think we should turn back?" His friend jumped to action. "Or head for shore?"

Another glance toward the fast-approaching hostile clouds and the skipper knew they couldn't beat the storm to shore. Being unfamiliar with this stretch of coast and worried about the danger of getting caught in shallow channels, he made the decision to maneuver through.

"It'll be over quick enough. We can ride it out."

His friend frowned, looking unconvinced as fat raindrops began to pelt loudly against the deck.

"We've seen and handled worse." But whom was he trying to reassure? *Too late for regrets now.* He shook himself free of all thoughts that this might have been a bad idea, and called out, "Take a look below."

After rolling back the mainsail, his mate opened the hatch to the cabin to check on their precious cargo.

He gave the thumbs-up moments later as he hoisted himself back up on deck only to be knocked to his butt by a rolling wave.

"I need the storm jib and trysail," he shouted, to be heard over the wind and rain.

The skipper tossed the sails to his friend, who wrestled with the gusts to get them secured in place. Each wave seemed larger than the next, and the rain was now coming down so hard he could barely see the prow of the boat as he worked to position the rocking craft against the raging winds.

The men had been fighting the storm for longer than expected, and their muscles were aching from the effort. They'd need to rest soon.

"After this next wave we're going to heave-to," he yelled. "Be ready to trim the jib."

They were so focused on keeping the sailboat afloat, neither saw that the hatch had swung open from the rough seas. They also failed to notice the little boy, who'd slipped free of his life preserver, struggling up the steps from the cabin. Nor could his shrieking cries be heard over the storm's roar.

"Hold on!" The skipper shouted as they prepared to ride a large wave. Just then a movement on deck caught his eye. He cursed under his breath and waved a panicked arm at his friend as he screamed, "Grab him! Grab the boy!"

But it was too late.

1

Cassandra

Whale Rock Village, Massachusetts ~ Present day

"I might have known there'd be a natural disaster the weekend I chose to get married." I was starting to believe that the century-old curse against the Mitchell family was as strong as ever.

"Yeah, what's with the National Weather Service choosing "Chantal," when clearly "Tropical Storm Cassandra" would have been much more fitting?" Lu teased as she zipped up my wedding dress.

"I should have listened to Daniel," I grumbled, smoothing down the pearl-pink chiffon of the simple tea-length dress I'd chosen. "He wanted a fall wedding."

"It would have made more sense," Evelyn agreed.

Lu Ketchner and Evelyn Hilliard were two of my older sister Zoe's closest friends, both homegrown in Whale Rock. They'd come along with me for the final dress fitting, pointless as it now was.

"Sure, take his side," I pouted.

"Who's going to argue with Jon Hamm?" As a huge *Mad Men* fan, Evelyn had been the first to point out my fiancé's resemblance to the actor. She added, "This is, after all, the height of tourist season on the Cape."

I didn't need to be reminded of that, since I barely saw my husband-to-be these days. When we'd first met, Daniel Benjamin had been an FBI agent in Boston; but since moving to Whale Rock, he'd retired and invested his savings into becoming a partner of Mitchell Whale Watcher Boat Tours, the touring and whale-watching company started over a century ago by my great-grandfather, Percival "Percy" Mitchell. I'd spent my entire youth working for the family business, practically cutting my teeth by my father's side, though we'd eventually had to sell it when Papa's every moment became consumed with caring for my ill and frail mother. I was thrilled that someone associated with the Mitchell family was again involved in running the business that bore our name.

I held up my thick mane, using my free hand as a fan. "On days like today, I'm tempted to chop off this tangled mop."

"Cassie, you wouldn't dare!" Evelyn was aghast. My sister and her friends had always coveted the rich auburn locks I'd inherited from my great-grandmother, Percy's wife, Celeste. I'd only recently learned that bit of genetic trivia upon discovering long-lost portraits of my great-grandparents, which had been misplaced after being rescued from the terrible fire in which both had tragically died. My great-grandparents were the originators of the Mitchell family curse, and theirs had been a dramatic end—leading to much-repeated Whale Rock lore—with Percy having run from the burning home, holding the charred form of his dead wife, and leaping from the nearby cliffs, proclaiming, "I am not finished!"

Evidently, he still wasn't finished, for the otherworldly spirits of my ancestors continued to be an imposing presence . . . though one I kept mostly to myself. I'd successfully held on to our familial home of Battersea Bluffs, and I was solidly convinced that the two of them made themselves known there through scents and sounds within the bones of the grand old Victorian. For instance, the pleasant yet pervasive scent of burning sugar had been shadowing me closely during these past weeks leading up to the wedding, which I interpreted as a sign that they approved of my pending nuptials. I frowned to think of their reaction to the imminent postponement.

"I was trying to accommodate Brit's schedule," I told Evelyn and Lu in defense of my insistence on a summer wedding. Brit Winters, my best friend since the first day of nursery school, had been accepted into a professor exchange program in Italy. But after falling head over heels in love with the brilliant Nico, much to my dismay she'd ended up staying there.

"I'm sure you're both disappointed." Evelyn offered me one of her warm, lavender-scented hugs.

"As is Zoe," Lu said, to which I responded with a snort and a dubious eye roll. My sister had canceled her flight at the first hint of a possible postponement.

"It's true," Evelyn said, nodding in agreement. "She was looking forward to being here for you."

"Nice try, Evvie," I said, turning and taking in my reflection from every possible perspective. "There was a palpable wave of relief coming through the phone when I told her about the storm."

"That was just your very vivid imagination," Lu argued.

"Maybe someday one of you will finally tell me what it is about Whale Rock and The Bluffs that has kept Zoe away all these years." I'd long been trying to pry information from these two tight-lipped ladies about why my older sister left home—*fled* was probably a better term—twenty-five years earlier. But neither one was going to spill anything, at least not today, for in ambled the taciturn tailor, who proclaimed my dress a tad snug across the tummy. When I refused his offer to let out the seams to accommodate said tad, he shrugged and ambled back out.

"You'd better stay away from that secret stash of Twizzlers," Lu warned in good fun.

"Our Baby Cass will never need to worry," Evelyn said, using the nickname Zoe's pals had given me years ago. Even now, in my late thirties, it had remained their habit to treat me like a child.

"True," Lu agreed and then added, as if I wasn't still in the room, "she's always had one of those enviable metabolisms."

"Whereas mine seems to have put on the full-stop brakes in recent years." Evelyn patted her own soft belly and made a comical face.

"You just enjoy your own baking too much." Lu sent her long-time friend a fond wink.

I quickly changed back into my skort and T-shirt and collected my wedding dress, carefully wrapped in pillows of plastic. After tucking it into the backseat of my aged but beloved Miata, I met the ladies out in front of the tailor shop.

"How about lunch?" I said.

"It will have to be a quick one." Evelyn checked her phone for the time. "We've got to help guests make arrangements to leave, not to mention the gazillion cancellations." Evelyn and her husband, George, owned Hilliard House, one of the most popular inns in Whale Rock. With that popularity came the headaches of finding ways to placate people who were having their vacation ruined by an act of God.

"And I've got some guys coming to help move some pieces to the gallery loft." Lu owned the LK Gallery in town and was well respected in the art world, both local and international.

"Then let's do the diner," I suggested, since it was a quick walk from the tailor shop.

But not quick enough for Lu not to pounce. "I'm rather impatient to see what you've been working on."

"You're kidding, right?" How could she think I'd had time for painting when I was still adjusting to Daniel moving in and planning a wedding with the guy? Not to mention keeping up with the demands of my tenants in the carriage house I'd converted into a rental. During the past year, I'd welcomed a wonderfully eclectic group of artists and authors, who have made life interesting on Lavender Hill.

"As it concerns my business, I am always deadly serious." Lu had a keen eye and was constantly on the lookout for new pieces to add to her gallery's collection. Last year she'd stumbled on my stacks of unfinished canvases, proclaimed me a genius, and pushed me to finish enough for a first showing. "It's been ten months since your exhibit, which, I don't need to tell you, is an eternity in the art world."

"Whatever happened to the old adage *Anything worth having is worth waiting for*?"

6

"Make them wait too long and you'll be yesterday's news."

"I get it, Lu. I will be forever grateful for your confidence in me, and I appreciate the nudge." We'd arrived at the diner. "After the wedding, whenever it may eventually be, I promise to return to my studio."

"I will hold you to that promise."

The Whale Rock Diner was unusually quiet, probably because folks were prepping before the storm descended. It was only a couple days away from hitting, with all the models showing Cape Cod at the center of the swath of the predicted storm path.

"Won't it be a kicker if the storm bounces out to sea?" I pushed my Greek salad around with a fork, having little interest in actually eating it. "Then we would have canceled the wedding for nothing."

"It was the right thing to do." Evelyn reached across to pat my hand. "Besides, you're not canceling—just postponing."

I tried to tamp down my rising insecurities. After my divorce, I hadn't expected to find someone with whom to share my life again, especially a person I could trust not to bankrupt my finances or my self-esteem.

We spent the rest of our luncheon discussing all that we had to do in preparation for the pending tropical storm Chantal. When the three of us parted company, I made a quick stop in to see Archie Stanfield, owner of Coastal Vintage Wares. He'd called earlier in the week and insisted I come by the store before the wedding.

"Cassandra Mitchell! Finally," said the man behind the counter, in his typical tendency toward the dramatic. Archibald Stanfield was one of Whale Rock's more unique characters, and I was quite fond of him. He'd made a long-ago pact with my Granny Fi to return any Mitchell family belongings or artifacts that had walked away during the tragic fire. As a result, we'd been able to reclaim countless items of silver, crystal, and china. It had been a while since he'd gotten in touch, and I was eager to see what new treasure he'd discovered.

"No rush now since there isn't going to be a wedding this weekend."

He made a clucking sound with his tongue. "The price we coastal dwellers pay."

"True."

"But there will be a wedding eventually," he said confidently, opening a drawer beneath the counter. He took out a small velvet box and set it on the counter before me.

"What's this?"

"Your 'something borrowed.'" He nodded for me to open it.

I teased the lid off to find an exquisite pair of pearl and diamond earrings. "These are gorgeous, Archie."

"Try them on," he said, holding up a mirror for me.

"I couldn't possibly. They are too precious. You know me . . . I'm likely to lose one." I put the earrings back in the box and closed it.

"You won't. Besides, Peeps and I insist." Peeps was the former Miss Peeper, my former high school principal and Archie's wife. "They were her mother's, and all they do is sit in the jewelry box. It would make us happy if you wore them."

"Okay. But you keep them here for me until we have a new date."

"Let's hope it's soon," he said.

"I'm trying to find another date that works for Brit. Did you hear she's staying in Italy?"

"I did hear that." Of course he had. Whale Rock was your typical small town, where everyone knew everybody else's business.

"I really miss her." I pushed out my lip.

"A couple of peas in a pod, you two." His eyes twinkled. "You were my favorite non-buying customers."

"Please tell Miss Peeper—I mean Mrs. Stanfield—how moved I am by the earrings."

"You can probably start calling her Joannie now." He winked.

"Right." *As if.* "Well, I'd better head back to The Bluffs. Lots to do before Chantal arrives. Are you staying?"

"We've yet to evacuate for a storm, and I doubt we will this time. We're on high enough ground."

"By the way, I hope you don't mind that I parked out back." With the craziness of the season, in-town parking was a nightmare. Archie often walked to work, leaving the coveted space behind his shop available. I was one of the lucky few allowed to park there.

"It's yours whenever you need it. You can use the back door." He waved me out as the bell on the door tinkled, announcing a customer.

On the short walk to my car, a sparkle caught my eye on the ground near a temporary dumpster behind La Table, the new location of my old flame Billy Hughes's catering business.

Later, I reflected on how different things would have been had I not been so curious.

What if I hadn't had the dress fitting today? *What if* I hadn't parked in Archie's space? *What if* I hadn't gone out the back door of his shop? *What if* I hadn't gone over to examine what was glittering next to the dumpster?

"The *what ifs* and *should haves* will eat your brain." It was a quote of John O'Callaghan's, from his book of poetry entitled, *Sincerely, John the Ghost*—ironically, a gift from Zoe, who'd always eschewed the notion of Percy's and Celeste's spirits.

The point is, if I hadn't done all those things, then I wouldn't have seen that glint on the ground and gone over to check out what it was. Most crucially, I would never have noticed a hand through the rusted-out hole in the dumpster.

A very dead hand.

2

Cassandra

Five minutes later, Whale Rock Police Chief Brooks Kincaid's cruiser pulled up next to my Miata.

"What's this all about?" he asked, whisking sandy-colored hair off his forehead in a lifelong habit.

"I don't know, Chuckles."

He responded with a stern look from my use of the nickname he so despised. It sprang from his famous belly laugh, for which he'd been mercilessly tormented as a child. These days, few dared to call the imposing man anything other than *Chief* or *sir*, but considering our long history, I was usually granted a pass when it slipped out.

"Sorry," I mumbled, then pointed to the hole in the dumpster. "You tell me."

He hiked up his khakis and crouched down for a closer look.

"What the . . . ?" He stood and whipped out his phone. "I need a forensics team ASAP."

After providing the pertinent details, he ended the call and then began taking photos of the scene.

"You don't need to stick around," he told me as he unwound yellow crime scene tape.

Just then, Billy Hughes popped his head out to see what was going on. He sent me a quizzical look, but it was Brooks who asked him, "How long has this dumpster been here?"

"About a week."

"Can you get an exact date and time for me?"

"Sure. What's up?"

"Find out that information, and then we'll have a chat."

I could tell Billy was taken aback, but he disappeared into his shop.

"Do you think the ring's a clue?" I asked Brooks, who had slipped on a pair of gloves and was scooping it from the crushed shells of the alleyway into an evidence bag.

"Maybe. Maybe not." He squinted up at me. "You didn't touch it, did you?"

I took an involuntary step backward. "I know better than to mess with evidence." Though had I not seen the hand first, there's no question I would have picked up the shiny item that had caught my eye.

Billy came out of his shop again. "I just spoke with the dumpster company and their records show a seven thirty delivery last Thursday morning."

Brooks made a note of it in his small, worn notebook, then turned to me and said, "I'm sure you have better things to do."

I did. However, staying here to find out who was in the dumpster was much more interesting.

"Not really," I said as the county forensics van pulled up the alley, blocking me in.

Brooks spent several minutes talking with a woman who, I presumed, was the head forensics investigator, while two men unloaded equipment and biohazard bags and donned protective gowns, goggles, and gloves.

Billy and I silently looked on until Brooks remembered we were there. He returned to where we were standing, pointed directly at me, and said, "Go run an errand. I want you out of their hair."

"Fine." I raised my hands in surrender.

Brooks then patted Billy on the back and guided him into the shop, saying, "Let's you and me have a little talk."

I leaned against the Miata, watching as old cabinets were lifted from the dumpster and contemplating where I could idle for an hour or so while the team did their work. I stalled as long as I dared, knowing Brooks would be livid if he found me still loitering at the scene when he came back out. My only exit, aside from going back through Archie's store, was to walk around the crime scene, and there was just enough space for me to squeeze by the other side of the van. As I rounded the back of the vehicle, a bulky rolled-up rug, from which the dead hand appeared, was being lifted out of the dumpster. I held my breath, hoping Brooks wouldn't come out before I got a look at who was attached to that hand.

"Come on," I whispered as the rug was slowly unrolled.

Finally, one of the techs said, "Male."

I stood on tiptoe, which bought me a glimpse of an unfamiliar face under a shock of platinum hair. *Thank God it's not anyone I know.*

"He hasn't been here long." This from the woman, who turned to the other tech and said, "Go get Chief Kincaid."

As badly as I wanted to stay, that was my cue to leave. I scooted out of the alley seconds before another cruiser pulled in. It was Officer Bland, Brooks's aptly named second in command, but he seemed focused on the task ahead and hopefully hadn't noticed me.

To kill time, I headed toward the harbor to see if Daniel was around. I found him and Johnny Hotchkiss in the office with their heads bent over the desk.

"Hey Cassie Lassie," Johnny said as I poked my head in, using the nickname he'd given me as a kid. In the years since my father had sold the business to him, Johnny had grown it to where a partner was needed, and fortunately the timing had been perfect for Daniel to step in.

"What's up?" Daniel asked.

I was dying to tell him about the body, but knowing what a chinwagger Johnny could be, decided to wait until Daniel came home later.

"I was in town for my final dress fitting and thought I'd stop by to say hello."

"Sorry you two had to postpone the wedding. Bad timing, this storm," Johnny said, giving a sad shake to his head. "We were just finalizing the schedule for getting the remaining boats moved or tied down."

Others in the harbor were doing the same. I spotted Robyn Landers docking her sailboat, presumably with plans to have it dry-docked during the storm. Robyn wasn't a Whale Rock native, but over a decade ago she and her now ex-husband had purchased a beach cottage here, which they'd named Land's End. I didn't know Robyn well, but we'd bonded a little over being divorcees, and I knew she'd gotten both the sailboat and Land's End as part of her settlement. During summer months she lived on the boat and rented out the cottage for some extra income.

A familiar-looking man I couldn't quite place was helping her at the end of the dock. "Who's that?"

Daniel followed my gaze. "A new hire."

"You remember Wes Creed?" Johnny asked.

I nodded. "Thought he moved to Florida."

"He's back." Johnny made a face. "Things didn't work out so well for him down there."

Wes Creed had been a few years ahead of me in school and was good friends with Johnny's youngest brother, which was probably how he got the job. Wes wasn't exactly a ne'er-do-well, but he'd been kind of aimless, moving from job to job, until an opportunity came up for him down South. Though his skin had leathered a bit from the Florida sun, Wes hadn't lost his looks or any of his thick, wavy hair. More sexy than handsome, and in good shape for a guy who'd passed forty, though I could see the slight beginnings of a beer gut forming.

"Like what you see?" Daniel had caught me staring.

"Who, Wes?" An incredulous little snort escaped. "As I recall, he was always trouble with the ladies."

"A regular 'love 'em and leave 'em' kind of guy," Johnny agreed. "Hopefully he's settled down by now."

"I'll let you two get back to your schedule." I planted a kiss on Daniel's worry-wrinkled forehead, then waved at Johnny. "See ya."

I still wanted to kill some time, so decided to make a quick stop in to All the Basics to pick up something for dinner.

"Not much left," Stella Kruk lamented as I took in the stark shelves, a contrast to the usually crammed-full shop. She was one of the greedier business owners in town, notorious for both her scandalous price gouging and mean-spirited gossip. Still, as the only market walkable from all the beach houses, she did a good business.

"Are you going to close up?" I asked while gazing into the freezer.

"Can't see the point in staying open when all the customers will be leaving. Plus, deliveries are going to be delayed." Stella sighed. "My daughter wants me to come stay with her until the storm passes."

"Good plan," I said, setting a frozen pizza on the counter along with a bag of arugula and a package of gorgonzola crumbles.

"What in heavens name do you hope to make with this?" Stella frowned as she bagged the items.

"Salad pizza." I grinned at her. "It's my specialty."

Thank goodness Daniel enjoyed cooking. But during the busy season, I tried to pull my weight in the kitchen, if salad pizza could be called cooking.

Stella rang me up, and thirty dollars later for three measly items, I headed back to my Miata. The forensics van was gone, and so were the two police cruisers, but the yellow crime scene tape remained as a gruesome reminder.

3

Cassandra

"Have you talked to Brooks at all?" I asked Daniel the next morning while sharing a quick breakfast over the kitchen sink. I'd told him about my discovery of the body when he got home yesterday, but with the storm now less than thirty-six hours from hitting, his attention was on other matters.

"Briefly." He shoved down the last of his toast and brushed the crumbs from his fingers.

"Any leads?"

"Apparently not. I think the case is temporarily on hold. The force has their hands full with enforcing the mandatory evacuation areas." He took a gulp of coffee. "We mainly discussed the tall ship's plans for moving out."

The Whale Rock Chamber of Commerce had finally succeeded in enticing a tall ship company to bring one of its old-fashioned schooners to town for a week of day and sunset cruising and on-board tours. Unfortunately, the *Lady Spirit*'s visit would be cut short because of the storm.

"I'm surprised they haven't already left," I said, yawning.

"The captain stopped by yesterday. Models for the storm's path after it hits the Cape are all over the place, so it's been hard for them to nail down a route."

"They'd better leave soon."

"They have to go today," he agreed, then finished his coffee and rinsed out the cup. "What's on your schedule?"

"Getting everything set up for our temporary lodgers."

"Good thing we have the carriage house and that you installed a generator and added a bathroom out in the barn," Daniel said. "We ought to be able to easily accommodate another six to eight people."

"Thank goodness *'It's no ordinary barn.'*" I quoted my Granny Fi as Daniel smiled. The first barn on the property had been lost to the hurricane of 1924, which had devastated Cape Cod and killed my great-grandmother's beloved rabbits and goats when the outbuilding collapsed. After that, Percy had insisted the new barn be built to survive a hurricane. And it had since survived many. Now it served as my studio, and I'd been slowly making it a more comfortable space—all part of a plan for recruiting artists to rent the carriage house and share the studio with me. The idea had come from Zoe and Lu, back when I'd almost lost The Bluffs to mounting debt, and it had become a wonderful financial asset.

"I'm sure the Parsons crew will be quite comfortable out there." Pete Parsons was the Harbor Master, and he and his wife, Emma, lived just blocks from the harbor in a low-lying area. They were the first people Daniel had invited, and they'd be bringing along some relatives who were visiting.

"I'll put the Princes in the guest suite upstairs." Daniel and I were close friends with the young couple; Jason was the newest deputy on the police force, and Laura was writing for the *Cape Cod Times*. I'd invited them to stay with us, since the beach house they were renting was also precariously low-lying.

"Edgar and Jimmy will be in the carriage house?" Daniel asked.

"Mm-hmm. I was hoping they'd come tonight, but they still have work to do closing up their place, so I don't expect them until tomorrow."

Edgar Faust and Jimmy Collins were other dear friends. When I'd learned that their Chatham home was in a mandatory evacuation area, I'd immediately reached out to invite them to stay with us. They would have been over this weekend anyhow for the wedding. In fact, we had asked Jimmy to officiate the vows.

"We could make room for more if necessary, but I'm hoping this storm will be kind to Whale Rock."

"You'll be here most of the day then?"

"Except for picking up food from Feast."

He sent me a quizzical look.

"Our wedding caterer," I reminded him. "Since we have to pay for what was already in the works, I decided to bring it out here to feed the evacuees. Someone might as well enjoy it."

"Damn storm." Daniel pulled me into a hug and kissed the top of my head. "It will work out. You'll see."

"I know," I said into his polo shirt, surreptitiously brushing away annoying tears. I wanted to agree, but as the room filled with an acrid burning scent, it was clear to me that Percy and Celeste were displeased by this turn of events.

It was difficult to ignore their negative view of the postponement of our planned nuptials. Maybe our union *was* cursed. *God how I hated that word!*

"Do you need me to come down to the harbor to help?"

"No, I think we've got it covered." He pushed me back to study me closely. "You're good?"

"Perfect."

"It will be a late night."

"Off with you then." I offered my most genuine fake smile and he was out the door.

Not ten minutes later, as I was loading up a basket with sheets and blankets, a call came in from Laura Prince.

"Cause of death was blunt force trauma," she blurted out.

"Wow, you're good," I told her as I hoisted the basket of linens onto my hip and headed toward the barn. Knowing I was unlikely to get anything out of Brooks about the suspicious death, I'd put Laura's bloodhound nose on the scent.

"I've cultivated some great sources," she said, not in a bragging way.

"Is there an ID yet?" I asked.

"Lee Chambers. Does the name mean anything to you?"

It didn't.

"My sources tell me that he was a small-time drug dealer and general thug who only started hanging around Whale Rock because of the party house."

I knew what she was referring to. This was the second year that a large group of frat boys had rented out Sea Breeze cottage on the beach, and the community was not pleased by the loud party atmosphere and unsavory elements they'd attracted to our family-friendly town.

"Do any of *your sources* know what might have caused that blunt force trauma? Was it a rock? A hammer?" I ventured.

"Too early to know."

"Keep me posted?" I said.

"Sure thing. But this stays between us."

"Always." I set the basket on the floor and surveyed the area where the mattresses had been set up. "Are you and Jason coming out tonight?"

"Doubtful. They've got Jason on evacuation duty, so you probably won't see us until tomorrow morning. And it might just be me."

"Such is the life of a rookie cop."

"And a rookie cop's wife." The sigh echoed through the phone.

While I made up the temporary beds, I couldn't stop thinking about Lee Chambers. It felt personal, since I'd been the one to discover his body. I didn't think I'd ever get the image of that dead hand out of my head.

4

Cassandra

The storm was fast descending on Whale Rock, and the harbor area was a chaotic scene, with volunteers scurrying about to secure boats and evacuate the last remaining stubborn beach dwellers.

Lu and I bent our bodies into the wind, heading toward the last cottages on the southern end of the beach, where we'd been sent to ensure everyone had evacuated.

"Isn't that your friends' dog?" Lu pointed up the beach. Sure enough, the Princes' gorgeous black German shepherd was prancing around where Laura and Jason's bungalow flanked Land's End cottage, the last house on this end of the beach. As we drew near, the Princes emerged from Land's End with another man and a pit bull, neither of whom I recognized.

"Hey guys," I called out to them, but only Whistler heard me over the roar of the wind. He ran to greet us, nuzzling my pocket for the dog biscuits I always carried with me these days. I lovingly patted his sleek, black coat before offering the treat and murmuring into his ear, "What a good boy."

Lu had walked ahead to greet the trio, leaving Whistler and me to straggle behind.

"Why are you all still here?" I shouted, approaching the group, who were now securing a sailboat and tying up the rigging.

"We're helping our neighbor." Jason made the introductions, keeping his voice loud to be heard above the crashing surf. "Lu Ketchner, Cassie Mitchell, this is Christopher Savage."

I reached my hand out, which Christopher shook with his left, raising his bandaged right. "The owner's kitchen knives are sharper than I'm used to."

"So, you're the lucky guy Robyn Landers found to rent Land's End." Robyn had lost her usual summer renter. "Openings are rare, especially right on the beach."

"In that case, I guess I am lucky." He was a pleasant-looking man with a deep tan and sun-kissed highlights to his hair, which was thick with the summer grease of salt and surf.

"You've got some good neighbors in Laura and Jason too."

"It's a good thing I saw him out here this morning," Jason added. "He was just bringing in Robyn's dayboat."

"You were out in this?" I sent him an incredulous look. "You must be some sailor."

"I hadn't been out long when I realized it was getting worse and turned back."

"He didn't know about the storm," Laura explained for him as she tied off the last of the rigging.

"I've been totally unplugged. No TV since I arrived." Christopher shook his head sheepishly. "But the winds were perfect."

Lu gazed over toward the sea cliffs of the dunes. "You *are* rather secluded out here. It's a good thing you turned back, or nobody would have even known to look for you."

Christopher's face darkened. "You've got that right. I've been caught in a few storms in my day and try not to relive the experience."

Jason grabbed two life preservers and tried a door at the back of the cottage.

"That's always locked," the newcomer yelled to him. "Just throw them into the outside shower stall."

"I hope you're packed up and ready to leave," I called out to Laura.

She came closer to be heard. "I've left three messages on your cell phone. Christopher hadn't made any plans to evacuate, so we've invited him to stay at The Bluffs. I hope that's okay?"

"Of course." I turned to Christopher, who said, "I hope you have room for another stray"—he then pointed to the dog, who was crouching between his legs—"or two. This is Gypsy. She's a bit timid. And not too keen about storms herself."

"You and Gypsy are welcome to join us." I looked around. "Where's your car?"

"I'm without wheels." He shrugged.

"He's hitching a ride with us," Jason said. "Our car's up at the harbor because they've blocked off the road. We came down to help Christopher with his things."

"Well, let's get a move on." I grabbed a pack and slung it over my shoulder. "This storm will be bearing down soon enough."

The five of us humans, plus the two canine companions, silently trudged our way back up the beach, working against the whipping winds. Even shouts could not be heard above the pounding surf.

We loaded Gypsy, Christopher, and his things into the Princes' car. It was decided that Laura would take them out to The Bluffs and get settled in while Jason went to help with evacuations. I volunteered to take Whistler, as the two dogs were wary of each other, and it didn't seem like a good idea to coop them up in the same car.

We all said our goodbyes, and they headed out. As Lu and I got Whistler settled into Daniel's Land Rover, Evelyn Hilliard ascended the public access steps from the beach, holding the hand of a young tow-headed boy who looked to be about six.

"This is Nicholas," she told us, to which the boy nodded shyly.

"You came into the gallery with your family a couple days ago, didn't you?" Lu chatted with the boy for a moment while Evelyn took me aside.

"Mom was beside herself because she couldn't find little Nicholas. She has her hands full with four little ones."

"That's a large brood to manage alone," I sympathized.

"George and I were rounding up stragglers, and we stopped by to check on them. They've been renting The Lookout." She pointed her thumb in the direction of one of the most coveted rentals in town, with its beautiful large roof deck and private steps down to the beach. "George helped her get the others to the inn while I went looking for this one. He was just standing at the edge of the water, staring out at the sea as if he was hypnotized." She glanced over at him. "It was a little spooky."

As Evelyn was telling me this, a metallic blue Porsche SUV pulled to a stop beside us, and out hopped an attractive, well-dressed man who looked vaguely familiar.

"Daddy!" Nicholas called out to his father.

"Hey, Bud." The tall, slim man lifted the boy up for a hug, then set him down again, looking around, confused. "Where's Mommy?"

"I've got her and the other boys up at the inn," Evelyn answered, then offered a quick introduction. "Lu, Cassie, this is Nicholas's father, Matthew Kleister."

The man nodded as he took off his glasses to wipe away the mist, but he was clearly more interested in gathering his family. "I'll drive up and get them out of your hair."

"The inn will be a more comfortable place for you to wait out the storm. We've got a generator and lots of food, water, and blankets. Even some games and toys." Evelyn smiled sweetly down at the child.

"Daddy." The little boy tugged at his father's shirt.

"Just a minute, buddy." Then to Evelyn, "I think we'd be fine staying where the boys are used to being. I just made it down from Boston without a problem."

"This storm may be upgraded to a hurricane, and Hilliard House has withstood many of those," I assured him.

"Your rental is much more exposed. I'd be afraid that deck might tear loose and take the roof with it," Evelyn warned. "I think you'll be safer with us."

A Whale Rock police cruiser pulled up, and Brooks hopped out, waving his hands at us as if herding a group of goats. "Let's get a move on, everybody."

"Okay," Matthew reluctantly agreed, before remembering his manners. "Thanks for your hospitality. Let's go, Nicholas."

"But Daddy," the child pleaded, "I've gotta tell you something."

"Later. Get in the car."

Nicholas cast a frightened look down to the beach.

"Don't worry, Bud. We'll be okay. Let's go be with Mommy, Lucas, and the twins."

"No, Daddy." It was barely a whisper.

Matthew squatted down beside his son and kindly but firmly said, "Nicholas, we are going right now. Understand?"

"Yes," Nicholas said, but I didn't think Matthew could see the one lone tear trailing down his son's cheek as he lifted him into the booster on the backseat of the vehicle.

"I've just got to collect my laptop and some paperwork from the house, and I'll be right up," Matthew told Evelyn.

But it was Brooks who answered. "Five minutes." He then turned to Lu and me and said, "It's really getting bad. Let's get you both home."

"I'll go try to drag my fiancé away from his precious boats."

"I'm out of here." Lu gave me a quick hug and then hopped into the cruiser with Brooks.

As I made my way down to the docks, from a distance I could see a woman gesturing wildly as Daniel was adding extra tie-down lines to one of the Mitchell touring boats, waving a piece of paper in front of him, but he just shook his head. I caught a glimpse of her frustrated face as she slipped into the harbor office but didn't recognize her. *Maybe one of the tourist boat owners?*

"Here, let me help," I yelled down to Daniel, and he handed me the end of the rope, which I secured to the cleat with a bowknot. "What was that all about?"

"What?" He was distracted by his efforts.

"That woman you were just talking with?" We were shouting to be heard over the waves crashing against the docks.

He glanced toward town, but the woman had disappeared. "She's looking for someone. Nobody I recognized." The wind gusts were making it hard for him to grasp the lines.

"We really should go now," I insisted.

"I'd've been done long ago if that damn Wes Creed had shown up to help. And yesterday, he skipped out early."

Perhaps Wes hadn't turned his life around as Johnny had hoped.

"Left two messages, the latter less kind than the first." He pulled a tarp up over the boat and began to tie it down. Finding good help had been Daniel's biggest challenge. He had no patience for the human resources aspect of his new role as business owner.

"Wishing you were back at the Bureau?"

He looked up and said, "Never. I'm exactly where I want to be. Just not in the midst of a hurricane."

"Hurricane Cassandra is what Lu is calling it."

"It appears Mother Nature wasn't too keen on our getting hitched."

It was a cavalier remark, but it left me briefly wondering if there was something more behind it. Like me, Daniel had been married before; was he reluctant to try again? The vibration of a heavy tread on the already swaying dock pushed aside that momentary flash of insecurity. I looked behind me to see Brooks purposefully striding toward us.

I raised my hands and called out. "We're leaving now."

Daniel finished tying off the tarp and stood, wiping his face with his sleeve. The wetness was no longer only due to sweat from the August heat and humidity. The storm clouds had begun to release large drops of rain.

Brooks beckoned impatiently and yelled, "The tides are rising, and with this surf the road out to The Bluffs will soon be impassable."

"We're outta here," Daniel said as we walked at a brisk pace in the direction of his car.

"Actually, Cassie needs to go," Brooks took hold of Daniel's arm, "but I could really use your help. We have an emergency."

"What kind of emergency?" I asked.

"A missing child emergency."

5

Renée

New York City ~ Mid-1980s

Renée had feared the day would come when she'd have to face her demons, but she wasn't prepared to see her younger sister's face looking back at her through the peephole of the apartment door. Isabella hadn't changed much in the fifteen years since they'd last seen one another; still petite with honey-gold skin and bright jade-green eyes. Renée could pretend she wasn't home, but how to be certain Isabella would give up and go away? No, best to let her in while Michael was at work.

"*Sorella mia.*" Isabella fell into her arms as soon as she opened the door.

Renée was surprised by the surge of emotion. How she'd missed her little sister. They clung to each other for several moments until the neighbor across the hall came out of his door.

"Good morning, Renée." The older gentleman seemed to wait for an introduction, but Renée merely bid him a pleasant day and ushered Isabella into her living room, closing the door swiftly behind them.

"You live very well, Renata." Her sister walked about the space, admiring the décor as she wiped away the remaining vestige of tears, her voice still clinging to the slightest hint of the accent they'd all brought with them from Italy.

"It's Renée now." It had been Renée since she'd fled her old life all those many years ago.

"And I'm Sister Bernadetta."

Renée looked at her sister in surprise. "But you're dressed normally."

"We are a progressive order," Isabella said.

"Is that what I should call you now? Sister Bernadetta?" Renée asked, still processing this news while trying to push aside feelings of guilt for having abandoned her younger sister.

"Whatever makes you most comfortable."

"I'll make us some coffee . . . Sister." If she was asking her sister to respect her own self-imposed alias, then shouldn't Renée in turn respect Isabella's calling?

"Such a lovely view." The woman, a stranger and yet not, gazed out the window to the tree-filled courtyard below while they waited for the coffee to brew. "I've come about Vito."

Renée's hands were shaking so badly she dropped one of the cups she was taking down from the cupboard.

Her sister rushed over and gently took hold of those trembling hands. "I didn't mean to upset you. But our brother is very sick."

"I'm sorry to hear that." This was true. Renée would never wish Vito ill.

"He wants to see you, to ask your forgiveness and put his troubled mind to rest."

Renée broke free of her sister's grasp. "Then please tell him I forgive him."

Isabella shook her head. "He needs to hear it from you. And you need to do it for yourself."

"How do you know what I need?" Renée snapped. She would not allow her heart to be torn open again.

"I've been praying. God will help you."

"Tell me, *sorella*, where was God fifteen years ago?"

"It is not for us to know." Her sister's face was so serene and beautiful, like the nuns portrayed in movies, but with the soul of a wise old woman. Renée envied her sister that confidence. Isabella opened her black pocketbook, which had the look of a thrift store bargain. "I'm going to Italy to see him in three days. Here is a ticket for you."

"Italy?" Renée stared at the ticket. "He went back?"

"Yes, after . . . everything that happened, he couldn't bear to stay here." Isabella lifted and released her shoulders in dramatic defeat. "But he has done quite well for himself back home. He bought us these tickets." Her sister took out a slip of paper with the name and address of a nearby convent. "This is where you can find me until I leave on Friday."

The two long-estranged sisters walked numbly toward the apartment door, where the younger took the older into her arms again. "I pray you will go with me, Renata."

Renée leaned against the door for a time afterward, wondering how she could manage a trip to Italy without telling Michael the truth.

* * *

Boston ~ Early 1960s

Vito, Renata, and Isabella huddled together, tired, hungry, and scared in the baggage claim area of Boston airport as they waited for their aunt and uncle to collect them. Vito did his best to keep them smiling with his jokes.

"How will we know Zia Rosa and Zio Enzo?" Isabella, the youngest, asked.

"I will show you." Vito, the oldest at seventeen, was very protective of his younger sisters. He flipped over his ticket and with the nub of a pencil drew caricatures, joking that, "We will recognize Zia Rosa by her crossed eyes and mustache. And Zio Enzo has a big crooked nose and very bushy eyebrows that waggle when he laughs."

However, they would soon learn that their Zio Enzo seldom laughed and was not at all pleased about the arrival of his new responsibilities.

"*Ha le bracce corte.*" It was an insult about their uncle's cheapness, meaning his arms were too short to reach his wallet.

"In English," Renata, the serious middle child, scolded as Isabella giggled. Renata had tried to insist they speak only English so they would learn their new language before arriving to this foreign country. She'd been tutoring them for weeks after they finally heard from their mother's sister in America. The three children had been orphaned when their parents both died in a train crash. Although Zia Rosa took on a second job to raise the money to bring her sister's children to Boston, it had still taken over a year for her to scrape up enough to pay for their travel fares, during which time the siblings had been separated among neighbor families trying to keep them from being taken into the orphanage system.

They'd been told there would be wonderful opportunities in America. Better schools especially. But only Isabella would benefit from an American education. They were barely in their aunt and uncle's home before Zio Enzo found situations for the three *parassiti* (parasites), as he frequently referred to them. *"Don't we have enough of a struggle with four children of our own?"* he spouted often enough.

Their aunt's husband was basically a lazy man, but when it came to farming-out his new wards, he became quite industrious. Zio Enzo was toughest on Vito, not appreciating having a handsome, light-hearted young man around. He was constantly berating the boy and even took to slapping him around. Vito wasn't one to take abuse and left of his own accord after finding a job with a fishing crew in South Boston. Isabella, the youngest at thirteen, had always been drawn to the church, and with strong Catholic connections, Enzo was able to find her a place in a convent. In exchange for working in the kitchen, scrubbing pots and pans, she was given food and shelter and was also permitted to attend classes at the adjacent parochial school.

For Renata, he found a live-in nanny position with the Welles family through connections with his brother, who was the gardener for another wealthy Boston family.

"But uncle, I can speak well in English. May I please go to school?" Renata begged.

"You're almost sixteen. You have no need for study." He hadn't even allowed his own daughter to finish high school. But this offered no consolation to Renata, who had a great love for books. She immediately sought out the local library and applied for her first American library card. If she had to, she would teach herself. However, her love of learning would also lead to a world of problems.

*   *   *

New York City ~ Mid-1980s

Renée wasn't certain how long she stood there, lost in her memories, before hearing the elevator ding. She rushed to her bedside table and stuffed the tickets Isabella had left her under some books. Luckily, she had a glimpse of her reflection in the bureau mirror and quickly fixed the tear tracks before the door opened to the happy sounds of her husband and son.

"Mamma! Look at my prize."

The little boy leaped into her arms, melting her heart as no other could. It wasn't until she was holding on tightly to her sweet young son that she could breathe easily, for only then could she be assured he was safe.

6

Cassandra

Whale Rock Village ~ Present day

"Oh my God! Who's missing?" I said at the same time that Daniel, his FBI background taking over, asked, "When was the child last observed?"

"It's the little Kleister boy," Brooks answered me first.

"But Evelyn found Nicholas," I said in confusion. "You were there, Brooks. Did he wander off again?"

"It's not Nicholas. It's the younger brother, Lucas." To Daniel, he said, "There's some confusion about that. George Hilliard was evacuating the mother and children to the inn while Evelyn went off searching for the older boy, Nicholas. But either George didn't realize there ought to have been four children in total, or he thought one was with the father. Either way, he said the mother was disoriented, and it was all he could do to get her and the little ones up to the inn. It wasn't until the father arrived with Nicholas that they realized Lucas was missing."

"How old is Lucas?"

"Three." Brooks looked grim.

"How could they lose track of a three-year-old?" I was aghast.

"Mrs. Kleister thought Lucas was with Nicholas," Brooks said. "Apparently he often looks after his little brother."

"But Nicholas can't be more than five or six." Too young to be unsupervised, let alone in charge of siblings.

Brooks and Daniel began to strategize but refused to let me go check along the beach.

"Absolutely not." Brooks and Daniel refused in harmony.

"Nicholas seemed to be disturbed by something down there." I pointed to where the boy had been looking. "He was trying to tell his father about it."

"Okay. We'll cover the beach first," Daniel assured me, wiping the rain from his face.

"You'll need more than just the two of you," I protested.

"A search team is being organized. People who are *trained* for this," Brooks emphasized. "It's dangerous out there."

I looked to Daniel for support, but he remained firm. It was obvious there'd be no budging by either man, so I got into the driver's side of Daniel's Land Rover, where Whistler was waiting in the passenger seat. Officer Bland pulled up in a Whale Rock police department cruiser, and Jason hopped out.

"See? Reinforcements are already arriving," Brooks said.

"If you leave now, you'll make it," Jason called out against the wind, pulling the hood of his rain slicker tighter. "But I wouldn't wait another minute."

Daniel leaned his arms on the window opening to block the incoming rain. "Look, your heart is in the right place, but I don't want to be worrying about you."

"But we should be together." I pouted. "Instead, *I'll* be worrying about *you*."

"You know I can take care of myself." Daniel reached in and gently took my chin to turn my face toward his.

"Fine." I turned my head away, not wanting him to see the tears forming, and started the car.

"That's my girl." He leaned in and kissed the side of my head. "Text me when you get home."

The drive back to The Bluffs was a fierce battle to keep the vehicle on the road due to the rising winds and increasing rain. I was grateful I'd taken Daniel's tank of an SUV. There was no way I would have made it through some of the flooded stretches of road in my old

Miata. *How on earth could a child survive out in this?* I shivered with dread while praying Lucas would be found somewhere safe.

It was a relief when The Bluffs came into view as I rounded the bend of the drive. I shook off the rain from my slicker on the porch and hung it in the mudroom before entering the kitchen to find that Laura had taken charge.

"Everyone's settled in," she reported, filling water jugs in case the pump generator failed. "I put Christopher and his dog in the carriage house with Edgar and Jimmy. Since Gypsy's skittish, I thought it best to keep her away from the Parsons crew with those three rambunctious kiddos."

"Good thinking," I said. "Edgar and Jimmy will be good company for Christopher and Gypsy. They love dogs."

"Especially Whistler." Laura smiled down indulgently at the shepherd even as he soaked her with the spray of rainwater he shook off.

"Who doesn't love Whistler?" The dog began wagging and nudged my hand. "Yep. We're talking about you, smart boy." I snuck him a treat from my pocket.

"You're spoiling him," Laura scolded good-naturedly. "Where's Daniel?"

I filled her in about the search for Lucas Kleister, the missing boy.

"Oh my God!" Laura was horrified. "That poor family."

"Did you have a chance to get to know them?"

She shook her head. "Only a little bit. I'd occasionally see the mom around town with that massive double stroller for the twins, but I was more likely to find Nicholas and Lucas playing together on the beach."

"The Kleister children seem to have been pretty free-range," I commented.

Laura agreed, but added, "I can't imagine keeping track of four little ones, three of them toddlers. I remember when my little brother was the same age as the Kleister twins—crawling on furniture, running wild, drawing on the walls. My mother nearly went crazy."

My phone's ship bell sounded, and I checked the incoming call.

My sister, I mouthed to Laura.

"Are you safe and secure at The Bluffs?" Zoe would be following the storm closely from California. Already, she'd called to check in a minimum of twice daily all week. The line between sistering and mothering had always been slightly blurred for Zoe, partly from being a decade older than me, but also because Mama died quite young.

"We are all good here."

As she was going through a litany of all the things I should be doing—which I didn't bother to tell her I'd already taken care of—a second call came in.

"Daniel's calling," I told her. "I've got to take it."

"Any luck yet?" asked Laura after I ended the call.

"Sadly, no. Daniel and Jason are staying in town to help with the search." I looked out the window, then checked the weather radar on my cell before retrieving a basket and a cooler from the pantry. "I'm going to take this food over to the barn."

Laura peeked inside, making a sad face before plucking a jumbo shrimp from the basket. "The hors d'oeuvres for your reception?"

"They'd go to waste otherwise." I shrugged. "I'm going to stop and tell the carriage house crew to come over here for a bite. It looks like we've got another couple hours before the full brunt of the storm hits."

Selfishly, I also wanted to spend a little time with Edgar and Jimmy and had no doubt they'd lift our spirits. A short while later, they joined Laura and me at the large oak table to partake in a portion of what had been planned for my wedding buffet.

"Tell us about the book you're working on," Jimmy said to Laura, shifting the discussion away from the gloomy subject of the missing Kleister child. "What's the premise?"

"I'm loosely basing it on a very interesting Greek family I met while traveling abroad last year. It's kind of like *The Durrells of Corfu* meet *Modern Family.*"

"You've found you enjoy writing humor?" asked Edgar, who had taken an interest in Laura's writing career. He was himself a columnist and author who'd written a book about enduring local mysteries, most prominently the story of my great-grandparents' dramatic demise.

"I do. Though I'm hoping it will be a heartwarming story as well." She quickly added, "But I promise not to neglect my day job."

"As long as you get your stories in on deadline, they won't care how much time you spend on your book." Through his connections, Edgar had been the one to help Laura land her new job as a reporter for the *Cape Cod Times*.

"Why don't you tell Cassie about your own new project, Edgar?" Jimmy nudged.

"It's only in the beginning stages." Edgar removed his glasses and began to polish them.

Just then the kitchen door banged open, and a gust blew Christopher Savage in, causing Whistler to spring into action, growling the warning he reserved for strangers.

"Sit, Whistler." The dog obeyed Laura's command but continued to utter a low growl. "Sorry. I'm not sure what's gotten into him."

Christopher offered his hand to Whistler, but the dog wasn't having it, his hackles raised.

"You've met Christopher before," Laura chastised the dog.

"It's probably the storm," Christopher suggested. "Gypsy's not herself either. I was hoping you might have some Dramamine? That usually knocks her out."

"Works wonders on Whistler when we take him for long car rides. Let me go see if I threw some into our bags." Laura left the room.

"So, tell them about your novel," Jimmy urged Edgar.

"Novel?" I asked. Edgar had won numerous awards for his reportage and history writing, but I'd never known him to write fiction before.

"It will be my first significant creative writing project," Edgar explained, "and it's going to be based on Barnacle Boy's story."

"Really?" I was a bit disconcerted to hear this and felt my face warm.

"Who's Barnacle Boy?" Christopher asked.

"Years ago, a drowned boy washed up on the shores of Whale Rock. The mystery of who he was or where he came from was never solved. The small unknown boy was laid to rest in the Mitchell family cemetery."

"My father discovered the boy's body," I added. "It was back in 1969, I think."

Edgar nodded his agreement, then said, "I've just started the research. It's going to be a long project."

"Why the name 'Barnacle Boy'?" Christopher asked.

"Well"—Edgar hesitated, cringing slightly—"because by the time he was found, barnacles had attached to his body."

Christopher made a face, and Jimmy clicked his tongue in disapproval. "Not a pleasant subject."

"Granny Fi had a lovely imagination, and she would entertain me with stories about the lost boy—as she called him—always with happy endings," I told them, to lighten the mood. "Her stories made me feel as if the lost boy had been deeply loved."

I went on to tell them the delightful one in which the lost boy had been raised by dolphins.

Just then Laura returned with the package of pills, and the lights began to flicker.

"We'd better all head over with you while we can remain standing," Edgar said as he and Jimmy took their empty plates to the sink.

"Let us at least make you a plate," I insisted, but it was Jimmy who began filling a container with a small feast for Christopher. "I'll add some mini lamb chops for Gypsy."

Jimmy dropped the serving spoon onto the tablecloth and uttered a curse, "*Uffa!*"

"My mother used to let that slip sometimes," Christopher told him. "I've never heard anyone else ever use it."

"*Uffa?* It's Italian. It's like *ugh*."

"Hmph." The man was bemused. "I wonder why an Irish girl from New York used it."

"Are you kidding? Italians and the Irish in New York are practically the same thing. I'm Irish and I grew up there," Jimmy told him. "It's the largest melting pot of the world. We called it Fondue City."

"I thought that was the name of the restaurant where you used to bus tables." Edgar joked.

"Ha-ha. Let's skedaddle." Jimmy looped his arms with Edgar's and Christopher's. "We'll form a wall against the wind."

Our guest wasn't certain how to take his two roommates, though I detected a hint of amusement in his expression.

A few minutes later, the sky lit up in a weird bluish glow, which was followed by a buzzing sound, and then a loud purple boom before the lights went out.

"*Uffa*," Laura muttered.

7

Cassandra

The next morning, I shielded my eyes from the few rays of brilliant sun peeking through a mostly cloudy sky, my hair whipping in the remnant winds. I'd walked the property to assess the damage and had ended up at Percy's Bluffs—named after my great-grandfather, Percy Mitchell—to check out the shoreline. Gazing down at the waters of the bay crashing on the rocks below, I spied two daring surfers taking full advantage of the rolling waves. A cold nose found my hand, and I bent down to give Whistler a loving pet. I turned and saw Laura leaning into the stiff breeze trying to catch up.

I pointed down to where the surfers were riding a wave.

"Brave." She shouted to be heard over the wind and surf.

"We're lucky the storm bounced back into the ocean."

Laura looked to the south. "There's a hint of blue clearing."

"By the way, I found the cause of the power outage," I told her. "That old pitch pine at the end of our lane came down on the wires."

"Jason says power is out for most of Whale Rock."

"Thank goodness for our generators," I said as we started back toward the house together. "Evidently the Parsons crew managed okay. I peeked in on them earlier, and they were all still snuggled in together."

"How could anyone sleep through those howling winds?" she said.

"They've probably learned to tune out the racket from years of living near the noisy harbor."

I then noticed the dark shadows circling my friend's eyes. "Did you get any sleep?"

"More than the guys did," she said. "They just got back now, for a quick change of clothes and something to eat."

"They're still searching for the little Kleister boy?"

Laura nodded. "Sounds like it was an exhausting night."

"This turnaround in the weather can only help." Though it was unimaginable how a child could survive such a storm.

As if reading my thoughts, Laura said, "Maybe someone saw him wandering and took him in?"

"Let's hope that's the case," I agreed.

"I hear the Kleisters believe he was abducted."

I stopped in my tracks. "On what basis?"

Laura shrugged. "Jason didn't go into details."

Back at the house, I found Daniel raiding our supply closet and stuffing batteries, flashlights, and anything he deemed useful into a backpack.

I rubbed his back. "Sorry about the all-nighter."

He offered a weary smile. "And here I thought I'd seen the last of those when I left the Bureau."

His face was etched with the ravages of fatigue and worry, and for the first time Daniel looked every bit his forty-five years.

"Did you eat?"

"I had a banana."

"Let me fix you something more substantial."

"No time." He turned and pulled me into a quick hug. "But I love that you want to look after me."

As Daniel and Jason were gathering up the gear, Lu arrived to help me pack up more of the wedding food to deliver to folks without power.

"Getting here was tricky," she announced. "Flooded roads and trees down."

"I feel helpless," Laura said to her husband. "Let me do something."

"Maybe you can help with the canvassing," Jason suggested. A group was being organized to go door-to-door to check on Whale Rock residents, to see if they were safe and to find out what their needs were. Each canvasser was also going to take along a photo of Lucas to determine if anyone might have seen him or have information about what happened to him.

There was a knock on the door, causing Whistler to jump to attention. Christopher Savage entered tentatively, took in the crowded kitchen while offering his hand to the dog. "Hey, boy."

Good mornings were exchanged, and introductions made.

"Are you hungry?" I asked.

"Thanks, but I'm good. Edgar and Jimmy brought some muffins."

It shouldn't have surprised me that Jimmy would come prepared.

"Speak of the devils," I said as Edgar and Jimmy entered the kitchen.

"What a night!" Jimmy made a dramatic shivering motion before turning to Christopher. "We worried you were blown away by the storm."

"Sorry. I took Gypsy for a walk before you were up and about." He turned to Jason and said, "There must be a lot of damage in town. I wanted to see if there was something I could do to help."

"We, too, wish to lend a hand," Edgar said, Jimmy at his side bobbing his head eagerly.

"You could join me in the canvassing for Lucas," Laura offered while grabbing some water bottles to take along.

"Lucas?" Christopher asked.

"Oh, that's right," Jimmy said. "You weren't here when we were talking about the little Kleister boy's disappearance."

"Lucas Kleister?" Christopher was obviously disturbed.

There was a clattering of the water pipes—a signal from Percy and Celeste, or an issue from the storm?

"That's right." Daniel asked, "You know the Kleister family?"

"I don't know the parents well." His forehead creased. "But I'd often see Lucas and Nicholas on the beach." He turned to Laura and said, "I'd be glad to do anything to help. Can I bring Gypsy?"

"Sure. I'll leave Whistler here to watch over The Bluffs."

"I've got to get going," Daniel told me. "I'm meeting Teddy Howell down at the harbor."

"Is Teddy helping with the search?" I had a soft spot for the young man whom I'd first met last summer when he was bartending at a dive bar in a neighboring town. I'd heard recently that he'd started classes at Cape Cod Community College.

"He's part of a diver rescue team recruited to search the surrounding waters."

This grim implication had all of us looking down at our feet. Nobody wanted to think about a small boy being lost at sea in the storm. It was a too familiar story for those of us in Whale Rock, with Barnacle Boy's little body washing up on our shores several decades ago.

"That won't be easy with the high surf," I said. For the safety of the divers, I was hoping the waters would calm as quickly as the storm had headed out.

"Times a wasting. Let's hit it." And with a quick peck on my cheek, Daniel led the search crew out the door. A minute later, he popped his head back in. "The Parsons are heading back to town."

"We'll be coming in as soon as we have the food and water supplies ready and loaded."

"Be alert out there with these high winds. Lots of trees are leaning precariously and could topple like that." He snapped his fingers.

"Will do." I gave him a thumbs-up and he was gone.

Lu's cell phone rang.

"That was Billy Hughes," she told me after ending the call. "He has some food to donate and wants to help deliver."

This announcement was followed by more clanging pipes. Were my spirit roomies issuing a warning against my old boyfriend? Maybe so, but quite possibly the storm had caused some damage. I added a call to the plumber to my to-do list.

Lu's phone rang a second time, and a few moments later she was collecting her purse and keys. "I've got to go open up the gallery for Brooks."

"Because?" I sent her a puzzled look. Why would the police need entry to an art gallery?

"There was damage to the police station roof—a huge leak—and they need a ground zero location to operate from until they can get it repaired."

"Very generous of you," I said, knowing how protective Lu was of the art gallery.

"When lives are at stake, we do what we must." Lu shrugged. Even in the aftermath of a tropical storm, she was a fashion plate in her crisp khaki capris, striped boatneck sailor top, and the added touch of an anchor-printed scarf. She gave a wave and scurried out the door, leaving me alone with Whistler.

During my lone task of making sandwiches with a seafood salad I'd concocted from the remainder of the wedding appetizers, Zoe called to check in.

"I'm so glad to get through!" she said. "I've been trying for hours. How are you?"

"Safe and sound."

"Thank goodness." Relief . . . followed by a scolding. "I would have thought you'd call to let me know."

"It's been a little crazy."

"The news is saying the Cape caught a lucky break."

"Well, I guess that's the sunny California news anchor take." I tried but didn't succeed in keeping the resentment from my tone. My sister liked having the whole country as a buffer between her and Whale Rock with its mysterious bitter past.

She ignored the jab. "They say the storm's path has been so unpredictable that lots of larger ships are still at sea trying to outrun or avoid it."

This had me wondering what course the *Lady Spirit* had finally taken out of Cape Cod.

"Of course," Zoe continued, "they did say it would have been much worse had the storm stalled."

"Power's out everywhere, and lots of trees are down, blocking roads and rescue crews." I put the phone on speaker so I could continue with my task. "Who knows what damage to homes?"

I waited for her to ask how The Bluffs had fared, but she felt the same hostility toward our family home as she did the town.

"Lu was here helping but had to leave to open up the gallery for Brooks because the station roof was damaged." I paused before adding another little poke: "But perhaps you've already heard from Brooks?"

My sister was going through a tough separation from her husband, Oliver, and I held suspicions that she and her high school beau had reconnected by phone.

"Now you're just being silly, Cassandra."

Was I? I thought not. But now was not the time to probe further.

"No deaths reported yet for your area," she told me.

"That's good. However, we do have a missing child. A little boy named Lucas."

"Oh no." Zoe's voice caught, making me feel guilty for giving her a hard time. Having been unable to have children herself, my sister spent one morning each week volunteering at a local nursery school. She called it her "baby fix."

"How old?" she asked.

"Three."

"So young," she gasped.

"I know," I agreed. "And conditions couldn't be worse for trying to find him, both on land and sea. My friend Teddy's on the dive team, but I can't imagine how easy that will be with the storm remnants kicking up such a rough surf."

"Teddy? I've never heard you mention him."

"I met him last summer. He was tending bar at a little dive in Eastham called Wizards."

"I know the place."

"Oh?" That was a surprise. It didn't seem like Zoe's kind of hangout.

"Back in the day, it was the only place that didn't card."

"Ah." I finished wrapping the last of the sandwiches. "Sorry to end this, but I've got to run some food and water supplies into town."

"Please keep me posted?" She then added, "Especially about that poor little boy."

"Sure will." I ended the call, shoving from my mind images of a lost little boy, frightened and hurt . . . or worse. As Granny Fi would have said: *"Troubled thoughts open the door wide for the devil."*

I sniffed the air. A cloud of burning sugar had descended, and more pungent than usual. Percy and Celeste had been very active of late, their messages mixed and unclear.

What are you trying to tell me?

∗   ∗   ∗

The Lu Ketchner Gallery was a fortress against storms. Originally a bank in the Greek revival style and built of sturdy stone and stucco, its location on High Street also offered the advantage of a higher elevation, protecting it from rising flood waters. The most important benefit was the powerful generator Lu had had installed to protect the fine art housed in the gallery, which meant it was currently one of only a handful of buildings in town with both lights and air-conditioning.

When I arrived with lunch to feed the police, Lu was flitting around the gallery like a worried hen, moving sculptures and paintings to safer locations.

"They'll be here soon for a strategy session," she said while nodding for me to help her move a table. "It's not that I don't trust them. But accidents do happen."

She had every right to be cautious. Lu was gracious and generous, but she had worked hard to build her business and reputation.

"It's not as convenient, but they could meet out at The Bluffs," I suggested.

"No, this makes more sense. Besides," she confided, "I like knowing what's going on."

"For once you'll know more than Evelyn."

"That will drive her nuts." Lu grinned mischievously. Evelyn enjoyed having Hilliard House be the hub of town goings-on. "I'm guessing it won't be long before she pokes her nose in here."

Not five minutes later, Evelyn was indeed carried in by the wind, along with a woman and three young boys.

"This is little Lucas's mother, Helene," Evelyn introduced us. "You remember Nicholas, and the little ones are the twins, Mason and Aiden."

They were a shell-shocked lot. Helene Kleister appeared dazed, confused, and agitated, and Nicholas looked miserably sad. Only the twins showed any life in their whining, which triggered their mother to snap at them. But who could blame her? She was gripped by the unfathomable terror of not knowing where her son was and the dreadful possibility that he was no longer alive.

My own thoughts were painting unimaginable scenes of the poor child being washed away by the storm—or worse—someone harming him. It would be too much for a mother to bear.

"Why don't we get you all settled over here." Lu took the distraught mother's arm and gently pulled her into a side gallery with a small but plump sofa.

"I brought these along for the boys." Evelyn told Lu, producing a canvas bag filled with books and puzzles. She added with a wink, "No crayons or markers, though."

"Bless you," Lu patted her friend's arm.

"Have the boys had lunch?" I asked, but Helene didn't respond.

"I doubt it," Evelyn whispered, helping me with the basket of food I had intended to deliver to the family.

"I'm hoping peanut butter sandwiches are okay for the little ones."

The twins were now peering curiously into the basket to see what other treats might be offered. Just then a gust of wind banged the door open again, thrusting Brooks and Daniel into the gallery. They were followed by Jason, Deputy David Bland, and a recently added female deputy, Lisa Kirkpatrick, whom I only knew from seeing around town.

"Can you handle this?" I asked Evelyn, indicating the kids and their lunch.

"Sure thing." She plunked herself down on the floor with the three boys, encouraging Nicholas to try a bite.

I took a seat next to Helene and touched her arm. She finally noticed me.

"See those people over there?" I pointed to the group gathering around a small conference table Lu had brought out from her office. "They are going to do everything in their power to find Lucas and bring him home to you."

Helene's eyes filled, showing her first real emotion. As I stood, she grabbed my hand. "Promise?"

I nodded, knowing I had no right to offer such an assurance. But I also understood what it was like to lose oneself into the deep well of hopelessness, and right now it was hope that Helene Kleister needed most, and her other three children needed her to be strong.

The gallery door opened, and I followed her gaze to watch as Matthew Kleister struggled against the wind to close it. He swept the windblown hair away from his glasses and searched the room, but when he found his wife, the look that passed between them was far from tender compassion; more like anger, defiance, and reproach. Helene was the first to look away, pulling one of the twins onto her lap. None of the boys seemed to notice their father's arrival.

I followed Daniel and Brooks into Lu's office, where they were conferring privately.

"How's it going?" I asked.

"Nothing yet, I'm afraid." Daniel looked serious. "So far, nobody seems to recall seeing a lone toddler."

"It was so chaotic that day," I said, even as I wondered how any-one could've missed a three-year-old child walking around by him-self. "What does the father have to say?"

Brooks spoke quietly, "The Kleisters feel strongly that it was a kidnapping."

It's what Laura had mentioned earlier. "What do you think?"

"We've spoken to each of them separately." Daniel shook his head, and then, "Neither of them have offered much in the way of justification for their theory. Or leads on who might be behind an abduction."

"Their stories and timing aren't gelling either," added Brooks. "Not to mention, there's been no communication from kidnappers and no ransom request."

"Matthew's argument is credible, though," Daniel said. "The storm and power outages could be responsible for delays in making contact."

Jason popped his head in. "Everyone's ready."

Brooks nodded to Daniel and left Lu's office. "Let's get this show on the road."

Before Daniel could follow, I took hold of his hand. "You're not optimistic, are you?" I said.

"I'm not anything yet—except focused on the work." His attempt at a smile was bleak.

While Brooks brought the team up to speed, I tried to be unobtrusive as I handed out sandwiches and drinks.

"Let's make this strategy session quick so we can get back out there searching with the volunteers." Brooks turned to Daniel and asked, "Have you heard anything from Wes Creed?"

"He's not answering his phone." Daniel looked down at a sheet filled with notes. "MIA for two days now. Parents deceased. One sister, no contact information. I asked Johnny's brother for a list of friends; it wasn't long, but none have heard from him since last weekend."

"Apparently, he got into a few scrapes down in Florida," Brooks added. "Keep on it. We need to find him and determine why he was a no-show and where he's been."

"Who is this Creed guy?" Matthew asked.

"A mid-season hire down on the docks," Daniel told him. "Until yesterday he's been pretty reliable."

"Wes is a native of Whale Rock," David Bland elaborated. "He's been away for a few years and just recently returned."

"But if he has a criminal record, he'd be a likely suspect, wouldn't he?"

"Let's not get ahead of ourselves," Brooks cautioned Lucas's father. "Jumping to conclusions about an abduction, without reliable evidence, puts us at a disadvantage. We are pursuing that scenario, but we have to be open to all possibilities."

"What about the party house?" Jason asked. "They've been the cause of lots of problems this summer."

Brooks frowned. "It's doubtful a bunch of rich frat boys would be involved in taking a child. But Sea Breeze is located close enough to The Lookout that maybe they saw something suspicious. Jason, you start rounding up that gang and see what they may know."

Jason nodded, then turned to Matthew and asked, "Have you had any problems with that group of kids in the cottage below yours?"

"Other than them being noisy? Not really."

"Not to interrupt," I said, "but there was a woman looking for someone down at the harbor yesterday morning."

"That's right," Daniel agreed. "She had a photograph of a man she was trying to locate."

"I saw her too," said Deputy Kirkpatrick. "I assumed she was worried about the person's safety with the approaching storm."

"What did she look like?" Brooks asked.

The deputy paused and looked chagrinned as she answered, "Kind of nondescript. Middle-aged."

"I saw her too, yet I'm also having a hard time bringing any distinguishing features to mind," Daniel said, rubbing his head.

"Did you recognize the man in the photo?"

Kirkpatrick shook her head. "Nobody I recalled seeing around town."

"To be honest, I was focused on getting the boats tied down and didn't get a good look," Daniel said, and I could tell by his expression that he was embarrassed to admit it.

"Have your teams ask about this woman, too, while they're canvassing," Brooks instructed the team.

All heads turned as the front door crashed open with another forceful gust, propelling Teddy into the gallery.

Brooks motioned for him to join the group. "Everyone, this is Ted Howell. He and a team of divers have been working on the coastal search."

Both Matthew and Helene Kleister leaped to their feet, their faces stricken.

"The water's still pretty rough, making progress slow," Teddy reported. "But so far we've found nothing."

Matthew's groan of relief echoed through the gallery. All he heard was that they had not found a body. There was still hope that his son was alive.

"Thank God!" Helene grabbed Teddy's arm and began to sob. The young man looked uncomfortable as he awkwardly patted the woman's shoulder. Neither of the Kleisters reached out to the other. It was as if a wall of ice stood between them.

I looked over to the boys playing and was relieved to see Evelyn and Lu were keeping them distracted. At least the twins were engaged; Nicholas still seemed to be floating in his own little bubble.

"How much longer will the divers stay today?" Brooks asked.

"Everyone's exhausted from battling that surf. The dive team leader has called for a rest period. After that, we'll go out one more time."

"Don't take any chances out there." When Teddy responded with a slight eye roll, Brooks changed tack and asked, "Has your crew eaten?"

Teddy shook his head. "We'll grab something."

I picked up the basket I'd brought. "Here, take this. There are plenty of sandwiches and waters left."

"Thanks, Cass." Teddy turned to me and said, "Sorry about the wedding."

I waved it away. "Seems minor compared to a lost child and a dead body found in a dumpster."

"Well, when you put it that way." He attempted a smile.

Brooks stood and clapped his hands. "Okay folks, let's go. We've got work to do."

8

Cassandra

I t was well past midnight when Daniel came home, heaving a sigh of defeat.

"Any news?" I quietly asked.

"Nothing." He sat on the edge of the bed and rested his head in his hands. This failure to find a lost child was weighing heavily on him. "Sorry to wake you."

"You didn't." I raised up and began to rub his back, feeling the tension in his shoulders. "You need to try and get some sleep, or you'll be useless tomorrow."

"I know." He patted my hand and said, "I'll try."

I knew he was truly exhausted, for only moments after Daniel pulled up the covers, I heard the deep breathing of sleep coming from his side of the bed.

Early the next morning, I slipped out of bed to fix a hearty breakfast for our houseguests. Shortly afterward I was joined by Laura, who'd apparently had the same idea.

"How's Jason?" I asked, ripping open a package of bacon as she began cracking the eggs into a crock bowl.

"Tired. Discouraged. I'm sure they all are."

"Have you come across any clues in your canvassing?"

"Sadly, no." A moment later she said, "One weird thing. When I was getting dressed just now, I saw someone coming over the ridge from your family's graveyard."

"Maybe it was Christopher out walking Gypsy?" I suggested.

"I didn't see a dog, and it looked more like a woman."

"In what way?"

"Just an impression." She shrugged. "It was still too dark to make out for certain."

I checked the captain's wheel clock, a fixture in The Bluffs since my great-grandparents' era. A few minutes before six. It was strange that anyone, male or female, would be prowling around the Mitchell family cemetery at this early hour. These worrisome thoughts were interrupted by the arrival of the first hungry man.

"The smell of bacon is a great alarm clock," Jason announced with a yawn and a stretch.

Laura got on her tiptoes to give him a smooch. "Did you sleep?"

"Like Rip Van Winkle."

"Then you have missed twenty years of your life." Daniel arrived, with damp hair and smelling of Irish Spring.

"I thought he slept a hundred years," I said while mixing the pancake batter.

"That was Sleeping Beauty," he corrected.

"You certainly do know your fairy tales."

"Right now? I feel like we're living one." He filled a large mug from the coffee pot. "A grim one, no pun intended."

This cast an even more somber mood on the group. Soon after the eggs were ready and a large stack of pancakes had been set on the table, Daniel and Jason brought us up to speed on the search and rescue efforts.

"It's not helping that power hasn't been restored to most of Whale Rock," Jason said. "Lots of folks are still out of town."

"How are the Kleisters holding up?" Laura asked.

"They're an odd couple," Daniel answered. "And their stories aren't lining up. It's hard to know who to believe."

"You'd think, with the seriousness of this situation, they'd be completely forthcoming." Laura wore a look of disgust.

"From what I witnessed yesterday," I told them, "there's trouble in that marriage."

Daniel nodded his agreement. He munched on a crisp slice of bacon before asking me, "Have you had a chance to spend any time with Christopher Savage?"

"Not really. How about you guys?" I asked Laura and Jason. "His beach cottage is next to yours."

"He hasn't been there all that long. Maybe a month?" Laura said. "He was my canvassing partner yesterday. That was the most time we've ever spent together. He's pretty quiet."

"A bit of a loner," Jason agreed. "He took the sailboat out every morning. Walked his dog. Other than that, we rarely saw him. Why do you ask?"

"The Kleisters mentioned that Nicholas has been spending time with him. Helene has been allowing Nicholas to go as far as Christopher's beach cottage alone."

"Now that I'm thinking about it"—Laura made a face—"I did see Christopher fishing with a little boy a few days ago. At the time, I just assumed it was a relative, but it could have been Nicholas."

"Apparently this Kleister woman is no helicopter mom." I added my two cents. "That's a long way and a lot of autonomy for a six-year-old."

"His father would agree with you," Daniel said. "He's made some offhand comments about his wife being too cavalier with the boys. She even let Nicholas go out alone sailing with Savage one day. She defended the decision because she was able to see the sailboat from the deck of her house."

"A little too trusting, I'd say." I wanted to give Helene the benefit of the doubt, but how could she just assume Christopher was trustworthy? "Not only was Christopher a virtual stranger to them, but he wasn't even someone well connected to Whale Rock."

Following those thoughts, Jason managed between bites, "Brooks asked me to do some checking on Savage's background."

"You should talk with Edgar and Jimmy since they've been rooming with him the past two days," I suggested.

"Edgar is nothing if not observant," Laura agreed.

"I'm guessing there's been no progress on the Lee Chambers case?" I asked, changing the subject.

"All resources are devoted to searching for Lucas," Jason said. "However, we did get a lead from someone who thinks they saw Chambers in town the day before the body was found."

"Who could miss that platinum blond hair?" It slipped out before I realized my mistake. I wasn't supposed to have been there when the body was removed from the dumpster. Fortunately, Jason hadn't picked up on it, and Daniel was checking his phone for messages. I rushed to cover my slip by asking Laura, "What are you doing today?"

"More canvassing, plus I have an assignment for the *Times*." She turned to Jason, "Can you ride in with Daniel?"

"I can give you a lift," Daniel said, tucking his phone in his pocket.

Jason gave his wife an appraising look. "You look a little green. Are you feeling okay?"

"I'm just tired," Laura assured him.

"Maybe because you've been up at the crack of dawn every day this week?" Then to Daniel and me, "Usually I have to drag her out of bed."

"Don't worry about me," she told him, giving him a slight push toward the door. "Worry about finding that little boy."

He kissed the top of her head and said, "I can do both."

I envied the easy loving way they had with each other. Perhaps sensing something in the way I watched Laura and Jason, Daniel sidled up to me and asked, "You okay?"

"It's nothing a good night's sleep won't fix. We could all use one."

"Maybe you should go back to bed for a little while," he suggested. "It's still early."

"Would *you*?" I placed my hands firmly on my hips. "I need to be out there helping. Edgar, Jimmy, and I have more food to deliver. The Congregational Church is putting care packages together, so we're going to help with those."

"Okay, I get it. Just be careful. There will be road crews out, removing the fallen trees and branches. Probably some detours."

"Daniel, *I'm* the one who's lived here all my life. If anyone can find their way around, it's me."

He winked. "Thanks for reminding me. It's your fault for making me feel so at home in Whale Rock."

"It *is* your home."

"My point exactly." Before he left, he planted a kiss that did make me think about going back to bed, but not alone.

After Jason and Daniel left, Laura turned to me and asked, "So tell me, Cassie, how is it that you know the victim had platinum hair?"

Leave it to the cub reporter to catch my slip.

"I doubt it's a secret," I said, defending myself. "Anybody who knew or saw this Lee Chambers guy would know his hair color."

"But you said you'd never seen the man."

"Fine." I caved and admitted what I'd observed the day the body was found.

"Did you notice anything else? What he was wearing?"

"I had to get out of there quickly." I tried to remember if there was anything else that stood out. "There was a ring on the ground near the dumpster that initially caught my attention, but it might not have any connection."

"What kind of ring?"

"It was silver, but other than that? Don't know. It was half-buried in the crushed-shelled alleyway. Before I got close enough for a good look, I saw the dead hand." I shivered. "Try as I might, I cannot erase that image from my mind."

"Where's the ring now?"

"Brooks bagged it as evidence. I assume he turned it over to the forensics team. Look, he'd be livid if he knew I stuck around, let alone that I was telling you this."

"You can trust me." She made a zipping gesture to her lips before grabbing her backpack and walking toward the door. "I'm just curious."

I had my doubts it was idle curiosity. More like stashing away details for a future article in the *Times*. But I had too much else to do to concern myself with Laura's plans, and that included setting up a work space for my two helpers who would be here any moment.

While waiting for Edgar and Jimmy to arrive, I found myself surrounded by the aroma of burning sugar, only it wasn't the usual pleasant scent I welcomed. It was sharp and disagreeable, which had me worried. The last time the spirits of the house emitted such an unpleasant odor, it had signaled a medical emergency.

"Please, not again," I whispered.

* * *

What followed was a long, nonstop day. When Daniel and I finally made it to bed, we could barely speak let alone contemplate the notion of romance I'd longed for earlier in the day. Even if we hadn't been exhausted, I doubt we'd have had the will, considering yet another day had passed with no signs of little Lucas Kleister. As tired as I was, sleep was elusive, with my thoughts painting unimaginable scenes of terror for the toddler. Had he been kidnapped? Had someone harmed him? Had he been washed away by the storm? It was all too much.

9

Renée

Renée was buckled in beside Isabella in the Business Class section of the nonstop flight from JFK to Rome, eyes still red and swollen. She knew it would be difficult to leave her family behind, but the parting was more heart wrenching than she could have imagined. She hadn't spent a single night away from her son since his birth six years earlier. Her husband had looked on with concern as the unstoppable tears flowed from both mother and son.

"So, does your husband know about Vito and me now?" her sister asked.

Renée flushed hot, but she wouldn't lie to her sister. "There will be time for that later."

Isabella sent her a questioning look. "So what *did* you tell him?"

"It's a long story," Renée said.

"It is a long flight, is it not?"

Renée nodded and ordered a Scotch to relax herself.

* * *

New York ~ Early 1970s

Brandan Kane had been a godsend. Renée had met the emerging design artist shortly after escaping to New York City. With his studio located just a block away from her office job, they'd often run into each other at the nearby corner bistro, and quickly a friendship had ensued. Eventually, the two became nearly inseparable.

"When are you going to move out of the Webster?" Brandan had asked over a shared tuna melt and fries.

"Hey, I'm lucky to have found it," Renée responded. The Webster was a private apartment building founded to provide affordable housing for unmarried working women, and she'd been grateful for the room when she first arrived.

"But how much longer can you take Chatty Cathy?" he mocked, moving his hand like a beak. He'd heard plenty of complaints about her incessantly chatty roommate sucking the limited air supply from the tiny one-bedroom flat.

Renée was desperate to breathe again, but until she found a better paying job, she was stuck at the Webster.

"I'm waiting for you to become successful so you can rescue me from the typing pool," she told him.

"Well," he said, smiling broadly, "I sold a collection this week."

"That's wonderful, Brandan!" She was genuinely pleased. "It's about time someone took notice."

"Soon I'll be needing an assistant." He raised his eyebrows expressively.

His confidence was well placed. It wasn't long before Brandan's talents were being celebrated by Manhattan's elite, and Renée had been lucky to go along for the exciting ride. Her role evolved from assistant to indispensable handler of his professional life, which expanded well beyond his art. The Brandan Kane Creations empire grew to include furniture and fabric design as well as complete home décor makeovers for select clients. Those few who could boast of having a Brandan Kane home paid prodigiously for the privilege.

Renée now had assistants working for her and had even begun dabbling in design herself. The nightmare of her early life, though never completely forgotten, had faded more than a young immigrant girl could ever have dreamed.

She grew to love Brandan, even having serious thoughts about a life together beyond their professional ties. However, what she'd seen as dating, he'd considered something far different. She'd been floored when Brandan finally admitted he was gay.

"You certainly hide it well," she told him, trying not to let her wounds show. Though he must have known how she felt about him.

"I hoped you might have guessed." He reached across the table to take her hand. "It doesn't change how I feel about you."

Renée wondered if Brandan had intentionally chosen Tavern on the Green for dinner that night. It was a popular dining spot for the art crowd, and there were frequent stops by friends and admirers to chat him up.

Upon reflection, of course, there had been signs. But Renée had not wanted to acknowledge the truth. With no family and few friends, she'd become emotionally dependent on Brandan.

"I will always watch out for you," he told her. And he had been true to his word.

Renée's heartache had been short-lived. Meeting Michael had changed everything. It had been at an exhibit for Brandan where she first met her future husband. He later confessed to having purchased a painting only for the opportunity of seeing her again, though he'd also assumed there was more to the relationship between Renée and Brandan. Thus, it took Michael over a year to ask her out on a date. However, once together, their relationship quickly blossomed, and six months later they were wed. After years of trying, Renée finally became pregnant with their son. This new life made her believe in second chances.

At her first opportunity after Isabella left, Renée had put in a frantic call to Brandan.

"I need to go to Italy," she told her friend.

"What's wrong?" Brandan asked.

"My brother is very ill."

"You have a brother in Italy? How did I not know that?" He sounded hurt.

"We've been estranged for years." She paused a moment before adding, "Michael knows very little about my past."

"And you'd like to keep it that way?"

"Yes." She felt her face flush warm for admitting this. "For now. Look, my past is complicated . . . and now isn't a good time to bring out all the skeletons."

"I get it." Brandan had a few of those himself. "What do you need?"

"A good reason to be in Italy."

Fortunately, he was able to locate a fabric design show in Rome as a convenient and plausible explanation for her need to fly out quickly.

* * *

Italy ~ Mid-1980s

"This Brandan sounds like he's been a brother to you." There was a whisper of regret in Isabella's tone.

"He's my best friend in the world."

When Renée and her sister landed in Rome, the two women had a much better understanding of what had been the steering force in each other's lives since the day of their unfortunate parting fifteen years earlier. For Isabella it had been her faith and commitment to God. For Renée it had been a need to power forward without a rear-view mirror.

A driver was waiting at baggage claim to take them to where Vito now lived with his family. Both sisters had reasons, though differing, for feeling deep trepidation.

10

Cassandra

The Bluffs ~ Present day

"The gods have been kind." Jimmy Collins raised his hands and lifted his head toward the skies in a dramatic pose. "Electricity is back on in Chatham."

Edgar and Jimmy had joined Daniel and me in the kitchen for one last cup of joe the next morning.

"More important, let's hope those gods have been kind to Alcyone." They'd named their home in Chatham after a story in Greek mythology because of Jimmy's fascination with mythological deities.

"Tempestas can be temperamental."

"And which Greek god is Tempestas?" I asked, unfamiliar with the name.

"Not a god, a goddess." He waved a finger. "And not Greek, but Roman. Tempestas is the goddess of storms. There was a temple dedicated to her by some Roman leader several hundred years BC. When his fleet was caught in a bad storm, he prayed to Tempestas, and she delivered the ships safely back to Rome."

"That must be where the word *tempestuous* came from. I knew it had to have a feminine origin," Daniel teased. I sent him a reproachful look, which prompted him to change the subject. "Now if only they could get the power back on in Whale Rock."

"It would make the search easier," I agreed.

"Once we check on Alcyone, we'd be happy to come back and help," Edgar said.

"Absolutely." Jimmy nodded his agreement before suggesting, "Maybe Christopher can help deliver food today."

"Speaking of Mr. Savage, did Jason talk to you?" Daniel asked.

"He did." Edgar stirred sugar into his coffee. "A rather reticent man, at least with me. He opened up more with Jimmy. My husband can get anyone to talk."

"So, sue me—I have a gift." Jimmy feigned indignation but went on to say, "He's a New Yorker. First time to the Cape. He told me he's a prep school history teacher, and he had a lot of questions about the area. Said he was looking for interesting stories for a class he's preparing on New England history. We talked a little about First Encounter Beach and the Mayflower. Of course, I also invited him over to Chatham to see the Marconi Museum."

"Considering kids' fascination with their smartphones and tablets, they could use a lesson in the history of the shortwave radio," Daniel said. "The original wireless technology."

"If for no other reason than to help them appreciate what they have now," Jimmy agreed.

"He also seemed curious about Whale Rock's history. Especially once Jimmy told him he was staying on the most significant property in Whale Rock." Edgar was momentarily pensive. "I have the feeling Christopher's purpose for coming here goes beyond a conscientious teacher looking for ways to spice up his class."

"How so?" Daniel asked.

"Nothing concrete. Just an impression."

"He has spent time at the library doing his research," Jimmy said. "Maybe the librarian could give you an idea of what he's been looking at."

"I know Bethany, and I'd be happy to ask her," I volunteered. "I'll be in town anyway."

Daniel nodded his assent before asking, "What else did you learn besides his being a teacher?"

"Um . . . Let's see. What else?" Jimmy tapped his chin. "He was interested in significant shipwrecks on Cape Cod Bay. Edgar told him about the famous ones—you know, the *Sparrow-Hawk* and the SS *Merrimack*?"

"He asked if there was any with local lore attached. The only one I could come up with off the top my head was the *Whydah Galley* and "Black Sam" Bellamy."

Sam Bellamy was an English pirate known as the Robin Hood of the Sea. In 1717, he and his crew captured the *Whydah*, which was carrying over four tons of silver, but the great treasure was lost at sea off the coast of Cape Cod during one of the most violent storms ever recorded in New England history. The recent discovery of the pirate's remains had been a hot news topic the past few years.

"What about Barnacle Boy?" Laura asked, having just caught the tail end of our conversation after returning from walking Whistler. "That's a local legend he might find to be of interest."

"Are you kidding? Edgar talked his ear off about Barnacle Boy."

"It was Christopher who asked," Edgar said a tad defensively. "Still, we don't know how the young lad came to be washed up on the Whale Rock shores. It may not have been from a shipwreck at all."

That was true—there had been many theories about Barnacle Boy, ranging from accidental drowning to shipwreck victim, to body dumped at sea to hide evidence of other crimes, but none had even a trace of evidence to verify. Edgar had his work cut out for him if he hoped to piece together the mystery. At least, because his was a work of fiction only inspired by a true story, he could choose which theory to follow.

"Have you made any interesting discoveries yet?" I was both curious and yet a little protective of Barnacle Boy's story. After all, he was as much a part of the Mitchell family lore as were Percy and Celeste.

"Perhaps." There was a twinkle in his eyes. "But I'm not yet ready to reveal anything."

* * *

Laura headed out shortly after Edgar and Jimmy left, and Daniel was getting ready to leave when Brooks's cruiser turned the corner of our long lane. Whistler ran to greet him, knowing there'd be a treat.

"Glad I caught you," Brooks said to Daniel after tossing the dog his biscuit. "Where's Savage?"

"He left a while ago for a walk with his dog," I answered.

Daniel asked, "What's up?"

"Couple of things." Brooks folded his arms and leaned against the cruiser. "First, there's been significant damage to his beach cottage. He can't go back until the roof's been repaired and inspected."

"How long will that take?"

"Hard to say. Construction companies will have their hands full for a while."

"He can stay in the carriage house until our next renter arrives," I offered.

"That would be great. I'd like him to be somewhere one of us can keep an eye on him."

"Are you considering him a suspect?" Daniel asked.

"More like a person of interest. Jason did some digging and discovered he has a tenured position at a private prep school in upstate New York called Bridgewater Academy."

"Edgar and Jimmy told us this morning he was a teacher," I confirmed.

"Apparently, he's well respected by students and faculty."

"Okay?" Daniel's dubious tone made it clear he wasn't seeing a problem.

"There are some concerns. It appears he took a sudden leave of absence from his teaching job during the middle of summer term."

"Could be lots of reasons for that."

"True," Brooks agreed without giving us any more information. He then turned to me and said, "Can you go see Johnny Hotchkiss?"

"What about?" I asked.

"Helene Kleister told us Nicholas had begged to go out on a big sailboat with Christopher, not the dayboat at Land's End, so I'm guessing he rented it from Johnny. If I'm right, I'd like to know when this was, and did he go alone or with someone else? If so, who, and how long were they out? Once you get Johnny talking, he'll be telling you the man's life story."

"Why me?" I asked.

"I don't want Johnny to suspect anything and start blabbing around town about it. If you go, it's just curiosity. If I go, it's official."

"Got it. Sure, I'll talk to Johnny." Then I asked, "Are you here to question Christopher?"

"I'm here to get his reaction to a few things."

"Well, here he comes." Daniel nodded to where the man in question had just come into view, over the ridge, from the land trust where he took Gypsy for walks on the trails. The pit bull was leery of Whistler, so I grabbed the German shepherd's collar and escorted him onto the porch and secured the gate.

Brooks and Daniel had moved to the carriage house where I joined them, uninvited, just as Christopher arrived.

"I have some bad news about your cottage," Brooks told him. "It took quite a hit by the storm, and you can't go back until the repairs are done."

"Hmph," Christopher mumbled.

"You're welcome to stay in the carriage house for a couple more weeks," Daniel told him.

"No charge," I added quickly, knowing it would be in the best interest of the investigation for him to stick around. "It was going to be empty anyhow."

"That's very kind of you." He then asked Brooks, "Can I go collect the rest of my belongings?"

"Someone will need to escort you, for insurance purposes," Brooks told him. I thought it more likely the police chief didn't want Christopher Savage to have unchaperoned access to the cottage.

"When can I go?"

"Maybe tomorrow? We've got a lot on our plate right now."

"Okay," he reluctantly agreed, not looking pleased.

"Do you know where Sea Breeze cottage is?" Brooks posed a non sequitur.

Christopher shook his head. "I'm not all that familiar with the names of the beach houses."

"It's located at the opposite end of the beach from Land's End, before the harbor area. A group of college kids have taken it over this summer. Skull and cross-bones flag on the pole?"

"Now I know which one you mean." He nodded. "The party house."

"Ever go to one of their parties?" Brooks asked.

"No." Christopher looked disgusted at the thought.

"Ever heard of a man named Lee Chambers?"

Christopher shook his head. "Should I have?"

Brooks shrugged.

"Who is he?"

"A drug dealer mainly, though he's had other offenses. Unfortunately, the party house has attracted some unsavory types." Brooks pulled out his phone and showed Christopher a photo. "Recognize him?"

"Never seen the man." I tried to read Christopher's expression, but there was nothing telling.

Gypsy was whining, and he turned to leave.

"One more thing," Brooks said to him. "Helene Kleister told us that her oldest son spent some time with you."

Christopher nodded. "Nicholas wandered down to my cottage the first day I got here. He told me where he was staying, and I thought it pretty far for a kid his age, so I walked him back up the beach."

"Did you see him after that?"

"Sure. We fished together a couple times. I took him out on the dayboat once—with his mother's permission," Christopher was quick to add, before asking, "How is Nicholas doing?"

"Not well. He's not talking. At all. It's pretty traumatic to have your little brother disappear."

The man nodded thoughtfully. "Do you think I could see him? Maybe I could get him to talk."

"What makes you think that?" Daniel asked.

"He was always pretty talkative with me. Sometimes it's easier for kids when it's not their parents."

"I'll check with the Kleisters. But I wouldn't count on it." Brooks frowned. "They're being exceptionally protective of their other three boys right now, as you can imagine."

"Of course."

"Did Nicholas ever bring Lucas with him to your cottage?"

"Once. I called his mom right away to make sure she knew. I wheeled them back on the beach cart." He hesitated a moment before saying, "Helene seemed a little out of it the times I spoke with her. Nicholas told me she was sick."

"Sick how?"

"He didn't seem to know." He raised his hands in a slightly exasperated gesture. "He's only six. But he worried about her."

Brooks started to walk toward his cruiser, stopped and turned around, and said, "Someone will be in touch when we're freed up to take you back to your cottage."

Christopher's shoulders dropped in a somewhat defeated gesture. As Brooks took off, I was reminded that Christopher didn't have a car.

"Let us know if you need a ride somewhere," I offered.

"I can take The Flex." He evidently knew all about the Cape's public bus routes.

"I'm heading to town for an errand in a bit if you want a lift," I told him.

Daniel said, "Might as well go with me. I'm leaving now."

"Thanks, but I've got some calls to make first," the man said, declining.

Thirty minutes later, as I was getting into my old pickup truck Christopher called out, "Is your offer of a ride still good?"

"Sure. Hop in."

On the short drive to town I tried to engage him, but he wasn't the chatty sort. However, we did make a plan to rejoin the canvassers searching for Lucas after we both finished our respective errands.

"Where do you want to go?" I asked, making the turn onto High Street, nearly deserted save for work crews.

"The post office."

I dropped him off and told him I'd meet him back there in an hour. But as I drove away, I saw in my rearview mirror that Christopher Savage did *not* enter the post office. Instead, he walked down Harbor Drive. *Was he defying Brooks and going to his cottage?* I considered following him, but I had two errands to accomplish.

Unfortunately, the first proved fruitless. During my stop at the library, I learned that Bethany was dealing with storm damage at her own home, and the summer volunteer covering for the librarian wasn't comfortable sharing the information I needed. The Mitchell Free Library was one of Granny Fi's legacies, but this volunteer was pretty firm in his stance. I didn't think it would help to tell him about my family's connection. I'd come back later when Bethany was there.

My second errand was more productive.

"Hey, Cassie Lassie. You've been hanging around so much, maybe you want your old job back?" Johnny gave me a fond punch to the arm.

"Which one? Tour guide or crew?" Though it pleased me to once again have a proper association with the family business, my memories of last year were not pleasant. I'd been flat broke and desperate to scrounge together every penny I could get my hands on when Johnny took me on, out of pity, to do scut work on the boats. "Never mind. The answer is N.O.!"

He grinned. "Aw, come on. It wasn't so bad, was it?"

"Yeah, a real breeze." I gave a sarcastic snort. The work had been brutally hard. "But I have to admit, it was a much-needed lifeline."

"If we could only get a lifeline to that lost little boy," he said while setting out two ratty folding chairs. We watched for a moment as a handful of men worked to ready the fleet of touring boats to return to work after the storm. "I let most of the crew go help with the search."

"I'll be joining them shortly. Along with Christopher Savage. Do you know him?" Johnny wasn't great with names, so I elaborated. "He's the one who lucked out and got Robyn Landers's cottage this year."

"Yeah, yeah, right. Tall, blondish?"

"That's him."

"A good sailor, that one." Johnny raked his hands through thick salt-and-pepper hair, then rubbed his chin. "He rented the Catalina a couple days ago, before the big storm hit. Brought it back in one piece, even after getting caught in a pop-up thunderstorm. He and a friend took it out."

"Who was that?" I asked.

"Shoot. You know me and names." Johnny had always been able to laugh at himself. "He came back on his own, though—said he'd dropped his friend in Orleans. Waited out the storm there and then sailed the Catalina back on his own."

"Not an easy boat to solo sail," I marveled.

"That's what I was saying. A fair good sailor he is. I asked him if he often lost his friends at sea."

"I'll bet he thought that was funny." I didn't, but I knew Johnny would take the bait.

"Not a fan of man-overboard jokes, that one." Johnny made a face. "Now you have me curious about the name of the friend." His eyes brightened. "The waiver."

Anyone renting a boating craft was required to sign a liability release. A moment later Johnny came out of his office, brandishing the waiver like a flag. He handed it to me, and I glanced at it. *Tyler Stendall.* The name didn't mean anything to me, but I committed it to memory before handing the paper back. I also caught Christopher's DOB—only two years earlier than mine, which surprised me. I would have thought him older, but I guess the sun and surf had left their imprint. Most sailors considered it a fair tradeoff.

As I walked back toward the pickup, Robyn Landers's red Mercedes convertible sped by. I waved, but she didn't see me. She was driving too fast for me to get a good look at who was in the passenger seat, though I was pretty sure it was a man. I was glad to think that she too had moved on after her divorce. Of course, the leggy, brunette, blue-eyed stunner wasn't bound to stay single long.

I arrived a bit early back at the post office, hoping to see which direction Christopher came from. Sure enough, he walked up from Harbor Drive. When he got into the truck, I noticed sand around his ankles. He'd definitely been to the beach, but had he gone to the cottage? And if so, what was his purpose?

11

Cassandra

It was three days after the storm, and there was still no sign of what had happened to Lucas Kleister. Daniel was now splitting his time between the search and helping Brooks investigate Lee Chambers's death, on top of his responsibilities at Mitchell Whale Watcher Boat Tours. Which was why I was surprised to see his mud-splattered Land Rover pull up to The Bluffs in the middle of the day.

"What are you doing home?" I called out as Whistler rushed to offer a greeting with warm, wagging tail thumps. Laura and Jason were extending their stay in our guest room until repairs could be made to their rental, which had also suffered some damage. Both being busy—Jason with his deputy duties and Laura writing an article about the aftermath of the storm for the *Cape Cod Times*—the pleasure of tending to Whistler's needs was left to me when I wasn't out helping with the search.

"Good to see you too." He took me in his arms for a kiss. "Most women would love to be surprised by a midday visit from their husband."

"Not my husband yet," I reminded him.

"We will have to remedy that problem, now won't we?" He walked with me into the house, his arm draped across my shoulder and Whistler close on our heels.

"First, let's find little Lucas."

Daniel's handsome face darkened. "It's so damn frustrating trying to look for clues of any kind with the mess the storm left behind."

"We ran into nothing but trouble this morning." My team had been combing the land trust preserve that abutted our property, but there were so many precariously leaning trees and large hanging limbs that it had been called to a halt.

He shook his head and walked toward the library. "I need Wes Creed's employment file to verify some information he's given us."

"You've spoken with him?" I asked when he returned to the kitchen, holding a manila folder.

"He showed up for work this morning, and Brooks has him in custody now."

"Where?" There was no way the police station could have been repaired that quickly.

"Damage was limited to the offices and interrogation rooms. The wing with the holding cells was spared. There's a separate entrance, so Brooks set up a temporary work space in one of the cells."

Lu must be relieved to have her gallery back, I thought.

"Johnny and I will be working extra hours until we can hire a replacement." Doubtful this late in the season, which meant I would be seeing Daniel even less than practically never. "Or Wes is released."

"*If* he's released," I added.

"We'll see. So far? He's cooperating and hasn't asked for an attorney." He held up the file he'd come to retrieve. "Brooks asked me to check out his alibi. Wes claims he was in Boston with some pals from a former job."

I was filing through my memories of his old Whale Rock jobs and thinking I might do my own digging, when Daniel interrupted my thoughts.

"He denies knowing anything about Lucas Kleister's disappearance or Lee Chambers's death, though he didn't seem alarmed to hear about either."

"Wes Creed has always been one cool cucumber."

"But not a good egg. He's got some priors. Also, Jason learned from the party house crowd that Wes had shown up at a recent kegger. Guess who else was there that same night?"

"Lee Chambers?"

"Bingo."

"Wes didn't deny knowing him?"

"No, but he also didn't admit to being chummy with him either. One of the frat boys claims to have overheard Chambers and Creed talking when they went outside for a smoke; it was something to the effect that Chambers had a new client, and he'd pointed up to The Lookout."

"Helene Kleister?" Sea Breeze cottage was located near the bottom of the steps that led down to the beach from the Kleisters's rental.

"It certainly seems feasible. The woman's been in a distracted haze every time I've seen her." Daniel frowned and shook his head. "Wes made an offhand comment about the Kleisters that makes me suspect he knows them, or at least one of them, better than he's admitting. That hunch was reinforced when I took some mug shots over to show the Kleisters. Chambers and Creed were the only two to inspire a reaction."

"By whom?" I asked.

"Well"—he heaved a sigh—"Matthew answered for them all, stating that he recognized Wes from when the family went out on a whale watch tour. He also remembered seeing someone who looked like Lee Chambers hanging around Sea Breeze. But it wasn't *his* reaction that interested me. It was Nicholas. He appeared startled by the mug shots, whipped around to look at his mom."

"What did Helene do?"

"She just stared vacantly."

"There is definitely something off there," I said, then glanced at the captain's wheel clock. "Can I make you something to eat?"

"Got something quick?"

I grabbed a bag of whole grain bread and pulled from the cupboard some peanut butter and beach plum jam. "PBJ is as quick as it gets."

"What's our tenant up to?" he asked as we took our plates out to the porch.

After telling Daniel about my trip into town with Christopher, I said, "I saw him again a few minutes ago, leaving on a walk with Gypsy."

"Brooks is regretting not pushing more to let Savage talk with Nicholas." He bit into the sandwich and mumbled through the stickiness. "Matthew Kleister refused, as predicted. He implied that Savage was a little too interested in their boys."

Just then Daniel's phone buzzed with a text. He narrowed his eyes to read it.

"Damn. The Kleisters have hired their own investigator," he said with disgust. "That won't be helpful."

"Don't forget, babe, this is just a part-time gig for you," I reminded him, knowing how deeply he could immerse himself in a case.

"It's hard to let go when a child's life is at stake." Daniel tapped his fist to his heart. The anguish he was feeling made me love him all the more.

Evelyn's familiar blue and white mini cooper rounded the bend of our lane and sounded her custom car horn, a yodeling loon.

Daniel rolled his eyes every time he heard it. He pointed at me and warned, "Do not let her talk you into getting a screaming orca horn for your Miata."

"How about a braying donkey?" I joked.

"Hey, you two," Evelyn called out as she toted a book bag from her car. "Looks like The Bluffs fared pretty well in the storm."

"A few fallen branches. Some loose shingles. That's the extent of our problems."

Evelyn plopped herself down onto one of the porch rockers. "I take it there's still no news about little Lucas?"

"Nope." It was hard for Daniel to admit defeat, and his expression showed it.

"Sorry," Evelyn mumbled. "I stopped in to check on the family this morning. Took them a meal. It's a very tense household."

"I'm sure they're beside themselves," I said.

"The bickering isn't helpful."

"They still butting heads?" Daniel asked.

"Terribly," Evelyn said. "The house is a disaster zone. That poor father has his hands full."

"What about Helene?" I asked.

"She seems lost. And those kids? They're a mess." She wrinkled her nose. "I gave the twins a sponge bath while I was there."

I could easily envision the scene. Evelyn had a talent for gently insinuating herself and seamlessly taking charge.

"Nicholas still isn't saying anything."

"We're trying to figure out a way to talk to him," Daniel said.

"Well, you'd best do it soon," Evelyn told him. "I overheard Matthew say the grandparents were coming to take Nicholas for a while."

"I'd better let Brooks know," Daniel said. "I've got to head out anyway." He leaned down and planted his lips on my forehead.

"Until these cases are solved, I could ease some of your burdens by helping Johnny out at the harbor," I offered. As soon as I spoke the words, my nose filled with a warning scent from Percy and Celeste. I wasn't sure what they were warning me about, but Daniel was not having it.

"No way. Your days of crew work are behind you," he said. "I've got it covered."

After Daniel left, Evelyn said in a knowing way, "I understand they're shorthanded down at the harbor."

"Oh?" I pretended ignorance, though not surprised she would know. Evelyn had informants all around town.

"I'm sure it's no secret," she said defensively. "I can't believe Daniel didn't tell you. Brooks was seen escorting Wes Creed into the station this morning."

"Wow." I continued to play dumb. "I just learned a couple days ago that he was back in town."

"Oh yes." Her face brightened at the prospect of spilling what she knew. "There was a little trouble down in Florida. I think he got involved with the wrong woman."

"Same old Wes."

"You can say that again. He came back with a hideous tattoo on his arm," she said in a disapproving tone. I could only imagine her reaction if she saw the phoenix tattoo I'd gotten last year.

As casually as possible, I asked, "Who was it that Wes used to hang out with before he left The Rock?"

"Well, he was always good friends with Johnny's brother, Charlie Hotchkiss." She thought a moment before adding, "Wes moved around a lot, but he did stay at Nauset Marine for a while. He likely had some pals there. He dated Lu's cousin for a while."

"I didn't know that." Lu might be a good source of dirt on Wes.

"Why the interest?"

"Just curious. I'd forgotten all about him until I found out he was working for us."

She frowned and leaned in. "You don't suppose he had anything to do with little Lucas? Or that suspicious death?"

Fortunately, I was saved from answering those prickly questions when Whistler stood and barked as a man and a dog appeared in the distance.

"Is that Christopher Savage?" she asked.

"Yep."

"I have a delivery for him." She held up the book bag. "He put in a request through the Massachusetts Library System for some books and periodicals. Bethany's home took a hit, so volunteers are pitching in, and George offered to deliver them."

"Funny, you don't look like George," I kidded, knowing Evelyn had probably been dying to see what was going on over here, what with a mysterious stranger bunking in our carriage house.

She ignored the jab. "Apparently he's been spending a good deal of time at the library, doing research."

"I don't suppose anybody mentioned the subject of that research?"

Evelyn grinned deviously and picked up the book bag. "We could sneak a quick peek."

However, Christopher had tied Gypsy and was now walking toward us in his easy stride. I introduced him to Evelyn, who reluctantly turned over the book bag.

"Bethany said you were eager to receive these, so I offered to drop them off to you," she explained in a flirty way, tucking a lock of hair behind her ear. Probably hoping for a hint of what she'd just handed over, she added, "Is it a special project you're working on?"

"Not really." Christopher thanked Evelyn, then retreated to the carriage house. There would be no snooping into his requested library delivery today.

"Quite the taciturn man," she said, slightly offended, watching him take Gypsy inside.

"He can't be pleased about being displaced from his vacation beach cottage. Have you noticed any work being done on it?"

"I haven't been to the beach, let alone had time to walk between helping with the search and getting things back up to snuff at the Inn." She checked her smartwatch. "Oh dear. I've got to get back to meet an electrician."

I was relieved that there would be no further questions about Wes Creed's potential involvement in either of the mysteries plaguing Whale Rock. I didn't know the answer, but I also didn't want to encourage Evelyn or feed the Whale Rock gossip mill. I was, however, glad for the little bit of background she was able to pass on about the man.

*　*　*

After Evelyn left, I took Whistler for a walk. I headed for the cliffs, but he had other ideas, tugging me insistently on a detour to the Mitchell family cemetery.

He stopped to sniff at Granny Fi's grave, as had always been his habit, while I took a survey of the graveyard. So many tragic stories in this plot of land. The storm had flattened many of the plants in the perennial garden my mother had started years ago, surrounding the graves of all the baby boys she'd lost. She'd blamed the miscarriages and stillbirths on the century-old curse against my great-grandparents.

The sun grazed the bronze Winnie the Pooh statue that stood guard over Barnacle Boy's grave. I let go of Whistler's leash and walked over to find a bouquet of wildflowers tied with raffia and laid by the stone. Had Edgar left this memorial to the lost boy? Such a sweet gesture would be just like him.

It wasn't until the walk back to the house that I was struck by another possibility. Perhaps the flowers had been from the stranger, the woman Laura saw the other morning walking along the ridge. I was now even more curious about this mystery woman and why she had paid a secret visit to The Bluffs.

12

Renée

The first year of Renata's nanny position with the Welles family passed easily. She enjoyed her two well-behaved charges, four-year-old Gregory and six-year-old Lisa, and was permitted adequate time to herself for her studies. There was more than a decade age gap between the younger Welles children Renata had been hired to look after and the eldest. Phillip Welles hadn't paid even the smallest attention to Renata during that first year, mostly because he spent a good portion of the time at a prestigious private boarding school in New Hampshire. But one summer day between his junior and senior years, their paths crossed in the outside world when she was returning books to the neighborhood library. For once, Phillip took notice of her.

She'd stumbled up the stairs to the library, her pile of books flying in every direction.

"Here, let me help, Renata," the familiar voice said.

Flustered, she looked up into the classically handsome face she had admired from afar. She wasn't aware he even knew her name.

"These are textbooks." Phillip frowned at the books, then looked at Renata. "How can you go to school if you're working for us?" He seemed genuinely confused.

"I need to work to help my family." She lifted her shoulders. "So I teach myself. With these."

"I'm impressed." He handed her the books he had gathered.

"Don't be. I'm terrible at math," she admitted.

"How old are you?"

"I have just turned seventeen."

"Your accent is very exotic."

Her face grew warm. How hard she'd tried to free herself from an Italian accent.

"I like it." He smiled, easing her embarrassment.

"Maybe I can help you with your studies," he suggested. "We could work after the little kiddles go to bed."

That's what he always called his younger brother and sister. Just like the little doll toys that were so popular back then. Isabella giggled when Renata told her about the nickname that next Sunday. It was her free day and she was expected to visit her family. Mostly she spent the time with Isabella who also returned to Zia Rosa's for Sunday dinner. Vito rarely came, avoiding their Zio Enzo at all costs, so Renata would try to squeeze in quick visits with her brother before her obligatory family dinner.

The tutoring sessions with Phillip began the following day and continued through the summer. He'd come to her room in the evenings and drill her on her weakest subject. She was a cinch at history and geography, and with her love of reading, she'd finished almost as many of the classics as Phillip had, even though he was a year ahead of where she'd be if she'd been allowed to attend school.

"I don't think we need to be working on this anymore," he proclaimed one night as summer was nearing an end.

She'd been crestfallen to think their evenings together would end. But that wasn't exactly what Phillip had meant. Hard as it was, however, she managed to resist his advances.

When September arrived, Phillip left again for school. Renata didn't see him again until the Christmas holidays. But his return home wasn't met with the usual joyous welcoming from Mr. and Mrs. Welles. In fact, the house was filled with an awkward tension.

With the children on their holiday break, Renata was kept quite busy and fretted that she wouldn't see Phillip before he left again for New Hampshire. But that time never came.

When Phillip knocked on her door New Year's Eve, he tearfully told her of his expulsion. He wasn't forthcoming with details, only that he and a group of his friends had been falsely accused of an expellable act and sent home. He was to finish his senior year at the local public school.

Phillip seemed to have lost his confidence, and Renata wanted to do what she could to help this boy for whom she was developing serious feelings. After Gregory and Lisa had been tucked into their beds at night, Renata looked forward to that light knock on her door, and she found herself permitting Phillip certain liberties that before she'd fought against.

Renata began to notice changes in the young man, especially after he told her about his acceptance to the University of Oxford in spite of the expulsion, brushing aside his father's having had to make a sizable donation to the university as well as calling in some significant favors from the family's British connections. When summer arrived, he spent most of his time at the country club, hanging out with old friends. Though the visits to her room continued, they became less and less frequent.

13

Cassandra

"It wasn't me," Edgar insisted. Less than an hour after I'd phoned Laura about the flowers on Barnacle Boy's grave, she and Edgar were standing on my porch, Whistler circling them excitedly.

"I was at the Whale Rock library, doing some research for the book, when Laura sent me a text," Edgar explained sheepishly, probably not wanting to seem vulture-like. He admitted that he *had* been hoping to spend some time in the cemetery but hadn't wanted to intrude.

"You never have to feel that way," I assured him.

He smiled fondly, warming my heart.

"I swung by and picked up Edgar on my way back from Eastham," Laura added.

"I was without a car. Jimmy dropped me at the library early this morning and then joined the search."

"Nothing new to report on Lucas, I'm sorry to say." Laura tried to brighten the conversation by saying, "But I did get a great story to add to my article."

As we ambled toward my family's graveyard, she went on to tell us about a large century tree that had uprooted and split in half a barn housing a goatscaping herd. Fortunately, it had a good ending since not a single goat had been harmed.

"Creating atmosphere is crucial to the writing process," Edgar said as we strolled around the family gravestones. "Being here helps me get a sense of the boy's spirit."

"How old was he?" Laura asked.

"The coroner's report gave a range between four and six years," Edgar responded.

"So very young." Laura's voice was tinged with the sorrow we were all feeling. "My own brother was only six when he drowned."

I suspected that's why Laura was so interested in helping Edgar with his book about Barnacle Boy. When she was eleven, she and her younger brother had been caught in an undertow while swimming. Her father nearly drowned trying to rescue his children, succeeding in saving only her. It wasn't until weeks later that the little boy's ravaged body washed up on shore, discovered by strangers. She had always felt responsible for the drowning.

By Edgar's next words, it was evident he knew the story as well. "Emily Dickinson said it so beautifully: '*I would have drowned twice to save you sinking, dear.*'"

Laura nodded, touching her fingertips to the corners of her eyes as I draped an arm across her shoulders and gave a tender squeeze.

"So close to the ages of Lucas and Nicholas Kleister," she finally managed.

"Let's hope for a better ending for the Kleister family," I said.

"Indeed." Edgar knelt to inspect the bundle of wildflowers I'd found there.

"You mentioned earlier about having uncovered some interesting details?" I asked, to bring the conversation back to Barnacle Boy.

"Oh yes. I spent the morning with the historian of the Congregational Church. The minister back in 1969 was the Reverend James Woodhouse. He performed the funeral. He's no longer living, but very fortunately for me, his daily journal of prayer and good works had been retained in the church archives."

I knew the name. Reverend Woodhouse had been the minister who'd married my parents. I wondered if their nuptials had been recorded in that journal and what he might have said about their union. Maybe I'd go check it out one day.

"His notes indicate he performed a blessing on an item that was found along with the child."

"What was it?" Laura and I asked in the same eager tone.

"It wasn't specified. But Reverend Woodhouse did make an interesting notation about it."

Edgar fished from his pocket a folded-up photocopy of a beautiful handwritten note, which read: *The young boy will be buried in the private cemetery of the Mitchell family on Lavender Hill, Whale Rock. I believe this service would be more appropriately performed by Father Callahan with burial in St. Mary's churchyard. However, this cannot happen without the approval from the diocesan bishop, and that is unlikely without proof the child has been baptized.*

"Seems archaic."

"All religions have rules and traditions that must seem strange to others," Edgar said. "This unknown item somehow ties the boy to the Catholic Church. It intrigues me, and I wish there was more to be learned about it."

"I know who we should ask," I told them.

Fifteen minutes later, we were standing at the counter of Coastal Vintage Wares, having a chat with Archibald Stanfield.

"It's nice to see somebody walk through those doors," Archie exclaimed. "Whale Rock has been such a ghost town—I only came in today to check on things."

"Another week, and you'll be back to cursing the summer crowds." Laura tried to make light of his complaint.

"As if?" He rolled his eyes. "This world is going to hell in a hand basket," he lamented. "Historic storms, missing children, a murder in Whale Rock!"

"We don't actually know for sure it was murder," I corrected him.

"Well, I doubt that the man crawled into that dumpster on his own to die." Archie was indignant. "And now a kidnapping! That poor Kleister family."

"Why do you say it was a kidnapping?" Laura asked.

"It's the scuttlebutt that's going around town. Not true?"

"There's not enough evidence to know anything at this point," I answered. No doubt Matthew and Helene or their investigator were spreading the abduction theory—a tidbit I'd be sure to pass along to Brooks and Daniel.

"Is there a particular item I can help you find today?" Archie wiped away imaginary dust from the display counter glass top.

"We're here on a mission." I went on to explain what Reverend Woodhouse had written in his journal. "We were hoping you might know what the item was."

"That all happened long before I opened my shop in Whale Rock," he said, deflating our hopes. But Archie was not about to disappoint us. "Your grandmother Fiona once mentioned something about it to me, though."

"She did?" That rascal Granny Fi knew something about everything and everybody.

"The child had been found in a terrible state, as we all know." Archie closed his eyes and shuddered dramatically at the mental image. "It was your father who found the boy."

Papa had been sailing past the rocky shoreline north of town when he spied the body.

"Saintly people, you Mitchells," Archie went on to say. "Making a welcoming place for the child in your family graveyard."

It had mostly been Granny Fi's doing, but I nudged Archie to continue. "What was the item they found with the boy?"

"There was a chain around his neck that had unbelievably managed to stay on." He raised his arms in wonder. "The chain had a medal, some saint or another, though I dare say it did little to protect little Barnacle Boy." Archie's face saddened again. "Why the interest?"

"I'm writing something about the boy," Edgar told him, and then added softly, almost to himself, "I wonder what happened to that chain and medal."

* * *

"Wouldn't they have buried it with him?" Laura said on the drive back to The Bluffs.

"Most likely." Edgar was quiet a moment. "The only way to know for sure would be to have the body exhumed."

He seemed to sense my shock at the idea, for he went on to defend his proposal. "DNA testing didn't exist back in 1969. We could learn a great deal."

"Wouldn't you need permission?" Laura asked. "And wouldn't there be all sorts of health department rules and license applications?"

"Perhaps," Edgar countered. "But the family is as unknown as the boy. I'd handle the details and the cost."

When I still didn't say anything, he added, "Of course, since he's buried on Mitchell property, I will respect whatever you decide."

"Let me think about it," I said. Perhaps it truly would help determine who Barnacle Boy was and how he ended up lost and unclaimed on our shores. Still, I wasn't sure disturbing the long-buried child was a good idea.

"That's all I can ask." He offered his kindly smile as we pulled back up to The Bluffs. "Well, I must be off. Back to the Mitchell Free Library for a little more research into local lore."

Laura departed with Edgar, leaving me to consider his suggestion to exhume Barnacle Boy. I walked back into the house, and my nostrils filled with the telltale scents of the spirits who already shared my home. I didn't relish the thought of yet another manifestation in The Bluffs, pursuing me to its purposes. My gut was telling me to let the poor little soul rest peacefully.

*　*　*

I'd made a few calls to Nauset Marine to see if anyone there might still be in touch with Wes Creed, but nobody picked up. No doubt they were busy enough after the storm. I would try Lu next to find out about her cousin's past with Wes Creed. But before I had a chance, my phone buzzed to life with a call from Zoe.

"No news about the little boy," I told her before she could ask.

"That was going to be my second question."

"What was your first?"

"Had I been *permitted*, I was checking to see how things were with you."

"Busy with the search and helping the displaced. I got a call yesterday to help unload a truck of supplies sent from the Midwest."

"I made a donation yesterday to the relief efforts on the Cape."

"That was nice of you," I said, while cynically thinking it a means of easing her guilt over not being here in person. I was surprised by the next turn the conversation took.

"Remember that Teddy person you mentioned the other day?" she asked.

"Teddy Howell?"

This was met with silence, making me think the call had been dropped, which had been happening a lot lately.

"Zoe?"

"I'm here." She then asked, "How old is this Teddy *Howell*?"

"I'd guess mid- to late twenties," I said. "Why the interest?"

"Do you remember Theodora Howell?" she asked. "Her family owned the Glass House in Wellfleet."

"Oh yeah." I remembered the house, but not the girl. My father had christened the place "The Glass House" because it was one of those ultra-modern homes designed almost completely of windows, to take advantage of the great Cape Cod views. But it stuck out like an ugly sore amid all the charming cedar-sided cottages. And it was only a summer house; the family's main residence was in Boston.

"What did you say her name was?"

"Theodora. Everyone called her Theo. She was exotic looking, with long black hair."

"Oh, you mean the beauty queen?"

"I'd hardly call her that." The response was icy. Was Zoe jealous of someone she'd known ages ago?

"Well, *she was* Miss Massachusetts," I defended myself.

"Until she had to forfeit the crown." *Meow. Meow.*

A hazy memory surfaced of my mother and Zoe talking about some type of scandal linked to the pageant. I'd been too young to pay attention.

"Were there nude photos? Or did she get pregnant during her reign? It was something like that, right?"

"Funny." Not exactly an answer to my question. "I don't think she ever married. In fact," Zoe continued, "I'm told she still lives in the family's Beacon Hill home. Pretty fancy address, don't you think?"

I hadn't a clue where she was going with this. "Is Teddy related to her?"

"She's his mother."

Now, that *was* a surprise. "I never would have made the connection." I realized then that it had been Zoe who brought this all up. "So, what did you want to know about Teddy?"

"Nothing." Her voice was crisp. "I was just curious how you knew him."

There was something deeper than curiosity going on.

"I'd better go. I've got a meeting with my attorney," Zoe said.

"Next steps?" I ventured, not knowing what she'd decided about her errant husband. Zoe was all about prying everything out of me about my life and yet telling me nothing about hers.

She surprised me when she said, "Yes, I think it's time."

"I'm here if you need me," I told her. "You are always welcome at The Bluffs, and everyone would love having you back in Whale Rock."

A bitter laugh was followed by "Right."

I'd always wondered if my sister's rushed marriage to the charming Oliver Young, who'd whisked her away to the West Coast, was driven by her strong desire to escape Whale Rock. Why she never returned still remained a mystery to me, although she'd once confessed that she sensed something evil lurking within the bones of The Bluffs. As the call ended, I was enveloped by the scents of the spirits with whom I shared my home, wishing I could convince Zoe they meant us no harm.

Though sometimes, like right now, I had no idea what they were trying to tell me.

14

Cassandra

The next morning, when Jason joined Daniel and me for breakfast, he looked bemused. "Laura's not here?"

"I haven't seen her yet," I told him.

"Maybe she took Whistler for a walk," Daniel suggested, not lifting his gaze from the paper.

Jason's eyes swept the room, verifying his dog wasn't there. "That must be it." He took out his phone and sent a text, then filled his plate from the pan of scrambled eggs and popped two pieces of bread into the toaster.

"How's the Kleister investigator?" Jason asked Daniel while slathering the toast with butter.

"Pushy. Which can be an effective quality for someone in his role." Daniel took his empty plate to the sink. "I've briefed him on what we have. Now he's on his own."

Ten minutes later, Jason had finished his breakfast but still hadn't heard back from Laura. He and Daniel had to leave, so I grabbed my sneakers and tied them on. "I'll go round them up."

"Text me when you find them?"

"You bet," I said and headed out toward the land trust trails. I'd forgotten to warn Laura about the dangerous trees and fallen limbs.

It wasn't long before I found Whistler, whining and circling Laura, who was sprawled out on the trail. Fortunately, she was conscious and alert.

"What happened?" I kneeled beside her to brush the dirt from her face, which was difficult because Whistler kept shoving his nose in. "It's okay, boy."

"I was checking texts and my foot got caught on a root. Down I went and my phone went flying off over there." She pointed to the high grass along the path, where I found it and brought it back to her.

"Have you tried to stand?"

"Yes, but I've twisted my ankle." Then she covered her face with her hands and began to sob. "I'm so stupid."

"Don't be silly. Anyone could trip over these gnarly tree roots. I've done it plenty of times."

"I'm pregnant." Her face stricken with dirty tear tracks on her cheeks, she cried, "I landed really hard, and I'm so afraid the fall harmed the baby."

Pregnant? Could all these strange scent signals from Percy and Celeste have been about Laura's pregnancy now that she's staying at The Bluffs?

I pushed aside these thoughts and found myself in Granny Fi mode. "Let's get you sitting up. I'll just text Jason—"

"No!" She grabbed my arm. "He doesn't know about the baby yet. And if I've lost it . . ."

"Got it. I'll just tell him I found you." But I'd need help getting Laura back to The Bluffs. Fortunately, Christopher and I had exchanged cell phone numbers when I drove him to town yesterday, and he quickly came to our rescue.

"I can't thank you enough," I told him after we finally got Laura tucked into the car. I was insisting on taking her to the urgent care center to X-ray the ankle and check to make sure all was okay with her pregnancy.

"Glad I could help."

I was finding it hard to imagine him a person of interest, as Brooks had indicated.

"Does Jason think Christopher had anything to do with Lucas's disappearance?" I asked Laura later, on the drive to the medical center.

"Jason doesn't talk much about his work now that I'm doing reporting for the *Times*. What I know about the case I've learned from listening to discussions around the kitchen table with you and Daniel."

The conflict-of-interest aspect of her job hadn't really occurred to me. "Is that awkward for you?"

"Sometimes. I miss hearing about his day."

"He was worried about you this morning. You were out awfully early."

"Morning sickness." She stuck out her tongue and made a face.

"Ah-ha." Now her early morning rising made sense.

"I saw that woman again, the one from the other day? I managed a photo, though not a very good one, and decided to follow her." Her tone turned mournful as she continued, "Obviously, it didn't turn out as I'd hoped it would."

*　*　*

Back at The Bluffs two hours later, I helped Laura hobble inside. She was wearing a walking boot to treat a stress fracture in her foot.

"At least it will keep you out of trouble for the next six weeks."

Laura laid a hand across her belly. "I'm just so relieved the baby is safe."

"Maybe it's time to tell Jason?" I suggested.

"I was planning to tell him after your wedding. I knew he'd never be able to keep a secret and I didn't want *our* news to take away from your big day." She took in a deep breath. "And then the storm hit, and there just hasn't been a good time."

I got Laura settled in, with her foot elevated and iced.

"I'll take care of Whistler," I told her. On my way through the library, my laptop came whirring to life of its own accord . . . or not. *What were those mischievous little spirits up to this time?*

At the same time, my phone buzzed. It was Lu returning my call about her cousin's relationship with Wes Creed.

"Not much to tell," she said. "It didn't last long. The Ketchner girls have good sense. Why are you asking?"

"He's been working for Mitchell Tours, and I was curious if he'd straightened up his life."

"Evidently not. Evelyn told me he's in the Whale Rock jail." So much for curbing the gossip about Wes's arrest.

"I heard." Talking to Lu reminded me of Zoe's recent comments about Teddy and his relationship to Theodora Howell.

"What's Zoe's history with Theo Howell?"

There was a pause before Lu asked, "Why are you asking about *her*?"

"Zoe was asking about Teddy and then reminded me that the Howells owned the Glass House. I didn't know they were Teddy's family."

"She told you that?"

"Yes. She has a bug up her butt about Teddy's mother, which seems silly to me. Theo was a summer girl from decades ago, and barely a blip on the radar."

"Oh, believe me, Theo Howell was always much more than a blip."

"Because she was Miss Massachusetts?" I asked.

"Well, there's that," Lu admitted.

"Was there a more personal connection?" I prodded.

"That's a question for your sister," Lu said, signaling a full stop to my probing. "I must get going. The Congregational Church is still putting together care packages. If you're bored, join me."

* * *

After ending the call with Lu, I sat down at my laptop and found the incoming mailbox was already opened to an email from Zoe. The subject line was "Genetic Testing," and her two-line note read: *Maybe there was a genetic defect involved in Mama's miscarriages. You should get tested.*

I clicked on a link Zoe had included and began scanning the article, which was about several types of genetic abnormalities that had been found to promote miscarriages. The room filled with the strong burning smell that had been shadowing me the last few days. *Did Percy and Celeste not want me to follow up on these genetic issues?* Feeling the need to escape the overpowering and confusing scent, I grabbed Whistler's leash.

"Let's go, boy," I called out to the dog, who was as eager for some fresh air as I was.

I was lost in thought about the article Zoe sent when I reached Percy's Bluffs, only to find Christopher Savage sitting in my favorite spot. As annoying as it was, I tried to shrug it off.

"Hey there," I said, sitting down cross-legged next to him while letting Whistler run free. "Quite a view, huh?"

"I could get used to it." He continued to gaze out at the bay.

"Taking a break from the search?" I asked.

"The buses aren't running today."

"Oh, right." I hadn't thought about that.

"Where's Gypsy?" I rarely saw him without the pit bull.

"She's having a rough day."

"How's that?"

"We came across an aggressive dog on the trails. A brief snarling match, but it takes her a while to recover." He finally looked directly at me. "A rough history."

"She's a rescue?" I asked.

He nodded.

"Had she been abused?"

He shrugged. "*Something* had happened to her. And she was half-starved. I found her in a kill shelter just hours before her sentence was to be carried out. The staff told me they'd found her tied to their door, a sign around her scrawny neck: 'Please find her a nice home.'" Christopher shook his head at the memory. "The Good Samaritan who left her there probably had no idea it was a kill shelter and that Gypsy's fate was left to overworked volunteer staff who had only three days to find that nice home for her."

"Is that how you came up with the name?" I asked. "Because she'd been wandering and scavenging?"

"That, and I knew it would make my mother happy." A brief smile brightened his face.

I sent him a questioning look.

"Do you know the song 'Gypsy' by Fleetwood Mac?" he asked. "It was my mother's favorite song."

Fleetwood Mac reminded me of my father. For Papa, it had been "Landslide," which he'd played repeatedly after Mama died. Just like in the song, he truly had built his life around her, his world crumbling after she was gone. Even now, whenever the haunting tune came on the radio, I immediately changed the station.

"How's Laura?" Christopher asked, interrupting my sad reflections.

"Stress fracture," I told him. "They gave her a walking boot. I can't thank you enough for helping me get her back to The Bluffs."

"No problem."

"Is this your first time visiting the Cape?" I asked. I knew the answer already from Jimmy, but why not take the opportunity to pry some more personal information from the man?

He nodded.

"What brought you here now?"

"My mother."

"Oh, does she live out here?" Strange that he wouldn't have mentioned her earlier, especially when the storm hit.

"No," he said, disinclined to offer more. He idly picked at the grass, perhaps hoping I'd leave him alone. We sat in silence for several minutes before he finally spoke. "My mother died recently. Brain cancer."

"How horrible." And then, "I lost my mother to cancer. It was years ago. I was only seventeen."

"That's tough."

"When did it happen?" I rushed to ask while chastising myself. *Way to go, making it about yourself, Cass.*

"Over a month ago."

Right before he came to Whale Rock, according to Laura's estimate of when he arrived.

"I truly am sorry."

He nodded and continued to look out at the rising tide of the Cape. I probably should have left him to his lone thoughts, but for some reason I felt compelled to stay.

We sat quietly for a bit before he said, "I came out here to get away for a while. Took a leave of absence from my job."

That made sense, and should alleviate Brooks's concerns.

"I heard you're a teacher. What do you teach?" I asked.

"History and geography at a small prep school in upstate New York."

"I guess they go hand in hand." *Was this the best I could do?* "I'm not familiar with New York. Where did you learn sailing?"

"Mostly on Greenwood Lake, but also on the Hudson."

"I've only sailed on the ocean. How does it compare to lake or river sailing?"

"There are swells and tides to contend with out there." He jutted his chin toward the sea. "Not to mention all the land hazards along the coast."

"Was this your first ocean sailing experience?"

He shook his head and started to rise, clearly done with our conversation.

"Nicholas's grandparents are coming to take him away," I blurted out, added awkwardly, "I know you're fond of him."

He turned a worried face toward me. "Where will they go?"

"I think they live in Connecticut." I didn't know why I was telling him this. To gain his trust? "That's not for public consumption."

He looked at me as if to say, *Do I seem like someone who goes around blabbing everything I hear?* "If I've learned anything in my two decades of teaching, it's discretion. Both *how* to be discreet, and *when* it's *appropriate* to be."

15

Cassandra

Christopher and I walked back in awkward silence. When we arrived at the carriage house, I mentioned I'd be heading into town shortly.

"Let me know if you need a ride," I told him.

But after we parted company, I didn't see or hear from him, so I took myself to town to help Lu at the Congregational Church. A detour for tree removal forced me to park on Harbor Drive, at the end of the beach, near Laura and Jason's cottage. Before trekking to the church, I walked to the edge of the road to check on the progress of the repairs. There were no work crews in the vicinity, but I did spy a couple huddled near the rocks at the shore. Had there not been something familiar in the man's stance and the woman's short dark hair, I would have walked away. But a moment later they turned around, giving me a good look at their faces.

"What the . . .?" I didn't know which was more surprising, that Wes Creed was roaming free or that he was having a rendezvous with Helene Kleister.

I didn't want them to see me, so I ducked up the street to call Daniel.

"I just saw Wes Creed. Did you know he'd been released?"

"Yeah. Brooks just called to tell me that they couldn't hold him any longer without charging him, and with no evidence . . ." he left the thought dangling. "He's been instructed not to leave the area."

"Well, he's still here, and keeping interesting company."

"How's that?"

"He was with Helene Kleister."

"Where was this?" His tone sharpened.

"On the beach by Jason and Laura's place." I went on to ask, "Do you think they could be having an affair?"

"It's possible. There's no denying Creed's a real charmer."

"Always a useful trait for a roving rogue like Wes." I had no doubt said rogue would be roving right out of Whale Rock again shortly.

"It may also be why Nicholas reacted so strangely to Creed's photo the other day." Daniel blew out a frustrated breath. "If they *are* having an affair, then Wes has been lying."

* * *

Lu had already left the Congregational Church when I finally arrived, but it was a nice surprise to see Robyn Landers there helping out.

I sidled up to where she was working on care packages.

"Sorry we never got around to forming our First Wives Club." I resurrected the joke we'd shared when we both became newly single last fall.

"Yeah, well you're the lucky one who found love again so soon," she kidded back. "Sorry about your wedding."

Robyn hadn't been invited, but nothing happened in Whale Rock without everyone knowing.

"Sadly, Mother Nature doesn't check the calendar for weddings." I then asked, "How badly was Land's End damaged?"

"Not as bad as most. I hear my renter is staying with you until it's repaired."

"That's right. How well do you know Christopher?" I thought it a good chance to do a little digging.

"Not well at all."

"I was surprised that an outsider was able to snatch it up."

"I didn't even have to advertise. I put the word out, and some folks from Orleans called and said they had a friend who was interested."

"Anyone I'd know?"

"The Montrose family?"

I shook my head and then asked, "Is your boat back in the water yet?"

"No. Not a top priority." She gave me a mischievous smile. "Luckily I have a new friend who's been letting me bunk with him."

I was about to ask more when Robyn got a call and walked away to talk privately.

"I've got to run," she told me when she got back. "Nice to catch up."

"We should go out for drinks some night," I told her.

"Let's plan on it." She looked around the fellowship hall of the church. "Once the aftermath of Chantal has been cleaned up and life in Whale Rock is back to normal."

It was late afternoon when I returned to The Bluffs. I'd just let Whistler out when his barking brought me to the porch in time to watch a Whale Rock police cruiser pulling to a stop. Brooks tossed the dog a biscuit and then walked purposefully toward the carriage house, only nodding a hello to me.

It was a hot, still day and I easily heard his booming voice asking, "Have a minute for a chat, Mr. Savage?"

"Right now, I've got nothing but time," Christopher responded before the two men disappeared inside.

A few minutes later, Daniel called.

"Brooks is here," I told him.

"I know. The Kleisters's investigator has been putting on the pressure. Brooks is worried he'll show up at The Bluffs and make a mess of our investigation."

"Anything prompting this?"

"I was at the Kleisters when the grandparents showed up, giving it one more shot to get Nicholas to open up." Brooks was using Daniel for the more delicate interviews, capitalizing on his FBI experience.

"Did he?"

"Short of a tantrum, Nicholas resisted leaving his family. Finally, he told Matthew that he couldn't talk because he and Savage had a secret pact."

That didn't bode well for Christopher. "Any idea what the pact was?"

"That's what Brooks is trying to find out."

"He's not likely to say much." I told Daniel about my chat with the man and what he'd said about discretion.

"To hell with discretion. If this *secret pact* has anything at all to do with what happened to Lucas, then Savage has an obligation to tell us. He's an adult, for crying out loud, and this isn't a game." Daniel didn't even try to hide his frustration.

"I don't think Christopher would put a child's life in danger."

"We don't really know him, Cass."

"True," I said to appease him.

"I also have a hunch that Nicholas was being sent away out of fear he'd say something incriminating."

"Does your hunch have anything to do with today's little rendez-vous between Wes and Helene?"

"Well, that's one possibility." He cleared his throat. "Creed did show up at the harbor shortly after you spotted them and has been hard at work all day. Speak of the devil, here he comes. Gotta go."

I took my sketchbook out on the porch, where I could catch Brooks before he left. I was itching to get back to my painting. It had been months since I'd had any quality time in the studio. My life had not been my own, what with the wedding plans. My art had fallen by the wayside.

I'd become absorbed in my sketch and didn't notice Brooks until he stepped onto the porch, alarming me enough to break my char-coal stick.

"You startled me!"

"That was my aim." He laughed.

"I haven't heard that laugh in a while, Chuckles."

He dipped his head in agreement. "Not much to be amused about lately."

"Right." I closed my drawing pad and set it aside. "Coffee?"

"It *is* my drug of choice." Looking exhausted, Brooks followed me inside and nearly collapsed onto a kitchen chair.

"Have you slept at all?" I asked, setting up the coffee maker.

"Barely." He rubbed his large hands across his face. "The whole team has been working around the clock trying to find Lucas. Not to mention we have the Lee Chambers case."

"Any progress?"

"This storm has slowed that investigation to a snail's pace. I've got Bland and Kirkpatrick working on it, but there've been no leads. We're hoping forensics will provide us with something to follow up on."

"Was Christopher helpful?" I asked casually, setting the cream and sugar on the table.

"Not particularly. I'm still not convinced this Savage guy knows as little as he's claiming. Though he insists he could get Nicholas to talk."

"Maybe you should let him try," I suggested.

"The parents have thrown down a gauntlet. Short of a court order, my hands are tied." He sighed. "What do you think of the guy?"

"He's not easy to read." I measured my next words carefully. "But being quiet and detached doesn't make a person evil."

Brooks stared pensively into the cup I had just set before him.

"If I didn't make that coffee myself, I'd swear you were reading tea leaves," I ribbed him gently.

"It's killing me not finding that kid." The pain was etched into the lines of his face. "It's been four days now. Too long."

Though he'd yet to officially change the investigation from search and rescue to search and recovery, I could tell my friend feared the cruelest outcome. There were too many scenarios to consider. Had Lucas been swept away by the storm? Abducted? Or worse?

"Remember that little boy in North Carolina who got lost in the woods last year? He was gone for several days before they found him. We can't lose hope yet."

"Right now, hope is all we have." Brooks pushed himself up from the table and stepped onto the porch as Teddy Howell's gray jeep pulled up to the house.

"What's he doing out here?" Brooks mumbled.

"Hey, Cass." Teddy beamed a familiar smile at me. Now that I knew Theo Howell was his mother, I tried to resurrect a memory of the young woman. But it was too long ago for me to determine which of the dark, exotic beauty queen's features this young man may have inherited.

Brooks asked, "You looking for me?"

In a flash, Teddy's smile disappeared. "I tried to call but got voicemail. Daniel said you were out here, so I thought it just as easy to come to you."

Brooks glanced at his phone and frowned. "What did you find?"

My stomach lurched when Teddy produced a clear evidence bag that contained what looked like a child's sweatshirt and a small sneaker.

"Where were these?" Brooks's voice was gruff in that way men get when trying to mask their emotions.

"The shoe was wedged under the water in between the rocks at the north end of the beach in front of Jason and Laura's place."

Which meant it was also near Christopher Savage's cottage.

"And the shirt was caught in some lines of a sailboat in the harbor."

"Good work, Ted." Brooks laid a hand on the younger man's shoulder, producing an awkward moment for the two of them. "I'll take it to show the Kleisters. See if they can identify either as Lucas's."

"It could be nothing, right?" I said. "I mean, lost shoes and clothing are a regular occurrence along the beach."

"Absolutely," Brooks said, though he didn't look at all confident.

"Do you want us to continue diving?" Teddy asked.

"Call it a day. I'll get in touch later. I'm heading in for a strategy meeting now." Brooks looked at the evidence bag. "After a visit with the Kleisters."

Teddy nodded grimly. It appeared he also thought this find was a bad omen.

The two men departed together just as Christopher left with Gypsy for another walk. Knowing he was usually gone for at least an hour, my internal debate began: *The carriage house belongs to me, after all. I have every right to go in there.* Yes, but this was nothing short of invading his privacy. *But what's the harm, unless I find something incriminating? And if I do, then it should be discovered, right?*

"I'll go in for ten minutes," I told Whistler and left him outside the carriage house to alert me if anyone came along. If Christopher returned, I decided I'd use the excuse that I was there to gather sheets from the bedroom Edgar and Jimmy had used, so the first thing I did was strip the bed before poking around the rest of the carriage house.

I knew Christopher had been bunking on the Murphy bed in the far corner of the living area. He was a very tidy man. The bed was put away, there were no dirty dishes in the sink, and his clothes were neatly folded in his open bag. There was no way I could rifle through there without it being noticed.

My attention was drawn to the stack of books and periodicals on the kitchen table, lying next to the book bag Evelyn had delivered. Most focused on the pirates and shipwrecks of Cape Cod. There was a book entitled *Graveyard of the Atlantic* and several more on the history and local lore. Edgar's book on the enduring mysteries of Cape Cod was set to the side. I noticed there was a bookmark, so I opened it to find he was reading the chapter about the fire at The Bluffs. *It made sense that he'd be curious about a story that occurred in the home where he was staying,* I told myself.

I then picked up a publication from the top of the stack and flipped it open to an earmarked page. Inside was a reprint of an article from the May 1970 edition of the *Cape Cod Times*, headlined "Mystery of Drowned Boy Remains Unsolved."

Late September of last year, the body of a child was found washed along the rocky northern end of Whale Rock. Local tour boat owner, James Mitchell, had spotted the body while sailing back to Whale Rock Harbor.

"Having sailed these waters my entire life, I knew it was too risky to approach the shore by watercraft." An hour later he returned by land with Sheriff Walt Lindsey. County coroner, Dr. Calvin Jones, made the preliminary determination of death by drowning, though in his statement he claimed that the condition of the body made it difficult to determine if the trauma inflicted on the child had been the result of tumultuous conditions of the sea or from blows that may have occurred before the child ended up in the water.

An anonymous source close to the investigation reported that much of the flesh from the extremities had been eaten away by sea creatures, allowing barnacles to attach to the exposed bone. From this rumor sprung the nickname Barnacle Boy, though never uttered with anything but compassion by the local townsfolk.

As of this writing, some eight months after the child's body was discovered, his identity remains a mystery. This follows an exhausted search campaign to identify the child by untiring local and national law enforcement.

"It is simply mind boggling that no one has come forward to claim this unknown boy," Sheriff Lindsey said at a press conference late yesterday, announcing that the town's petition to have a proper funeral and burial for the child had been granted by the state. "This child matches no missing person claim going back well beyond what would be considered a normal time frame based on the pathology results. There has been no connection made to any other missing persons or unidentified human remains discovered within the same time period."

Led by Miss Fiona Patrick, mother of James Mitchell, the town put forth a request to give the child a proper Christian funeral and burial and have raised funds to cover the cost. In accordance with Massachusetts law, the body will not be cremated because of potential religious belief of the family should they be located at a later date or come forward to claim the child. No further details will be disclosed by investigators.

I knew the story well but had never seen this particular article. I wouldn't have given it much more thought had the room not filled with the familiar scent of Percy and Celeste. I dropped the magazine when Whistler began to bark an alert and now scrambled to pick it up and return it to the pile. Then I grabbed the bed linens and let myself out. I needn't have rushed; it was only Laura. She was sitting in a porch rocker, generously doling out her attentions to Whistler.

"How's the foot?" I asked.

"It would be better if I could take pain medication." She flinched. "What were you doing in the carriage house?"

"Collecting Edgar and Jimmy's sheets." I lifted the stuffed pillowcase as evidence.

"Uh-huh." She wasn't buying it.

"Oh, all right." I sat in the rocker next to hers. "I was doing a little scouting."

"Find anything?" She leaned forward, unable to conceal her eagerness.

"Nothing incriminating." I told her about the books on pirates and shipwrecks that Evelyn had delivered.

She actually yawned before saying, "Yeah. Edgar said he was working on a special project for his class. Kids would love studying that kind of thing in school. So?"

"He also seems to have been studying up on the Mitchell family's tragic history and Barnacle Boy. He's clearly interested in local lore."

"Hmm. It's funny. When I called Edgar to tell him I couldn't meet him today, he was grumbling about not finding what he was looking for at the library. I wonder if Christopher beat him to the very materials he's trying to track down."

"Could be."

"I suppose you've already heard that Wes Creed was released?" Evidently, Laura hadn't been resting all afternoon—more likely on the phone with her sources.

I nodded, debating whether to tell her about my sighting of Wes and Helene together, when she surprised me by what she said next.

"Remember the ring you saw by the dumpster where that drug dealer's body was found?" She didn't wait for an answer. "Well, it isn't a ring as in jewelry. It's a key ring. With a key attached."

"Does it have anything to do with Lee Chambers?"

"I don't know, but I intend to find out."

Not if I do first.

16

Renée

Italy ~ Mid-1980s

Renée marveled at the beautiful Italian countryside. On the drive to Vito's villa, her senses were indulged by the natural riches of her homeland: meadows filled with wildflowers, rolling hills in the distance, the fresh scents of lemon and orange trees, olive groves and grape vineyards. There was a tug of nostalgia as she remembered her parents and the happy life they'd had in their small village. How different her life would have been had they not died. She could easily have become a farmer's wife, and perhaps Isabella would not have been drawn to life in a convent if they'd stayed in Italy. Only Vito lived out his destiny in their native country, and soon she and her sister would have a glimpse of what could have been for their own lives.

As the minutes ticked by, Renée's anxiety grew. She worried about seeing Vito after so many years. Though she'd said she would forgive him, it might not be so easy to do when they were face to face. Would deep-rooted resentment overpower that protective sealed-off chamber?

Isabella reached over and gave her hand a comforting squeeze, as if she could sense Renée's angst. "It will be fine, Renata."

"How can you be so certain?"

Her sister smiled serenely and subtly raised her eyes. "Because He is with us."

Oh, how Renée wished she had such faith. But for now, she would have to rely on her sister's trust in God and hope Isabella's conviction would be enough to carry them both through this difficult day.

Renée did not let go of Isabella's hand until they were escorted to a veranda by a woman dressed in a crisp white dress, who she'd assumed was Vito's nurse. Though exceedingly pleasant, the woman spoke very little, communicating mainly via nods and smiles. She motioned for them to take a seat and went back into the house.

"This is stunning." Renée stood at the edge of the terrace, which overlooked a beautiful hillside of olive groves. Isabella had told her of Vito's success in producing and exporting high-quality olive oil.

Moments later the lovely lady who'd greeted them returned, holding Vito's hand. Renée gasped at the sight of her brother. Except for how thin he was, Vito looked nearly identical to their father before he'd been killed. His hair was still thick with short curls, though now it had turned completely white.

Isabella and Vito greeted one another in their native tongue. Renée had lost so much of her first language, but she understood enough to realize that the woman was Vito's wife, Martina.

"Renata." Her brother held open his arms.

Renée remained frozen in place, overcome by a surge of emotions. She covered her face and began to sob with abandon. They let her have her space, though she sensed their hovering presence while all the misery she'd kept carefully locked away was unleashed. Like the opening of Pandora's box, there would be a penalty to pay. When her catharsis ended, she was in a mild state of hyperventilation, with burning eyes and a headache. And yet she felt lighter, almost airy. Only Vito remained on the terrace with her, watching her with compassionate eyes.

"I'm sorry you had to witness that." Her voice was raspy. She held in her hands a crumpled handkerchief she didn't recognize, and was now seated but had no memory of how or when that happened. "How long did my meltdown last?"

"The sun is still high in the sky." He smiled kindly.

"Quite a first impression I've made on your wife."

"She is happy you are here." He added, "Because it makes me happy."

"And your children?"

"Three boys. You will meet them later, at dinner. Martina has a beautiful meal planned."

Renée took in her brother's gaunt appearance. "Isabella tells me you've been ill."

"It's the *cancro*." Even in his melodic Italian accent, the word sounded ghastly.

"Are you in treatment?" she asked.

"Experimental. The doctors tell me it's working."

"I'm very glad to hear that, Vito." And she was. It was amazing how comfortable she felt being there with her brother and sister, strangers to her for many years.

"And I'm glad you came. It has been hard, having no word of your life. You just vanished from us."

"Staying would have destroyed me."

He nodded his understanding. "Every time you looked at me, you would remember."

"That's not it," she said, though if she were honest, Vito had hit close to the mark. "Look, I don't want to dredge up that terrible time." She could not bear a repeat of her earlier breakdown. "I needed to erase that chapter of my life to survive. I never blamed you." It was true. She had only blamed herself.

"You've forgiven me, then?"

"There's nothing to forgive, *fratello mio*."

"Ti ringrazio." Relief eased the worry lines of her brother's face, reminding her more of the young Vito who had so often made her laugh. "Now we have both been liberated from our demons."

Would she ever be totally free? Renée wondered what she had said during her breakdown for Vito to think this.

During the next three days, the siblings reminisced about their youth. Vito gave them a tour of his land and the olive oil pressing plant. They ate breads dipped in that liquid gold and pastas coated thickly with it. There were wonderful cheeses and wines.

Vito's sons were engaging and talented boys, ages eight, ten, and thirteen. Spending time with them made Renée lonesome for her own family. She found herself phoning home more than she should have, always directing conversation back to what her husband and son were doing while she was away so as to avoid lying more than was necessary.

When the hour of departure arrived, Vito held out a thick brown envelope to Renée. Intuiting it held something she wouldn't want to see, she resisted, holding her arms firmly at her side.

"You will one day want to read these." He gently folded her hands around the envelope. "When the time is right, you will know."

She could not conceive of a time when curiosity would win out over self-preservation, but she swiftly tucked the envelope away in her carry-on bag.

"It might provide you with peace." Isabella encouraged her on the plane trip back to New York.

"Peace?" Renée was incredulous. "How does one find peace? Believe me, for the past fifteen years, I have tried."

The sisters remained quiet for several minutes before Renée asked, "Do you know what's in there?"

Isabella shook her head.

Renée removed the envelope from her tote bag and shoved it onto her sister's lap. "I give you permission to open it. Read everything. All I ask is that you never tell me anything about it."

She then ordered a double scotch and followed it with a sleeping pill, neither of which helped her achieve the oblivion she sought. Finally, she gave up and removed the sleep mask. Noticing Isabella's reading lamp was still lit, Renée turned to ask a question but found her sister wiping dampness from her cheeks.

"What's wrong?" She'd momentarily forgotten what Isabella had been reading.

Her sister returned the envelope and said, "You are not ready to read these, Renata. But Vito is right. One day you will be. And you should. But not yet."

* * *

Boston ~ Mid-1960s

Renata counted and recounted the days on the calendar. Never had her monthlies been so late.

"*Brutto stupido,*" she mumbled, slipping into her seldom-used Italian. How could she have been so naïve? She had fallen for Phillip Welles's charms, believing that he truly cared for her. But now he was at Oxford, and she was carrying his for certain unwanted child. Phillip hadn't even had the decency to say goodbye. She'd learned secondhand from the cook, the day after he'd left for England.

Renata understood she was alone in this bad situation, made worse by her aunt and uncle's strict Catholicism. They'd have no tolerance for a child born out of wedlock. Neither would her employer. She'd need to find a new place to live and work. And soon. She vowed to never tell anyone, especially Mrs. Welles, that Phillip had gotten her in trouble. Who would believe her anyhow?

But Marjorie Welles was an astute woman, picking up quickly on the early signs of morning sickness.

"I won't pry into your life, Renata, but does your young man plan to marry you?"

"No, ma'am." She sniffed, looking down at her feet in shame, fearing her employer might read the truth in her eyes.

"As I thought." It hadn't been spoken unkindly, but simply as the unvarnished truth of the matter.

A week later, Mrs. Welles came to Renata's room and instructed her to pack up her belongings. She burst into tears, thinking she was being sent back to her aunt and uncle's house from where she'd surely be banished in shame.

"Now, now. It would be unwise for you to stay here. You know how people gossip." Her employer gazed about the room as if suspecting someone might be peeping in through the curtains. "I presume returning to your family is not a viable option?"

Renata shook her head.

"That's what I thought." Mrs. Welles stood and opened a drawer, making a tsking sound at the meager belongings. "I've made arrangements for you to stay with a good friend of mine. Catherine Ferris and I have known each other since grammar school. She's a physician and will take good care of you during your pregnancy in exchange for you watching after her twins."

Renata was shell-shocked at how sympathetic the woman was to her predicament. *But would Mrs. Welles be treating her so kindly if she knew the whole story?*

Despite her fears, Renata could not have predicted how advantageous her new situation with Dr. Catherine Ferris would be, nor could she have imagined how much joy this unexpected child would bring to her life. She stayed on with the Ferris family for five wonderful years, Catherine and her husband becoming more than employers—mentors and friends, taking her under their wing and treating little Antonio as an equal to their own children. It was idyllic.

Until Marjorie Welles showed up for a visit. That was the day everything changed.

*   *   *

New York ~ Mid-1980s

After the two sisters collected their baggage at JFK airport, Renée asked, "When do you return to Boston?"

"I'm taking the morning train."

Renée knew the right thing to do would be to invite Isabella to her home, introduce her to her family. But she was too drained from travel and the emotions of the past few days to have another round of introductions.

"They have a room for me at the convent," Isabella said, sensing her hesitancy. Still, she wasn't about to let Renée completely off the hook. "You have taken the first step toward healing. Now it's time for the second."

"And that would be?"

"Tell your husband about everything. Honesty is the only path to freeing yourself from your burdens."

"I've lived the lie so long, it's become my truth. The past is the lie now."

"Does that mean we'll part again for good today?" Her sister's sad eyes broke Renée's heart.

"There are work reasons for me to travel to Boston. We'll meet again there," Renée assured her sister.

"I will take what the Lord offers." Isabella dabbed at her eyes. "I've missed you all these many years. The past few days have been a tonic for my soul."

"And mine. But you must understand, my decision to keep the past separate from the present has nothing to do with you."

Her sister sighed softly, then suggested, "Do you want me to take the envelope, for safekeeping?"

Renée couldn't help smiling. "You're worried I'll destroy it?"

Isabella lifted her shoulders. "The thought has crossed my mind."

In truth, it had crossed Renée's as well. "I promise you, I will not destroy the contents of Vito's envelope."

The two sisters shared a cab, stopping first at the convent. They hugged for such a long time, the cabbie rolled down the window and gruffly called out to them, "Hey, the meter's still runnin', ya know."

"*Dio vi benedica,*" Isabella whispered. ["God be with you."]

"*Anche con te.*" ["Also with you."] Renée kissed her sister on both cheeks. "I'll visit you soon."

*   *   *

When she arrived home, it was to warm hugs and a home-cooked meal.

"We made you spergetti, Mamma. 'Cause you were in Italy, far across the ocean." She held her son tightly until he squirmed free. "I gotta grate the cheese."

"It seems my two bachelors managed fine without me." She barely concealed her hurt feelings.

"Never." Michael took her into his arms. "You are the gravity to our universe."

Later, as Renée unpacked her suitcase, she considered tossing

Vito's envelope into the building incinerator in the morning. But she had promised Isabella, and it was probably a mortal sin to betray a nun. Instead, she tucked the envelope into a hidden security compartment in the bottom of her jewelry box.

She'd had a large enough dose of her past. It was time to shift into forward mode again. She was good at focusing on the future; it was how she'd managed these past fifteen years. Michael had called her the gravity in their world, but that wasn't true. What kept their universe intact was pure momentum. She feared that if she stopped hurtling forward and began to think about the past, that's when everything would fall apart.

17

Cassandra

I was trying to figure out how I could find out more about that key chain as Laura told me what else she'd learned while working the phones.

"Wellfleet's a mess. They've had so much more damage than Whale Rock," she said. "I'll be going tomorrow to interview the displaced and some of the volunteers. The Catholic Church has become a shelter. I spoke with the priest, and he's hoping a mention in my article will bring attention to how badly their community has been hit."

"I'll let the Congregational Church in town know. They'd want to help, and it would be another good destination for those food and care packages they're assembling."

"I'm told the road's washed out and half the town is stranded while other people can't even get to their cars. Johnny Hotchkiss is ferrying people who need to leave in one of the whale watcher crafts."

"He's a peach." But her mention of Johnny reminded me that I'd never passed along the name of Christopher's sailing partner to Brooks.

"I've got to run to town," I said. "Need anything?"

"Nope." Laura patted her laptop. "I'm going to try to get some work done."

Ten minutes later, I was back in town again for my second visit of the day with Brooks, who was fortunately still at the police station.

"Miss me?" he asked.

"Of course." I sat down across from his makeshift desk and noticed the bagged evidence that Teddy had brought to Brooks on the bench beside me. "Were these Lucas's?"

"Helene Kleister identified the shoe as his."

Not good. Not good at all.

"But she didn't recognize the sweatshirt." He raised his eyebrows. "We'll still submit it for DNA testing to be certain."

"Can I see you a sec, Boss?" Deputy Lisa Kirkpatrick popped her head in and nodded hello to me.

"Be right back." He stood and followed her far enough down the hallway that I was unable to make out the conversation.

While waiting, I picked up the evidence bag and fondled the small gray sweatshirt through the plastic. When I set it back down, it slipped off the bench along with a smaller bag. I picked them up and in doing so realized the smaller bag held a key ring. Probably *the* key ring from the alley, and there was a key attached.

"Thanks, Lisa." Brooks's voice was growing closer, barely allowing me time for a quick snap with my phone camera before tucking the bag underneath the sweatshirt again.

"What a mess." Brooks sighed deeply as he sat heavily in his chair.

"What's going on now?" My heart was racing from almost being caught snooping through the evidence.

"I managed to get a judge to help us with a court order to have Nicholas brought back so we can talk with him."

"A judge allowing you to set up this meeting seems positive, right?"

"Except for the fact that as soon as I presented the Kleisters with the order, I discovered that Helene's parents have a high-powered law firm in Boston. So now there has to be a hearing about the court order with another judge."

"Why would the Kleisters do anything to slow down the investigation?"

Brooks blew out another exasperated breath. "I wish I knew, Cassie. Not cooperating does nothing but cast suspicion on them. And like you said, slows down the progress we've been making."

"I did learn why Christopher Savage has taken a leave of absence from his teaching job. His mother died."

He merely nodded.

"I also found out the information you wanted me to get from Johnny." I gave him the name of the man who had gone out sailing with Christopher on Johnny Hotchkiss's Catalina the day before the storm.

"Tyler Stendall. S-T-E-N-D-A-L-L?"

"That's right. Apparently, Christopher dropped him off in Orleans. It may be the same guy who brought him out to the Cape."

"Okeydokey," my exhausted friend said. "I'll get someone working on it."

*   *   *

I had to wonder if Brooks even made it to bed that night, with his call coming in so early the next morning.

"It's not looking good for Christopher Savage," Daniel told me as he headed to the shower.

I threw off the sheets and, quickly pulling on shorts and a T-shirt, followed him into the bathroom. "Why? What's happened now?"

"Do you want to hear the bad, worse, or worst news first?" he called out, to be heard above the shower.

"Does it matter?" I asked, brushing my teeth.

"Jason spoke with another straggler from the party house last night. This new guy claims he saw Savage having an altercation with Lee Chambers. Savage kept stabbing Chambers in the chest with his finger and said something to the effect of 'Leave it alone' or 'Leave him alone.'"

If this was true, it meant Christopher had lied to the police about not knowing Lee Chambers.

"Okay, what's the worse news?" I splashed water on my face.

The shower stream stopped, and Daniel pulled a towel off the shower door.

"When the workers showed up to begin repairs on the cottage Savage is renting, they found what appears to be the mate to the shoe the divers found."

A queasiness came over me with this revelation. "Are they sure it's a match?"

"Brooks is heading down to pick it up now." He wrapped the towel around his waist and walked to the closet. "There might be an easy explanation to that, but Brooks wants me to talk with Savage while he checks out the cottage."

"Wouldn't they need a warrant?"

Daniel held up his hands. "I didn't ask."

"So what's the *worst* news for Christopher?"

"Jason has uncovered the existence of some sealed records from an incident early in Savage's career."

"What kind of incident?"

"Nobody he currently works with knows anything about it." Daniel emerged from the closet in polo shirt and khakis. "Brooks wants me to see if my contacts at the Bureau can get a look at them"—he made finger quotation marks—"unofficially."

*   *   *

Moments later, Daniel was scarfing down a slice of toast and filling a travel mug with coffee while I was reading a note from Laura.

"Laura's already gone for the day, and Jason spent the night at the station."

"It's nice to have the place to ourselves." Daniel grabbed me and nuzzled my neck. "Too bad we can't take advantage."

I couldn't help giggling, which was also a nice change of pace. But our brief moment of fun was interrupted when Whistler issued a growling alert a moment before there was a knock on the door.

"Could I hitch a ride to town sometime today?" Christopher asked me before noticing Daniel in the kitchen.

"I was just coming over to see you," Daniel said, wiping his hands with a kitchen tea towel. "But we can do it here."

"Do what?" Christopher had a wary look.

"Some information has come to light that you might be able to help us with."

"Sure," he agreed, but he didn't look all that eager.

"I'll just go take care of some paperwork," I said as the two men pulled out chairs across from each other at the large oak table.

"Don't leave on my account." Christopher's pleading look said "Stay."

Daniel merely shrugged, which I took as an invitation.

I filled a mug with coffee for Christopher, pushing the cream and sugar closer.

"Thanks. What can I help with?" he asked, stirring cream into his coffee.

Daniel placed Lee Chambers's photo on the table.

Christopher frowned at it. "I've been shown this photo before."

"That's right. And you told Chief Kincaid you didn't know this person?"

"Correct." He peered intently at Daniel over the top of his mug as he took a gulp of coffee.

"I just wanted you to look at it again and be certain."

"I'm certain." He pushed the photograph back across the table with a conviction matching his tone of voice.

"Well," Daniel scratched his head, "there's a witness who's come forward and stated they saw you and this man having an altercation."

"Then that *witness* would be mistaken. I've never met, seen, or heard of this man until the other day when I was first shown his picture." Christopher's patience was being tested, which may have been what Daniel intended.

"Okay." Daniel raised his hands in a calming gesture. "I appreciate your patience with us as we try to sift the facts from the fiction. Could be mistaken identity."

It was fascinating to observe Daniel question someone. It was a poker game, all hedging and bluffing.

"The second problem we've run into has to do with the cottage you're renting. The workers showed up today to begin repairs and found something concerning."

Daniel opened a photo on his phone and passed it across the table.

Christopher squinted. "A shoe?"

"A child's shoe."

"Where was it found?"

"Under your deck steps. A piece of decking had broken, and when they pried it off to replace it, that's when they found it." Daniel took his phone back. "Odd place for it, wouldn't you say?"

"I suppose."

I opened my mouth to ask a question about whether the storm winds could have blown the shoe under the steps, but caught myself. It wouldn't be wise to interrupt.

"Any idea whose it is?" Daniel asked.

"Can I see it again?" Daniel pulled up the photo once more.

Christopher enlarged the image to study it closely before saying, "I can't be certain, but it might belong to one of the Kleister boys."

There was a subtle twitch to Daniel's jaw that had me wondering if he was surprised by such a forthright response.

"Care to elaborate?"

"Remember when I told you the other day that Nicholas brought Lucas to the cottage once, and I wheeled the two of them back to their place on the beach cart? What I didn't mention was that Lucas cut his foot that day. That's why I used the cart. The boys were climbing on the rocks barefoot, but Lucas slipped and cut his heel on the sharp edge of a broken shell." He closed his eyes and rubbed his forehead as if trying to bring the scene to memory. "I grabbed a towel from the line to clean it, then bandaged it up. I thought we'd gathered all their things, but now I can't recall."

Daniel was silent. I couldn't tell whether he believed the story or not.

"You can ask Nicholas," Christopher said defensively. "He'll tell you what happened."

"For one thing, Nicholas is now with his grandparents."

I held my breath waiting for Christopher's reaction.

"Where?" he asked, and I relaxed, knowing he wouldn't betray my confidence.

"I'm not at liberty to say. Besides, he isn't talking to anyone."

"He'll talk to me," he persisted.

"Unfortunately, that's not going to happen." Daniel placed the photo of Lee Chambers back into the file. "Work on your rental will be delayed."

The man seemed to deflate with this unwelcomed news. He was likely eager to return to his solitude.

"Why?" he finally asked.

"The police are there now, and depending on what they find, it may be declared a crime scene." Daniel said this matter-of-factly, but Christopher's head whipped around.

"Are you accusing me of something?" He was angry now.

"Just asking some questions," Daniel told him.

"Well, I have a question for you. Do I need an attorney?"

"Entirely up to you. If you think you need representation, then by all means, hire one."

"I don't *need* representation because I am not guilty—of anything. But if someone is framing me, which I'm getting a sick feeling is the case, then I don't know how to defend myself."

Daniel wrote down the name of a lawyer friend of ours and passed it across the table. "She's excellent."

"Can I go now?" Christopher picked up the paper and tucked it into his shirt pocket. He looked so miserable, my heart wrenched for the guy.

"Sure. Just don't leave town."

After he left, I asked Daniel, "Do you really think he's involved?"

"I'd have a better idea if we could unseal the documents about that past incident. It would open a clearer window to the guy's history." He took in a deep breath. "And we really need to speak with Nicholas."

"You didn't bring up the sealed records."

"Too soon. We need to see if we can get our hands on them before we show those cards."

I drummed the table with my fingers.

"What are you thinking?" he asked.

"Christopher Savage is either telling the truth, or he's a very skilled liar and a cool cat when cornered."

"I've observed both." Daniel gathered his papers and his phone, not giving a hint of which extreme he felt better suited the man.

To use an old sailing expression, I'd cut the guy some slack and see how he handled the sail. Christopher was guarded—no question. But was he evil?

*   *   *

After helping to pack up boxes of provisions at the church, I stacked as many as would fit in the bed of the truck and drove them over to Wellfleet. I found Laura chatting with folks temporarily sheltering in the Catholic Church, and playing with the children. She was a natural with kids; I could tell she was going to be a great mom.

When she saw me, Laura waved and came over to help me unload.

"These are going to be a big help," she shouted, in order to be heard over the chain saws attacking a fallen tree.

"No heavy lifting for you. Just the lighter bags." I pointed to the cab of the truck.

"I'm pregnant, not sick," she complained, lowering her voice.

"I was thinking about your foot," I said as we carried the first load into the church.

She frowned down at her boot.

"Is Jason over the moon at the news?"

"I have not had a moment alone with him. He's beat from around-the-clock shifts." She made a pouty face. "I want it to be special."

I glanced across the large church social hall and noticed a dowdy-looking woman who seemed vaguely familiar, but I couldn't place how I knew her.

A pleasant, fresh-faced man sporting a priest's collar approached us. "Let me help you with these."

"Father Sebastian, this is my friend Cassandra Mitchell. She's delivered a truckload from the Whale Rock Congregational Church."

"A much-needed blessing. We are praying everyone will be able to return to their homes soon." He followed us out to the truck and hefted a large box. "Mitchell, you said? Like the Mitchell Whale Watcher Boat Tours?"

"That's right."

"Johnny Hotchkiss is one of our most devoted parishioners."

I wondered how Johnny found time to squeeze in an hour for Mass anytime during the season.

"I hear he's been ferrying the stranded out of town."

"A godsend. Truly."

It took several more trips to finish unloading. Back in the social hall, I searched for the woman who had stuck out to me, but she was no longer there.

18

Cassandra

On my way back to The Bluffs to collect more supplies for the shelter, I was detoured past The Lookout, where I noticed Helene Kleister chasing after one of the twins. I quickly pulled to a stop and hopped out in time to grab the little tyke before he ran straight into oncoming traffic.

"You're a speedy little guy," I said as he squealed to be released.

"Mason, you are going to be the end of me." The harried mother took the squirming toddler from my grasp. After catching her breath and taking in the scene, she looked at me and said, "Lucky you caught him. Thanks."

"Traffic is moving slowly because of the detour," I said to ease her distress. "Having two *under* two can't be easy."

"Oh God! Aiden." She ran as fast as she could while holding a wiggling child, and I followed her around to the beach side of the house.

Fortunately, the other twin was amusing himself on the deck with a smartphone. Unfortunately, I also spotted a pair of sharp scissors lying on the deck not far from where he was playing, so I picked them up to place them out of reach while casually asking, "Where's Matthew?"

"Out with the search teams." She combed fingers through her short dark hair and kept her focus on the twins, who were now fighting over the phone.

"I've got a few minutes. Let me help you put some of this away," I offered and gently removed the object of dispute from the twins' grasps and handed it to Helene.

"I can manage," she said, though not defensively and certainly not convincingly. Nor did she stop me as I began to gather up the remnants of their lunch.

"Of course you can," I said before going inside to tidy up a bit. *Evelyn was right. The house was a disaster waiting to happen.* The first hazard I noticed was a bottle of pills, unlabeled—not even a child-resistant cap. I didn't hesitate to move it to a safer location, but not before opening it, tapping one out, and tucking it into my pocket. I looked out to the deck to ensure Helene was occupied with the twins before slipping into the master bedroom.

I checked both night table drawers and found another similar bottle hidden in the back behind some books. Using a tissue, I pried off the cap to find it contained the same type of pill. I rushed back out to the kitchen for a plastic zipper bag to preserve any fingerprints with the thought of tying the pill bottle to whoever was on the supply end of these drugs. I then tucked the bag containing the pill bottle into the waistband of my shorts.

I spent the next few minutes loading the dishwasher and cleaning off all the kitchen counters. A peek into the refrigerator assured me that they at least had adequate food for the next few days, though I wondered how the parents of a missing child could manage to keep anything down. I was just about to sneak into the boys' bedrooms for a look when Helene brought the twins in from the deck.

"I'm going to try to coax them down for a nap," she told me over their shrieks of protest. After taking in the now sparkling kitchen, she offered a defeated shrug. "Thank you."

I wrote down my cell phone number on a whiteboard next to the pantry. "Call if you need anything."

She nodded and then pulled the two resisting bundles of energy down the hallway.

* * *

For the second time in as many days, I was surprised to see Daniel walk into our kitchen in the middle of the day.

"If you're hungry, all I can offer is an encore to yesterday's lunch." I hadn't yet made it to the grocery store and wasn't ready to face Stella Kruk again. With all that was going on in Whale Rock these days, she'd be salivating for details about everything from poor little Lucas to the mysterious dead man, to my postponed wedding. On the other hand, maybe Lee Chambers had stopped by her store. *Hmm . . . perhaps a visit to All the Basics was in order after all.*

"I'm hungry all right." He sent me a randy smile, then checked the captain's wheel clock. "Unfortunately, I don't have much time."

"This will have to do"—I set out all the fixings and pecked him on the cheek—"for now."

He pulled me into a hug but quickly pushed me away and felt along my waist and pulled out the bagged pill bottle. "What the heck is this?"

"I borrowed them from Helene Kleister." I then proceeded to tell him about what happened just an hour earlier.

"You use the term *borrowed* quite liberally." I couldn't tell if he was dismayed or proud of me.

"I don't think she'll miss them yet. She has a large supply." I dug out the single orange pill I'd tucked into my pocket and handed it to him. "Look familiar?"

"Might be Adderall." He pulled out a pair of reading glasses to inspect more closely. "See the 'AD' printed on the side? Big abuse problem with these."

"Do you want to give them to Brooks?" I held up the bag. "Or should I?"

"I'll be seeing him later." He took it and held it up to the light. "If we're lucky, there will be prints other than Helene's on the bottle."

At least I'd be off the hook to explain to Brooks how I managed to take them.

Daniel gazed out the window at the carriage house. "Where's Savage?"

"I haven't seen him since this morning. Maybe he's meeting with his *new attorney.*"

The sarcastic edge to my tone prompted Daniel to ask, "You feel confident he's not involved?"

"I just don't get the sense that he's an evil human being. He's quiet, but he seems relatively normal."

"Ted Bundy syndrome," he mumbled, taking a plate down from the cupboard.

"What about Ted Bundy?"

"He was a nice-looking and charming guy, seemed perfectly normal. Nobody would have guessed that he was capable of bludgeoning someone to death with a baseball bat." Daniel shook his head as he slathered bread slices with peanut butter and beach plum jelly. "That name you found?" he said between bites. "The guy who went sailing with Savage last week?"

"Tyler Stendall. You've tracked him down?"

"No, he's not answering his phone. But we were able to speak with his parents. Mother, that is, and stepfather. I get the impression they're somewhat estranged from their son."

"How old is this Tyler?" I unscrewed the peanut butter jar lid and scooped out a gob with my finger.

"Just turned twenty-eight." Daniel made a face. "Hey, we do share that jar."

"Sorry," I mumbled through the thick paste. "So, the parents weren't all that helpful?"

"Only in the sense that they generated more questions. The mother did say that Stendall loved the Cape. Apparently, she and his father brought him out here when he was a boy."

"Where's his father now?"

"He died in Afghanistan." Daniel pulled a carton of milk from the refrigerator and gave it a sniff. Deeming it fresh enough, he poured himself a glass to wash down the PBJ. "Stendall has no record of a criminal past, no arrests. His mother said that he wasn't a bad kid, just not terribly motivated. He dropped out of college and has remained aimless ever since."

"What does he do?"

"He was tending bar somewhere in Rhode Island last they heard. That was a year ago."

"Where do the mother and stepfather live?" I let Whistler lick the remnants of peanut butter from my finger.

"Upstate New York." Daniel took the jar of peanut butter away from me, possibly to ensure I didn't dig in again, especially with the finger that Whistler had just licked clean. Then he began to make a second sandwich. "The most useful part was that Stendall attended the Bridgewater Academy. Same prep school where Savage teaches."

"Did the parents know Christopher?"

"Here's where it gets interesting." Daniel waved his sandwich at me. "The mother was doing all the talking until I asked that question. When she repeated Savage's name, the stepfather took the phone from her and said, 'That's a closed chapter.' Then he disconnected, and they've not answered our attempts to call them back."

My willingness to give Christopher the benefit of the doubt was challenged with this bit of information. Had the relationship between Christopher and Tyler gone beyond teacher–student? Why had the stepfather reacted so heatedly, and why was he refusing to talk about it? "Do you think there's a connection between Tyler Stendall and the sealed documents?"

"Not sure. My contacts at the Bureau got a New York judge to review the contents. He'll allow the file to be unsealed, but only if Savage signs off on it." Daniel finished off his sandwich and brushed the crumbs from his hands. He drained the glass of milk, took it to the sink, and rinsed it out. "With the caveat that it cannot be used for any purpose other than to prove or disprove his involvement in the missing Kleister boy case."

"How does that work?"

"Won't know until we see it. There'd be a good deal of redaction, I'm sure. We'll just have to hope that whatever's left sheds light on Savage's character—for good or bad."

I sat quietly for a moment before offering a suggestion. "Look, Christopher trusts me more than he does you or Brooks. Let me try to convince him to do it."

Daniel drummed the table but didn't say no.

"If you take him down to the station, all he'll see are the holding cells," I continued. "It could backfire. He might refuse to let you open the file."

"You've got a point. Let me pass it by the chief."

He took his phone into the library to confer with Brooks. When he returned, he gave me a thumbs-up. "Okay. It's your game."

I pulled out my phone and sent Christopher a text and received a quick response.

"He's walking Gypsy and will be back shortly. You probably shouldn't be here when he gets back."

"You're right. Call me when you have his answer." Daniel pushed back his chair and grabbed his keys. I considered it a good sign. He couldn't be too worried about the guy if he was willing to leave his fiancée in the company of someone he'd compared to Ted Bundy moments earlier.

"What if he says no?"

"Having second thoughts?"

"No," I lied. "I'm your best bet. I just wondered what Plan B was."

"I believe we've gone well beyond B at this point. Maybe Plan F?" Daniel looked defeated.

"What aren't you telling me?"

"Tomorrow Brooks will announce a change in status from search and rescue to search and recover."

My stomach heaved at the thought. "Do the Kleisters know?"

"Not yet."

"I don't envy Brooks having to tell them." Helene was barely holding it together as it was. How would she survive this blow?

"Nor do I."

"Wishing you were taking a tour group out instead of all this crap?"

He tilted his head. "Sure do."

*   *   *

Fifteen minutes later, Christopher and I were sipping lemonade on the front porch.

I decided it was best to take the direct approach. "I'm aware there are sealed documents from an incident early in your teaching career."

"And how would you know that?" He reached down to give Whistler some pats.

"It's a small town. And given my connections to local law enforcement . . . I'm a bit of an insider on the Lucas Kleister case."

He didn't say anything but fixed me with a cool stare, green eyes mirroring my own.

"The file is an unknown, which casts suspicion on you. My understanding is that a New York judge has reviewed the file and will allow it to be unsealed if you give your permission."

"Why would I want to do that?"

"It could be beneficial to you."

He stared out toward the bay for an uncomfortable moment before looking at me directly and asking, "Do you think I've done something to Lucas?"

How to answer this? "It doesn't matter what I think."

"Maybe not, but I'd still like to know."

"I don't have any reason to believe you did," I said carefully. "I also don't possess any information to convince me you didn't."

"At least you're not trying to play me." He returned his gaze to the bay.

"Why would I try to play you?"

"As you said, you have close connections to law enforcement."

I took a deep breath. "Look, I don't know you at all. But from the brief interactions we've had, my gut tells me you couldn't have harmed a child. That's why I think you should unseal the documents."

He wiped the sweat from the glass of lemonade before taking a gulp. The silence between us was awkward, and I was prepared for him to leave. But he surprised me when he spoke.

"There was a disciplinary action brought against me early in my teaching career."

I stayed silent and didn't prod, hoping the best strategy was to allow the man to tell his story at his pace.

"I was young and green, barely out of the chute as a teacher. But I made up for that inexperience with idealism and enthusiasm. I was going to form minds and mold characters." He laughed cynically. "However, I was completely ill-equipped to counsel a student with personal issues. The problem was, I was blinded to that fact by unfounded confidence. As a result, I made a foolish mistake."

I waited.

"Look, what I did was reckless, but it was only to protect a student from a difficult situation. I'd been trying to do what I thought was right, only it turned around on me."

"What was the accusation?" I prepared myself for the worst.

"Inappropriate behavior and sexual misconduct with a minor." *Not much worse than that for a high school teacher.* "It was a false accusation," he quickly added.

"If you were exonerated, why were the records sealed?"

Again, those cool green eyes locked onto mine. "To protect the student."

"A student had a crush on you and, when spurned, made up a story?" I ventured a guess.

"It wasn't the student who filed charges. It was the parents." He rubbed his face with his hands. "It also wasn't a female student."

Ah-ha.

"The kid confided in me that his stepfather was verbally and physically abusing him. He ran away from home, and I let him stay with me for a few days until we came up with a plan. But then the you-know-what hit the fan."

Pieces of the puzzle were starting to click into place in my head. "You couldn't persuade him to go to the police?"

"His stepfather *was* the police."

I wondered if that was why Christopher seemed so defensive around Daniel and Brooks.

"Was this student Tyler Stendall?" *Why not go out on that limb too?*

Christopher's astonished face was answer enough.

"How do you . . . how would you know anything about Tyler?"

"An educated guess."

"Based on what?"

"He signed a release form when you two went sailing last week. The police have been trying to contact him, but he isn't answering his phone. His parents didn't react well to hearing your name. Have any idea where he might be?"

"It was such a mistake coming here," Christopher said, resting his weary head onto his hands. "Ghosts from the past should not be disturbed."

It appeared we Mitchells weren't the only ones haunted by their past.

19

Renée

"Bless me father for I have sinned." Although Renée had long ago abandoned her Catholic faith, she hoped to find comfort in the holy sacrament of confession. She was surprised to find no confessional booth but instead met with a priest in what was called a Reconciliation room. She had waited for the long line to dwindle so she could be the last to make her confession.

"In the name of the Father, and of the Son, and of the Holy Spirit. Amen."

When Renée didn't speak, the priest asked her, "How long since your last confession, my child?"

"Forty years." She met his eyes. "I'm a little rusty at this."

The priest smiled kindly. "Is there a particularly troublesome sin you've committed?"

"I've lied to my family—a very big lie—about who I am and what I've done."

"Is what you've done a mortal sin?"

A sob escaped as she nodded. "And now God is punishing me. With brain cancer."

The priest waited for her to regain her composure. "Are you prepared to confess that sin today?"

She shook her head.

"I would counsel you to trust in God's mercy."

"I'm sorry, I've wasted your time."

As Renée stood to leave, the priest took her hand. "Let us say the Prayer of Contrition together."

Afterward, he told her, "Your penance is to tell your family about this secret you've been keeping. God will forgive you."

"But will *they*?" she asked, knowing the priest could not answer.

It was a slow walk home, during which Renée came to a decision. Telling her husband and son the truth would serve no useful purpose other than to relieve her burdened conscience. But in doing so, she would be burdening her family. She could not do that to them now. They had enough to deal with in the coming months as she went through chemotherapy.

When she returned to the apartment, she removed Vito's envelope from the secret compartment of her jewelry box, where she'd kept it hidden for decades.

"This will be my penance," she whispered. It was time to face the truth, however awful it might be. She opened it, creating a deep paper cut in the process and spilling a drop of blood on the envelope. Being superstitious, she dabbed it behind her ears as her mother would have done.

After reading the shattering contents, she flung her wretched self across the bed and wept for hours. It was a release of all the emotions that had remained bottled up since her meltdown with Vito. She understood that the cancer was her just punishment. It first took her brother, who had battled the devil for many years. Now she would await her own death sentence. If there was a God, she prayed it was a merciful being.

* * *

Boston ~ Late 1960s

Renata had been surprised to find Mrs. Welles sitting with Catherine Ferris in the courtyard when she brought the children out for some fresh air. It was a school holiday, and they'd been frozen in front of the television since breakfast. The Ferris twins were now ten, and her son Antonio had just turned five. They acted like siblings, squabbling at times but mostly loving and playful with one another. Today they were getting along famously and ran to the outdoor play set.

"Renata, come say hello." Catherine pulled out a chair for her to join them.

"What a pleasant surprise," Renata said, trying to calm herself. "You look very well, Mrs. Welles."

"As do you." The woman looked at her appraisingly. "You have really come into your own."

"Our Renata here is now taking courses at Massachusetts Community College."

"That's wonderful." Her former employer seemed genuinely pleased. "What are you studying?"

"Mostly practical courses, accounting and clerical."

"I've also encouraged her to take some design classes. Renata has an artistic flair. I'll have to show you some of her watercolors."

"I have to think of the future," she said, though pleased by the compliment. "The children soon will be too old for a nanny, and Catherine will find a better use for our rooms."

"I will hate to see you go." Catherine smiled fondly.

"My, how progressive. On a first-name basis, are we?"

Renata felt her cheeks grow warm. Although Mrs. Welles had been her protector during a difficult time, she still considered Renata a lowly employee.

"Don't be so archaic, Marjorie," Catherine scolded, as only a close friend could. "Renata has become a good friend to us."

Just then, Antonio ran up with blood dripping from his nose.

"Oh no, another one?" Her son was prone to nosebleeds. Renata pulled some gauze from her pocket, always at the ready.

"He must have his father's eyes." Marjorie Welles smiled, noticing the boy's startling blue eyes.

It was true, Antonio had inherited Phillip Welles's eye color, which popped stunningly against his light caramel skin and the bronze hair he'd inherited from Renata.

"Let's get the bleeding to stop," Renata said, taking Antonio inside the house, hoping Mrs. Welles wouldn't recognize any other familiar traits.

From the kitchen, she heard Mrs. Welles say, "Phillip used to get horrible nosebleeds as well. We had him tested and learned it was a genetic disorder. Not hemophilia."

"Von Willebrand disease?" Catherine asked.

"Yes, that's it. Of course, as a doctor you'd know about it." Mrs. Welles said. "It was Type One which is the mildest form, and eventually he seemed to outgrow it."

Renata had stopped breathing and prayed. *Please, please, please, Catherine, don't mention that Antonio recently tested positive for Von Willebrand disease.* She was grateful when she heard the conversation turned to other topics, but only let out her breath once Mrs. Welles finally left. Although surely Catherine herself would now connect the dots to Antonio's paternity.

Later, when the children were doing their homework, Catherine sought her out.

"Join me for a cup of tea?"

The two women sat quietly until Catherine asked, "Did Phillip rape you?"

Renata shook her head. "It was consensual."

"But he did take advantage of you." It was not a question and was uttered in disgust. "I'm not betraying my friendship with Marjorie by telling you that Phillip has earned something of a reputation for his behavior."

This resurrected the memory of Phillip's expulsion from the private school in New Hampshire. Renata wondered if he'd gotten another girl in trouble.

"Does he have other children?"

"I don't believe so. I'm aware of at least one other pregnancy." Catherine looked away and said, "It was terminated though."

"He never knew I was pregnant. He'd left for England before I even knew for sure myself." Now she wondered, what would she have done if Phillip had pressured her to end the pregnancy? A shiver passed through her at the thought of how hollow her life would have been without Antonio.

"Do you think Mrs. Welles suspects that Antonio is Phillip's child?"

"I don't know, but it won't take long for her to start piecing it together. Marjorie Welles is a very intuitive lady."

Renata agreed, which worried her greatly, but Catherine tried to reassure her.

"It's unlikely she'd do anything about it. The Welles care very much about appearances."

As kind as Mrs. Welles had been to her in the past, Renata's own intuition was telling her not to trust the woman.

* * *

New York ~ One year ago

Before beginning her cancer treatments, Renée found an excuse to travel to Boston for a visit with her sister. She decided to treat herself to a night at The Four Seasons and invited Isabella to join her, but her sister declined, making Renée feel guilty about the indulgence.

"Why don't you stay with me? It will be like old times, when we were girls and shared a room," Isabella offered instead.

The thought of spending the night at a convent made Renée uncomfortable, but she finally relented and was pleasantly rewarded to learn that Isabella lived in an apartment. It was modestly furnished, but sunlight filled the cheery and welcoming living space. French doors opened onto a small terrace, making it feel more spacious. The bedroom had two twin beds, just like the room they'd shared as young girls in Italy.

"Why did you move out of the convent?" Renée asked.

"I wanted to live in the neighborhood I serve." Isabella was a trained social worker and had recently taken a position at a community services agency. "Let me make us some tea."

Over tea and scones purchased at a nearby bakery, Renée told Isabella about her diagnosis.

"I wanted to see you before I began treatment. I'm not sure when I'll be able to travel again." *If she'd ever be able to travel again.* "First a surgery to remove the tumor and then radiation. After that, the doctors will assess to determine the next steps."

"Dio ti guarisca." ["May God heal you."] "You must let me come and be with you."

"I'll be in touch." When her sister made a disbelieving face, Renée added, "I promise."

"I will pray for you."

They were sitting together on a loveseat and Renée reached over to take her sister's hand. "I opened Vito's envelope."

The two sisters stared at one another before Renée crumpled into tears. "It was cowardly to run away. I should have stayed to face the consequences. Instead, I left Vito to bear the burden."

"You mustn't think like that," Isabella murmured. "You were so young."

"That's no excuse." She blew her nose.

"You couldn't have known what would happen that day. Or afterward."

"Then why is your God punishing me?"

"How have you been punished?" Isabella took a rare stern tone. "You have much to be grateful for. Haven't you had a good life? Did God not bring to you a devoted husband? A son you have raised to be an honest and brave grown man?"

Renée had never introduced her husband and son to her sister, but she'd kept Isabella updated through the years since their reunion, a distant witness to all the joys and challenges of Renée's life.

"You've suffered great sadness in life, but God did not give you the cancer." A few moments later Isabella said, "If it will ease your conscience, I can arrange for you to make your confession."

This caused Renée to laugh. "I've already made a fool of myself to one priest."

She shared what had happened when she'd attempted to confess her sins.

"You did not commit a mortal sin. It's time you stop punishing yourself. Self-flagellation is an archaic tradition." Isabella sighed deeply. "The priest you spoke with was very wise in telling you that the only way to liberate your soul is to tell Michael the truth. He loves you. He will understand."

"The risk is too high." Renée shook her head. "I couldn't bear to lose my family. I have lost too much already."

*　*　*

Early the next morning, the two sisters parted warmly. Isabella left for her work at the community center, and Renée told her she'd take the train back to New York. But she had one more planned stop before heading home to begin her treatment. For who knew if she'd even have the chance again?

"I'm Isaac," the Uber driver introduced himself and confirmed the address. "Is this a one-way trip?"

"No, I'll want you to wait and bring me back to South Station, if that's convenient."

"I am at your service." The driver had a warmth about him. "Some light classical music for the ride?"

"That would be nice. How long will it take?" she asked.

"About an hour each way. It's a really pretty drive." Isaac put the car in gear and said, "Sit back and relax."

Relax? Not likely. This was her personal road to perdition. There would be no pleasure in the task ahead of her.

20

Cassandra

I couldn't get that woman from the Wellfleet church out of mind, which reminded me of why I had come back to The Bluffs in the first place. The priest had given me a list of items they could use, so I started in the barn to collect the now deflated air mattresses that had been set up for the Parsons crew.

My heart sank to see my unadorned easel in the corner. How long had it been since I'd picked up a brush? I walked over and began sorting through the canvases resting against the back wall of the studio and picked up one of the paintings commissioned by the Chamber of Commerce to promote the recent tall ship visit. It had been a pleasant project and fun to see the posters with my rendering of the schooner all around the Cape. Why then were my nostrils filling with my ancestors' strong warning scent? I looked around to see what might be causing them concern. Nothing seemed amiss.

"What? What are you trying to tell me?" I asked aloud.

* * *

A few hours later, I'd returned from making my second delivery to Wellfleet and was quite pleased with my success in figuring out why the woman from the church shelter looked familiar. While in the pantry trying to scrounge up something suitable for dinner, I'd been sifting through all that had happened in this long day. Sadly, none of it brought us any closer to finding little Lucas Kleister.

Whistler leaped to his feet, and a moment later Laura hobbled in.

"Hey, boy." The shepherd circled her, waiting patiently as she extracted a treat from her pocket. "Where is everyone?"

"In here." I stepped down from the small ladder, holding a can of chickpeas and a box of couscous. I gave her a moment to settle in before announcing, "I found her."

"Found who?" She sat down so she could elevate the booted foot and give Whistler a head rub.

"The woman who was passing around a photo the day of the storm."

"You're kidding. Where was she?"

"Well, I didn't actually find *her*, but I know who she is. Kind of. Do you recall seeing a smallish woman wearing a dated skirt and sweater at the shelter today?"

"Gray cardigan?" she asked.

"That's right." I set the staples on the counter and leaned against it.

"Who could miss that? It was ninety degrees today." She chewed her lip before adding, "But I only saw the woman from a distance."

"Well, she looked familiar, and it was bugging me that I couldn't place her. When I went back to deliver another load of supplies, it was with hopes of talking to her, but she wasn't there."

"Too bad."

"However"—I raised my index finger—"I did chat with some other people and get this. One of the men told me that she'd show everyone who came into the shelter a picture of a man she was trying to find." I lifted a shoulder. "It has to be the same woman."

"Did you see it? The picture?"

"No."

"Could the man describe the guy in the picture?"

I shook my head. "He thinks Father Sebastian might have a copy. He wasn't there either, but I left word for him to call me." I took a seat beside Laura to show her a picture of the woman another person at the shelter had texted to me. "Take a look."

Laura's mouth fell open in an almost comical way when I showed it to her. "I don't believe it."

"What?"

She pulled out her phone, flipped through until she found what she was looking for, and held it next to mine.

"It's the same woman I saw walking your property those early mornings."

I squinted, comparing the two photographs.

"The light's bad and it's a little blurry, but check out the head. Same tight bun."

I leaned back and blew out a breath. "We have to find her."

"What's this?" Laura accidently flipped back to the previous photo on my phone, which happened to be the evidence bag holding the key ring. Her eyes widened. "The dumpster key ring!"

"It must be. I wouldn't have guessed it *was* a key ring if you hadn't told me." I explained how I came to have the photo. "Look closely and you'll see a 'C' written on the key label."

"Lee Chambers?" Laura yawned, though whether from fatigue or the boring clue, I couldn't tell. I, too, had been hoping the key ring would tell us more.

"Or Wes Creed," I suggested.

She looked again at the photo. "Could be anything really. The rest of the label's been covered by writing on the evidence bag. I'll see what I can find out."

*   *   *

After Laura went upstairs with Whistler, my phone buzzed with a call from my sister.

"What's up, Zoe?"

"I wanted to apologize to you."

"O-kay?" Now this *was* unusual.

"I know I often cut you out of my life, and I was unfair to you yesterday." She took a breath. "Thank you for inviting me to The Bluffs. I'm just not ready."

"I hope you will be one day soon," I said.

"Me too."

Since Zoe was in a rare contrite mood, I asked about her meeting with the attorney. "Are you going ahead with the divorce?"

"Yes, and it's going to be expensive. For Oliver, that is." This was followed by a cynical giggle.

"Well, he should have thought of that before he cheated."

"I don't think he honestly believed I would leave him."

"You should move away from there." *Before he charms you into another reconciliation,* was what I wanted to say. Instead, "Move back here, Zoe. When you *are* ready."

"Have you read the articles I sent you?" she asked, putting an end to that discussion.

"Most of them. You think it's possible that Mama's miscarriages were the result of a genetic abnormality?"

"It does seem much more logical than a curse cast upon our family by a drunken Englishman."

"Well, when you put it like that," I deadpanned, though the room filled with a strong disapproving smell. Percy and Celeste evidently didn't get the joke.

"Regardless, you're pushing forty."

"Thanks for the reminder."

"I'm just saying, if you and Daniel are planning to start a family, you should get tested. And soon." She cleared her throat. "I'd very much like to be an auntie one day."

"I'd like that too." I paused just a second before venturing into the taboo territory of my sister's inability to conceive. "Did you have miscarriages, Zo-Zo?"

She didn't answer right away, making me certain I'd overstepped. Finally, she said, "Yes, but not like Mama."

"How do you mean? Not as many?"

"Hers took such a toll on her, both physically and emotionally."

"Did you learn that from Mama's diary?" I asked. Mama's journal had been a point of contention between us ever since I learned it had been sent to Zoe, rather than to me, after Granny Fi died. I never would have even learned of the journal's existence had it not been for

Edgar. Last year, when Edgar returned to me some Mitchell family correspondence found in his files from the book he published years ago, *The Enduring Mysteries of Cape Cod*, they had included excerpts from a journal Mama kept. Once I knew it existed, I'd yearned to get my hands on it.

"There was no need to read a diary to figure it out. I witnessed it, Cassie." There was a finality in her tone that warned me off asking anything further. I guess we were back to Zoe cutting me out of her life again. Mama's too.

* * *

It was late when Daniel finally made it home. Laura had long gone to bed, and who knew if Jason would make it back tonight, with the long hours he was keeping.

"Have you eaten?" I caressed his tired face.

"Not really hungry."

"I whipped up a chick-pea salad that's pretty yummy." I pulled out a kitchen chair, and he landed heavily into it. I grabbed the power salad from the refrigerator and set the bowl in front of Daniel, then took a seat across from him. "Where've you been?"

"The Martinez took a hit and needed to get in for repairs if we're to be up and running again next week. Since Johnny's been ferrying people from Wellfleet, that left me."

"And it took until now?"

"No. Brooks asked if I'd meet with Matthew Kleister's father."

"Why did Brooks want *you* to meet with him?"

"He had some other pressing issues that came up." He held up his hands to fend off any questions. "I don't know what they were. Will Kleister asked for the meeting. He and his wife brought Nicholas back because the boy wasn't adjusting well being separated from the family. The senior Kleisters were lucky to find a room in Orleans for tonight and will bring Nicholas here to Whale Rock in the morning." Daniel pushed the chickpeas around with his fork, not eating anything. "Apparently Nicholas had a terrible nightmare last night and said something about waiting for a signal from Lucas. He also mentioned Christopher. However, when he fully awakened and was asked about it, he wouldn't talk."

"Did Mr. Kleister tell you anything else?"

"Actually, he gave me quite an earful," he said, finally taking a bite of the salad. "This is good."

"It's a Karoo recipe." I'd made a trade with the owners of my favorite South African restaurant: a small painting for the recipe. It was well worth it. "Anything you can share?"

"If you promise to keep this on the down low."

I jokingly made a scout's three-finger salute.

He pointed his fork at me. "I mean it. Tell nobody. Especially not Laura." I guessed he was concerned about her job at the *Times*.

"When have I ever blabbed?" I was a little defensive.

"Sorry. I'm tired and this is extremely sensitive information."

I tried not to show my eagerness to be in on this new confidential revelation and waited patiently as he kept eating.

"Helene Kleister"—he scraped the last chickpeas from his plate–"has had addiction problems in the past, and he's concerned that she may have started again over the summer."

"Adderall?"

Daniel nodded. "Her father-in-law tells me they believe it began following a difficult delivery of the twins. Apparently, she didn't cope well with the responsibility, even with help. Evidently, she was very driven professionally, and being out of the career loop these past two years took a toll on her self-esteem. It wasn't an easy transition from high-powered attorney to stay-at-home mom. She was able to hide it pretty well until she returned to work. There were some critical errors, and she was placed on a leave of absence. But the family has high-level connections. Her parents own the law firm where she worked." He raised his brows in a knowing way. "She went through rehab, and it was all swept tidily under the rug."

"Did you tell him about the supply of Adderall I found?"

"No. I'll pass along the details to Brooks and let him decide what to do with it."

"Do you think it's possible Helene accidently hurt Lucas?"

Daniel sucked in a breath. "I don't know. Anything is possible."

I thought of what I'd found at The Lookout earlier. The scissors and the bottle of pills, both in easy reach of the Kleister children. Also floating back to mind was the memory of how distressed Nicholas had been the day the storm hit. The room filled with the unwanted acrid burning odor, which I hoped wasn't a signal I was on the right track.

I diverted the conversation to the mystery woman, telling Daniel what I'd figured out about her so far.

"It would be good if you could track her down and find out who she was looking for, even if only to eliminate it as a possible lead to Lucas."

"Or Lee Chambers," I added. "Has anything more been learned about him?"

"He's a native of Massachusetts. Lots of priors. He'd been serving a hefty sentence for selling drugs but was recently paroled as part of a reformed repeat drug offender law."

"And there he was, dealing again."

"Allegedly. And even so, a suspicious death still needs to be solved, even if he's a criminal."

"Not good company for Wes Creed to be associating with . . . allegedly." I then filled him in on my discussion with Christopher earlier in the day, which now seemed more like a week ago.

"Have you told Brooks?" he asked, placing his plate in the dishwasher before opening the freezer and taking out a pint of mint chocolate chip.

"I called and left a message. Haven't heard back from him." I joined him at the counter, with my own spoon poised to dive in. "Something's going on with him."

"Besides having to admit defeat on the missing child case and having an unsolved death to deal with?" He took a bite of ice cream, then shook his head. "This is not good for Whale Rock, and that's a lot of pressure."

"Yeah." I savored one last bite of the frozen treat before tossing my spoon into the sink. "I've known him a long time. There's something else going on."

Daniel kept his gaze on the nearly empty pint and said nothing.

"You know something," I accused.

"Moi? You jest." Daniel finished off the ice cream and shook his head. "When have I ever been able to penetrate the unyielding force field erected by all you Whale Rock-ettes?"

It was his playful name for the natives, but his joking did nothing to lessen my suspicions that Daniel knew something about Brooks. They'd initially been adversaries in a tug-of-war for control over a local missing persons case last year. But after Daniel retired from the FBI and moved to Whale Rock, they'd settled into an easy bro-ship.

I supposed as police chief it was difficult for Brooks to form many attachments beyond his old group of high school cronies. I consoled myself with the understanding that whatever it was, I'd eventually find out. Such was the nature of living in a small, tight-knit community.

21

Cassandra

I picked up my phone from the bedside table to check the time after awaking to the sound of Daniel's muffled voice coming from the bathroom.

"These insanely early morning calls are getting to be a regular thing," I said when he emerged with his own phone in hand.

"Good thing I'm used to rising at the crack of dawn."

"Yes, but what about your roommate?" I rolled onto my side.

"She'll have to adjust." Daniel reached down to smooth my messy hair from my face and sat on the edge of the bed. "Remember the guy from the party house who claimed he witnessed an altercation between Savage and Chambers?"

"Uh-huh." I rubbed the sleep from my eyes.

"He's nowhere to be found, but all his belongings, including his cell phone, are still at the house. What kid that age goes *anywhere* without his phone?" Daniel said. "Also, our new carriage house tenant was spotted in town last night."

"Maybe he had a meeting with the attorney?" I mumbled.

"Or maybe he had something to do with this kid going missing."

This seemed a considerable leap, but not relishing another Ted Bundy lecture, I said, "Another mystery for the incomparable Daniel Benjamin to solve?"

I stretched, exposing my phoenix tattoo, which Daniel absently traced with his index finger. As he did this, the lovely scent of caramel descended on me, offering a brief respite from worry.

"I'm just one of a team working on this."

"I thought you retired from the FBI. Or was that the other guy I was supposed to marry?"

He now came at me with fingers poised to tickle, causing me to shriek and roll off the other side of the bed.

"You're evil."

"And you love it." He grinned wickedly and headed for the shower.

I found Laura down in the kitchen, munching on a slice of peanut butter toast and giving the crusts to Whistler. There was a half-filled carafe in the coffee station.

"Jason already gone?" I asked.

"An early summons from Brooks."

"I didn't even hear him come in last night. Must have been even later than Daniel." I noted her steaming mug and asked, "Is it okay for you to drink coffee?"

"The internet is divided, but I'm choosing to play it safe." She tipped her mug in my direction. "Herbal tea."

"Good morning," Daniel said to Laura before turning his attention to Whistler, who greeted him with his usual robust enthusiasm, "Hey, boy."

He grabbed the last of the muffins Jimmy and Edgar had brought, took a bite, then winced comically.

"Stale?"

"Like a rock." He tossed it into the garbage bin. "I'll get something in town."

"Uncommon Grounds is open again," Laura told him.

"Ah, my favorite coffee shop." He rubbed his hands together. "How's work progressing on your cottage?"

"Workers were there yesterday." She held up crossed fingers. "We should be out of your hair soon."

"Nah. You're great company."

I would miss them terribly, especially Whistler, who was now nuzzling my fingers for a treat.

"Gotta run." Daniel blew a kiss and was out the door.

"Did you hear that the storm could possibly head back this way?" Laura flipped her tablet around so I could see the news headline.

"No way!" I hadn't had television on since before the storm and had been getting only snippets of the news the few times I'd gone online. "I knew that the storm had slowed down after it bounced off our coast."

"Stalled over the Atlantic now. All those boats that went out to sea to avoid the storm? They're stranded out there, waiting for Chantal to make up her mind."

"I hope the *Lady Spirit* made it safely to a port," I said, thinking again about the tall ship that had had a delayed departure from Whale Rock. The pleasant scent that had visited just a short while ago had now been replaced with a stronger, urgent, cautioning odor.

I looked over at Laura, who was grimacing.

"The foot bothering you?" I asked.

She shook her head and that's when I noticed she was holding her belly.

"Just a cramp. I've been getting them the past couple of days."

Ah. Perhaps that was what was behind Percy and Celeste's warning. What did I know about how discerning spirits could be?

"I think you'd better go see the doctor today."

"My ob-gyn says it's normal." She waved it away. "Did Daniel have anything interesting to share?"

I didn't tell Laura about the latest MIA witness because I didn't want her sniffing around the party house. But I did wonder if the mystery woman had any connection to the young man who'd disappeared.

"I wonder," I said, letting the thought float away.

"What?"

"Still can't get that woman from the shelter off my mind. Daniel did say it would be helpful to find her and the photograph she was passing around, at least to cross it off the list as a lead or clue."

Laura sported an expression that spelled trouble.

"I know that look. What are you thinking?"

"Let's go find her." Laura grabbed her backpack.

A stress fracture and boot were not slowing that one down, and if I wasn't the one driving, she might have left without me.

It took longer than expected to get to Wellfleet because of road crews. I thought we were going to be turned back, but Laura showed her press badge and we were waved on.

When we arrived at the church and found Father Sebastian, he only had disappointing news for us.

"What do you mean *gone*?" I asked.

"This morning I found her cot neatly made, and the family who was bunking next to her said she hadn't slept here last night."

"Did she leave her belongings?" asked Laura.

"Nothing that we could see. But let's go have another look." As we walked through the maze of cots and air mattresses, Father Sebastian asked, "Why are you interested in finding Sister Bernadetta?"

"Sister? She's a nun?" I asked.

The priest smiled kindly. "Many nuns have abandoned the traditional habit."

Laura went on to explain. "An unknown woman was seen the day of the storm in Whale Rock, passing around a photo of a man she was looking for. We think it was this woman, Sister Bernadetta."

"I see." He nodded thoughtfully before asking, "Who was in the photo?"

"That's what we're trying to find out," I told him as we checked the area around the nun's cot. "We were hoping you'd have a copy."

"No. Sorry. She did show it to me, but I didn't know the man."

"Could you describe him?"

"It was a black-and-white photocopy, so I couldn't tell you hair or eye color, though he was definitely white. I'd guess middle age." He shook his head. "Sorry, I didn't look all that closely—just enough to know I didn't recognize the man."

Laura pulled from her backpack photos of Lee Chambers and Wes Creed. "Was it either of these men?"

"I don't know." He lifted a shoulder and said, "Look, I was busy and glad for the extra helping hands. During what little downtime there's been, I'd find the sister kneeling in the church, and had no thought of interrupting her prayers. If something was troubling her, I wish I had known."

"You've heard about the child that went missing in Whale Rock before the storm hit?" I asked.

"Just a couple days ago, when Johnny started helping people here. Our prayers have been with the family." He tilted his head. "You think Sister Bernadetta is somehow involved with the missing child?"

"We don't have any reason to believe so," Laura answered him.

"Is this a police matter?" he asked.

"Look, Father, we're here unofficially," I explained. "The Whale Rock force has its hands full searching for the lost child and also investigating a suspicious death."

He nodded. "I heard about that."

"My husband is on the Whale Rock police force," Laura told him. "And Cassie's fiancé is a retired FBI agent who's been called in to help."

"What we're trying to do is determine if the person Sister Bernadetta is looking for has any connection to either of those cases."

"And if there is no connection?" he asked.

"Then maybe we can help her find the person she's been searching for," I answered.

"Anything you can tell us might help," Laura prodded gently.

He scratched his head. "She showed up here at the church the day of the storm, asking if she could stay to wait it out. We were already sheltering families from lower-lying homes who hadn't evacuated. She went straight to work helping us."

"Do you know where she's from?"

"I remember the order, but if she did tell me where, I can't recall."

"What was the order?"

"The Sisters of Saint Joseph."

"Are they local?"

"I'm not sure, but I would assume they have New England orders. Wellfleet is a new congregation for me. I only recently relocated from the Midwest."

He followed us back outside, and Laura handed him her card. "If she shows up or you hear anything from her, please give me a call."

"I will." He looked at the card before tucking it into his shirt pocket.

We thanked him and said goodbye, but before we even made it to the truck, he was calling out for us to wait.

"Did you remember something, Father?" I asked as he approached.

"No, but I think that's hers." He pointed to the car we'd parked behind, a blue Honda with Massachusetts license plates. The car had been left unlocked, so with the priest's permission we did a little investigating into the totally pristine, albeit nearly antique Civic.

"Trusting lady. Here are the keys," Laura said after opening the glove compartment. She tried starting it, but the engine wouldn't turn. "It's not the battery. Oh, I see the problem. The gas gauge is on empty."

"So she either left on foot or hitched a ride with someone," I said.

The priest's expression made clear his dubious position.

"Now what?" Laura asked after returning the keys to the glove box.

"We can pray," Father Sebastian suggested.

"Thank you, Father. Pray for little Lucas too," I said.

"Of course. We have been praying for him daily," he assured us as we took our leave.

"I'll check with local cabs to see if they picked up anyone last night from Wellfleet," Laura said as we headed out.

"Good idea. You do that, and I'll call the bus station." They'd been running a limited schedule, but if an evening route was operating last night, maybe we'd get lucky and find a driver who remembered the woman.

"Drop me off in town?" Laura asked. "I'll pick up the car from Jason. Hopefully, the force will be getting another cruiser soon, and we won't have to be sharing the Subaru all the time."

*　*　*

On my drive back to The Bluffs, I put in some calls to see where search crews might be working today, hoping to go out and help. If Christopher was around, I'd see if he wanted to go with me.

I found him sitting outside the carriage house, Gypsy panting at his feet.

"I don't know where it's hotter, out here or in there." He thumbed toward the carriage house.

"Sorry about that." A heat wave had followed the tropical storm, and it showed no signs of relenting. We had never had a need for air-conditioning at The Bluffs because of the ocean breezes. I'd installed a unit in the carriage house to keep renters comfortable on sweltering days, but a power surge during the storm had fried the compressor, and we were at the bottom of our electrician's very long list. Being uncomfortable didn't rank up there with having no running water, refrigeration, or lights. By all counts, we were one of the luckier locals.

"Any news on Lucas?" he asked.

I shook my head. "I thought you might want to hit the trails with me. They're allowing searchers back into the land trust now that most of the hazardous trees have come down. We might have to go off trail in some places."

"Sure, I'll go," he said, but Gypsy stood and cowered at the sound of a WRPD cruiser pulling up the drive.

"It's okay, girl," Christopher said, stroking the dog's ears as Brooks walked over to where we were sitting.

"Morning." He nodded to us, his face serious.

"What can I help you with, Chief?"

"Would you know anything about the disappearance of Zach Renner?" he asked bluntly.

"I don't even know the name. Who is Zach . . .?" He raised a palm in question.

"Renner," Brooks repeated the last name. "He begged off a night out with his friends, claiming a headache, and hasn't been seen again."

"Why would you think I'd know anything about it?"

"Because he's the individual who identified you as having an altercation with Lee Chambers shortly before Chambers was murdered."

Murdered? I wondered what details had emerged. Or was Brooks playing heavy-handed with the term to make Christopher nervous?

Christopher blew out a deep breath before saying, "How many times do I have to tell you people? Whoever the kid saw, it wasn't me. Perhaps you should broaden your search instead of focusing on me. You'd have a better chance of finding whoever it really was."

Brooks's jaw tensed at the insinuation that the Whale Rock police were not doing their job.

"Maybe *Zach Renner* had something to do with Lucas going missing," Christopher continued. "But I assure you, *I* did not."

An uncomfortable moment passed before Brooks pulled a small notepad from his shirt pocket.

"Where were you last night? Specifically, after six."

"I was in town until about eight or so."

"Doing what?"

"Having dinner at The Diner."

"Can anyone corroborate this?"

"Yes." Whether to annoy Brooks or for dramatic effect, he hesitated before finally providing the name. "Tyler Stendall."

"You knew we wanted to talk with him!" Brooks exploded at Christopher, who in turn looked sharply at me. There went the good will I'd been trying to build.

Brooks caught the look and probably realized his slip, since it was I who'd told Christopher about the police looking for Tyler when I was trying to get information on the sealed documents.

"What was the purpose of this meeting?" Brooks asked in a more composed voice.

"I was planning to ask for his permission to release the sealed documents."

"Did he consent?"

"I didn't have the opportunity to ask."

Brooks raised his eyebrows.

"It wasn't the right moment. He's going through a tough time, and I've often been his sounding board."

"Would you say it's unusual for a teacher to stay connected with a student so many years later?"

"It's rare," Christopher agreed, "but we had a rare bond, stemming from his need to confide in someone when he was a kid."

"It seems kids like to confide in you."

Christopher met Brooks's stern gaze. "Yeah, I guess they do. Kind of goes with the job of being a teacher. You know, molder of minds and character?"

Brooks ignored the sarcasm. "What time did you get back here last night?"

"I got the bus around eight."

So the bus was running last night.

"Where was Tyler going?"

"He said he was meeting someone."

"Do you know who? Where?"

"I didn't ask. It was none of my business." Christopher sized up the police officer. "I have good reasons for not pushing Tyler right now. He's fragile."

"So is the ice you're standing on. You might want to start thinking of your own situation." Brooks flipped his notebook closed to answer an incoming call.

He held his phone to his chest and said to us, "Hang tight a minute." He then walked to his cruiser where he was out of earshot.

I broke the uncomfortable silence while we waited by attempting to explain to Christopher. "I was acting as a buffer for you. Giving you some time to track down Tyler before they did."

"It's fine." He kept his eyes on Gypsy, who was still panting nervously.

"I hear they're trying to arrange for you and Nicholas to talk." It wasn't cool of me to be telling him this, but I hoped to regain his trust.

He finally looked up.

"Act surprised when you hear it?"

"Is it likely?" he asked.

I fluttered my hand. "It could go either way."

"There are some questions I'd like to ask him."

"Like what?"

"Nicholas has a wild imagination. Some of the stories he told me were way out there. I simply dismissed them as the inventiveness of a child's mind."

"I understand. But if there's anything you can comfortably share that might help the investigation . . ."

"I've been upfront with the police on anything that could be construed as a clue. I've given them my impressions of the Kleisters."

"Which are?"

"They seemed like nice, normal people, though the mother was a bit distracted. Who wouldn't be with four kids?"

"True." No doubt the reason Adderall was her drug of choice.

"Especially with how inquisitive Nicholas was, each question leading to ten more. He was intrigued by pirates." He smiled and began mimicking Nicholas. "Christopher, how bad would someone have to be to walk the plank? What's a stowaway? If a stowaway was found out, would they have to walk the plank?"

Hearing what a chatterbox Nicholas had been made his present silence seem all the more ominous. "It's too bad he's closed down." I hesitated before asking, "So what was the pact about?"

"Without going into any specific detail, I assured Nicholas he could always come by the cottage if he was frightened."

"What would he have to be frightened about?"

"Monsters." He shrugged when I made a face. "He's a six-year-old boy. Monsters are still a very real thing for boys that age."

I was enveloped by the scent of burning sugar. *Monsters, ghosts, spirits. Who was I to judge?*

I pulled out my phone to show Christopher the photo of Sister Bernadetta. "Did you by chance see this woman on the bus last night?"

He narrowed his eyes and stared for longer than I would have expected. "She looks a little familiar." He rubbed his chin. "But I can't place her."

Brooks cleared his throat to announce his return, and Christopher handed back my phone.

"Who's that?" Brooks craned to see the photo.

"That woman from the day of the storm," I told him.

He did not look at all pleased that I'd shown the photo to Christopher Savage, but got right to business. "I have to take you to town, Mr. Savage."

"Why?"

"Cassie, can we have a minute?"

"Sure." I reluctantly stood and walked back toward the house, trying to make out what Brooks was saying. I stayed on the porch, watching the two men in serious discussion.

A few moments later, Christopher walked over and said, "I need a favor. Can you keep an eye on Gypsy? Let her out?"

"Of course, but what's going on?"

He made a popping sound with his mouth before answering, "I'm being arrested."

"Why?"

"The shoe they found under my deck stairs? It's Lucas's. They also found blood evidence around and under the deck stairs."

"What does that prove?" I asked.

"Let's get going." Brooks walked toward us, not giving Christopher the opportunity to answer.

"I'll just put Gypsy inside," he told Brooks, and then to me, "Thanks for checking on her."

After Christopher walked away, Brooks gave me a stern look and said, "Keep this under wraps."

"I'm not now, nor have I ever been part of The Rock grapevine." In fact, I was always more likely to be a subject of the chatter. "Nobody will hear anything about this arrest from me, but good luck trying to keep it a secret."

His eye roll said it all.

"Does this mean you've given up on finding Lucas alive?"

"Not yet."

"You obviously think something happened to him, or you wouldn't be arresting Christopher."

"Give me a break." He brushed his hair off his forehead, his expression pained. "I'm getting pressure from all sides."

"What about Helene? Have you looked at her? The pills? How about Wes Creed?"

"Last I checked, you were not a member of the Whale Rock police force," he snapped.

"I get it." I decided it would be in my best interest to back off. "Sorry for pushing."

"Look, I appreciate all the help you've given"—he rubbed his temples—"but I've been lax with sensitive details around you. Just don't make me regret it."

"You can trust me, Chuckles." I stood and gave him a hug. "I know this is tough for you."

He gave my back a quick pat and gently pushed away, pretending to cough to hide his emotions. Glancing over to the cruiser where Christopher had just gotten into the passenger side, he told me, "I'll have Savage back here by noon."

"What?"

"We can't hold anyone in a cell overnight right now. With all the construction, it's not secure enough. I'm taking him in to have an ankle monitor put on."

*　*　*

Brooks was true to his word. I took Gypsy out with me to scour the land trust, where I met up with a group of volunteer fire fighters. When I returned late morning, Christopher was back on the carriage house porch, though he'd changed into long pants, no doubt to hide the monitor.

"We turned up nothing." I plopped down in another chair while Gypsy danced around him.

"I don't think his body will be found."

I found this a startling remark. "Why do you say that?"

"I don't know." He kept his eyes on Gypsy while rubbing her belly. "Just a feeling."

"Because you think he's still alive?"

"Because I hope he is." He looked at me and added, "And not just because it would get me off the hook."

I merely nodded.

"Can I see the photo of that woman again?" he asked.

"Sure." After a minute of him studying Sister Bernadetta, I said, "Figure out why she looks familiar?"

He shook his head.

"I'll text you the photo. If it comes to you, it could help us find her."

"Why are you looking for her?"

"You might not have heard us talking about the stranger who appeared the day of the storm."

"The first I heard of it was earlier today when you mentioned it."

"Well, she was passing around a photograph of a man she was searching for. It's a bit of a mystery that we're trying to solve, especially as it may or may not relate to Lucas's disappearance or whatever happened to Lee Chambers."

Before I was able to say anything else, Daniel's Land Rover rounded the curve. He got out and walked purposefully in our direction.

"You've got an audience with Nicholas over at District Court. The judge is waiting for us now."

22

Cassandra

After Daniel left with Christopher, I was debating what I should do next, when a Federal Express truck pulled up.

"Delivery for Cassandra Mitchell?" He wasn't our regular FedEx delivery person.

"That would be me." I smiled and took the package. "You guys must be playing catch-up after the storm."

"You've got that right. Your usual guy was called up—Coast Guard Reserve. Helping to move the larger Coast Guard vessels out."

I nodded. "I heard lots of the larger ships were moved out."

"But they can't get back because the storm path has been so erratic."

"Chantel is one fickle lady," I agreed as he headed off, and the aroma of Percy and Celeste poked at my nostrils.

"Okay, I'll open it." Inside the mailing envelope was a gift-wrapped box. I cautiously removed the creamy toile-printed paper to find a burgundy, leather-bound book, tied closed with a leather strap. It wasn't new, the leather worn at the binding. I caressed the book before gently untying the strap and flipping it open to immediately recognizable handwriting. *Mama's journal.*

I picked up my phone and made the call.

"You can't know how much this means to me," I said when Zoe answered.

"I think I do." Not one for expressions of sentimentality, my sister returned to the practicality of the gift. "Mama documented a great deal about her pregnancies. I thought it would be helpful for you to read those entries especially. Some of the information might even be valuable when you decide to see a genetic specialist."

I hugged the diary tighter, wanting to end the call so I could have a few moments alone with Mama's words.

"I hear it doesn't look good for finding that little boy," Zoe said.

"You've been talking to Evelyn. Or was it Lu?"

"Neither."

"Then who? Brooks?"

"Yes, Cassie," she said, "but there's nothing to it."

"Brooks hardly has time for a ten-minute nap, so I can't imagine he'd call you if there was *nothing to it*."

She puffed out a sigh and said, "Okay. We talk. So what?"

"So nothing."

"He's going through a lot right now, and it's not as if he can confide in anyone back there."

"Okay." I had been thinking the same thing, to be honest.

"I can tell you're reading more into this. Trust me Cassie, Brooks and I are just friends."

The lady doth protest too much, methinks.

"I don't know who you're trying to convince. Me or you? Either way, I'm not buying it."

"I really don't want to talk about this anymore."

"I understand," I said, even though I didn't. To change the subject, I asked, "Did Brooks say anything else about Lucas?"

"Just that he keeps hitting one dead end after another and that the parents aren't helping the situation." She made a tongue-clicking sound. "I just don't get it."

"Nobody does, Zo-Zo."

I promised to keep her informed, and after ending the call, I tucked Mama's journal in a drawer in the library. For now, it would have to wait. While talking with Zoe, my decision on what to do next was made. I texted Teddy Howell, thinking he must know something about the party house crew.

Ten minutes later I was parked at Kinsey Cove, where a group of divers had been searching along the coast and were now breaking for lunch. I shivered at the thought that it was in this cove that Papa had discovered Barnacle Boy's body.

Teddy waved when he saw me and walked over to the truck, holding a half-eaten cheese sandwich.

"How's it going today?" I asked, pointing my chin toward the other two divers.

"No news is good news, right?" He shrugged and took a bite.

I nodded. "Let's hope."

"What's up?"

"I'm sure you've heard about the party house on Whale Rock beach?"

"Sea Breeze? Yep, I'm aware."

"Do you know any of those guys?"

He wiped his mouth with the back of his hand. "They're younger. I went to high school with the older brother of one of them, but he was always a real jerk to me."

"What's his name?"

"Jeremy Montrose."

"Montrose?" I'd heard the name recently, but with all the new information swirling around in my head I couldn't call it to memory.

"Why the interest in the party house?"

"Just curious."

"Right." He gave a crooked smile that was so reminiscent. "What would your buddy Brooks say if he knew you were snooping?"

"You're not going to tell him, are you?"

"No way." Teddy had finished his sandwich now and was wadding up the wrapper.

"Is there any way you can find out about someone staying at Sea Breeze? His name is Zach Renner."

"I don't know the name, but I can nose around for you." He pulled out his phone. "Zach Renner. R-E-N-N-E-R?"

"That's right." He glanced over to where his dive buddies were putting on their gear. "I'll let you know what I find out."

"Thanks, Teddy." I hesitated, almost said *good luck*, but thought better of it. "Stay safe out there."

He gave a casual salute and then ambled over to join the other divers.

I watched for a few minutes while they readied themselves to return to the search, thinking of what Christopher had said just a short while ago: "I don't think his body will be found."

What would make him think or say such a thing?

*   *   *

It was early afternoon when I returned to The Bluffs just as Daniel was dropping Christopher off at the carriage house.

"After all that, Nicholas Kleister still wouldn't talk." Daniel plunked himself down onto one of the porch rockers and popped the top off an icy Pepsi he'd grabbed from the fridge. He gulped it half down and then held the cold bottle against his cheek. "Will this heat wave never end?"

"Not for a couple more days, or so say the sage forecasters. So, tell me," I prompted, anxious to hear what happened.

"The judge gathered us in his chambers with the parents and their attorney all seated behind Nicholas so as not to be a distraction. But the boy kept turning around and looking at his parents, then shaking his head. He finally beckoned me close and whispered in a tiny, desperate voice, 'Just me and Christopher.'"

"That must have been hard for you."

"Broke my heart." He took another sip of the soda. "After about twenty minutes of unsuccessful coaxing, the judge asked Nicholas's grandmother to take him out to the lobby to allow the grown-ups a chance to discuss the matter."

"And?"

"The judge said it was obvious Nicholas felt uncomfortable speaking with his parents in the room and suggested allowing the boy to talk with Savage alone, in his presence."

"The Kleisters were opposed?"

"Oh, yeah. Adamantly."

"How did it end?"

"The judge brought Brooks in and asked him and the Kleisters's attorney to each present an argument for and against allowing the private meeting. Brooks made a great suggestion of bringing in a child psychologist to monitor and proposed someone who's worked with him on other cases. The other attorney knew of the psychologist and agreed that she had an unimpeachable reputation, but still he argued against the meeting."

"How could they not want to uncover every possible lead to find Lucas?"

"I believe the judge is puzzling over that very point. He's going to review precedents and case law. We're all on call until he decides."

"Do you have a feel for which way it will go?"

"The judge is a difficult read, which makes him a good one in my opinion. He did, however, ask Brooks to have the psychologist available in case."

"I'd take that as a positive sign."

"I can't see that it would do anything but help our investigation for him to allow it. And Nicholas clearly has something gnawing at him. It could go a long way in helping him deal with whatever is torturing him." Daniel finished off the Pepsi, following it with a quiet belch of satisfaction. "Any more luck with your mystery woman?"

"She's a nun."

"Really?"

"Uh-huh. Sister Bernadetta."

"You'd think I'd have noticed a habit."

"I've done a little studying, and her order, the sisters of St. Joseph, don't wear the traditional garb. Anyhow, I texted her photo to the bus driver on last night, and he didn't recognize her."

"Maybe she took a cab?"

"Laura's looking into that angle. So far only one cab service sent anyone to Wellfleet last night."

"Sounds promising."

"It would be if the driver was answering his phone. Today is his day off. Hopefully, he'll check messages and call Laura back."

I quoted one of my Granny Fi's oft-spouted sayings: *"One step forward and two steps back."*

"True enough." He gave his back a stretch. "Every thread seems so tenuous here. First, we have Lee Chambers's suspicious death. Then we have a missing toddler, and a little boy who won't talk but might likely be a witness to, or at least know something about, what happened to his brother. But every new potential witness disappears: this mystery nun, Tyler Stendall, Zach Renner."

I decided not to mention my conversation with Teddy until I had some concrete information.

"It's like that movie *Six Degrees of Separation*."

"More like six degrees of *disappearance*. All with connections leading back to one Christopher Savage."

"Brooks told Christopher that Lee Chambers was murdered. It's now a homicide investigation?"

"I hadn't heard that." He frowned. "But I've been focused on the Kleister case."

"Speaking of which, what was the evidence that connected Christopher to warrant an arrest?"

"His blood was found on the shoe. So was Lucas's."

"How did they determine that so quickly?" DNA testing wasn't normally such a speedy process.

"Through my FBI connections, we were able to get access to a rapid DNA testing machine."

"There's such a thing?"

"It's fairly new technology, but yes, it's a thing."

I digested this new information for a minute, thinking there could be an easy explanation for the blood, and then remembering what Brooks had said about being under pressure. It at least gave the appearance of progress while the search continued.

"How about Wes Creed? Has anyone seen him around lately?" I asked.

Daniel rubbed a hand over his face. "Crap. I was supposed to check in with him today."

"He's been seen." Jason stepped out on the porch.

My head jerked around. "I didn't know you were here."

"Laura dropped me off a while ago for a much-needed shower and change of clothes."

"You were saying about Wes Creed?" Daniel said.

"Yeah, he's still around, but it's the company he's keeping that's not good." He joined us in one of the porch rockers. "At least not for our friend Christopher Savage."

"How's that?"

"A witness spotted the two of them having an argument."

"Interesting." Daniel glanced at me. "Who's the witness?"

"Edgar Faust. He was leaving the library parking lot and had turned up Harbor Drive when he saw two men in a heated shouting match. He drove to the station to report it, and I went to check it out, only to find Wes Creed there alone. He denied having been with anyone, let alone involved in a quarrel."

"Could Edgar have been mistaken?" I asked.

"I showed him the mug shot of Wes Creed. He was adamant that was who he'd seen with Christopher."

"What time was this?" Daniel asked.

"Between seven thirty and eight."

"Nearly sunset," I said. "Not good light."

"Still, Edgar's got a writer's eye for detail," Daniel countered. "It's the nature of the beast to be a good observer."

"Don't I know it," Jason mumbled, displeasure seeping into his tone. *Poor Laura.*

"The question now is, what to do with it?" Daniel leaned forward, elbows resting on thighs, snapping his fingers absently.

"Brooks is aware," Jason said. "How did it go today?"

Daniel gave him a quick rundown.

"That's a shame."

"It is," Daniel agreed. "Because my gut tells me that little guy holds the key to this mystery."

"You two weren't there the day the storm hit, when Evelyn was gathering Matthew and Nicholas to come to the inn," I said, recalling again the wild panic in Nicholas's eyes. "The boy kept looking down toward the beach, tugging on his dad's sleeve and trying to get him to listen."

The warning scent had returned. I closed my eyes. *What am I missing?*

"Christopher mentioned offhandedly that he told Nicholas he was always welcome to come to his cottage if he were frightened."

Daniel was eyeing me curiously. "Are you suggesting Lucas may have been hiding there when the storm hit?"

"I don't know." I shook my head. "It's a crazy idea."

"What could frighten a little boy so much?" Jason wanted to know.

"Monsters." I repeated what Christopher had said.

"Those imagined? Or of the human kind?" Daniel asked. He picked up his phone to check a text. "Well, we are about to find out. The judge wants us back."

"Already? I hope that's good news for . . ." I stopped. There were so many possibilities of what Nicholas could reveal. Had Helene accidently lost track of Lucas while she was high? Was it a kidnapping gone wrong? Could Christopher have been involved in any way?

"For?"

"I was going to say for Nicholas to finally let go of those secrets that are eating away at him, but only if it means finding little Lucas."

23

Renée

Renée took a leave of absence from work and began her cancer therapy without admitting the truth about her past to her husband. Halfway through treatment, she received a message from her sister. She was grateful Isabella had taken care to disguise their relationship in case someone else were to open the card. It would seem that an old acquaintance had recently learned about her diagnosis and was sending a note of well wishes. But Renée understood it was intended as a subtle reminder that her sister was only a train ride away should she be needed.

On one of her good days, Brandan came for a visit. Michael had arranged it since he had an important business meeting and wouldn't be able to pop home to check on her.

"I've missed you," she told her old friend when he arrived.

"And I, you," he said, though unable to hide his surprise at the change in her appearance and hugging her tentatively.

"I've lost weight, but I won't break, Brandan."

"Of course you won't. Love the wig!" He recovered quickly, reaching out to touch it. "Ooh, and it's real. Nothing but the best for you."

He'd brought takeout from their old favorite bistro where they'd first met all those years ago.

"A tuna melt and fries for the lady."

"You remembered." She batted her eyes coquettishly.

"How could I forget? It was all we could afford." He laughed as he produced a second lunch. "Only today we don't have to share."

He kept her amused while bringing her up to speed on all the gossip at Brandan Kane Creations.

"How is Amber doing?" she asked of her assistant.

"You've trained her well."

"She'll make a good replacement."

"Nonsense. Merely a placeholder until you come back." He squeezed her hand. "She misses you. Everyone misses you."

She held a hand to her heart. "Give them all my love." Her work family had become an important part of her life.

After they'd finished lunch, Renée suggested a walk.

"Should you be out among the masses and all those germs?" Brandan was unsure.

"To the post office, just a few blocks away." It was the perfect opportunity to send her response to Isabella.

"I can mail something for you," he offered.

"I need some air," she insisted. "Please?"

"You are queen for a day, and your wish is my command." He bowed dramatically, making her laugh.

As they exited the apartment building, Renée breathed in deeply. "You can't imagine what it's like being cooped up inside all day."

"You're right. I can't." He tucked her hand through the crook of his arm. "And I wish you didn't have to be. But it's not forever."

Brandan was right. It wouldn't be forever, but likely not to a good end. For now, she would live in the present, breathe in real air, and walk with her best friend among the streets of Manhattan. It had become her city.

"Here we are," Brandan said as they arrived at the local post office. "Can you handle all these steps?"

She'd never before given a second thought to the entrance steps, but today she was already a bit winded from the short stroll.

As she hesitated, Brandan slipped the letter from her grasp and said, "Be right back." He trotted up the stairs and down again.

"Using me to do your dirty work?" he scolded good-naturedly, having obviously checked the addressee. Brandan knew about Isabella, which brought pangs of guilt that Michael knew nothing of her past.

"What's the point in keeping this from him now? Michael adores you. He'll understand." It was a mild rebuke.

Will he? She said nothing, though, and Brandan dropped it. As they made their way back, a headline caught her eye at a local newsstand.

Phillip Welles New Ambassador to the UK. She had to steady herself as she picked up that day's edition of *The Boston Globe.* How long had it been since she'd thought of Phillip and the Welles family?

"What is it?" Brandan took hold of Renée's arm again.

"Nothing," she said, handing him the paper. "Buy this for me?"

He fished in his pockets and withdrew a few loose dollar bills to make the purchase.

Renée was shaking now as the unexpected tidal wave of emotions overtook her. Thank goodness Brandan was there to guide her, for she could barely see the sidewalk through the tears as they walked back to the apartment.

* * *

Boston ~ Late 1960s

"I don't think it's a good idea," Renata said to Catherine Ferris after Mrs. Welles had invited her and Antonio to lunch at their home.

"What could it hurt?" Her friend was a practical woman and trusting in her nature. "Even if she's figured out that Antonio is Phillip's child, what do you think she'd do?"

Renata shrugged uncertainly.

"Don't worry. There are laws protecting your rights. Besides, Marjorie Welles fears scandal more than death. You should go. There could be some advantages for Antonio."

Renata was still concerned but put her faith in Catherine's wisdom and accepted the invitation. She should have trusted her own intuition. The afternoon turned into an ambush.

It began pleasantly enough, with her former employer doing everything possible to make Antonio feel comfortable.

"Let's have lunch outdoors where Anthony can play with some toys I brought down from the old nursery."

"It's Antonio," Renata corrected her.

"Of course, my dear." Mrs. Welles patted her hand. "Let's just enjoy this delicious luncheon Meg made for us."

Renata had stopped in for a quick hello to her former coworker, though the reception was rather chilly. She blushed to think that Meg might possibly have known about Phillip sneaking up to her room back in her nanny days.

When the ice cream sundaes were served, Mrs. Welles turned her full attention to Antonio and asked, "Are you in kindergarten yet?"

"He will start in the fall," Renata answered for her son.

"Are you having fun, Anthony?"

The child nodded eagerly as ice cream dripped down his chin, and the woman reached across and playfully wiped away the stickiness.

"How would you like to come back and visit again?"

"Yeah!"

"Yes, thank you," Renata corrected.

"Yes, thank you," the small voice echoed.

When Antonio went off to play with a toy airplane in the large enclosed yard, Renata told their hostess, "Thank you so much for a lovely afternoon, but we should be on our way."

Ignoring Renata's attempt to depart, Marjorie Welles bluntly asked, "Did you ever hear from Anthony's father?"

Why on earth won't the woman call him Antonio? She tried to keep the annoyance out of her tone when answering, "*Antonio*'s father was never in the picture."

"But you do know who the father is."

The conversation was entering dangerous territory, so Renata reached for her purse and said, "I don't see that this is anything to interest you."

"Don't be upset. I only want to help."

"Help? With what?"

"I hear your son has a genetic disorder that causes abnormal bleeding."

"Antonio," Renata called to her son, but this did not stop Mrs. Welles.

"Our Phillip has something similar. It's called Von Willebrand disease." The woman's expression was morphing into Snow White's evil queen. "You remember Phillip from when you worked here, don't you?"

Renata dabbed away the perspiration forming on her forehead.

"Of course you do."

At that moment, Phillip and his father entered the courtyard.

"I don't think we need introductions," Mrs. Welles said as the men joined them at the table.

Still handsome, Phillip nodded curtly while Renata folded her hands in her lap to hide the trembling.

"Antonio!" she called to her son again, and this time he came running. "It's time for us to go home now."

She thanked God he didn't protest. But as she tried to stand, Mr. Welles took hold of her arm, forcing her to remain seated.

"Mamma." Antonio tugged at her sleeve. "I thought we were going."

"In a minute, darling." She pulled her son close to her.

"You should have told us," Mrs. Welles said, seemingly oblivious to how a child might react to this conversation.

"Antonio, give Mamma five more minutes of grown-up time and go play with the airplane."

And away he went, squealing with delight.

"There was nothing to tell you."

"One only need look at Anthony to know that Phillip is his father. And he's admitted to having relations with you at the time you became pregnant."

Renata looked at Phillip, who kept his eyes averted. She swallowed back the bile that was rising in her throat before saying, "You cannot prove anything."

"We wish to do right by the child." Mr. Welles spoke in a kind but firm tone. "He is, after all, our grandson."

"And what of the medical attention he will need?" asked Mrs. Welles.

"I have taken good care of Antonio."

"Of course you have," Mr. Welles agreed. "But you must see that we are in a much more advantageous position to give Anthony a good life filled with opportunities."

"He will have opportunities. What is most important is that he is loved, and he knows he is loved."

"Was there a reason you decided to keep this from Phillip?" Mrs. Welles blurted out, seeming almost hurt. "From us?"

"Phillip left for England without a word of goodbye to me. He never wrote to me. It was apparent he had no interest in anything beyond what he sweet-talked me into doing in my room."

Phillip remained silent but finally turned those icy blue eyes on Renata, his face filled with contempt.

Mrs. Welles's color rose. "We are not proud of Phillip taking advantage of you."

"I had no intentions of forcing him into an unwanted marriage or fatherhood."

Mr. Welles cleared his throat. "Well now, as you can imagine, marriage at this point is not an option. Phillip is engaged. No matter how reckless his past actions, we cannot expect him to give up his future."

"But we would like to bring Anthony here to live with us. Gregory is just nine now and Lisa is twelve. They'd love to have a little brother."

Renata was confused. At first, she'd thought they just wanted to be involved in Antonio's life, which was bad enough.

Now it was Mrs. Welles who would not look at her as she said, "You will be well provided for, and we could make arrangements for visitation."

"Antonio is *my child*." She stood and collected her things and called out to her son. When he ran up to her, she cupped his face in her hand and smiled at him.

"*Ti amo, Mamma.*"

"*Ti amo, Tonio.*" She then took her son's hand and said, "Thank you for lunch, but now we must be going."

"I'll see you out." Phillip finally spoke and followed them to the car.

After Renata secured Antonio into his seat, Phillip took her roughly by the arm. "You can do it this way, or we can simply take him from you."

"You are hurting me." She pulled free and rubbed where surely a bruise was forming. "If you cared at all about the best interests of this child, you'd leave us be."

"He's a Welles and my family has deep pockets. You will lose him one way or the other. You might as well take the money."

"I would rather die." She spit out the words, not knowing what had come over her.

She was shaking so badly she could barely insert the key into the ignition. If she hadn't borrowed Catherine's car, she wouldn't even return to the Ferris's house. Fortunately, nobody was home when she arrived. She quickly packed two bags, one with Antonio's clothes and toys and the other with her own possessions.

She jotted a quick note to her friend. *A family emergency requires us to return to Italy. Sorry I couldn't wait to say goodbye. Thank you for everything, especially your trust and your friendship. Love, Renata and Antonio*

Renata was a complete wreck by the time she showed up on her brother's doorstep later that day.

"Hey, hey, my little Tonio." Vito picked up the child and tossed him into the air, catching him just in time, provoking shrieks of panicked glee. But one look at his sister and he knew there was something seriously wrong. "What is it?"

"He's going to try and take Antonio from me."

"Who is?"

"Il diavolo." ["The Devil."]

*   *   *

New York ~ Six months ago

Renée was breathless from her foray out into the world.

"Let me put the kettle on. What you need is a nice cup of English Teatime."

While Brandon tended to the tea, Renée spread the newspaper out on the breakfast table and read through the article. She would add it to the envelope Vito had given her, the one she kept stashed away in the secret jewelry box compartment.

"What's that?" he asked, watching as she carefully clipped the article.

"A ghost from my past." She studied the photo of Phillip Welles's family and something caught her attention. Standing behind Phillip's wife, children, and now grandchildren, was a middle-aged man who looked strikingly familiar. It could be a younger version of Vito.

"My God," she whispered, her heart racing. "Antonio?"

"Who's Antonio?"

Renée looked at her friend with sad eyes. "My son."

Brandan fell dramatically into the chair across from her. "I am not leaving here until you tell me everything."

24

Cassandra

Before Christopher left with Daniel, he stopped by the house to give me a heads-up that Edgar might be stopping out to The Bluffs.

"He asked to borrow some materials I checked out from the library. They're on the carriage house kitchen table."

"I'll make sure he gets them."

He glanced down toward the ankle monitor before asking, "Could you walk Gypsy too?"

"Of course." Then to ease the awkwardness, I said, "I know you'll do what you can to help Nicholas."

"I will try." He smiled sadly and tipped his head, then walked off to join Daniel at the Land Rover.

Gypsy was getting used to me and greeted me sweetly. The call from the judge had summoned them quickly, leaving no time for Christopher to put things in order, but I found the place neat and tidy as usual. The pile of books was on the kitchen table, as promised.

When I returned from walking Gypsy and was bending down to fill her water bowl, I noticed the strap of something sticking out from the lower kitchen cabinets. I opened the cupboard to find Christopher's messenger bag. I used my cell phone camera to take a shot of how it was placed in the cupboard before lifting it from its hiding place.

The cautioning scent of my great-grandparents now intensified when I opened the bag and sorted through the papers. On top was a brochure for the *Lady Spirit*. There was also a manila envelope with a handwritten note in a language I didn't recognize. I unfolded a yellowed newsprint article I did recognize; it was the same article I'd seen before from *The Cape Cod Times* about the unclaimed boy who washed up on Whale Rock shores so many years ago.

What was Christopher Savage's particular interest in Barnacle Boy?

I returned my attention to the manila envelope and gently opened the clasps to find letters in the same handwriting and unfamiliar language. I took out my phone to photograph the note and then began replacing the items, when a text came in from Edgar, telling me he would be there in ten minutes.

After carefully returning the messenger bag to the cupboard, I gave Gypsy a biscuit and said, "Promise not to tell?"

A few minutes later, Edgar and I were sitting at my kitchen table, Whistler nuzzling Edgar's hand for another treat.

"I now carry a supply of these because of you." He patted the dog's head, then drank down a glass of ice water. "It's cruel to have this heat wave while all those workers are still trying to clear away the mess left by Chantal."

"Thank goodness power has finally been restored to the Cape." Power lines had been repaired in a somewhat staggered order.

"Luckily your library was one of the first."

"I hear you were working there late last night and caught a little action on the wild streets of Whale Rock." I raised my eyebrows.

"Indeed." He shook his head disapprovingly. "I don't know that Creed fellow, but I was disappointed to see Christopher involved."

"You're sure it was him? I only ask because it does seem out of character." I took a sip from my water glass while Edgar considered the question.

He gazed upward, forehead scrunched as if trying to resurrect the scene, then looked at me and said, "On a ten-point scale, I'd rank my certainty as a seven."

"Very precise, Edgar." I had to laugh.

"I wish I had thought to take a picture with my phone, but it was probably too dark anyhow." He then turned his attention to the pile of books. "What have we got here?"

"These are what Christopher asked me to give you."

Edgar flipped through one of the books, which automatically opened to some articles stuck between the pages. He unfolded a sheet of paper, read through it, and then passed it across to me. "Does this mean anything to you?"

"*The Boston Globe*, 1969?" I checked the upper corner first and then perused the short piece about two men arrested after stealing a boat for a joy ride. "I don't recognize the names. I doubt these guys were Whale Rock locals."

Edgar was scanning a second article.

"Is that one related?"

"Doesn't seem to be." He slid it across the table.

The second article was more recent, also from *The Globe*, about a prominent Boston family.

I shook my head. "Haven't a clue who these people are either." I glanced down at the two articles, lying side by side on the table. "The two stories don't seem to be related in any way."

"Other than the Boston connection." Edgar began flipping through the other books but found no other articles. "Anyone could have left these in the book."

"True," I said, though the thick ashy scent that had enveloped me was evoking doubts. "Mind if I keep these?"

Edgar eyed me suspiciously over his half-glasses but didn't question the request.

"Of course." He gathered up the books. "I must be on my way. Jimmy's waiting for me to collect him."

"Did he go out with the search teams again?"

Edgar nodded. "He's been hard hit by little Lucas's disappearance, even though he's never met the child."

"You married a good, kind man."

"That's my Jimmy, all right." He glanced furtively at the papers on the table. "Keep me posted if you learn anything."

I wasn't sure whether he was referring to Lucas or if his curiosity had been piqued by the articles.

*　*　*

After Edgar left, I returned to our private library, hoping for a little time with Mama's journal. But that was not yet to be. My laptop came to life with digital images of the paintings I'd worked on for the tall ship brochure loading onto the screen, accompanied by a nearly choking odor filling the room.

I took my laptop to the kitchen to try to escape the pervasive odor so I could think, and began to retrace the messages from Percy and Celeste during the past couple of days. They'd sent a warning when I found the brochure for the *Lady Spirit* in Christopher's bag less than an hour ago, and now these images on my laptop. Didn't they also send a signal when the FedEx guy was talking about ships going out to sea? In fact, every time the *Lady Spirit* was a topic of conversation, the overwhelming calling card scent had emerged.

I hesitated only a second before picking up the phone. Luckily, Daniel answered. "What's up?"

"Has Christopher been allowed to speak with Nicholas yet?" I asked.

"No. Long story, but we're waiting on another ruling. Why?"

"I can't really explain this to you, but I have a hunch."

"Honestly, a hunch is probably better than anything else we have at the moment, so shoot."

As I told him my theory, the scent surrounding me sweetened. I hoped and prayed my spirit guides were sending us on the right path . . . and to a good end.

25

Cassandra

"Finally, some good news. We've found Lucas!" The call from Daniel came at about five p.m.

"Oh thank God!" I exclaimed. "Please tell me he's all right."

"He will be. I still can't get over your idea to check the *Lady Spirit*." He blew out a low whistle. "You never told me about your psychic powers."

Not psychic powers, just a couple of amazing guides from the spirit world.

"I can't reveal all my secrets."

"Well, your hunch certainly had amazing results. I'll tell you all about it—it's too long for the phone. Why don't you meet us at Rock Harbor Grill?"

"I'll be there in twenty." Rock Harbor Grill was a favorite gathering spot in Orleans, not far from District Court.

When I arrived, I found Daniel, Jason, and Brooks sitting out on the back deck. Daniel stood and pulled out a chair for me, signaling the waiter.

"Bring out a bottle of your finest champagne," Daniel told him. "We need to toast this lady."

"A glass of the house chardonnay will be fine for me," I told the waiter, and then to the guys, "Tell me what happened."

Before anyone answered, Teddy popped his head out the deck door, but when he noticed it was Brooks who had his back to the door, he began a subtle retreat. Jason spied him and called out, "Hey man, you've got to hear this!"

He gave a quick wave and said, "Let me grab a beer first."

At the sound of Teddy's voice, Brooks turned and motioned him over. "We've got a pitcher."

"You want to tell the story?" Brooks offered Daniel the honor as the waiter set a glass of white wine in front of me. "You witnessed all of it."

"It's amazing," Daniel said, shaking his head in wonderment. "Lucas has been found. Alive!"

"That's awesome! Where was he found?" Teddy was probably wondering how they could have missed him, with the combined efforts of volunteers combing the island door-to-door, trekking through woodlands and marshes, and his team of divers searching every shoreline nook and cranny.

"Nova Scotia."

"*What?*" Teddy and I said in harmony.

Just then Laura arrived, and demonstrating her nose for a story, she blurted out, "I just heard the great news!"

Brooks mumbled, "Of course you did."

I wondered how long he would tolerate Laura's conflicting position with the local paper.

She leaned in for a smooch from Jason after he pulled up another chair for her.

"I ran into Deputy Kirkpatrick, and she told me Lucas was found alive. That's all I know."

"For now." Brooks folded his arms and, with a stern look, told her, "This is all off the record. Let's allow the family a little bit of privacy."

Laura blushed. "Of course."

"But if you come down to the station tomorrow, I'll give you an exclusive statement," he said, softening.

"That would be great," Laura said, then placed her hand atop her glass when Jason moved to fill it from the pitcher of beer.

"Daniel was just starting to tell what happened."

"It's an amazing story," Daniel reemphasized. "In the midst of the mediations at the courthouse, Brooks took a call from the authorities in Halifax advising him that the *Lady Spirit* had just come in to port, and Lucas had been taken to the hospital."

"The *Lady Spirit*?" Teddy said.

"That was the name of the tall ship that was visiting Whale Rock the week leading up to the storm," Brooks answered. "Cassie did some brilliant deductive reasoning."

"Just a fluke." I waved the compliment away and took a sip of wine, though all eyes were eagerly focused on me. "Earlier today, when we were hashing through all the possibilities of what could have happened to Lucas, I was reminded of Nicholas's odd behavior the day of the storm," I said. "He was clearly bothered by something and kept looking down at the beach with panic."

"You weren't far off target on that one," Jason said to me, then told the group, "Cassie had also suggested Lucas might've been hiding in Christopher's cottage during the storm and then wandered off."

"Glad I was wrong on that last point."

"Lucas had been hiding in Land's End?" Laura asked, clearly frustrated by not being able to piece together the story.

"Not there." Jason laid a calming hand on his wife's arm.

Daniel picked up the thread again, "Anyhow, when Cassie called, she urged me to have Christopher ask Nicholas if he'd been on the *Lady Spirit*."

"How did you make that leap?" Teddy asked.

"That's what I want to know," Laura lifted her hands palms upward, totally stumped.

"Bear with me." I smiled at them. "Today the Federal Express guy mentioned that ships were stranded out at sea, which got me thinking about the *Lady Spirit* since it was so late to leave Whale Rock, and I wondered if it ever made it safely to port. Then I remembered Christopher telling me about Nicholas's inquisitive-ness, especially as it had to do with pirates and walking the plank and stowaways. It reminded me of the onboard cocktail party I attended on the day the *Lady Spirit* arrived. I was invited because I did the artwork for the promotional campaign. We were given a delightful tour by an actor in a pirate costume, and he pointed out a storage hold where stowaways hid." I took another sip of wine. "This had me thinking that if the Kleisters took a tour of the ship, then Nicholas probably also learned about those places to hide."

"But why would Lucas be hiding at all?" Laura persisted.

"That I don't know," I told her.

"When did they realize Lucas was onboard? And why didn't they report finding him?" Laura asked.

"Good questions. The ship's satellite communication system failed, and there were no working cell towers within reach," Brooks lifted his shoulders. "As Cassie said, many ships headed out to sea when the storm was hugging the coast, and *Lady Spirit* was directed to do the same. However, with it being such an unpredictable storm, there was no certain path back to land, especially after it stalled. I don't have specific details yet, but from what I understand, when Lucas was found he was unconscious and dehydrated. Luckily, they had an EMT on crew and were fully medically prepared to treat him."

"There are still many unanswered questions." Daniel picked up the thread. "For instance, we still don't know *how* Lucas ended up on the ship."

"There will be a full investigation," Brooks said, jumping in. "We assume Nicholas knows, but we don't want to push him too hard. The boy was visibly traumatized by the whole ordeal."

Daniel was shaking his head. "Can you imagine the poor kid's panic when the ship sailed?"

"The Kleisters must be in shock. A *good* shock, but still . . ." Teddy said. "I imagine they'd already expected the worst case in all this." He shook his head in disbelief. "I know I had."

"It was the first time I'd witnessed those parents show the slightest civility to each other," Daniel noted.

"There's an odd disconnect there," I added. "Beyond the stress of their child disappearing."

"Definitely something deeper at play," Brooks agreed.

"But why didn't Nicholas tell anyone where Lucas was?" Teddy asked.

"Kids that age think differently," Brooks answered.

Teddy tossed him a look that I couldn't interpret, but Brooks continued, unperturbed. "He was probably terrified of what would happen to him, especially after witnessing everyone's reactions. It was no wonder the kid clammed up."

"Well, whatever the reason, Nicholas does feel safe talking with one person," Daniel said. "Christopher Savage."

"Will the judge allow it?" I asked. "Will the Kleisters?"

"It's happening as we're sitting here," Brooks answered. "The parents weren't happy about it, but now that Lucas is safe, they didn't have a reasonable argument."

"In my opinion? There's still something eating away at that kid," Daniel said.

"Let's hope he's able to get it all out now while Christopher is speaking with him," Jason said.

"Indeed," Daniel agreed, then told us, "The transcripts will be sealed until the judge decides how to proceed with them."

"So that's why Christopher isn't here celebrating with us," I said, thinking he, as much as anyone, had a right to celebrate the discovery of Lucas.

Daniel checked his phone. "He's going to call for a ride back to The Bluffs when the interview is over."

"I'm calling an end to this short celebration." Brooks pushed back from the table. "Along with all the unanswered questions about what happened to Lucas, I might remind you we have a couple of missing persons to track down, *and* there's a killer still out there."

On that somber note, the group dispersed.

"It truly is unfathomable." Laura caught up with me in the parking lot. Her eyes were bright, possibly at the prospect of a story.

"It's the best possible ending anyone could have hoped for."

"No kidding." We were all still in a happy shock.

"What are you up to now?" I asked.

"I'm on my way over to Nauset beach to meet the staff photographer at Liam's Clam Shack."

"I can't believe Liam's is gone," I whined over the loss of a family favorite. The storm had done irreparable damage to the beloved clam shack, and it was not going to return to its famous beach location.

"After that, I have a certain cabby to have a little chat with."

"So you found him?"

"Actually, my husband did the heavy lifting on that one."

I sent her a quizzical look.

"Evidently, Brooks has Jason working on this for some reason."

So that's why he was annoyed at my showing Christopher her photo this morning.

"Anyhow, he tracked down a cab driver who claimed to have picked up Sister Bernadetta."

"Did he tell you that?"

"Jason isn't telling *me* anything. I overheard him talking to the cabbie." She pursed her lips. "Brooks doesn't trust me."

"Maybe you should stop eavesdropping," I teased.

"Oh, but I'd miss so many scoops," she kidded back.

"Trust me, it's not you—it's just your job. Police and the press don't always live by the same rules and timelines. He did offer you an exclusive," I reminded her.

"True. Better run." She started to walk away but turned back and said, "By the way, I found out a little more about that key chain. I'm told the label had the letters 'LEC' on it."

"Lee Chambers?"

"A safe assumption since his middle name was Edward. What the key opens, I don't know. Yet."

I caught a subtle twinkle in her eye that made me smile.

"I take it you still haven't told Jason about the baby?"

"What makes you say that?"

"If he knew, he wouldn't have offered you a beer."

"Maybe *you* should work for the *Times*."

"There's enough drama in my own life. I don't need to be getting involved in the craziness of the rest of the world."

Little did I know how much more drama was in store.

26

Cassandra

After tending to Whistler, I headed to the carriage house to take Gypsy out one more time, thinking about the ordeal Lucas Kleister had survived and wishing there was a way to send a signal of gratitude to Percy and Celeste. As I walked around the side, Daniel pulled up with Christopher, and Gypsy nearly dragged me over, trying to get to her master.

"She's one devoted pup." I handed over the leash.

Christopher kneeled and allowed the dog to cover his face with slobbery kisses.

"I'm pretty sure she sees me as her rescuer." I was reminded of how he'd adopted the dog just hours before she was to be euthanized.

"Dogs have a keen sense of who their protectors are," I agreed.

"Speaking of which," Daniel said, "Where's Whistler?"

"He's already been walked, watered, and fed."

"That's more than I can say." He rubbed his hands together. "How about the three of us mosey into town to support one of the local eateries? They could use the support after this past week."

Christopher's eyes widened, obviously taken aback by the invitation. Or maybe just leery of spending more time with Daniel.

"Please join us," I insisted. "We have much to celebrate."

"That would be nice." He looked down at his khaki pants and asked, "Do I have time for a quick change? Shorts would be more comfortable in this heat wave."

"Good idea," Daniel said. "Think I'll do the same."

When the two men returned, looking and feeling much cooler, I noticed Christopher's ankle monitor had been removed. Daniel suggested taking two cars since he had some work to do at the harbor after dinner.

"Perfect. I'll meet you guys at the diner." The Whale Rock Diner was one of a handful of restaurants that had been able to open its doors, albeit with a limited menu. When we arrived, it was bustling with the exciting news that the young Kleister boy had been found. Even with all the problems of the recent storm, the Whale Rock grapevine was still as tightly strung as ever. Many people were stopping by our booth to offer their congratulations to Daniel.

"I had nothing to do with finding Lucas," he kept telling everyone. "It was pure luck."

We had agreed not to talk about the specific details. It would all come out soon enough, but we hoped to give the Kleisters a little breathing space, especially Nicholas.

Archie Stanfield saw us sitting at the window booth as he passed by and rushed in to share the good fortune.

"It's nothing short of a miracle!" he said, in his dramatic way. "Peeps and I had given up all hope that the little angel would be found."

"You weren't alone," I told him.

"Hello there." He acknowledged Christopher as if he knew him.

"Hello, I'm Christopher Savage." He offered his hand.

"Oh. Sorry, I had you mixed up with someone else. Nice to meet you." Archie looked more closely at Christopher and then pointed to his neck. "That's an interesting piece."

"It's a family thing." Christopher fingered a silver medallion and then tucked it back inside his shirt, fastening the next button up. I'd noticed the chain before, but since he usually wore T-shirts, I'd missed the attached medal pendant.

"Then you probably wouldn't want to sell it," Archie grinned. "I must apologize. I'm always on the lookout for unique treasures. It's an occupational habit."

"Archie owns Coastal Vintage Wares just up the street," I explained.

"I'll be sure to stop by one day." Christopher smiled.

"Please do. Speaking of which, I've got to go lock up the store. I just popped in to pick up dinner for me and Peeps." He gave a wave and then stopped at the counter where they had his takeout order ready to go.

I'm not sure how Daniel finally managed to finish his burger through all the interruptions. Pure hunger, I supposed.

"I'd better get over to the harbor," he said, pushing back from the table. "I promised Johnny."

"Don't work too late," I told him when he leaned in for a kiss.

"Couple hours." Then to Christopher, in a serious tone, "I appreciate you seeing my lady home safely."

After Daniel left but before I could get one question in, Lu sashayed over to our table, looking cool as a cucumber in a sea-horse print summer sheath.

"You remember Christopher?" I said to her.

"Of course—we met the day of the storm as he was evacuating." She eyed him appreciatively before adding, "I heard your cottage took a hit."

He merely nodded.

"Such great news about little Lucas!" She brought her hands, prayer-like, up to her chin. "It's nothing short of a miracle."

"An incredible story," I agreed.

Lu lowered her voice and leaned in closer to the table to ask, "Is it true he somehow got lost aboard that tall ship?"

So much for giving the family some breathing time.

When neither Christopher nor I responded immediately, she lifted her shoulders innocently and said, "That's what Ev told me."

"It's true," Christopher said, surprising me.

"But there are still many unknowns," I added.

"Of course." She nodded, then brought the conversation around to one of her favorite topics. "Are you working on something I can take a peek at?"

"Since you last asked a week ago? No."

"What? Are you letting a little hurricane interfere with your genius?" Lu pursed her lips, then said to my dinner companion, "Cassie is one of our great local artistic talents."

My face was burning.

"I didn't know that," he admitted, tilting his head as if assessing me with a different eye.

"It's true, and I would love to do another exhibit. It's been close to a year now since the last smashing success, and people have been asking."

"What people? Ev and George?" I snorted slightly at my own joke.

"Cassie's self-deprecation has always been part of her charm," Lu explained. "She's really quite gifted. Have her show you some of her works."

I shot her a cautioning look.

"Well, I must be off. Nice to meet you," she said to Christopher, to which he stood politely. She then signaled me with her eyes to follow.

"I'll walk out with you," I told her, then excused myself to Christopher. "Be back in a sec."

"Sorry. Old habits," Lu apologized when we were out on the sidewalk. "I didn't mean to embarrass you."

"It's fine. What's up?"

"Remember, you were asking about Wes Creed dating my cousin? Well, word around town is that he has a new friend."

"Anyone I know?"

"I'll give you a hint. She's tall, gorgeous, and drives a red Mercedes convertible."

"Get out of here!" This was a shocking revelation. "I thought she had more sense than that."

"It's true. Wes Creed and Robyn Landers are an official Whale Rock item."

"She mentioned having a new friend, but Wes Creed?"

After giving it a moment's consideration, it shouldn't have been all that surprising. Robyn was single and spent a lot of time at the harbor, where her sailboat was moored, especially during the months when she rented out Land's End. Wes would have plenty of opportunities to woo her. I just hoped it wasn't for the wrong reasons. Robyn had made out well in her divorce, and I'd hate to think Wes was taking advantage. An image came to mind of Wes Creed huddled closely on the beach with Helene Kleister.

"Maybe he's just a summer boy toy," Lu suggested.

"Wes isn't young enough to be a toy."

"I don't think age has anything to do with it." Lu seemed to take umbrage. She'd been known to date her share of younger men. "He's a handsome bad boy with a sexy smile. Why shouldn't Robyn have some fun?" As if to emphasize her point, Lu craned her neck to peek at Christopher through the diner window. "He cleans up well," she said. "Single?"

"Why? Looking for a boy toy of your own?" Christopher was several years younger, but that had never stopped Cougar Lu in the past.

"Just wondering." She wiggled her eyebrows.

Right. "I would guess he's single, but the subject never came up."

"Oh well. Must run," she said, looking at her phone. Then over her shoulder she called out, "I want to see what you're hiding in that studio of yours."

Through the diner window, I caught Christopher watching closely as Lu walked away. Hmm. Had he fallen under her bewitching spell?

When I returned to the diner booth, I pushed away my half-eaten burger and fries. "Sorry about that."

"She seems nice."

"Who? Lu? She's great." Not wanting to go there, I reached for something to divert the conversation. "You must be happy to have that ankle monitor off."

"I'm all for new experiences, but that is one I hope never to repeat." He shook his head. "I had a feeling Lucas would be found—or maybe I just didn't want to think otherwise—but how it all came about is mind-boggling."

"Was Nicholas protecting Lucas from something or someone? Was there a monster involved?" I asked, referring to an earlier comment he made.

His look said, *Really?* "You know I can't talk about what Nicholas told me."

It was a mild rebuke, and he was right. I should have honored his need to protect the confidential nature of the conversation.

"His parents have to be beyond relieved," I said to break through the uncomfortable silence that followed.

Christopher remained quiet.

"You don't like them, do you?" I ventured.

"I don't understand them." It wasn't really an answer. "But I can't say anything more about it."

"I get it."

After a moment, he said, "I will tell you this. When I made that statement about monsters, I had no idea how rooted in the truth some of Nicholas's imaginings were."

That sent my own imagination into high gear, considering all the possibilities. Still, knowing I wasn't going to get anything more out of Christopher, I suggested we head back to The Bluffs.

"I was wondering, is your father still living?" I said to break the silence that had settled in during the drive.

"He is." A troubled shadow crossed his face.

"Does he live near you in New York?"

"Manhattan, actually. My parents are city people to the core. My mother was especially."

"But not you?"

"I grew up there, but the tempo is too fast for me. I prefer the bucolic countryside to blaring horns and exhaust emissions."

"That's what I love about the Cape, though it can get a little busy in the summer."

"Still more low key than the city. I could get used to it."

"You wouldn't be the first." How lucky for me that Daniel had been charmed by Whale Rock. "How's your research coming along?"

"There've been some distractions." He sent me a sidelong glance that had me squirming.

"Have you learned anything you think will interest your students?"

"There's a lot of untapped history associated with this area. Nuggets not often found in your typical textbook." It was a vague answer, but one that could explain why he had the Barnacle Boy article. It was a "nugget" of interest that wasn't widely known, though not necessarily one that would be considered of historical importance.

"I'm sure you've already heard the story of my great-grandparents, Percival and Celeste Mitchell."

"Edgar and Jimmy gave me the long version when we were bunking together during the storm." He offered a rare smile. "I plan to buy a copy of Edgar's book and have him sign it before I leave. Whenever that is."

"You'll be staying on in Whale Rock a while longer then?"

"Whether I want to or not," he said with a sigh. "It's been *requested* I stick around."

With all the good news about Lucas, I'd forgotten Christopher was still tied to the Lee Chambers case.

As we drove up the lane to The Bluffs, I said, "How about I give you a personal tour of the Mitchell family burial grounds? I just might be able to add another tidbit or two about our family legacy."

"I'd like that." He gave a sad lift to his shoulders, making me feel sorry for him. "I'm not going anywhere."

* * *

Laura was waiting for me in the kitchen when I walked through the door and was greeted enthusiastically by Whistler.

"Want to go on a little adventure?" she asked before I had a chance to set my purse on the table.

"What did you have in mind?"

"The cab driver finishes his shift in a few minutes and said he'd meet with me if I come to him in Eastham."

"Where's Jason?"

"Where do you think?" She made a face. "I thought he might have a night off, but Brooks has him and Deputy Bland following some lead in the Chambers case."

"Why do I feel like you're using me for my wheels?"

"Hey, you're the one who figured out that the mystery woman was Sister Bernadetta. Don't you want to help find her?"

I checked the captain's wheel clock. Eight thirty. I texted Daniel: *How's it going?*

He responded: *Promise to be home by 10.*

"We have an hour," I told Laura and off we went. Luckily the cabbie agreed to meet us right on Route 6 in the parking lot of the Superette. The small grocery story was famous for staying open every day for nearly seven decades, even during strong storms like Chantel.

"If Jason was working on this, how did you get the number? Or don't I want to know?" I asked as we waited.

"Probably not." She looked chagrinned, which told me it was likely from snooping in Jason's phone.

A black car with "Cape Cab" in yellow lettering soon pulled up beside us, and out popped a short, bald, gum-chomping man abuzz with energy.

"Which one of you's Laura?" he asked.

"That would be me." She gave a wave and said, "This is Cassie."

He nodded.

"Thanks for meeting with us, Pat." She pulled up a photo on her phone and showed it to him. "This is the woman we're looking for."

"Yeah, yeah. Same photo that cop texted me." Pat continued, "I left a message with Officer Prince but haven't heard back. You two ladies cops too?"

"Not exactly," I said. "But we're helping them with this."

"So you remember the woman?" Laura asked.

"Sure do. She was a nun, but no habit or nothin'."

"How do you know she was a nun?"

"She told me. Said she needed to find a convent. Some priest told her she'd find one in Orleans."

I frowned. "Where's the convent in Orleans?"

"That's the thing." Pat threw his hands into the air. "There isn't one. The last convent on the Cape closed a few years back. I should know. My mother's cousin was a nun."

"So where did you end up taking her?" asked Laura.

"The Transfiguration Church over in Rock Harbor."

"I didn't know there was a convent there." I knew the church; it had a dramatic angel sculpture atop the hundred-foot-tall bell tower. But aside from having once attended an organ concert in their sanctuary, I've had no association with the church or any of its members.

"Not really a convent, so to speak, but there's this group of celibate sisters who live there on the compound. I drive by there all the time." He waved an arm in the direction of Rock Harbor. "I take a regular to get her hair done every week. You can see the sisters walking the property in their white robes."

"Do they have a shelter set up there?" I asked, wondering if the nun had been looking to offer her help elsewhere.

"I don't know," he said, puzzled. "I had another call, so I just dropped her."

"Did she seem pleased when you took her there?"

"I wouldn't say *pleased*." He rubbed his shiny head. "*Relieved* might be a better word."

*   *   *

After leaving the Superette, we decided to pay a visit to The Transfiguration Church where Pat had taken Sister Bernadetta.

"Even if there is a shelter there, it seems strange that she would pack up everything at one church shelter, leave her car there, and hire a cab to take her to another one."

"Unless she discovered that the man she was searching for was at this church?" I suggested.

"That would be too easy." Laura smiled.

As it turned out, nothing was going to be easy as concerned finding this Sister. We arrived to find the church locked up tight and nobody answering any of the doors we knocked on.

"We can try again tomorrow," I said on the drive home.

She nodded, then segued to another subject.

"Did you ever find out why Christopher had that Barnacle Boy article?"

"It could be as simple as a point of interest to share with his class. Why?"

"Working on this story with Edgar has brought some weird old feelings to life."

"About your brother?" I was referring to the brother she'd lost to a drowning accident as a young child.

"Only partly." She lifted a shoulder. "I have this hunger to learn who Barnacle Boy was, where he came from, why nobody ever came looking for him."

"It's your reporter's instincts shifting into high gear."

"Haven't you been curious? I mean all these years, and nobody knows who he is or where he came from."

"Sure, I'm curious. I'm also a little protective of him." Deep down, I felt I already knew him.

"Protective? I don't get that."

"I'm not certain I can explain it." I paused to consider. "It's just that the mystery has made him a Whale Rock legend." *A Mitchell legend.* "Whenever Granny Fi took me to the graveyard to visit the other family members, we always stopped at Barnacle Boy's gravesite too. Only we never called him that. To us, he was always *the lost boy.* My Granny would tell me made-up stories about the lost boy and his life." I knew that no matter what real-life story was uncovered, it would never measure up to the ones she told me.

Laura was reflective a moment before offering her own perspective.

"When I was in college, I came across a true crime story from the 1950s, about a little boy whose body had been found in a large cardboard box in Philadelphia. Although he was badly bruised, someone had taken the time to clean the body, trim his nails and cut his hair, and then carefully wrap him in a blanket and fold his arms across his stomach. But the investigation went nowhere. No leads, no clues—nothing. To this day the Boy in a Box mystery remains unsolved."

"That is such a tragic story."

"No more tragic than Barnacle Boy's story," Laura pointed out.

She's right, I thought as we pulled up to The Bluffs and got out of the car. When you lived your entire life with a tragedy woven into your own town's folklore, you must become inured to it. Granny Fi's stories created a character that had in a way diminished the lost boy's terribly sad fate.

"I wrote something about it for one of my creative writing classes. The shadow of sadness still clings to me. Then we came here, and when I first saw Barnacle Boy's grave in your family's cemetery? It made me want to solve at least one of the mysteries." She held my gaze a moment before asking, "Is that crazy?"

"Not at all." Certainly no more crazy than the overwhelming burning sugar scent that enveloped me as we walked inside. Laura took Whistler upstairs, and since Daniel wasn't yet home, I decided to treat myself to some time with Mama's journal. Before I could, however, I found my laptop open to another email from Zoe. It read: *Check out this link. Dr. Zane is a specialist in the field. She might be able to help you.*

I read with interest what Zoe had forwarded, and with even more interest what Mama had written about her pregnancy struggles, all the while accompanied by the sweet encouraging aroma of Percy and Celeste. *Okay. I'll contact Dr. Zane.* I'd also send off an email to Brit. Nico, her new Italian lover was a genetic scientist.

"What are you doing?" Daniel asked from the doorway.

"Oh!" I jumped. "I didn't even hear you come in."

"You were engrossed." He nodded to the journal in my lap.

"It was my mother's. Zoe sent it to me." I gently closed it and set it on the desk before shutting down my laptop.

"It's late." He reached out his hand, and the sweet scent followed us up the stairs.

27

Cassandra

"Couldn't he stay a little longer?" I nestled my face into Whistler's neck. With the okay given to the Princes to return to their beach cottage, I'd driven Laura and Whistler back to town.

"You can visit him whenever you like."

"It's not the same." I released the poor dog from my clutches and stood to help unload the truck.

"I know. But at least you still have Gypsy staying with you." Laura tried to cheer me up.

"She *is* a sweet girl once she gets used to you."

"I think it's time for you to get a dog of your own."

Growing up, I'd never been allowed to have a pet because Mama was allergic. And my first husband had not been a pet person. Whistler had been my first experience with a dog, and I'd been unprepared for how much he'd meant to me.

"I'll help you find one," Laura said, interrupting my musings. "There are so many shelter dogs who deserve a loving home like you and Daniel could give."

"We'll see." It was tempting.

"Can I leave the truck here? I've got some errands to run." With some streets still closed off in places, parking was iffy.

"You bet. Let's check in with each other later."

"Sounds good." Laura had more interviews for her article, and I planned to return to the church in Orleans to see if I could track down Sister Bernadetta.

I gave Whistler one last hug and bid Laura goodbye.

* * *

While in town, I decided to pop in to see Brooks. I rounded the corner of the station in time to see Wes Creed exiting and walking in the opposite direction. *Hmm?*

"Do I even want to know what he was doing here?" I asked, when I found Brooks in his temporary office-slash-cell.

Brooks frowned. "Who?"

"I just saw Wes Creed sauntering out of here like he didn't have a care in the world."

"I was trying to put some pressure on him to admit to an altercation with Savage."

"And?"

"No go."

"Maybe it wasn't Christopher," I suggested.

Brooks responded with a noncommittal grunt, keeping his attention on the paperwork littering his small makeshift desk.

"It looks like they're making progress on the roof," I said. "When will the work be completed here?"

"They say another week." He looked exhausted and sounded frustrated. "Did Daniel tell you that Matthew Kleister is on his way to Nova Scotia to bring Lucas home?"

"Miracle of miracles." I walked to the corner of the cell, leaning against the bars. "I mean that literally."

"You can say that again." The fatigue-induced creases on his face were momentarily eased by the happy thought. Just then, Jason blasted in.

"EMTs just rushed Helene Kleister to the ER!" he reported. "Suspected overdose."

My jaw dropped, but he hadn't seen me because of the angle from him to where I was standing. Brooks cleared his throat and tilted his head in my direction.

Jason closed his eyes as he flipped his head back.

"Don't worry." I held up my hands. "I'm a steel trap."

Both men rolled their eyes.

"Seriously, I promise not to say a word."

"That Kleister family has brought more devastation to The Rock than the damn tropical storm," Brooks grumbled, struggling to his feet. In doing so, he knocked a mass of files to the floor. "Damn it. I'll be glad to have my office back."

Jason and I bent down to begin collecting the mess.

"You guys go ahead," I said. "I can clean this up."

Brooks hesitated a second.

"I get it. Sensitive material." I raised my hands.

"Stack it all up on the desk," he said. "The door will lock automatically behind you when you leave."

I gathered up the files and fortunately only a few loose pages had fallen out. But I couldn't help noticing one report that had photocopies of a familiar-looking keychain. The label did indeed have the letters "L," "E," and "C" on it as Laura's sources had reported to her. However, they weren't written like initials. The "L" and the "E" were on the first line, and the "C" was on the second line with part of the label torn away.

"Hey, Chief," a woman's voice came from down the hallway.

"He's not here," I called out.

Deputy Kirkpatrick poked her head in as I was gathering the last of the files.

"Hi, Lisa." I stacked the pile on the table. "Brooks had to rush out and he knocked all this on the floor."

"Do you know where he went?"

I shook my head. "He left with Jason not even five minutes ago."

"Huh. Must have just missed them." She looked suspiciously at the files.

"I think I got them all." I checked under the desk one more time. "Well, I must run."

I scurried out of the station, certain Lisa Kirkpatrick thought I was up to something. Maybe it was feelings of guilt for reading that report. When I spied Laura walking toward the library, I ducked down an alley, not trusting myself to keep a lid on what Jason had just disclosed about Helene Kleister. But what I found on my quick detour was another surprising sight. At the small back patio of the Cape Breeze Café, I saw Christopher seated at a table with someone I didn't recognize—a younger man, slightly built and with reddish hair. The two looked like they were having a rather serious discussion, and fortunately hadn't noticed me. I looked for an easy escape, and my only option was through the back door of La Table. *Crap!*

"Can I help you?" I turned toward a familiar playfully sarcastic voice, foiling my hopes of sneaking in unnoticed. I smiled at Billy Hughes, my long-time on-again, off-again ex-boyfriend.

"Just passing through." I waved, trying to make my voice just as playful. "How are you, Billy?"

"Not bad, not bad." He narrowed his eyes. "What trouble are you up to today?"

"Avoiding trouble would be a better way to put it."

"You always seem to find it." He pointed his thumb to the alleyway. "You know—the dead dumpster dude?"

"What have you heard about it?" I asked, thinking he might have learned something I hadn't.

"Nothing since they questioned me. First Brooks, then David Bland and that new lady deputy."

Of course they'd be very interested in Billy. He rented the dumpster.

"Did you know the victim?" I asked.

"First time I heard of him was when the police showed me his picture," he said, and then asked me, "What do *you* know about it?"

"Not much more than that."

"Right." His lips formed a line of skepticism.

"Gotta run." I gave another quick wave and exited the shop. "Ta-ta."

When I hit the sidewalk, I was flushed. Making things worse, Daniel just happened to be walking past.

"Hey you!"

He smiled and gazed up at the sign, then back at me, eyebrows lifted. "Planning a party?"

"And here it was supposed to be a surprise." I tried to make light. "What are you doing?"

"Heading to lunch at Cape Breeze." He swiveled his neck, checking to see who might be listening before saying, "I have a meeting. But that's all I can say."

Is that so? Exactly where I just saw Christopher and the mysterious stranger in an intense tête-à-tête?

"I understand." I nodded seriously and then, to get his goat, asked, "With Christopher Savage?"

"What? How did . . ." He blew out an exasperated breath. "And so the psychic abilities continue?"

"Actually, I was just coming to tell *you* that I saw Christopher with some guy out on the back patio." I thumbed in the direction of the alley. "Is that Tyler Stendall?"

A curtain of total exasperation descended. "How about letting *me* do my job?"

"Hey, last I checked, you'd retired from the FBI. Running Mitchell Whale Watcher Boat Tours was your job."

"Either way, I'm not saying." Then, in a tone of indignation, he told me, "Why don't you go plan your little party with Billy."

On that special note, he turned and walked toward the Café, making me feel small.

Perhaps I'd pushed him a little too far.

28
Renée

"Please no more," Renée begged of her husband. She'd had it with hospitals, doctors, needles, treatments. But Michael wasn't ready for her to give up yet.

"Dr. Medford is very optimistic about this new protocol. So far, it's been working beautifully."

She didn't have the heart or the strength to deny him his wishes, though she was bone tired and weary of it all. The cancer had moved in and made itself quite comfortable. She knew it wasn't going anywhere, no matter Dr. Medford's or Michael's optimism.

"Where's my boy?" she asked, hoping to forego another round of debate.

"I'm right here, Ma." Her son pulled his chair nearer to her bed and took hold of her hand.

She closed her eyes, at peace knowing he was close. How long she'd slept, she wasn't sure. At one point she awoke to hear her husband and son in a heated discussion.

"She's trying to tell me something," her son said to Michael. "Who's Antonio?"

"I don't know," she heard her husband respond. "Maybe someone from her past. Maybe nobody. I don't think you can take anything she's saying seriously right now. You've just arrived, but I've been living with this for weeks. The medications are making her confused."

"Why not take her off the antianxiety meds? That way she can stay conscious for a while."

"We tried that," Michael said, exasperated. "She becomes extremely agitated without them."

"Did you ever think she might be agitated because she can't focus on what it is she wants to tell us?"

Frustrated, Michael left the room, giving Renée the opportunity for a private moment with her boy.

"Tofie?"

He smiled. "You haven't called me that for years."

"Not since you forbade it." She sent him a sly look.

"I was trying to be a cool middle-school jock."

"How'd that turn out for you?" Neither she nor Michael had wanted their son to play football for fear of concussions. But a broken leg during his first junior varsity game had put a quick end to a future football career. She waved it away. "You were meant to spend time with books."

"True."

She took hold of his arm. "There is something you must know, in case . . ." She let the thought drift.

"This treatment is working, Ma."

"I know." She knew it was what he wanted to believe. "Even so, I've kept something from you. Something important."

"What is it?"

"My son," she whispered.

"Yes, I'm here, Ma." He misunderstood, but Renée was unable to gather the courage to speak the words that had been bottled up inside her for so many years.

"Does it have to do with this Antonio you keep mentioning?" He frowned in that way that caused a crease between his eyes, just like when he used to work through a homework problem.

"Yes." She heard Michael's footsteps approaching and lowered her voice. "Look in my jewelry box. You'll find the newspaper article. Antonio is in the photograph."

She cringed at the pity reflected in her boy's eyes. It was the same way Michael looked at her these days.

"You must believe me." She reached for him, and he took hold of her hand.

"Okay, Ma. Okay."

"Time for a snack." Michael entered, holding a small tray with a fruit and yogurt parfait. Also on the tray, a bottle of pills. Renée was relieved she'd finally been able to tell her son about the jewelry box. Now he'd find out about his brother. It was only right that he should know.

But something was nagging at her. Other secrets in that jewelry box. *What were they?*

*　*　*

Boston ~ Late 1960s

"He's going to try and take Antonio from me," Renata told her brother. *"Il diavolo."*

"You must calm down, *sorellina*." Renata's brother patted her cheek, then turned to his nephew. "Tonio, here are some crayons and paper. Draw me a nice picture of a big boat, heh?"

"Oh Vito," Renata fretted, "How can I calm down? These are powerful people with means. Phillip Welles's family invited us to lunch. But it was a trap. They figured out that Antonio is Phillip's son, and they want to take Tonio away from me. They said he'd be better off, that they could give him a better life."

She pushed the curtains aside to make sure nobody was lurking on the street below.

"You're his mamma. They can't just take him from you."

"They offered me money for my child!" she shrieked, causing Antonio to look up from his drawing.

Vito took her gently by the arm and guided her to the small kitchen. "You're frightening the boy, Renata."

"Of course, you're right." She rubbed her forehead. "We have to leave tonight, and you have to help us."

"Whoa, whoa, whoa." He took down a whiskey bottle from a high cupboard and poured a generous amount in a juice glass. "Here, drink this."

She did as she was told. It was a punishing burn, followed by a synthetic calm. Finally she told him, "Phillip threatened me. He said I might as well take the money because they would end up with Antonio either way."

"He was bluffing, maybe?"

"I can't take that risk. Antonio is my world." She finished off the liquor. "We will leave with or without your help."

"Okay, okay." He made a calming gesture with his hands. "Give me some time to think of a plan. Go play with your boy while I make some calls."

She sat cross-legged on the floor with Antonio and he let her pet and hug him without fussing. "How would you like to go on an adventure?" she asked him.

Those brilliant blue eyes widened with excitement. "Where, Mamma?"

"It's a secret. But I promise it will be exciting."

"When will we go?"

"Soon my darling boy. Very soon."

"I'll draw a picture of where I think it will be." Antonio returned his attention to his artistic creation, and Renata tried to hear what Vito was saying, wondering to whom he was speaking on the phone. Thirty minutes later he signaled for her to join him back in the kitchen.

"Thomas and I have come up with an idea." Thomas was Vito's best friend, and he'd always had a soft spot for Renata. She knew he'd do anything for her. "He'll be here shortly, and then we will go over the plan."

When Thomas arrived, he looked at Renata in a way that always gave her heart a tug. She felt it must hurt her more than it did him that she did not return his feelings.

"But he's never even been on a boat before," Renata fretted when Vito and Thomas laid out their plan. "He's only five years old, and so small."

"I have been piloting boats now for six years. You must put faith and trust in your big brother. Thomas knows someone who has agreed to lend us his boat in Plymouth." Vito tugged at her sleeve and pointed at the map he had laid out on the kitchen table.

"We'll leave early. There's a shortcut through the Cape Cod Canal"—his finger traced the route—"and we can meet you right here in New Bedford. From there you and Tonio will continue on together to New York."

"I have family in New York," Thomas told her. "They own a business and can offer you work and a place to live. It's modest, but clean and safe."

"That's all we need, Thomas." She hugged him. "How will I ever thank you?"

"It's nothing," he stammered, blushing scarlet. "I'll come and check on you as often as I can."

"We'd like it if you did." She felt something stir within her. Maybe there was potential for something between them after all.

"We have to do this quickly." Renata turned her attention back to her brother.

"Is tomorrow soon enough?" he asked. "It is Sunday and we will have the day free."

She'd like to leave right now but understood the plan required them to wait one more day.

"They will be watching my every move." Again, she peered out the window.

"That is why you will go separately. You'll take a bus, and Thomas and I will bring little Tonio. See? It's all worked out." Vito winked at his sister and assured her all would be fine.

Thomas purchased the bus ticket for her and dropped her and Antonio at the convent, where they spent the night with Isabella. Where could they be safer than at a convent?

She began to feel hopeful. Fantasies of a new life in a new place danced in her head as she thought of the plan for a new life with Antonio. But interrupting the pleasant imaginings meant to quiet her anxiety was Thomas's face when Vito was outlining the plan to her. What had been behind his look of concern?

*　*　*

New York ~ Three months ago

When Renée aroused from the torpor, her husband and son were talking again, though with more civility now.

"I think you should let it go," Michael said, though his voice had lost its fighting spirit. "At least for now."

"I can't let it go, Dad. It's obviously something she wanted me to know. And *I need* to find out what I can." He was quiet a moment before adding, "Maybe it's the closure she needs."

"Maybe," Michael said, but with defeat in his tone. "What do you plan to do about it?"

"What are you two up to?" Renée made her wakefulness known.

"I've got to go check on something in the kitchen. A surprise for you," Michael announced and sent her a sweet wink. "Be right back."

"Ma, I checked your jewelry box, but there's nothing there."

"Bring it to me." She motioned with her hands.

But when he came back with it, she'd forgotten already what she'd sent him to get.

"Yes, we must go through my jewelry," she covered for her confusion and opened the lid, delighted by the contents of the box. She held up a triple strand of pearls. "I want Cecelia to have these. And my diamond stud earrings."

"Ma, Cecelia and I divorced five years ago."

"That's right." She rushed to cover her mistake again and tried to make a joke. "No wonder she hasn't been by to visit."

She pulled out a drawer and clasped her hand to her heart. "I'd forgotten all about this."

"What is it?"

She held up a silver chain with a round medallion and then instructed, "Bend down so I can put this around your neck."

"Ma, I'm not one for jewelry."

"Antonio has Isabella's," she mumbled, gazing into space. "But something went wrong."

"Ma. There's nothing else in here."

She pulled out the secret compartment. *Empty? But how?*

"Brandan," she whispered.

"Brandan knows?"

She nodded.

"Then I'll find out from him."

She was suddenly gripped with fear. Even though she couldn't quite latch onto the reason, she felt sure it was a bad idea. She reached out to grab hold of her son, but he was too far away. *Come back. Come back. Come back.* It was only after he turned and blew a kiss before gently closing the door that she realized her unuttered plea had remained trapped in her head. Because she had now lost the ability to articulate her thoughts, her son was going to believe he had her blessing.

When she later awoke from another long nap, Michael appeared with her dinner tray, his face shining with the love he'd always had for her.

"You look rested." He fluffed her pillows and helped her to a sitting position. "I've made your favorite. Tuscan bean soup."

"It smells delicious."

"It should. I used your recipe." He smiled indulgently.

She took a sip and nodded her approval, then asked, "Where's my Tonio?"

"You mean Tofie," her husband corrected her.

Did she? "Of course."

"He went to see a friend. He'll be back later."

"That's nice." She smiled through her hazy confusion. Had her brain tumor permanently erased yet another part of herself?

29
Cassandra

Present day ~ Whale Rock

I stopped by the harbor later that afternoon to make nice with Daniel.

"Hey, Handsome," I called out.

The frown when he looked up from his work on the tour boat dashed my hopes. I hopped aboard anyhow to offer my help. Most of my life had been spent working in some capacity on these boats, and I didn't need any instruction. We worked quietly together for a while before he surprised me by asking, "Want to come out for a quick spin?"

"Have I ever turned down an offer to go out on the water?" I replied, encouraged by the invitation.

"Let's untie her," he said as he took his place at the helm. A few moments later, we were out on the open waters of Cape Cod Bay, testing the engine that had recently been repaired.

"The motor sounds good," I said, joining him at the wheel.

"Hold on!" he told me before taking it full throttle. As we neared Provincetown, he finally slowed down and found a calm place to drop anchor.

"Okay," he said, "Let's clear the air."

"One minute." I held up a finger and ran to the ship's head, where I threw up. Fortunately, there was still a secret stash of Scope in the same hiding place as when I crewed on the boat. I splashed water on my face and returned to the deck, still a little shaky.

"Everything okay?" Daniel caressed my cheek. "You're looking a little green."

"Seasickness, I guess."

"When does that ever happen?" Daniel handed me a peppermint from the supply kept on board to help the less seaworthy tourists.

"Never, right?"

"Do you want to head back?" he asked.

"Not yet. It's kind of fun playing hooky with you for an afternoon."

He pulled me to him. "Sorry about being a grouch earlier."

"It was my fault for pushing your buttons." I looked up into those piercing gray eyes and said, "I'm sorry."

"We're good." He hugged me tighter. "It's been a rather tense time."

"You think?" I shook my head. "A postponed wedding. A disastrous tropical storm. A missing child—thankfully now found—and a suspicious death. What's next?"

"Hopefully, now that Lucas Kleister is safe, finding the person who killed Lee Chambers."

"How's that progressing?"

"Working on it." Code for not wanting to talk about it. "I'm concerned about you."

"The nausea has passed now."

"I'm talking about something more serious."

"What do you mean?"

"We took the Cat out of dry dock today, and I sailed it back to The Bluffs. There's damage to the rigging."

"Poor *Queenie*. I've missed her," I said. The *Queen Jacqueline* had survived through all the Mitchell generations, and it was on *Queenie* that I'd learned to sail. "Not that serious, Daniel."

"That's not what I'm concerned about." He continued, "While I was waiting in the kitchen at home for one of the crew to pick me up, there was this beeping sound coming from the study. I went to investigate and found your laptop open."

"I must have forgotten to turn it off last night," I told him, though I remembered specifically that I had. Percy and Celeste were causing me trouble.

"I saw an email from your sister about a Dr. Zane open on the screen."

"It's nothing," I assured him.

"Then what is the research she mentioned, and why might this doctor be able to help you?" He was truly worried, which touched me.

"Really, I'm okay." I gave him a reassuring smile, then proceeded to fill him in on the information Zoe had come across about a genetic abnormality that might explain our mother's miscarriages and her suggestion that I consult a genetic specialist. "Apparently, this Dr. Zane is highly regarded in the field."

"When were you going to tell me about this?" He squared his shoulders and folded his arms.

"We've had a lot going on," I reminded him. "Zoe just brought it to my attention a few days ago and only sent the contact information for the genetic specialist yesterday."

"So, are you planning to get tested for this genetic abnormality?"

Seriously? Daniel had eschewed the whole curse idea when I'd told him my family's history, so he should have understood my wanting to seek a scientific explanation.

"I thought it would be important to know." I hesitated before adding, "Especially if we decide to start a family one day."

He said nothing, which made me all panicky inside.

"I realize it's a subject that hasn't come up . . ."

He asked, "You envisioned us having kids?"

I closed my eyes briefly and smiled inwardly at images of Daniel pushing a stroller and tossing a ball. "I think you'd be a great dad."

A doubt-filled grunt escaped his lips. "I didn't have the best parental role models. Maybe it's not in *my* genetic makeup."

Daniel's father had left when he was a toddler, and his mother had worked two jobs, leaving him to be raised by his grandmother. Not unlike my own upbringing; though Mama and Papa had been present, and they'd loved Zoe and me, it had been Granny Fi who'd been most involved in rearing us.

"We both learned all we need to know from our grandmothers," I said. When he didn't respond, I continued, "Besides, there are no hard and fast rules when it comes to raising children. Everyone has to wing it, right?"

"Don't forget, I'm older than you."

"You're only forty-five Daniel." I reached over to sweep the hair off his forehead. "A young forty-five at that."

"I'm not feeling young after this week." He smiled before growing serious again. "Look, I've just never really thought about children. I guess I pictured our life together as it is now."

I didn't say anything, mainly because I was struggling with my emotions. The last thing I wanted to do was to cry.

"Hey." He squeezed my hand. "I want you to be happy."

"I know." I squeezed back and waited, but he had nothing else to say. If only he had added, "And if having a family makes you happy, that's what I want for us too." But he didn't, which left me sad and confused.

I needed to change the subject before my emotions got the best of me, so I asked, "How did your lunch meeting go?"

"Okay." He was not inclined to offer more, but curiosity had me gently pressing on.

"Now that Lucas has been found, do you even need to see the sealed documents?"

"That's up to Brooks." He was twirling a strand of my hair around his finger. "It's still not clear if Christopher played some role."

"Really?" I twisted my head as far as I could to look at him.

"We'll know more if the judge releases those transcripts."

"So, if you weren't discussing the sealed documents, why were you meeting with him?" I persisted.

He sighed, probably realizing the questions weren't going to stop until I was satisfied. "Remember the party house kid who disappeared?"

"The one who claimed he saw Christopher having an altercation with Lee Chambers? Zach somebody?"

"Zach Renner. He's been staying with Tyler Stendall over in Orleans."

I was not expecting that. "How are they connected?"

"According to Tyler, the two have been having a summer fling of sorts."

"Ahh."

I recalled what Christopher had shared. It would make sense if Tyler's macho stepfather had a hard time accepting that his stepson was gay. Perhaps Tyler wasn't ready to come out yet, and that's why he'd been reluctant to release those sealed documents. But I left it unspoken because I didn't want to betray what Christopher had told me, and I was uncertain what he'd shared with Daniel. If anything.

"Anyway, Zach got spooked about coming forward and has been hiding out at Tyler's place, but it sounds like Tyler has talked him into meeting with Brooks."

"What has him frightened?"

"He received an anonymous note telling him to keep his mouth shut or else. A lucky break that Zach held on to it. Now it can be submitted for handwriting analysis." Daniel added, "Brooks still considers Savage a possible suspect in the Lee Chambers case and wants to set up a lineup to let Zach identify him."

"If Christopher was involved, why would he have brought Tyler to meet with you?"

"I understand that you have befriended the guy. But think about it. It would be in Savage's best interest to be eliminated from the lineup."

"I guess."

"And keep this to yourself. If you warn Savage, the whole thing goes to hell."

"Okay," I said a little defensively.

"Zach will need to be convinced it's safe coming into town."

"Here's a thought," I said slowly, realizing it was a bit out there. "With the station still under construction, why not stage the lineup out at The Bluffs? Then he wouldn't have to worry about anyone seeing him back in town."

"Hmm." Daniel rubbed his stubbly chin. "Actually, not a bad idea. I'd have to find a reason for getting Wes Creed out there."

"You and Brooks suspect him?"

"He had an association with Lee Chambers. He was in town at the time of death determined by the coroner. He'd been to the party house. Let's just say we're curious to see how Zach reacts to him."

I didn't probe further but did offer a suggestion. "You just told me *Queenie* suffered a bit of damage. Why not have him come out to work on her?"

"You're full of good ideas today." He tussled the top of my head.

"But won't you need more than just Wes and Christopher?"

"I'm sure we can round up a few other guys. There are lots of workers clearing up after the storm." He took another look at me. "Your color is returning. Ready to head back?"

"If we must."

Daniel's phone pinged just as we were ready to raise anchor.

"What is it?" I asked.

"Will Kleister updating me on Helene. She's going to be okay."

"Thank goodness." I thought about the four Kleister children and how this would affect their little lives and futures. You didn't have to be a psychologist to know how having an emotionally withdrawn parent could have a detrimental long-lasting impact. You only needed to live it. Zoe and I had been lucky to have our Granny Fi. Hopefully, Nicholas, Lucas, and the twins would have the same loving support from their grandparents.

* * *

I left Daniel to finish up at the harbor and walked up the beach toward the Princes' cottage to get my truck. First, I stopped to see if Laura was home. She wasn't, but Whistler jumped up when he saw my face pressed against the window.

"Hey, Buddy." I unlocked the door and let him out for a quick run down to the edge of the receding Cape Cod tide. While he romped, I contemplated my next task, which was to drive over to Orleans. When Whistler returned, I had to coax him back inside with a treat. As I closed up the cottage, the yellow crime scene tape at Land's End caught my eye, as did something shiny catching the sunlight behind the cottage.

I stood on a deck chair for a better vantage and spied a familiar red Mercedes convertible hidden behind the cottage. I then stepped back behind the vine-covered latticework that surrounded the outdoor shower, where I could watch unobserved. I waited for what seemed an eternity, but was probably no more than five minutes, before my patience was rewarded. Robyn Landers slunk out of the cottage and ducked under the tape, casting a nervous gaze about to see if anyone was watching. Satisfied she hadn't been noticed, she hurried to her car and peeled out.

Now, what was I to do with this interesting development?

* * *

While driving toward Orleans for another try to track down Sister Bernadetta at the church, I was reminded where I'd heard the name Montrose. Seeing Robyn stimulated my memory that it was the Montrose family who had referred Christopher to rent her cottage.

A call from Teddy interrupted my contemplations.

"I've got some information for you," he said. "Where are you?"

"Driving north on Route 6, almost to A Hole in One."

"You're not far from my place. You want to stop by?"

"Be right there." I decided to make a quick stop at the donut shop first.

Ten minutes later I was driving slowly along the road to First Encounter Beach, trying to remember which marsh-facing cottage was Teddy's. Then I spied his mud-spattered gray Jeep.

"Here you are," I handed him an iced coffee as he greeted me at the door. "Light and sweet, right?"

"*Gracias.*" He motioned me to follow him out to the deck. "This place doesn't have AC. We might catch a breeze out here."

I'd only been to his cottage once, and it was just as I had remembered it; a beachy feel, lots of books scattered about, and not exactly tidy. Outside the marsh was teeming with crabs and seabirds at low tide.

"I did a little nosing around about the party house crew." He took a gulp of the icy cold drink. "Ahh. Just how I like it."

"And?" I prompted.

"They aren't a bad crew—just young college kids."

"From where?"

"Some small school in Rhode Island. From what I gather, they're all from wealthy families and have been able to hang here for the summer and party."

"Drugs?"

"Normal stuff. Mostly pot." He took another drink. "I'm told that there was one bad egg in the group, and he was responsible for inviting a sleaze element to the house. He's not coming back though."

"Who told you this?"

"I called the classmate I was telling you about. Jeremy Montrose."

"Is Jeremy here for the summer too?"

"Nah. He graduated a few years ago. He's a stockbroker in Boston. But he gave me his brother's phone number."

"What about Zach Renner?"

"He's been hanging out with a friend of Jeremy's who's been bunking at the Montrose place in Orleans."

"Can you find out from Jeremy the name of that friend?" I was pretty sure it was Tyler Stendall, but independent confirmation would help.

He pulled out his phone, large thumbs amazingly nimble as he texted.

"That was quick," Teddy mused. "Jeremy must be making up for being such a jerk in high school." He showed me the text confirming it was Tyler. "Know him?"

"I know who he is." I nodded. "Did Jeremy say how he knows Tyler?"

"I think he said they bartended together during a couple summer breaks when Jeremy was still in college."

"Thanks for the information."

"Was it helpful?"

"I'm not really sure." Of course, I wasn't certain what exactly I'd been hoping to find out. "But thanks."

As I was leaving, I noticed a painting propped on his fireplace mantle, with the familiar image of Whale Rock Harbor.

"You have one of my paintings?"

"I'm proud to own a Cassandra Mitchell original." He smiled, sweeping his blond hair back from his forehead in a habit he had.

"And I'm honored that you do."

Lu had mentioned selling a couple smaller harbor paintings recently. Could this be one? Regardless, I was truly touched.

Back in the truck and on my way to Orleans again, I was processing all that I'd learned this morning. Tyler Stendall, Christopher's former student and the subject of the sealed documents, was also a friend of Jeremy Montrose. It was likely the connection that got Christopher a referral to rent Land's End. Tyler was also seeing Zach Renner, party house resident who identified Christopher as having an altercation with Lee Chambers before he died.

Now, to figure out what it all means . . . if anything.

* * *

I'd googled the Montrose house address and found it was right on the way to The Transfiguration Church, but on my quick drive-by saw nothing of interest.

There was a lot of activity when I arrived at the church compound, and when I was finally able to get the attention of a woman dressed in a white robe, I learned why.

"We are having a private community event today. But you would be most welcome to return tomorrow to tour the church and our gift shop."

"I've toured your beautiful church before, thank you." I pulled out my phone and enlarged the picture of Sister Bernadetta taken at the Wellfleet church shelter. "I'm looking for this woman."

She squinted. "I don't recognize her, but I'm just visiting."

The woman noticed my obvious disappointment and said, "Let me see if I can find someone else who can help you."

A few minutes later, another similarly dressed woman approached and asked to see the photo.

She smiled. "Ah yes, Bernadetta of the St. Joseph's sisterhood. She did join us for quiet reflection. We have a few rooms for visitors, and we welcomed her."

"Do you think I could see her?"

"She left this morning because of our special event, even though we told her she could stay. But she said she had somewhere she needed to return to."

"Return to?" I said. "Where was that?"

"Why, I don't know, and she never said. We've been very busy preparing for the ceremony."

I thanked the woman and left, defeated again by the greater powers that be.

My drive back to Route 6 took me past Cap't Cass. The rustic seafood shack had been a slice of Cape Cod life for decades. Papa used to kid me, saying he'd buy the place for me one day since I wouldn't have to change the sign. Dinner had completely slipped my mind, and hunger pains were my host, probably made worse by my little bout of stomach emptying on the boat earlier. Just the smell, as I walked into the restaurant, set my tummy to growling loudly.

While waiting for my to-go order, two young men came in. Having just seen Tyler Stendall earlier today, I easily recognized him as one of them. The other guy was also slight of build but taller, with black hair, and looked much younger. *Zach Renner perhaps?*

They took the table right behind mine, with my back facing them. The small dining room was busy; still, they were close enough for me to hear their conversation.

"Let's head into Beantown tomorrow. We can stay at Jeremy's. It'll sure beat this heat."

There was no verbal response.

"Come on, Zach."

Aha!

"Can't. I've got something to take care of."

"What?"

"Just some stuff. I'll probably stay with Kev tonight."

"Why? You tired of me?" Jokey but somewhat desperate.

"It's not that."

"Then what?"

"Can you just leave it?"

"Sure. No sweat. I'm cool."

"Here you go." The waitress plopped a large brown bag down on my table, thus ending my eavesdropping session.

*　*　*

When I got to The Bluffs, I found Laura and Whistler waiting for me on the porch.

"Did you forget where you're living now?" I leaned down to give Whistler a head rub. "Or did you just miss me?"

"Of course we missed you," Laura said.

"Hungry?" I held up the bag, now spreading with grease. "It's not Liam's, but I stopped at Cap't Cass for clams."

"Just as delish," she said, following me inside. "Looks like you have enough for an army."

"I was starving." I set out the fixings of a traditional fried clam dinner; coleslaw, French fries, biscuits, and plenty of tartar sauce. "What's the scoop, Scoop?"

"Ha! But don't call me that in front of Jason. He's paranoid enough as it is."

"Did Brooks give you a statement?"

"He postponed due to an emergency." She pushed out her lower lip.

I was guessing the emergency had something to do with Helene Kleister.

"I'm going to pay for this," she said, filling her plate. "I never had heartburn until I got pregnant. And no, I haven't had a chance to tell Jason yet."

"How's your article coming?"

"Making progress," she said. "How about your day—were you able to find Sister B?"

After hearing what happened, she shook her head. "This is one slippery nun we're dealing with."

"No kidding. I'm exhausted from chasing after her." I crammed three fries into my mouth and mumbled, "My hope is that she'll return to Wellfleet for her car."

"Have you spoken with Father Sebastian?"

I swallowed before answering, "Left him a message to get in touch if she comes back and to please not let her leave until I see her."

Just as we'd finished scarfing down our fat-laden meal, my phone's ship's bell signal chimed.

"Brooks is good with the lineup out at The Bluffs tomorrow afternoon," Daniel told me. "As unorthodox as it might be."

"Great. I'll go tidy up a bit out there." I wondered now if the lineup was the "stuff" Zach Renner had been referring to.

"No, don't do that," he said, then added, "Just the opposite would be better."

"What do you mean? Make a mess?"

"Or at least find some work that can be done. We need an excuse for bringing a couple of the workers out to add to the unofficial lineup."

"I'll find something."

"Keep it on the down low," Daniel cautioned.

"Will do. By the way, Laura popped out to have dinner with me."

As Laura was waving crossed hands and mouthing, "Don't say anything," Daniel was saying, "Especially not her."

"Got it," I told him. "Will you be eating in town?"

"Johnny just brought us some pizzas." After the call ended, I told Laura, "I have some things to take care of out in the barn."

"Let me help."

"Not with that boot," I said, hoping she'd decide to shuffle off.

"At least let Whistler and me keep you company. Jason is working late tonight, so I might as well hang out here." She hesitated briefly as we passed the carriage house, turned and opened her mouth as if to say something, until she saw my warning look. I did not want her bothering Christopher Savage.

I flipped on the barn lights and began looking for projects, moving boxes down from the shelves. To fend off questions, I told her about seeing Robyn at Land's End earlier.

"Are you going to tell Brooks?" she asked.

"I don't know. It could be nothing." Though Robyn had been acting suspicious. "Did you know that she was dating Wes Creed?"

"Really?" Laura made a distasteful face. "I never saw him at Land's End. In fact, I've never seen them together at all."

"Maybe it's a secret fling?"

Laura began inspecting some of the unfinished canvases stacked in the back of the barn.

"I can't wait for you to paint a portrait of us after the baby comes." Whistler let out a very loud sigh, causing Laura to laugh. "Do you think he knows he's about to have some competition?"

"I wouldn't doubt it. He's the smartest dog I know."

"What are you doing, anyhow?" she asked, indicating the mess I'd created.

"Looking for something," I fibbed, wiping the dust from my hands. "But not very successfully. I'll come back out tomorrow."

As we walked back to the house, Daniel's Land Rover pulled up, and Whistler trotted over to greet him.

"Ladies," Daniel greeted us before bending down to pet Whistler. "And gentleman."

"Have you by chance seen Jason?" Laura asked. "I think he's avoiding me."

"I doubt that." Daniel smiled at her. "But no, our paths haven't crossed today. It's a good thing your husband is young, with all the hours he's been putting in."

"I'll be glad when Whale Rock returns to the nice peaceful place we love."

"Here's a little happiness for you," Daniel told us. "I saw Matthew Kleister with Lucas and the twins. Everyone looked healthy and happy. They were jumping around like it was Christmas."

"Poor Matthew, though," Laura lamented. "Returning home to find his wife in the hospital."

Daniel sent me a swift look and I responded with a subtle headshake.

"How did you learn that?" he asked.

"It's out there." She was not about to reveal her source, and Daniel didn't look pleased.

After Daniel took himself off to shower, I warned my friend. "I'd try not to let on how much *in the know* you really are. You can tell Daniel and me anything, but when it concerns information related to a case? Tread carefully. Especially if you want to protect Jason's career."

"What about *my* career?" she pouted.

"Look." I sighed. "There's so much conflict of interest between your work at the *Times* and Jason's job at the Whale Rock PD. One of you is going to have to give. But that's for you and Jason to work out, sooner rather than later."

She looked down at her feet. "I guess you're right."

I changed the subject. "What happened to the novel you were so excited about writing?"

She lifted her shoulders. "Between writing for the paper and helping Edgar with his research, there's not much time left over."

"If it's truly something you want to do, make the time."

"I'll have plenty of time for writing after the baby comes."

Don't count on it. I left that thought unspoken, for who was I to know what was involved in caring for an infant? I wondered if I'd ever have the chance to find out.

30

Cassandra

I woke up the next morning with gloomy thoughts, not helped by a displeasing aroma that came and went in waves. Fortunately, a diversion presented itself by way of a call from Zoe.

"I'm checking on you since you didn't return my calls yesterday."

I checked my phone quickly and saw two missed calls. "Oops. I must have silenced it by mistake."

"I understand little Lucas was found." Her voice had a chill to it, which meant I was in hot water for not updating her.

"Yes. An unbelievable story."

"So I heard from Brooks." *Hmm? Brooks again?* The mind reader on the other end of the call said, "There's nothing to it, Cassandra. End of story."

"It shouldn't be."

"Shouldn't be what?"

"The end of your story with Brooks. There's so much more to write."

"Sometimes it's hard to separate out the bad parts of your history, no matter how much you really want to." She sighed dramatically. "You'd never be able to understand."

I initially bristled at her insinuation that my own personal history wasn't littered with regrets and difficulties I'd like to forget.

"Maybe I would if given the chance. I'm here to listen, should you decide to share that history with me."

"Not today."

"Fine." The heat and humidity had drained me of the will to press further. Besides, I'd know soon enough if those mysterious parts of Zoe's history with Brooks would be revealed in Mama's journal.

"What's that banging noise?" Zoe asked.

"I'm cooking." I'd decided to take a meal to the Kleisters and was checking my meager stores to see what I might make. I'd finally decided on lasagna and brownies, since they were the only two dishes for which I had the ingredients.

"Are you going to schedule an appointment with that specialist?"

"Probably."

"What do you mean, *probably*? If it was me, I'd be doing everything in my power to ensure I'd be able to carry a pregnancy to term."

"It's been a little crazy around here, Zo-Zo, and less than two days since you sent the information."

"Well, time is a precious commodity," she snapped.

"You okay?"

"Sorry. It's just . . ." A sniffle escaped. "I can't help thinking how different my life would have been had I been able to benefit from this new research."

Certainly, the process of going through a divorce wasn't helping her state of mind. If the young floozy that broke up her marriage ended up pregnant by Oliver, it might just send Zoe over the edge.

"I don't want you and Daniel to suffer the same disappointments that we did."

My doubts about Daniel's desire to start a family was not a topic to bring up today with Zoe. Maybe not ever.

"I'll call soon. I promise," I told her. "But I want a promise from you too."

"What's that?"

"If I do have a child, you'll have to come to Whale Rock to be a part of his or her life."

There was a long pause before she said, "I'll try."

* * *

I tried Father Sebastian again before I buzzed into town to drop off the food to the Kleisters. No answer.

"Hi there," I said as Matthew greeted me at the door. He looked at me searchingly, so I reminded him. "Cassie Mitchell. We met the day of the storm."

"Of course." He picked up one of the twins, who pulled his glasses off, giggling at the prank while the other twin hugged Matthew's legs.

"We were all so happy to hear the news," I told him.

"Thank you. The whole town has been great." He finally noticed I was holding a basket. "Come on in."

"I put together a pan of lasagna," I told him, then whispered, "and a batch of brownies."

I was surprised to see Helene curled up on the sofa with Lucas.

"Is she sleeping?" I whispered.

Matthew shook his head and took the basket into the kitchen, followed by the curious toddler twins, both chiming, "What's that, Daddy?"

"Hey there," I said to Helene, keeping my voice low. "What a miracle, huh?"

"He's been through a lot." She smiled sadly, dark shadows circling her eyes. "I guess we all have."

"Where's Nicholas?" I asked.

"Matthew's parents took him to play miniature golf. He needed a little fun."

"Bwownies!" squealed the twins from the kitchen.

"I guess the secret's out of the bag." I grinned at Helene.

"Thank you for being so kind," she said.

"It's just lasagna." I waved her thanks away.

"I mean the other day."

"I can't imagine having four incredibly active little ones. You still have my number?"

She nodded, her eyes filling.

"Call anytime." I took hold of her hand and gave it a squeeze.

She nodded again.

When I popped into the kitchen to say goodbye to Matthew, I checked to make sure my number was still on the whiteboard. It was, and I pointed to it and said, "That's mine if you need anything."

"Appreciate it." He then asked, "Christopher Savage is staying out at your place, right?"

"Temporarily, while his cottage is being repaired."

"Thanks," he said, but didn't offer an explanation for why he wanted to know.

* * *

Walking back to my parking spot, I passed All the Basics just as Robyn was coming out.

She smiled when she saw me, then pointed in the direction of Stella Kruk's store and held up two filled, cloth grocery bags. "I'll probably have to mortgage Land's End now."

Stella's prices were a standing joke in town.

"Plus, she had the nerve to ask me about my love life. What business is it of hers?"

"Well, you know Stella," I said, though it was exactly what I'd intended to ask if the topic came up again.

"Speaking of which"—Robyn motioned for me to follow her around the corner—"you've lived here all your life. What do you know about Wes Creed?"

"Is that the new friend you were telling me about the other day?" I ventured, hoping not to come across like scandalmonger Stella.

She nodded. "Do you know him?"

"He was a few years ahead of me in high school, so mostly by reputation."

"I'm not surprised he had one." She scrunched her freckled nose. "Wes is cute and fun, but I don't know."

I was dying to ask what she'd been doing at her cottage yesterday, but just couldn't pull the trigger.

She looked around to make sure nobody was in earshot before asking, "Is Wes in trouble?"

"What's this about, Robyn?"

"I've been staying at Wes's place since the storm, and after that little Kleister boy went missing, his father showed up there looking for him. Then, a couple days later, this other guy slid his business card under the door, with a note saying he was working for the Kleisters."

"Probably the investigator they hired."

"Investigator?" Robyn's eyes widened. "That doesn't sound good."

"What did they want to know?"

"The Kleister guy—Matthew—asked if I was with Wes the day before the storm."

"Were you?"

"No. But I didn't tell him that. I didn't know this guy from Adam, and he shows up and begins interrogating me?"

"Did you tell Wes about it?"

"Yes, but he didn't seem bothered, so I didn't worry about it. Especially now that the little boy has been found safe. But yesterday morning a couple of police officers showed up to take Wes to the station."

"Have the police talked to you?"

"No! Why would they?" She was starting to freak out a little.

"Just wondering." I paused a moment, considering the wisdom of my next question. "It's none of my business, but has Wes borrowed money from you?"

Her flushing cheeks were answer enough.

"Look, I like you, Robyn. Unless you're head over heels for this guy, I'd cut him loose. If you need a place to stay, come out to The Bluffs."

"That's a really sweet offer. I should be okay, though, now that my boat's back in the harbor." She lifted the bags. "My provisions. I don't know how much longer I could have stood being cooped up in Wes's tiny attic apartment."

"When can you go back to Land's End?" I was fishing for when Christopher's lease was up.

"September first, assuming the damage gets repaired." She cringed guiltily. "I went over yesterday. I didn't think the crime scene tape would still be up since the little boy had been found."

At least I had my answer now.

"The force has been busy with other matters as well," I told her. "You should tell Chief Kincaid, though."

"I sneaked in and out quickly." She waved it away. "I'm sure I didn't disturb anything, even though it was a wasted trip. Can you believe they lost my boat keys while it was in dry dock?"

Keys?

*   *   *

When I got home, Christopher was just leaving to take Gypsy for a walk. I checked the clock, feeling assured he'd be back in time for the staged lineup. It would also give me a bit of quality time with Mama's journal. After my conversation with Zoe this morning, I was even more curious to see if Mama had documented any of my sister's teenage angst. As I took the leather diary from the drawer, the study filled with the aroma of burnt sugar, pungent again. Presumably because I was about to delve deep into my mother's sad past and its connections to the ancestral spirits who still resided within the bones of Battersea Bluffs. No sooner had I started to read when my laptop buzzed to life. I tried to ignore it, but it kept whirring on and then off. Percy and Celeste were at it again.

I put aside the journal and walked over to the desk. This time, the screen was showing my email. A new email from Brit was in my in-box.

"What, you're not savvy enough to actually open the emails?" I mused aloud.

I clicked on Brit's email: *So glad to hear the good news about that little boy. OMG—what a journey! On that other matter, I mentioned Dr. Zane to Nico, and he says she's highly esteemed in the field. (Helps that my boyfriend is also a geneticist!) I'm attaching some research papers he says you might want to read before your appointment. Call him if you have any questions. BTW—have you set another date yet?*

Then she'd inserted a gif of Lady and the Tramp sharing a plate of spaghetti.

I typed out a response: *Thank you for the confirmation and the new information. No date set yet. You will be the first to know (after me that is)!*

I didn't have a chance to return to Mama's writings because Daniel arrived home to set up the barn for the staged lineup.

"Brooks had Jason send Laura on an errand," he told me. "That way she won't show up, spoiling our plans."

"I hate that their jobs are making everything so thorny."

"They'll work it out." He rubbed his hands together. "So what have you come up with for the workers to do?"

"You're not going to like it."

His hands were now resting on his hips. "What?"

"I thought they could load up all those boxes of antiquated files you've been talking about tossing. Then you can take them to be shredded." I smiled sweetly to take the sting out.

He wiped a hand across his face and narrowed his eyes, casting a glance toward the barn and then back at me.

"I guess it is time to shed some of that baggage," he said. "Let me go take a quick look to make sure nothing important gets tossed."

Not five minutes later, a sports car rounded the bend of the lane. *A Jaguar?* When it pulled to a stop, I had to smile. Brooks could issue an order to prevent Laura from crashing the lineup, but there was nothing to prevent Edgar and Jimmy from making an impromptu visit. As happy as I was to see them, their timing couldn't have been more inconvenient.

"New wheels?" I called out to them.

Edgar made a face and pointed a thumb in Jimmy's direction. "This one just had to get a Jag."

Edgar came from old money and all the sensible, practical choices that went along with it. Jimmy, on the other hand, was looser with his husband's purse strings.

"Come now, Edgar. You know you love it." Jimmy leaned in, air-kissing me near both cheeks. "Muah, muah. Hello, Miss Cassandra."

"I love the car," I whispered in his ear. "You'll have to take me for a spin."

I then turned and gave Edgar a hug. "You know you love to spoil him."

"I suppose you're right." Edgar made a face of mock annoyance. "What wind blew you to The Bluffs?"

"Certainly not a cool breeze," Jimmy fanned himself. "This heat wave is ridiculous."

"I'm returning these materials to Christopher." Edgar lifted a cloth book bag from the car.

"Were they helpful?"

"Indeed. I gleaned some interesting and surprising facts from these documents." He glanced toward the carriage house. "Is he here?"

"I saw him leave about an hour ago with Gypsy. He won't be gone much longer in this heat and humidity." At least I was hoping he'd be back soon. Otherwise our whole improvised lineup plan was certain to fail. "Would you like for me to give these to him? That way you won't have to hang around."

"Actually, I also wanted to ask him something," Edgar said. "Do you mind if we wait?"

"Of course not. How about something cold to drink?" I motioned for them to follow me inside, but Jimmy plopped down on a porch rocker and Edgar followed suit. *Oh well.* "Tea? Lemonade? Champagne? We have plenty left over from the wedding that wasn't."

"Ooh, how decadent. I'll have a mimosa!" Jimmy said with glee.

Edgar lifted a shoulder and said, "When in Rome."

My two friends weren't going anywhere soon. I'd try to keep them distracted, and perhaps they wouldn't pay any mind to the men as they arrived. There was only an indirect view of the barn door from the porch, and the rockers faced straight out to the Cape.

When I returned with the filled flutes, fizzing with bubbly, we clinked our glasses, and Edgar said, "To the enduring mysteries of The Bluffs."

I was about to ask how his new book was coming along, when we heard a caravan of vehicles drive up.

"We hired some guys for a small project in the barn," I explained before they could ask.

I had a better vantage point from the porch swing and counted four workers along with Brooks, who was out of uniform. They were huddled around the barn door when an SUV pulled up. I was surprised to see it was Matthew Kleister.

Edgar craned his neck to get a look at what was going on and said, "Oh, is that Christopher now?"

"No," I told him. "Christopher doesn't wear glasses. It's Matthew Kleister, Lucas's father."

"Such an amazing story." Jimmy held his hand to his heart. "And so fortunate."

Edgar took his glasses off to polish them with a handkerchief and then had a second look.

I started to wonder if our lodger was going to show. It would muddle up everything if he didn't arrive soon. "Excuse me for just one minute," I said to Edgar and Jimmy. "I forgot to tell the workers something. Be right back."

"We'll be right here." Jimmy looked content, sipping his mimosa while gazing out at the stunning view. But I felt Edgar's curious gaze at my back.

As I walked over to join Brooks and Matthew, I passed the Kleisters's Porsche SUV. The windows were closed and the motor running to keep the AC going, but I spied Nicholas's little head in the back seat, bent over one of those handheld gaming devices.

"Hi again," I said to Matthew.

"The brownies were a hit. I couldn't persuade the boys to wait." He smiled, then went on to explain, "Nicholas wanted to see Christopher again before we leave."

"Heading back to Boston?" I asked.

He nodded, not noticing Brooks's head shoot up in surprise.

"Anyhow, my son kept pestering." He raised his hands in a defeated gesture.

"Christopher will be glad to see him," I assured him.

Brooks surprised me with his next suggestion.

"Maybe you should come into the barn and wait where it's not so hot," he said to Matthew, who looked at the car where Nicholas was waiting.

Brooks raised his brows at me, then glanced toward the car. I took my cue, though I didn't know what the play was. "Why don't I take Nicholas to the house for a nice cold drink?"

Matthew hesitated. "Sure. That's fine, I guess." Though he didn't seem fine about it at all, he opened the SUV door and turned off the engine. He then asked his son, "Do you remember Miss Cassie?"

Nicholas nodded, which was a relief to both his father and me.

"She's going to give you something cold to drink," Matthew said, smiling encouragingly.

"Let's have some lemonade," I said, reaching out my hand. Nicholas unstrapped himself and came with me willingly.

"Great," Brooks said and patted Matthew on the back, guiding him into the barn while I escorted Nicholas toward the house. He'd be a wonderful distraction for Edgar and Jimmy while the whole sting operation went down out in the barn.

"Well, hello little man," Jimmy said when we got to the porch, making a clown-like face and grinning broadly, provoking a bashful smile from the little boy.

Nicholas followed me into the house. As I poured his glass of lemonade, I watched out the kitchen window as another car pulled up. This time it was Jason and the young man who I'd seen with Tyler Stendall at Cap't Cass's last evening. Zach Renner looked around cautiously as Jason ushered him into the barn. This had all been choreographed beautifully except for one missing character: Christopher Savage.

"My, this is an active little scene," Jimmy said as I popped out to offer the two men a refill on their mimosas.

"Yes, indeed," Edgar agreed. He opened his mouth to say something else but was stopped when one last person made an appearance.

This time it was Wes Creed, who, I'd almost forgotten, had a role in all this. He swaggered over to the porch.

"Hello, Miz Mitchell." He dipped his head and offered a charming smile. Nobody could deny he was attractive, in a bad-boy kind of way.

Remembering my manners, I offered the introductions, first turning to my friends and explaining, "Do you two know Wes Creed? He works on the docks with Daniel." Then I turned to Wes. "Edgar Faust and Jimmy Collins."

"Pleased to meet you," Jimmy said while Edgar took a hard look at the man, probably recognizing him from the other night when he'd reported an altercation between Wes and Christopher Savage.

"Gentlemen." Wes touched the bill of his Red Sox ball cap. He slowly turned back to me. "Daniel sent me out to take a look at your little *Queenie*."

I cringed at his cavalier use of my pet name for the Cat. "Yes, he told me you'd be here."

The screen door whacked behind me, and I turned to see Nicholas standing frozen to the spot, eyes fixed on Wes.

"Hey there, Nicky boy," Wes said playfully.

But Nicholas didn't respond. In fact, he appeared to be trembling, and I wondered what it was about Wes Creed that frightened him.

"You'll find the tools you need in the barn," I told Wes, remembering that the priority was to get him over there. "Near the back there's a workbench. Daniel's out there now—he can show you."

Wes held my gaze for an uncomfortable moment. Before turning on his heels, he had one parting comment. "You be a good boy, Nicky, you hear?"

After Wes Creed sauntered away, Edgar cleared his throat, prompting me to look in his direction. He jutted his head toward Nicholas, who was now standing in a puddle of pee.

The three of us shifted into high gear. I took Nicholas inside for a quick wash and found some cropped exercise tights that fit him like loose pants.

"These will do for now, don't ya think?" I handwashed his shorts and undies before throwing them into the dryer, all the while sharing some of the more memorable awkward moments of my own childhood, hoping to take the sting out of his accident.

The tale that finally brought a giggle was about the time I got trapped in a cat briar bush for hours until Granny Fi tracked me down. "My long braids had gotten so entangled in the briars, the only way my Granny could free me was to chop off my hair down to the scalp. You can imagine the reaction of all my classmates when I showed up at school the next day nearly bald."

When we returned to the porch, Edgar and Jimmy had hosed off all traces of the incident and had prepared a plate of PBJs. Of course, with Jimmy, nothing was ordinary. He'd found my cookie cutters and had cleverly cut the sandwiches into adorable animal shapes.

"We thought you might want to join us for a snack," Edgar said with a wink.

"Would you like milk with that?" Jimmy asked, to which the boy shyly nodded.

I followed him into the kitchen and asked, "Can you keep an eye on our little friend for a minute?"

"A pleasure." He poured a glass of milk, then spied a package of Oreos, which he plucked from the pantry. "Cookie magic for the wee one."

How lucky was I that Jimmy and Edgar had appeared today like two fairy godfathers? As I walked back outside, I spotted Brooks with Matthew Kleister and Christopher Savage, who must've arrived while I was inside with Nicholas.

I was immediately struck at the sight of Matthew and Christopher together: both tall with slender builds, weathered tans, and short, sandy, graying hair—Christopher's more tousled than Matthew's. The fact that they were both wearing khaki shorts and white polo shirts only added to the striking likeness.

No wonder Edgar had been confused. As if on cue, he sidled up to me and murmured, "I may have been mistaken about who was involved in that argument the other night."

"You should tell Brooks as soon he's finished up here." *Though Brooks may easily have made the same deduction himself.*

"Indeed, I will." He then asked, "What *exactly* has been going on out in your barn, Cassie?"

"I wish I knew, Edgar." It was the truth. I didn't know the results of the staged lineup, though I was itching to find out which of the men, if any, Zach Renner had identified as being involved in a fight with Lee Chambers shortly before his death.

"Did Nicholas say anything?" I asked.

"A few giggles at Jimmy, but nothing more. Do you know what that was all about?" He tipped his head back toward the porch. "The little bladder accident?"

"No, but I'm going to try to find out."

"How about Jimmy and I take a stroll to give you the opportunity to speak to the child?"

I laid a hand on his arm. "That would be great, Edgar."

"Hey, Jimmy," he called out as I walked toward the porch. "Come take a walk with me. I'd like to show you something."

"If we're not back in an hour, send a search party," Jimmy said in sotto voce as he passed me.

I gave him a furtive thumbs-up and stepped onto the porch, where Nicholas was keeping a vigilant eye on his father and Christopher.

"Have you had your fill of Oreos?" I asked, brushing away some chocolate crumbs from his chin.

"Can I take some home to my brothers?" What a sweet older brother this little guy was.

"You can have the whole package," I told him, and his eyes popped open wide. "Speaking of your brothers, I bet you're *so* happy to have Lucas home."

He bobbed his head spiritedly.

"Can I ask you something, Nicholas?"

He peered at me with suspicious eyes. I wasn't the first adult this past stressful week who had tried to pry information from the little boy.

"I was wondering, why don't you like Mr. Creed?"

He didn't answer, so I tried again with a more direct approach. "Does he frighten you?"

His began rocking side to side while sucking on his lower lip. I didn't think he was going to answer until he finally looked at me and said, "He's a bad man."

The simplicity of the statement, delivered in his small child voice, was chilling.

"Why do you think he's bad?"

"Because." A typical six-year-old's response, I supposed.

"Did he try to hurt you? Or Lucas?"

"Can I talk to Christopher now?" he asked, still rocking.

"Soon, honey." Though I was dying to know what was going on in that little head, I was not going to pressure him into talking about it. Whatever *it* was. He'd been through quite enough these past few days.

Matthew and Christopher started to slowly make their way toward the porch, deep in conversation.

"Be right back," I said to Nicholas and then hopped off the porch to meet them halfway. I wanted to give Matthew a heads-up about Nicholas's accident to save the little guy from embarrassment. "His shorts should be dry before you take off."

"Oh, wow." He frowned. "He's too old for that to be happening."

I didn't dare say anything about what prompted it until I'd had a chance to talk with Daniel or Brooks. Not to mention, Christopher was still standing there, and I had no idea about the outcome of the lineup and whether Zach had identified him as the person who'd fought with Lee Chambers before he was killed.

"Nicholas is very eager to speak with Christopher," I said instead.

"Yes, I know," Matthew answered, wearing the harried look of someone who was nearing the edge of what they could handle. He then walked to the porch and kneeled beside Nicholas. "Christopher wants to spend some time with you while I go check on Mommy. Is that okay?"

"Yeah." He bobbed his head.

"In a little while Grampy's going to come and take you home." He ruffled his son's hair and said, "If I know Grampy, there will also be a stop at the ice cream shop."

Nicholas grinned at his father.

Matthew nodded at Christopher, who smiled broadly as he walked toward Nicholas.

"Thank you for looking after him," Matthew said to me, massaging his neck as Brooks joined us.

"Ready?" he said, and the beleaguered man nodded.

What the heck was going on here? My eyes searched Brooks's, but he gave me nothing. The two men walked to the WRPD cruiser, and a moment later only a trail of dust remained. They were followed a few minutes later by Jason, exiting with Zach Renner. That left Daniel and Wes Creed alone in the barn. I found myself striding purposefully in that direction, my heart racing. *Nicholas had called Wes a bad man. But Brooks would never leave Daniel alone with Wes if he was truly dangerous, right?*

I slowly opened the door but didn't see the two men, though I heard calm voices, which was a relief. As I approached from the rear of the barn, I heard Wes say, "It was all Lee's idea. I wanted nothing to do with it."

Wanted nothing to do with what? A loose floorboard groaned under my weight, enough to bring Daniel from the alcove where he and Wes had been talking. He furtively raised a halting hand, which had me quietly retracing my steps back to the door.

"It was nothing," I heard Daniel tell Wes as I made my exit. As much as I wanted to know what this was about, I didn't want to endanger whatever Daniel was doing by being found eavesdropping.

I looked toward the porch where Christopher and Nicholas were sitting, heads nearly touching. Another conversation I would love to overhear, but yet another one that was none of my business.

Uffa.

31

Cassandra

I met up with Edgar and Jimmy as they were strolling along the cliffs, and The Bluffs was deserted when we returned.

"Quite the contrast to earlier today, wouldn't you say?" This from Jimmy.

"Indeed," Edgar agreed. "I don't suppose there's anything you can share?"

"Sorry, no." The fact of the matter was, I still didn't really know what happened here today.

"Well, I'm afraid we need to head back to Alcyone. My agent is coming for a visit that was arranged long ago."

"Is she eager to know where you stand on the Barnacle Boy project?"

"Push, push, push," Jimmy said. "That's publishing for you."

"I've hit a stumbling block." Edgar frowned. "She just wants a status update. And one of Jimmy's culinary masterpieces."

"She's a vegetarian, to boot." He made a face, though I knew he'd be up for the challenge.

"Will you make sure Christopher gets that bag of books I left on the porch? I'll call him later with my question."

"Of course." I bid them goodbye and took myself into the house, where I was startled to find Christopher sitting at my kitchen table, working on his laptop, Gypsy lying contentedly at his feet.

"Did Nicholas's grandfather come for him already?"

"Yes," he said, adding, "Daniel said I could work in here. There seems to be a problem with the WiFi in the carriage house."

"Sure, sure. That's fine," I said. "Care for an iced tea? Lemonade? A nice cold beer?"

"I could go for a beer."

"Beer it is." I grabbed an icy pint glass from the freezer, then listed the brands we had on hand. "Blue Moon, Corona, Stella Artois, and Sam Adams. I think that's it."

"A Stella would be great."

I set the beer and glass on the table, then went in search of some snacks in the pantry, returning with a bag of pretzels that I opened and poured into a bowl.

"Ahh." He said, eyes closed, savoring the first sip. For the first time since I'd met him, he looked relaxed. "You're not joining me?"

It certainly was tempting. Nothing like a cold beer on a hot day was what Papa used to say.

"I'll stick with water for now." I filled a glass from the tap and joined him at the table.

"What?" he said, after a moment of my just looking at him.

"I know you don't like questions, but that's all I've got."

"What do you want to know?" He slowly spun the bottle.

"What did Nicholas tell you?"

He shook his head. "That I can't share."

"Okay. Then how about, do you know where Brooks and Matthew Kleister went?"

"I think he was arresting him."

"For what?" I was stunned.

"Involvement in that Chambers guy's death. You know, the one everyone thought *I* was involved with," he said with more than a hint of irony.

"Not *everyone* thought that," I said. *Not Matthew Kleister either.* I felt shell-shocked, having never considered him a suspect, probably because I thought he'd been in Boston at the time of the murder. "He admitted to it?"

"Not sure. But the kid who thought he saw *me* having an argument with the victim has now positively identified *Matthew*."

"The glasses?"

"How did you know?"

"I'd never noticed it before, but today, when I saw the two of you side by side?" I whistled. "There's an incredible likeness."

"So I'm told." He looked bemused.

I imagined it was hard to see your own likeness in a stranger.

"Even Edgar thought Matthew was you when he showed up today with Nicholas." I then recalled Archie's reaction to Christopher at the diner and wondered if he also had the two mixed up.

"Did he admit that he was the one arguing with Lee Chambers?"

"He did."

"Did he deny he was the killer?"

Christopher held up his hands. "I was observing from a distance until Matthew called me over and asked if I'd talk to Nicholas. But he didn't kick up a fuss. Just asked that he not be handcuffed for Nicholas's sake." He tipped the glass back for another swig of beer. "Hopefully now they'll release me from house arrest." He attempted a smile. "Not that this isn't a special place. In fact, I wouldn't mind renting your carriage house next year."

"Better get your deposit in soon. It's a very popular rental."

"I can see why. But the reason I want to come back is personal."

My phone buzzed. It was Father Sebastian. I held up a finger to Christopher.

"I've got to go take care of something," I told him after I ended the call. "Make yourself at home."

* * *

Daniel called as I was en route to Wellfleet. "Where are you?"

"I am on my way to meet Sister Bernadetta. Finally. How about you?"

"At the station," he said. "Matthew Kleister has been arrested."

"I heard. I just can't believe it. Do you think Matthew killed Lee Chambers?"

"It would be a real shock, but who knows at this point? His lawyer is here, so I have no idea if he's talking or just negotiating right now."

"I presume Brooks is with him?" I hadn't yet had a chance to tell him about Robyn losing her keys.

"Yep."

"Why are you there?"

"Wes Creed."

"Oh yeah. I was wondering what you two were talking about."

"I didn't think this mess could become any more convoluted." He let out a loud sigh before saying, "Gotta go."

I would love to know what all had transpired in the barn today, but I'd have to wait. Hopefully not as long as the rest of the world.

32

Renée

New York ~ Two months ago

"You have a visitor, Renée." Michael was smiling at her from the bedroom doorway.

"Not today." She moaned and turned her back to him, but soon she felt his weight on the bed beside her.

"But this is someone who made a special trip to see you."

"Special?" *Antonio?* She opened her eyes and looked up at her handsome husband. "Is it him?"

"Who do you mean?" A wariness seeped into his tone.

"Tonio?" she whispered, but the moment the name was spoken, she wished she could take it back. That regret was mirrored in her husband's eyes.

In shame she closed her eyes tightly, and he moved away. Moments later the mattress shifted again, but with a lightness this time.

"My sweet Renata." The voice sounded so lovely and familiar.

"Mamma?"

"It's me—Isabella," the soft voice murmured near her ear.

Isabella? Renée did not open her eyes; against those closed eyelids a memory was playing out, and she didn't dare disturb it for fear it would end. Little Isabella was there and so was Vito. They were all so young and carefree as they ran through the olive groves, laughing. What were they doing? Oh yes. Hiding from their parents.

"Renée, sweetheart." It was Michael's voice again. Had hearing Isabella's voice been part of her dream?

She opened her eyes to find both Michael and her sister hovering over her. It took a few moments for the haziness of sleep and the hangover from her medication to clear from her head, but finally she understood this was not part of her dream.

"You've met my sister?" Renée asked her husband.

His face contorted in confusion.

"Sister Bernadetta." Isabella smiled beatifically. She must not have revealed herself.

"I must be such a mess." Renée's hands flew to her head to straighten the scarf that hid her baldness.

"You are as beautiful as ever," Michael said, taking hold of her hands and smiling.

Isabella nodded her agreement and said, "What you need is to get up and get dressed."

Renée noticed Michael's look of concern but decided that per-haps she really did need to get out of this bed and at least try to act human again.

"It will be fine," she said to her husband as she tossed the covers aside and allowed her sister to escort her to the master bathroom. "What time is it?"

"Almost noon," Michael answered as he lingered to supervise.

"Why don't you fix us a little lunch?" she suggested. His deflated expression prompted her to add, "I need to do this."

"Of course." He touched her cheek and then took himself to the kitchen.

Isabella told her, "I hadn't heard from you, and I was worried."

"But he doesn't know that you're my . . ."

"Sister?" She shook her head. "He knows me only as Sister Bernadetta. We didn't get into how we know each other."

"But, what *have* you told him?" The panic was returning, her breaths coming short and quick.

"Nothing, Renata." Her sister patted her hand. Isabella silently helped Renée through the routines of bathing, fixing her wig and dressing. She even added a touch of makeup.

"Now, there's my Renata." Isabella stood behind her as they both gazed at the mirror's reflection.

She had to agree. It made a world of difference to be out of that bed. To look and feel like a woman again. Maybe it was time to give it a go without the antianxiety meds. They were making her too tired to live what little life she might have left. She recalled the conversation between her son and husband and knew it would take some convincing to get Michael to support this choice. Still, she must try.

*   *   *

Boston ~ Late 1960s

"It's time for you to move out of this place," Renata told her sister after Antonio fell asleep between them.

"But I like it here." Isabella smiled serenely, caressing her nephew's hair.

"Still, you can't stay forever. Unless you're planning on becoming a nun." Renata made a sour face.

"It's convenient for taking my courses." Isabella had just enrolled at a nearby community college. "And I can save money for tuition by staying here."

"You'll be a wonderful social worker one day," Renata told her sister, "but you need a life, friends, *boyfriends*."

"I'm content for now." Isabella changed the subject. "Call me when you and Antonio are settled?"

"Of course. And you'll come to visit soon?"

Her sister nodded, brushing away a tear.

"What's this all about?" Renata reached across her son to offer a tissue, knowing it would be hard for her as well, leaving her baby sister behind.

"I'm used to having you and Antonio closer." Isabella sniffled.

"It's only a half day away by bus. And besides, you'll have Vito right here should you need anything."

*   *   *

Early the next morning, Isabella brought biscuits and hard-boiled eggs into her room. Antonio gobbled up the simple breakfast without complaint, but Renata's stomach was churning from nerves, leaving her unable to eat anything.

Her sister handed her a brown paper bag. "Sandwiches for your bus ride. It's not much, but it will tide you over until you arrive."

"Thank you." Renata tucked the bag into her purse.

"I have something for Antonio." Isabella pulled a small box from a drawer in the plain bureau.

The little boy's eyes brightened at the thought of a gift.

"Your mamma, Uncle Vito, and I were each given one of these before we left Italy, to protect us as we flew across the ocean to America." Isabella put the medallion chain around Antonio's neck. "Now you will have mine to protect you as well."

"Don't give up yours. He can have mine," Renata said.

"I insist. You are both starting a new adventure and need the protection. I'm not going anywhere, and even if I did, I wear my cross. Besides, I have all the sisters here to pray for me."

"You have one too, Mamma?" Antonio was mesmerized by the necklace.

"I do." She pulled hers from under her blouse for him to inspect and compare to his own.

Before Renata could protest again, Vito arrived to collect her little boy.

"I want to go with Mamma," Antonio wailed as he clung to her. "She's going on a secret adventure."

"As are you, my sweet boy." She knelt and brushed away his tears. "You're going to meet me there. Uncle Vito and Thomas are going to take you for your very own adventure."

"Thomas too?" He rubbed his red eyes.

"Yes, my little man." Vito lifted Antonio and raised him high. "Thomas will be there too."

In minutes, the pendulum had swung from devastation to delight, and Renata was relieved. Otherwise, she would not have been able to leave her son in such a distressed condition. Still, it was hard for her to be parted from her little one, even for these few hours. But she was desperate and trusted no one as much as she did her brother.

It took all of Renata's emotional strength not to cry or appear worried as she took Antonio into her arms for a goodbye hug. She clung to him, breathing in his signature scent of one hundred percent little boy. Crayons and gum, shampoo that hadn't gotten all rinsed out last night, the lingering smell of Cheerios and milk on his lips. It was just so intoxicating, and she didn't want to let go.

"Mamma," he said, squirming free and all but breaking her heart, "it's an adventure."

Which, of course, was what she'd been telling him.

"That's right." She smiled brilliantly, all for the sake of her child. "A fabulous adventure."

Heart-wrenching as it was, she reminded herself that all she had to do was get through this one day. Then she and Antonio could begin a new secret life elsewhere, far from the clutches of the Welles family.

After waving one last time before Vito and Antonio rounded the corner, she finally allowed the tears to flow, making her walk to the bus station difficult. But for her to be at the meet-up location, she could not miss her bus. In her rush and with blurry vision, she stepped into the street right in front of a blaring taxi. She felt herself being lifted back up onto the curb.

"Hey there, now," said the man who was still holding onto her arm. "Where you off to in such a hurry, little lady?"

She looked into his eyes, trying to determine if she recognized the man. Could he have been sent by Phillip to follow her? Or was he just a kindly man trying to help?

"I'm off to work," she told him, turning away and wiping at her eyes. *How likely was he to believe that with her toting a suitcase along?* "I can't be late."

"Better late than dead." This time she didn't look at the man but rushed across the street, trying to lose herself in the mass of city commuters in the crosswalk. She continued to check over her shoulder as she took a more circuitous route to the bus station, but there was no sign of the man from the corner.

Even when she'd handed over her ticket and was seated on the bus that would deliver her back to Antonio, she couldn't relax. Her whole body was vibrating as she wiped the sweat from her hands onto her pants. She tried to calm her breathing so as not to draw attention to herself. Closing her eyes, she envisioned the reunion with her son, their new life together. *An adventure*, as she'd told Antonio. She'd do everything in her power to make it so.

*   *   *

New York ~ Two months ago

"You must tell Michael everything," Isabella was urging her.

"I can't! It's not possible." Renée brought her hands up to cover her face. "I'm too ashamed."

"He loves you. Help him understand."

"Where's Tofie?" She needed her boy to help her through this.

"Who?" Isabella had never heard her use the pet name.

"My son," Renée cried. "Where's Christopher?"

33
Cassandra

Whale Rock Village ~ Present day

Though I recognized the nun immediately, she was much smaller than I remembered. It would be hard to guess the woman's age, her conservative attire and hair pulled back severely into a bun possibly adding years to her appearance. But she had clear, intelligent green eyes and the smooth rosy skin with which some older women were blessed. The most stirring quality was the absolute kindness of her expression.

"Sister Bernadetta, this is Cassandra Mitchell." Father Sebastian made the introduction. "She's the one who's been looking for you."

"Hello," we said in unison and then smiled.

"I'll give you some time to speak privately," Father Sebastian said, then closed the door, leaving the two of us alone in his office.

"I'm curious—why have you been looking for me?" the nun asked, the smooth skin of her forehead crinkling.

"You were in Whale Rock—that's where I live—on the day of the big storm," I said.

She nodded.

"I saw you that day. Briefly. But I understood you were looking for someone," I shook my head. "It seems like months ago now, even though it's only been a little over a week."

"Yes, it's been a difficult time. Storms leave much destruction in their paths." She smiled sadly. "Storms also swallow up many secrets."

I thought it a strange thing to say but didn't pursue it. "Who is it you're looking for?"

"My nephew." She threw up her hands in distress. "I'd show you his picture, but it was caught by the wind one day and carried out to sea. It was the only photograph I had of him."

"What's your nephew's name?" I asked.

"Christopher. Christopher Savage."

I honestly couldn't speak for a moment as I processed this, but my expression must have given something away, for the nun asked eagerly, "Do you know him? You know Christopher?"

"Yes," I admitted. "He's staying at my home."

We both stared at each other in disbelief.

"I'll take you to him," I said at the same time she asked, "Will you take me to him?"

We laughed together, and then she started to cry. I draped an arm over her slight shoulders and said, "First, let me make a call."

I went outside the church to call Christopher while Sister Bernadetta gathered her things.

"Can you just sit tight for a while?" I wanted to make sure he didn't leave for a long walk with Gypsy.

"Sure. What's up?"

"I'm bringing someone back to The Bluffs to see you. Someone who has been desperately looking for you."

"Who would be desperately looking for *me*?" Christopher asked.

"You're about to find out," I told him. "We'll be there in about fifteen minutes."

* * *

"Are you Christopher's father's sister or his mother's?" I asked Sister Bernadetta on the drive.

"His mother's. Renata." She waved a hand in agitation. "I mean Renée."

That was odd. "I'm so sorry to hear that you lost her recently."

The nun nodded and gazed out the window, brushing at a threatening tear.

"You've been pretty hard to find." I told her about my trips to Orleans to distract her from her sadness.

"We are a tightly knit group, the Sisters of St. Joseph," she said. "I've grown dependent on my sisters, and after a week of being away from them, I felt the need to spend some time with a community who would uplift me and yet allow me some solitude."

I smiled at her. "I only have one sister, but I do understand that need."

"I've been such a mess this week without them here to anchor me." She shook her head. "Father Sebastian had mentioned something about this church in Orleans which I misunderstood to be a convent. The night I decided to go in search of it, I found my car gas tank on empty. I hadn't even checked before I left Boston. I was lucky to have made it out to the Cape."

"Why did you decide to drive out the day before the storm?" I asked.

"I wasn't thinking straight. I'd just learned that my sister had died."

"I thought Christopher said she died over a month ago."

"She did. But . . . it's a long story, and I'm afraid I will only have the energy and the will to tell it once."

"How long has it been since you've seen Christopher?" I asked as we drove up toward The Bluffs.

She turned to look at me. "I've never met my nephew."

34

Renée

New York ~ Six weeks ago

Renée had become terribly thin and was always cold. She was enjoying the warmth of the brightly lit sunroom overlooking the courtyard below when the shrillness of the phone interrupted her peaceful afternoon.

"That was Brandan. He's stopping by for a visit," Michael told her as he draped a shawl across her shoulders. "You're shivering."

She nodded as she watched a hummingbird at the feeder on their balcony, though she wasn't shaking from the cold. No, it was fear. But of what? Was death coming for her? Would she be punished for her sins?

Not long afterward the doorbell chimed, followed by the murmurings of her husband and best friend. She supposed Michael was preparing Brandan for the condition he would find her in.

"There's my girl," Brandan said, leaning down to kiss her sunken cheek. "I brought you cinnamon brioche from Levains. Your favorite."

He opened the white pastry box to display the baked goodies. "Take a whiff."

"Yum," Renée said, pretending enthusiasm. The truth was, she had no appetite for sweets—hardly any appetite at all. And there would be no point in asking what *Levains* was. Even if he told her, she wouldn't be able to remember.

"I'm just going to run to the corner market," Michael popped his head out to tell them. "Be back in a jiffy."

"He's giving us some alone time for you to say goodbye to me," Renée said.

"Nonsense." Brandan eschewed the thought. "He says the new treatment is working."

"It's hard enough to keep up the act for Michael," she pleaded with her friend, "don't make me do it for you too."

"Whatever you say, Renée." He squeezed her hand, and for the next few minutes he brought her up to date on what was happening at the business. "Everyone sends their best to you. Some would like to visit."

"No visitors." She'd been adamant. "Only you and Christopher."

"And Isabella?" he asked.

She looked at him crossly. "Sister Bernadetta."

"What do you want me to do with this?" he asked, pulling the age-worn manila envelope from the inside pocket of his sports jacket.

"What is that?" She narrowed her eyes.

"The envelope you kept in a secret compartment of your jewelry box. You gave it to me last time I visited."

"Did I?" She was focused on the hummingbirds. "Did you know that hummingbirds almost never stop moving? It's how they survive."

"Just like you, huh?" She'd said something similar to him on the day she'd told him about her life before Michael and Christopher. When he'd urged her to tell them, she'd said, "There's no going back. If I don't keep moving forward, that's when my world will fall apart."

She nodded as the ghost of a smile played on her lips.

The day she'd given Brandan the envelope containing all her secrets, she'd only shared bits and pieces about that past life. She'd assured him that all would be explained by the contents of the envelope.

Today he had come for guidance on what to do with it.

"Should I give it to Michael? Or Christopher?"

"Christopher," she whispered.

"Okay." Now that he knew her wishes, he hoped for a little clarification. "But what does it all mean, Renée? I've looked through everything in the envelope, but it makes no sense to me."

"Christopher will figure it out." She finally tore her gaze away from the fluttering activity at the birdfeeder. "He'll know what to do."

Brandan unfolded a sheet of paper and handed it to her.

"What is this?" She reached for her glasses.

"I met someone who helped me find out who the man in *The Globe* article is," her friend answered. Then gently he told her, "His name isn't Antonio."

She rubbed her forehead as she looked at the photo, trying her best to summon the memory of why it had been so important. Then she saw Phillip in the center of the picture, bringing fragments of memory together.

"But the photo looks so much like Vito. It must be Antonio."

"There's a letter from Vito, but I couldn't read it. I don't know Italian." Brandan asked patiently, "Will the letter solve the mystery?"

She shook her head and the tears came. "I don't know. I don't know. I just don't know."

Michael rushed in, having just returned from the market.

"It's okay. I'm fine." Renée dabbed at her eyes with a tissue and said, "I get so frustrated when I can't remember."

"All you have to do is ask, and we'll fill in the blanks for you." He caressed her cheek.

She glanced at Brandan. Was it pity for Michael she saw in her friend's expression? It was too late now to tell her husband about her tragic life before he'd rescued her. She'd take the coward's way out and let Brandan give him and Christopher the envelope after she was gone.

"How about a cup of tea?" she said to her husband.

"Coming right up." Michael offered a loving smile and squeezed her toes before motioning for Brandan to join him in the hallway.

"What's going on?" she heard Michael ask.

"What's going on? Open your eyes, man," Brandan said. "That woman, whom we all adore, is slipping away from us."

Michael said something she couldn't make out, and then Brandan returned and took hold of her hand. For the next hour, the two friends reminisced about all their wonderful memories of their early days in New York.

"What would I have done without you?" she asked.

"Fate would have taken care of you." He winked.

"Fate has not always done so." She shook her head and handed him back the envelope she'd tucked under her shawl to hide from Michael.

"You're sure?" he asked.

Renée's face lit up, and Brandan turned to see what had caught her eye. Christopher was leaning against the doorframe.

"Hey, Ma."

"My beautiful boy." She lifted her arms, and her son came to her as Brandan tucked the envelope back into his jacket. He tapped his chest, assuring Renée that he'd keep his promise, then touched his fingers to his lips and blew a kiss. It was the last time the friends would see each other.

35

Cassandra

Laura's car was there when I pulled up to The Bluffs, and I found her sitting at the kitchen table with Christopher. They both stood when I entered with Sister Bernadetta.

"It's so nice to finally meet you." Laura took the woman's hand and smiled, while I explained, "This is Laura, who I told you was helping me look for you."

Sister Bernadetta nodded politely but could not take her eyes off of Christopher.

"And this is Christopher."

He also stared, as if he was trying to figure out how he knew her. And then, as if something clicked inside his head, he said, "Are you . . . Isabella?"

Isabella? Sister Bernadetta nodded but looked as surprised as I was. She brought her hands together at her chin and then tentatively reached up to place them on Christopher's cheeks.

The tautness in his face seemed to relax with her touch, as though the nun passed him some serenity through her fingertips.

"You're my aunt?"

The nun covered her face with her hands as a moan escaped. Christopher patted her arm before turning to pick up his messenger bag, which had been draped across one of the kitchen chair backs.

He withdrew an envelope that contained the letters I'd seen when snooping earlier.

"You wrote these to my mother?" He held the letters reverently.

She nodded, tears making her eyes shine brighter.

He pulled from the envelope an aged photograph of two girls and a boy, who looked to be in their teens. "Is this you with my mother?"

She gazed at the picture, a sad smile forming. "So long ago."

My heart broke for the woman, and I was relieved when Christopher went to her, draping an arm across her shoulder and leading her to a chair. He took the seat closest to hers and rested his clasped hands on the table.

"Such waste," she managed to say through the sobs. "All these years. Gone now."

Though Laura stood mesmerized by the scene, I felt intrusive and busied myself with the teakettle. Even though we were in the midst of a heat wave, there was always something comforting about a hot cup of tea.

"Your father told me the treatment was working when I last visited," Sister Bernadetta told Christopher. "And she seemed to be feeling much better."

"You've met my father?" It was clear that Christopher found this surprising news.

"Yes, but he knows me only as Sister Bernadetta," she told him. "Your mother didn't want to reveal who I really was. She told me all about you, though. I'm sorry our paths never crossed."

"The treatment *wasn't* working," Christopher admitted, "and I'm sure Ma knew that it wasn't. But my father needed to believe that she was going to get well again."

"Perhaps that's why I believed it as well. Your mother and I had agreed that I'd return on her birthday." Sister Bernadetta sighed. "I tried many times to call her to make our plans. Then I got the message that her cell phone had been disconnected, so I called the home number. That's when I learned that she had died."

"I'm so sorry nobody told you," Christopher said.

For a couple minutes, the only sounds were Sister Bernadetta's sniffles.

Finally, in a gentle voice, Christopher said, "What I don't understand is why you came out to the Cape, looking for me, on the day of the storm."

"When I spoke with your father, he said that you had argued, and you hadn't been taking his calls."

"That's true. I needed some space," he said, his tone tinged with shame. "I just couldn't believe he'd kept this from me."

"He didn't," his aunt assured him. "It was your mother who stubbornly refused to tell him about her past."

"Why?"

"She had a complicated fear of losing you, of losing your father's love." She shook her head. "But your father knew that your mother's friend, Brandan, had given you an envelope with some articles and letters."

Christopher nodded.

"When your father told me that you'd gone to Cape Cod to find out who Antonio was . . . I just knew I needed to find you first. To explain." Sister Bernadetta closed her eyes and took in a deep breath to compose herself. When she opened them again, she looked with interest at the chain around Christopher's neck.

"A St. Christopher medal?" she asked. "Have you always worn it?"

"No. Ma gave it to me right before she died." He pulled the chain from his shirt so she could examine it. "She said it was to keep me safe."

"He's the Patron Saint of travel, and your namesake." As Sister Bernadetta said this, the scent of burnt sugar tickled my nostrils.

He smiled warmly. "I was told I was named for my grandfather on my father's side." He reflected a moment before saying, "Ma wasn't the least bit religious."

"Perhaps not, but she was superstitious," his aunt replied, then asked, "May I show you something?" She reached her hand out, and he obediently took the medal from his neck. She flipped it over and pointed to the back. "See this mark right here?"

He squinted and then nodded.

"It's the mark of a local medal worker in the small town we came from in Italy. Before we left, he made us each a special medal to make sure we arrived safely to America."

"You have one too?" he asked.

"I did once, but I gave mine to Antonio." This brought on another emotional reaction. "Though it did not keep him safe."

"In her last weeks, Ma mentioned an Antonio. Who was he?"

Though I was also bursting with curiosity, I quietly set the steeping teapot on the table while signaling Laura to bring the tray of cups, sugar, and milk.

"We'll be out on the porch if you need anything," I whispered to Christopher while tugging a disappointed Laura by the sleeve to follow me.

He sent me a look of gratitude.

From the kitchen window that opened to the porch above the rockers where Laura and I sat, we could only hear bits and pieces of a story both of us were dying to know.

Still, Laura sat with pen and paper, jotting down the snippets she could hear. *Vito. Uncle. Italy. Boston. 1969.*

"What do you plan to do with that?" I whispered, indicating her notes.

"Don't know," she whispered back. "Force of habit."

A while later, Christopher brought Sister Bernadetta out to the porch and said, "My aunt would like to see the famous cliffs."

Laura stood and said, "I can walk out there with you."

"Thank you, I'd like that." The nun smiled, and the two headed off.

"Can you get in touch with Chief Kincaid?" Christopher scratched his head, watching as the two women walked toward Cape Cod Bay, before turning his gaze toward me. "I have to get home. I need to talk with my father."

After Christopher and Brooks spoke, he and I waited in the kitchen for Laura and the sister to return.

"Evidently, my mother had an entirely different life before my father and I came on the scene." He bore the slumped posture of a betrayed man. "I had an uncle who lived in Italy. Heck, I have a whole extended family I never knew about."

"Parents are hard to figure out." Hoping to mitigate his pain, I suggested, "Maybe she had a good reason for keeping that other life to herself. Your aunt didn't tell you?"

"She wants to talk to me and my father together."

I sensed he was holding onto something he wasn't prepared to share, so I ventured elsewhere.

"What made you choose Whale Rock?" I asked.

"My mother had saved a couple of old newspaper clippings that mentioned this town."

I knew that, and felt a flush from guilt for having snooped.

"I was going to go to Boston, but when Tyler told me about the beach rental in Whale Rock, I changed my plan."

"Boston? Whale Rock?" I lifted my hands in question. "Is there a connection?"

He picked up the worn envelope and tapped it against his chest— a lifeline to his new past.

"There was also a more recent article from *The Boston Globe*. She'd circled someone in a photograph of a front-page article." He opened the envelope and removed the newspaper clipping to show me. It was an original of the photocopied article Edgar and I found in the books he'd borrowed from Christopher.

I looked closely at the caption.

"The man isn't identified," Christopher said, "but he may be part of the ambassador's entourage."

I handed the article back. "Who did she think this might be?"

He looked at the clipping again, shaking his head. "Antonio, whoever he is. I'm hoping I'll find out soon enough."

"What did your aunt say about the articles?"

"I didn't show her. When I started to open the envelope, she stopped me and told me she would tell me and my father everything."

"Was there a link between the Whale Rock articles and the Boston article?"

"That was what I was trying to find out." He lifted a shoulder. "But so far I've struck out on that front."

I wondered what else might be found in that envelope. Then I remembered the other article I'd kept about the Cape Cod shipwreck, but since Christopher hadn't brought it up, I couldn't let on that I knew about it.

As he fingered the medal that had so interested Isabella, the room filled with the scent of burning sugar. *What? What? What?* A memory was nagging its way to the surface.

"I have a favor to ask," he said to me, patting Gypsy's head when she jumped to attention. "Can I leave her here with you for a couple days?" He tipped his head toward the dog, whose tail shifted into high gear, seeming to understand she was the topic of conversation.

"I'd be happy to take care of this sweet girl." I reached down to pet the dog, and she wriggled onto her back, begging for a tummy rub, which I granted. "Truly, I wouldn't mind at all."

The dog nudged him eagerly as Christopher assembled his belongings and wrote out Gypsy's care instructions. "No table scraps. Her stomach is as skittish as her personality."

He got down onto the floor and rubbed her ears, whispering calming words. They had an enviable bond. I felt terrible for separating them, but also couldn't deny being excited to have a canine companion in The Bluffs again, even if only for forty-eight hours, when Christopher would return for her.

"Have you left her with anyone before?"

My concern about how the dog would react must have shown, for he went on to assure me, "Only once, with my parents, but there was no destructive separation anxiety. She'll remain very calm and quiet, possibly a little depressed."

Calm, quiet, and a little depressed; at the moment, the description could just as easily fit Gypsy's owner.

36

Cassandra

I dropped the long-lost aunt and nephew back at Sister Bernadetta's car—after stopping for a can of gasoline—and reassured Christopher that Gypsy would be well taken care of.

When I cruised up the lane after a quick stop for groceries on my way back, I found Laura sitting on the porch with Gypsy.

"Thanks for letting her out," I said while carting the grocery bags up the steps.

"She really is a sweetheart." She stood and took one of the bags from my grip. "I wish she wasn't so scared of Whistler."

"I suppose, like the rest of us, she comes with her own baggage." I set the bags on the counter and tossed her a dog a treat, which she gobbled up and nudged my hand for more. "How was your walk with Sister Bernadetta?"

"Interesting," Laura answered as she helped me stash the food purchases. "After hearing the story of Percy and Celeste, she asked if we could visit your family burial grounds."

"You didn't mention knowing anything about her previous visits?"

"Of course not." She held up a box of Cap'n Crunch cereal. "Seriously?"

"Daniel's breakfast of choice." I pointed to a high cupboard. "I make him work for it."

"Anyhow, she was drawn to the graves of your baby brothers. I didn't share anything with her, but she understood the tragedy behind those tiny markers. She kneeled at the graves and prayed for a while."

"She's a nun. I'm fairly certain that's what they do."

"I guess. But it made me wonder if there was a similar loss in her past that caused her to seek a life as a nun."

"It wouldn't be the first time tragedy brought a woman to seek a cloistered spiritual life."

"She also wanted to know about Barnacle Boy."

Finished with stowing the groceries, I wadded up the cloth bags and stashed them in the pantry. "Everyone does."

"True." She nodded. "But . . ."

"But what?" I leaned against the counter and folded my arms.

Laura plopped down in one of the kitchen chairs. "Remember how someone left a bunch of wildflowers on Barnacle Boy's grave? Mostly butterfly weed with a little Queen Anne's lace." They grew abundantly on the Cape in the summer.

A little chill came over me as the otherworldly scents of Percy and Celeste arose to confound me.

"You think she's the one who left them there?" I asked.

"I don't know."

"Why didn't you just ask her?"

"I should have, right? I felt kind of uncomfortable grilling a nun. Probably my own upbringing by a Baptist minister." She shook her head. "Anyway, I thought I saw her pluck one of those withered blossoms and tuck it into her Bible."

Laura was chewing her thumb as she reflected.

"I know that look," I accused.

"Promise not to tell Daniel?"

"O-kay." I narrowed my eyes.

"The DNA results are in."

"What difference does it make now that Lucas has been found?" I was only aware of samples taken from his little sneaker and the boat Christopher had sailed.

"I'm talking about the murder. From the rug Lee Chambers's body was rolled up in before being tossed into the dumpster?"

Oh, I mouthed.

She pursed her lips before adding, "The results were rather interesting."

"How on earth do you know this already?"

"I cannot reveal my sources."

"Your sources? Or your unscrupulous ways?"

"I may bend the rules a bit, but I do have my principles." She waggled a finger and grinned mischievously. "Regardless, I can't tell you how I came upon the information."

Came upon? Now that was rather telling.

"Okay, protect your sources if you must, but surely telling me doesn't go against your anemic principles."

She began finger-doodling the wood pattern of the table, making me wish I hadn't insulted her integrity.

"Wes Creed's DNA was found on the rug," she told me at last.

"Interesting." I automatically thought of Robyn, which brought to mind her lost keys, and an idea began to percolate.

"Along with DNA from Helene Kleister." Hearing this reminded me again of seeing Wes and Helene together, but I lost that thread when Laura said, "Also Nicholas's."

That was unexpected. How were Helene and Nicholas Kleister connected to Lee Chambers? Had he been Helene's supplier?

"Not Matthew?" I asked, unsure of how far-reaching Laura's sources were.

"Nope," Laura continued her finger-doodling.

"I can't imagine the Kleisters consenting to giving their own DNA samples."

"They didn't. The police got them from their water bottles the day they met with the team at the gallery. Apparently, Lu was clever enough to put them aside for Brooks to bag and test."

"I think *CSI* used to be her favorite crime show." I deadpanned. "What about Nicholas? Wouldn't parental permission be required to swab a child?"

"His grandfather provided the sample."

I digested all this for a moment, trying to envision a scenario in which these three individuals would have been standing on the same rug with Lee Chambers. Where could such a rug even have come from?

I was puzzling on this when Laura dropped another bombshell.

"Christopher's DNA was also found."

Whoa! "Christopher?" Hearing her owner's name, Gypsy's canine intuition kicked in, lifting her head to lick my hand. First Zach Renner misidentifying Matthew as Christopher; now Christopher's DNA, not Matthew's, found with Lee Chambers's body?

"Stay with me." Laura snapped her fingers in front of my eyes.

"Sorry, I was just thinking. What were you saying?"

"I was saying that this poses quite the conundrum for the police, since Matthew Kleister was arrested today for the death of Lee Chambers." She peered closely at me. "You don't seem surprised. You already knew this, didn't you?"

I nodded. I wasn't going to reveal my sources either, and I was relieved when she didn't ask.

"What do you think? Is Matthew Kleister capable of killing someone?" she asked.

"I don't know him well enough to answer that. Wouldn't anyone be capable if the circumstances were dire enough?"

Laura lifted her shoulders and checked the captain's wheel clock. "I need to go pick Jason up at the station. He's actually working a normal shift today."

"Here's an idea. Why don't the two of you join us for dinner?"

"I don't want you going to any trouble," Laura insisted.

"How hard is it to make veggie and swordfish kabobs and a salad? Easy peasy lemon squeezy," I said, stealing one of her own favorite phrases.

She giggled and texted Jason, who responded promptly. "We're all set," Laura said. "Jason will get a ride over with Daniel later."

As we assembled the kabobs, Laura and I continued to talk through the possible scenarios for how the DNA from four different individuals ended up on the rug that had been used to dispose of the victim's body.

"Maybe we're going about this all wrong," I suggested. "Let's start with the victim. What do we know about him? Why would someone want to kill him? What was the relationship between Lee Chambers and the Kleisters?"

"To start with, we know he was a small-time drug dealer who'd been hanging out at the party house," Laura began. "And we know that Helene Kleister is a drug user. We also know that Lee was chummy with Wes Creed, so he also might have known Robyn."

I didn't betray my conversation with Robyn, though I would need to pass on to Brooks what I'd learned. I poured the marinade over the kabobs, placed the pan in the refrigerator, and then gathered the salad ingredients.

"I did find out a little tidbit about the key evidence. Remember telling me that the label had the initials 'LEC' on it?"

"Right, which led us to assume the key chain belonged to Lee Chambers."

"Maybe not. I saw a photo of the label, and it looks more like this." I grabbed a pencil and a piece of scrap paper and printed "LE" on the first line and "C" on the second. "Part of that second row had been rubbed out."

"Hmph?" Laura chewed her lip for a minute then shook her head. "Guys at the party house claimed to have overheard Chambers tell Wes Creed that Helene Kleister was his new client." She began chopping a tomato. "Which could also give her a motive."

A puzzle piece clicked into place for me. "That's probably how Nicholas recognized his mug shot."

"He did?" Laura stopped mid-chop. Obviously, an unknown detail to her, leaving me kicking myself for slipping.

"Not to be shared with anyone." I pointed a severely warning finger at her.

She held up surrendering hands. "Yes, it's true. I'm the new pariah of Whale Rock."

"Sorry." I reached over and gave her arm a pat. "I can't afford to have Daniel find out I told you, or for Brooks to learn Daniel shared it with me."

"I get it, I really do." She smiled and scooped the tomato into the salad bowl.

With the salad finished and the kabobs marinating, I filled two glasses with ice. "Tea or lemonade?"

"Lemonade," she answered, then suggested, "It might be cooler outside, with a sea breeze."

But when we took our cold drinks out to enjoy on the porch rockers, the air was still and heavy. Gypsy nestled at my feet and sighed deeply, probably wondering where her master was.

"Is this heat ever going to end?" Laura held the cold, sweating glass to her neck. "Boy, could I go for a nice cold beer right now."

"You said it," I agreed.

"Go ahead," she urged. "Why should you suffer just because I can't drink?"

"I'll refrain in solidarity." I asked, "So have you told Jason yet?"

"No, but maybe tonight if he doesn't fall asleep before his head hits the pillow." She offered a sad smile, then pretended to nod off, adding a comical snore. "We knew his rookie year would be tough. The only positive note I can find is that it does allow me time to work on my reporting."

A minute later, Daniel's Land Rover rounded the curve in the lane. Our two guys stepped wearily onto the porch. Gypsy stood and then, with her tail tucked low, resettled herself behind my chair.

"You a one-man woman, Gypsy?" Daniel didn't miss much, but went on to say, "Some more good news."

I leaned forward, anticipating something related to the murder case.

"There's an all clear for Whale Rock Beach." Bacteria levels had risen from storm water runoff into the ocean, closing all the nearby beaches.

I sneaked a peek at Laura, who was frowning her disappointment.

"This is great news for local businesses," Jason said, collapsing into one of the porch rockers as Daniel got them two frosty brews, clinking his bottle to Jason's. "People should be flocking back now, with this heat."

Daniel settled into the last of the porch rockers and took a long swig before adding, "Mitchell Whale Watcher Boat Tours has three cruises this week, and my guess is we'll be back to a full schedule next week."

"Glad to hear it. Now, if only this spell of good news could carry over to the Lee Chambers investigation," I ventured, hoping for a hint of an update.

"If only," was all Daniel said on the matter, while Jason remained mute and avoided eye contact with his wife.

"Laura and I had an eventful afternoon," I told them, recognizing a dead end when I saw it. The two of us took turns telling the guys how we had finally managed to track down Sister Bernadetta and what had transpired between her and Christopher.

"That's unreal," Jason said, shaking his head in disbelief.

"No kidding," Daniel agreed, doing the same. "Too bad nobody recognized Christopher earlier. Where are they now?"

When I told him they were on their way to New York, he and Jason exchanged a look. I knew better than to try to pry anything out of them now, especially with Laura's reporter's nose picking up the scent.

I searched for a safe topic of conversation, which brought to mind my chat with Edgar and Jimmy earlier today. After telling them about Jimmy's shiny new ride, I also shared, "Edgar brought up the subject again of exhuming Barnacle Boy's grave."

"What does he hope to achieve?" I couldn't tell from his tone whether Daniel approved. Having been a solver of crimes, I thought he'd enjoy seeing a solution to a cold case.

"He'd like to have DNA testing done. The boy was discovered long before it was being used to identify victims."

"Edgar really hopes to solve the mystery," Laura added. I knew how badly she also yearned to discover the truth behind what happened to the poor lost boy.

"I don't see the point. After all, he's writing a novel that's only inspired by the story." This from Jason.

Daniel nodded his agreement, then added, "Even if he exhumes the body and submits it for DNA testing, it would be quite an involved project trying to track down a match from back then. Not to mention the cost."

"Edgar's willing to foot the bill."

"Another challenge lies in the body having been in the ocean for who knows how long before it was discovered," Daniel pointed out. "A corpse suffers a great deal of trauma in the ocean, not to mention what damage can be caused by sea creatures."

The story of Barnacle Boy was starting to get under my skin as well. I tried to imagine what had happened to him. *Who was he? How did his little body end up in Cape Cod Bay? Why hadn't anyone come looking for him?*

"Archie told us the boy had been buried with it," Laura said, interrupting my thoughts. I'd caught the tail end of her recounting what Edgar had learned from the minister's records and what our subsequent discussion with Archie had revealed about the medal that had been discovered with the child's body.

"Edgar should talk to Teddy," Jason suggested.

"Why is that?" I asked.

"He's thinking of becoming an underwater criminal investigator."

"Really? I didn't even know it was a thing," Laura said.

"It's not a huge leap. Teddy's been part of the search and rescue dive team for the past year while also taking classes in marine biology."

"What's involved?"

"He'll need to become either an emergency first responder or a law enforcement officer before he can even be admitted into a certification program," Daniel answered.

"Wouldn't it be great if he could join the WRPD too?" Laura smiled at Jason.

"I'm not sure if there are any plans for expansion," Jason said, wiping the sweat from his beer bottle onto his pant leg before taking a swig. "Besides, he's getting a lot of grief from his mother about this new career direction."

"That's true," Daniel agreed. "Brooks mentioned something about Ted coming to him for advice. Apparently, he asked Brooks to talk to her on his behalf."

My ears perked up at these references to Theo Howell, considering she'd been a recent topic of conversation with Zoe, and I was now very curious about the woman.

"Anyone else starving?" Daniel asked as he stood and walked toward the grill.

The conversation mute button was turned on as we enjoyed our meal out on the porch. Though we all cleared our plates, exhaustion had set in, and both men were fighting to keep their eyes open.

As soon as we were finished, Laura tugged Jason to a standing position. "Time to go."

He followed and called out over his shoulder, "Thanks for the grub, Cassie."

"I'll call you tomorrow," Laura added.

I waved them off, clipped the leash to Gypsy's collar, and suggested to Daniel, "Why don't you go on up? I'll meet you on the sleeping porch in a few minutes."

He stood and stretched. "Sounds good."

"See you in five." I barely got the words out before Gypsy dragged me off the porch, making a beeline for the carriage house, probably hoping to find Christopher there. I couldn't help but wonder about the family secrets his mother had kept from him. Didn't we Mitchells know all too well about those?

The spare carriage house key was peeking out from its hiding place, so I tucked it back under the mat. This brought my thoughts back to the Lee Chambers case. The label on the evidence key had an "LE" and a "C" on it. "LE"—Land's End? "C"—Cottage? If I was on the right track, what would this mean for Christopher or Robyn or any number of people who might have had a copy of that key?

By the time I made it back upstairs, Gypsy following so close she nearly tripped me, I found Daniel splashed out on the bed, still fully clothed. As I was yanking off Daniel's boots and humming softly in harmony to his gentle snoring, something else Laura said earlier finally registered with me. My mind had been wandering elsewhere when she was talking about Edgar and Barnacle Boy, but now her words had come back to me: *"Archie told us the boy had been buried with it."*

What Archie had revealed to us when we visited his shop last week was that Barnacle Boy's little body had been discovered with a chain carrying a medal around its neck—the one Edgar hoped to find if I allowed the body to be exhumed. Archie mentioned something about the medal being a protective patron saint. Could it have been the same medal as worn by Christopher that had provoked such an emotional reaction from Sister Bernadetta? Was that what Percy and Celeste had been trying to get through to me?

Daniel must have brought my laptop up with him, for it was on the dresser, whirring to life and opening to the email from Dr. Zane.

"I'll call tomorrow," I whispered to the spirits in the room and shut the computer down.

Whimpering came from the corner of the room where Gypsy was cowering.

"It's okay, Gypsy girl." I kneeled beside her and rubbed her ears as I'd watched Christopher do, hoping to calm her, all the while inhaling the familiar scent of Percy and Celeste. I'd once read that dogs were highly perceptive of ghosts and spirits. "Don't worry, Sweetie. They're harmless." *When they aren't stirring up mischief for me, that is.*

37

Cassandra

When I awoke, it was to a half-empty bed and a quiet house. I reached down to pet my furry friend only to find her gone. I leaped from the bed and made haste down the stairs, but neither Daniel nor Gypsy were to be found. Spotting Gypsy's lead missing from the hook by the pantry door reassured me that Daniel had likely taken her for a walk, which I confirmed by calling his cell phone.

"You have Gypsy, right?" I tried to keep the worry from my voice.

"Yep. I tried to take her to the land trust trail, but she kept tugging me back. So finally, I gave in and let her lead me to where she was quite determined to go."

"Where are you?"

"The Mitchell family burial grounds," he said with a chuckle. "Gypsy felt the need to pay her respects at every stone." He uttered a mild curse before calling out to the dog, "Heel."

Had Christopher taken Gypsy there before? As I pondered that, I spied a square of newsprint under the kitchen table and had to crawl beneath the large round mass of oak to reach it. It was the article Christopher had shown me yesterday, which must have slipped from his file and fallen to the floor unnoticed.

"I just found something interesting." I frowned at the photograph.

"What'cha got there, girl?" I heard Daniel mumble to the dog. "Looks like we also found something interesting."

"What is it?"

"I'll show you when we get back to the house."

I went back upstairs and changed out of my PJs into something nice for a change. My first choice was abandoned when I couldn't get the zipper up. I really did need to stop with the Twizzlers, or my phoenix tattoo—positioned between my pelvic bones—was going to look very odd. I noticed the mint-green sundress I'd selected for the rehearsal dinner. *Might as well get some use out of it.* Besides it was cool and flowy, perfect for this hot and humid fat day.

The first thing I did when I went back down to the kitchen was to take a fat-free yogurt from the fridge, telling myself it was as good a day as any to start a diet.

When Daniel returned with a reluctant and panting Gypsy, he said, "She tried to go to the carriage house."

I stooped down to rub her ears. "He'll be back soon, baby."

I filled Gypsy's food bowl with kibble and sprinkled on a little parmesan cheese, which had seemed to do the trick last night when she initially refused her dinner. It didn't work this time. Gypsy pushed her bowl away with her nose and hopped up on the window seat, where she had a straight view to the carriage house.

"Now that's true devotion." Daniel tipped his head toward the dog. "Let's hope Christopher returns."

"Why on earth wouldn't he?" I didn't dare bring up what Laura had told me about the DNA.

He shrugged, signaling the end to the discussion, and then gave me the once-over.

"Wow." He whistled. "Don't you look nice. Going somewhere special today?"

"No, just tired of feeling grubby."

He leaned closer and said, "Mmm. You smell nice, too." When I reached for a hug, Daniel held up his hands. "Not until this *grubby man* has showered."

"A manly man, you mean." I raised on tiptoes and kissed his cheek. Before turning to set up the coffee maker, I pointed to the table. "See that article from *The Globe?*"

Not wanting to lose the original, I'd tucked it away for safekeeping and laid out the copy of the article I'd found tucked in one of the books Edgar had borrowed from Christopher.

"Christopher showed me that yesterday. It was with some papers of his mother's."

"Who's the guy circled?" Daniel squinted to read the print.

"That's the question. He evidently meant something to Christopher's mother."

"Really?" Daniel was intrigued.

Do you think you could have one of your buddies at the Bureau look into who he is?"

His gaze shifted from the article to me, but he fingered the paper and nodded. "Should be pretty easy if he's in any way associated with Ambassador Welles." He gulped down his coffee, then emptied the rest in the sink. "I'd better hit that shower and get to the courthouse. The judge renders his decision about the transcripts today." He was talking about the record of the conversation between Nicholas and Christopher.

As I watched Daniel's SUV pull away, it dawned on me that he'd forgotten to tell me what he and Gypsy had discovered in the graveyard.

* * *

After Daniel left, I put in a call to Brooks to tell him about Robyn Landers losing her keys.

"He's here," Officer Kirkpatrick told me. "But he's in conference."

I asked Lisa to have him call me and then left a message on his cell phone, telling him I was heading to town and had some urgent information.

"What's this urgent information?" Brooks asked when he called back.

"Remember that key ring that was found near the dumpster the day Lee Chambers's body was discovered?"

"Yes."

"Well, I have an idea. Can you bring the key to Land's End? I'll meet you there."

"I'm way too busy to play games, and I'm due at the courthouse soon."

I'd have to be a little more forthcoming to convince him, even if it revealed my snooping. "If I recall, the letters 'LEC' are on the label."

"I thought you didn't touch it."

"I didn't, but the other day when you knocked over all those files? A photo slipped out and I saw it." He didn't say anything, so I went on to explain my hunch. "At the time, I didn't even think about the 'LE' standing for Land's End. It wasn't until Robyn told me yesterday that she lost her keys that I was struck with the possibility it might be one of hers. 'LEC.' Land's End Cottage."

He blew out a long breath before finally saying, "Fine. I'll check it out."

Five minutes later, his cruiser pulled up next to my Miata—I was finally able to ditch the truck.

"How did you get here so fast?" he asked.

"I was already here when you called me back."

He shook his head and muttered an exasperated oath as he marched with a quick stride to the cottage door and tried the key. "Nope."

I followed Brooks around to the beach-facing side of the cottage, him telling me, "Yeah, we originally thought it was Chambers's key too, but it didn't fit with his apartment door or anything else of his."

I couldn't hide my disappointment when the key didn't work on that door either.

"Well, it was worth a try anyhow," he said, checking his phone. "But now I've got to go. I'm running late."

As we rounded the far side, I saw another door partially obscured by the outdoor shower. I recalled Christopher telling Jason on the day of the storm that it was a storage closet and was always kept locked.

"Hey wait," I called out to Brooks who was opening the cruiser door. "There's one more door here to try."

Resignedly, he came back and inserted the key and turned it, this time to the gratifying sound of an unlocking click. *Was that the "Hallelujah Chorus" I was hearing?*

Along with shelving, neatly filled with boxes of personal items, several rugs were rolled up on the floor. Brooks flipped over the corner of one and swore. He then took a photo and made a call, all the while keeping me in suspense.

"Lisa, I just sent you a photo of a carpet. Can you check to see if it's similar to the one in the Chambers case?"

My eyes must have popped, for he brought a finger to his lips and then pointed to me while sporting a very stern expression.

"Yeah, I'm still here," he said into the phone, chewing his lower lip while listening to whatever Lisa was telling him. "Okay, then. Get a forensics team out to Land's End." He nodded. "Yes, again. And I need someone to bring Robyn Landers in for a little talk."

He disconnected and said to me, "I mean it. Not a word."

"Promise." I held my hands up in surrender, though I was feeling very guilty about involving Robyn in this mess. "Could you leave me out of it when talking to Robyn?"

"How do you suppose we do that?" he asked, hands on hips.

"Robyn said the keys were lost while her boat was in dry dock. She must have reported it at the boatyard."

He rubbed his chin. "All right. I'll have David call to see if any keys have been reported missing."

"You're a gem." To show I was truly on his side, I added, "Robyn mentioned that Matthew Kleister and his investigator paid her a visit. Also, Wes has borrowed money from her."

"Interesting." He nodded but said nothing more.

"Again, please don't mention that I told you that either."

"I think we've become skilled enough to ask questions without revealing a source."

I felt a little thrill at being considered an official source for the WRPD.

"I didn't realize you and Robyn were such good buddies," he said.

"Casual friends, but I like her."

"Okay, so beat it before anybody sees you here." He sped off in his cruiser, and I got in the Miata and drove up Harbor Drive, spying some activity at The Lookout. An older couple was loading up suitcases into an SUV while Helene and Nicholas were keeping the twins and Lucas corralled and out of mischief. The only Kleister I didn't see was Matthew.

The streets of Whale Rock were busy again with people returning for the last weeks of summer, forcing me to turn up Main Street to park. I then walked back down to The Lookout.

"Hey there," I called out in greeting.

Helene gave a wave but kept her attention on the little ones. It was Nicholas who took me by the hand and dragged me toward the older couple and told them, "This is Cassie."

"We've been hoping to meet you," the woman said. "I'm Matthew's mother, Jeanne, and this is my husband, Will."

"Cassie Mitchell."

"Daniel Benjamin's wife, right?" Will asked. Now, that was a first. I couldn't wait to tell Daniel, who'd often complained about being second fiddle, constantly hearing, *"So you're Cassie Mitchell's friend."*

"Soon-to-be." I looked out toward the water. "Chantal interrupted our wedding plans."

"Storms don't stay long, but they sure do leave their mark." Will's words bore a rueful quality and reminded me of what Sister Bernadetta had said. "Lots of shattered pieces in their wake."

"It's hard to believe that a name as pretty as Chantal could be attached to such devastation." Jeanne looked over at Helene. "I read it means 'to sing' in French. Well she sang all right, blowing the lid right off some carefully guarded secrets in our world."

Will cleared his throat and gave a subtle nod toward Nicholas, who had kneeled to inspect a grasshopper.

Jeanne's hand flew to her mouth as her face reddened. To her husband she mouthed the word *sorry* and then said to me, "Will has diagnosed my condition as *say-it-like-it-is-itis*."

"Not a bad thing to have."

"Sometimes," she agreed. "But not today." She noticed that Nicholas had lost interest in the grasshopper and took his hand. "Let's go help Mommy."

"My wife means well—just forgets to put the brake on sometimes." Will raised his eyebrows and shoulders in a *what can I say* gesture. "She's right, though. The storm brought us much heartache when we thought we lost Lucas. It also opened our eyes to some secrets that were just as damaging to our family."

"How's Lucas doing?" I asked.

"We are thrilled by how well he's rebounded from the whole ordeal. Back to the ways of a normal toddler, with all the good and bad that entails." He grinned as he took in the scene of his grandchildren playing. But when his gaze focused on Nicholas, the smile faded. "I hope to eventually be able to say the same about Nicholas. A boy his age shouldn't have to grow up so quickly."

"He's a good boy," I said. "He'll be okay."

"My daughter-in-law tells me you've been a help during this awful time. We appreciate that you took an interest."

"It's the Whale Rock way," I said.

I said my goodbyes to the family and walked back to my car, thinking about what Sister Bernadetta had said about storms swallowing up secrets. Conversely, for the Kleisters, a storm had exposed their secrets. These ruminations were interrupted when I spied Jason heading toward the police station and ran to catch up with him.

"Wow, they've made good progress on the repairs," I said, walking through the front door with him and finding Deputy David Bland sitting at the station desk.

"Now that the roof's fixed, we've been able to move out of that dungeon."

I was secretly disappointed that I couldn't see who, if anyone, was being held in the cells. Matthew Kleister? Wes Creed? Thelma and Louise?

"Where's your lovely wife this morning?"

He frowned. "She's lying low today. Under the weather again."

I almost slipped with *Probably morning sickness*, but stopped myself in case Laura hadn't been able to share the good news of his pending fatherhood.

"I'll pop over and check in on her," I told him.

"That would be great." He opened his wallet and pulled out a five. "Could you stop and get her an Americano at Uncommon Grounds? Cream, no sugar."

"Sure," I told him as the desk phone rang, though I'd be getting her an herbal tea instead.

"Whale Rock Police," Officer Bland answered and after a few seconds rolled his eyes. "That's not a matter for the police, Ms. Kruk."

In addition to being a nosy Parker of the nth degree, Stella was also forever calling in complaints to the police department.

Backing out the door quickly, I could only imagine what could be Stella's crisis du jour.

38

Cassandra

I sent Laura a text: *Where are you?*

The reply text was immediate: *Courthouse. Can't talk.*

So much for being under the weather.

A few minutes later, however, she followed up with another text: *Meet me at Chocolate Sparrow. Good news.*

As I headed over to meet Laura, still debating whether to share the news about Robyn's keys with her, Daniel's Land Rover passed. I honked and he stopped and backed up.

"Finished at court?" I asked after we both opened our driver side windows.

"For now. Here's the information I found about the guy in the newspaper clipping." He handed me a printout. "Doesn't mean anything to me, but maybe it will help answer some questions."

"Thanks." I gave it a cursory look and set it on the passenger seat.

"What are you doing in town?"

"Laura's under the weather, and Jason asked me to check on her." *It was the truth after all.* Besides, Daniel would find out about the keys and carpet soon enough, and I didn't know how much Brooks planned to share about my involvement.

"She must have had a quick recovery," he said wryly. "I just saw her at the courthouse."

"Yes, I just found that out. I'm on my way to meet her now. She says she has some news. Would you know anything about that?"

"Yes, but I won't spoil it for her." He smiled and tipped his head. "Go ahead."

"Hey! You forgot to tell me what you found at the graveyard."

Daniel held up a finger and turned away. When he turned back, he handed me an envelope. "I think you'll find it to be an interesting discovery."

I held on to his fingers, and he gave mine a squeeze as someone behind us laid on the horn.

"Oops." I gave a quick wave and drove off.

*　　*　　*

I found Laura at the popular coffee and ice cream shop, nervously tapping the table like a drum. "What took you so long?"

"I was gathering some information of my own."

I decided to keep the news about Robyn's keys to myself, so instead I passed across to her the envelope Daniel had just given me. Inside was a strand of black rosary beads with an ornate silver crucifix.

"Sister Bernadetta's?" she asked, fingering the beads.

"I would assume so. Daniel found them in the family graveyard."

Laura looked down at them again and asked, "Where in the cemetery did Daniel find these?"

"He didn't say. Why?"

"I was just wondering if she dropped them or left then intentionally."

I texted Daniel: *Where did you find the rosary beads?*

A few seconds later he responded: *Barnacle Boy's grave.*

I held the phone for Laura to see, and we both shrugged.

I then showed her the document Daniel had given me and explained about *The Globe* article. "I don't think it's who Christopher was hoping it to be."

"Well, I have some good news for our friend Christopher," she said.

"He could use some."

"It's been officially determined that he played no part in Lee Chambers's death."

"That's great! How do you know?"

"Brooks told me on the condition I sit on the story for a day or two. But he's promised me an exclusive, so I'm happy to wait."

"I doubt you're happy about it." I smiled.

"I am happy about this, though." She slid a file across the table, looking around to make sure nobody was listening and whispered, "A copy of the transcripts."

"How on earth did you get this?" I whispered back.

"Not my sources. This time it was a very careless courthouse clerk." She tapped the file. "Go ahead. Open it. I'm not going to get her in trouble," she assured me when I hesitated. "I'll return it as soon as you read it and tell her it was left on the bench by my bag, and I picked it up by mistake. She'll be grateful to have it back, but I want to get it to her before she realizes it's missing."

My heart was pounding as I began to peruse the documents recording the interviews with Nicholas Kleister. The first was a record of the brief discussion he had with the child psychologist while his parents and Judge Simmons were present.

Dr. Clifton: What did you talk about with Christopher?

Nicholas Kleister: All kinds of stuff.

Dr. Clifton: Fishing?

Nicholas: Yeah. And sailing. He took me out on his boat once. It was so cool.

Dr. Clifton: What else did you talk about?

Nicholas shrugged.

Dr. Clifton: Did you talk about Lucas?

Nicholas: Maybe. I dunno. Christopher's mom was real sick.

Dr. Clifton: He told you that?

Nicholas: Yeah. We have to look after our moms.

Dr. Clifton: Is your mom sick too?

Nicholas: Yeah, but different.

Dr. Clifton: Different how?

Nicholas: (Shrugs and glances at his parents)

Dr. Clifton: Would you do anything to protect your mom?

Nicholas: (Nods) I don't want mommy to be sent away where we could never see her again.

Dr. Clifton: Who told you that?

Nicholas: mumbles (inaudible reply)

Dr. Clifton: Can you say that again?

Nicholas: Mommy. But the bad guy was talking about taking Lucas.

Dr. Clifton: Who's the bad guy?

No audible reply.

Dr. Clifton: Is that why Lucas was hiding on the boat?

Nicholas: I need to talk to Christopher. Can I? Please?

Dr. Clifton: Did Christopher ask you to keep a secret?

Nicholas: We have a pact.

"It's a good thing Lucas was found safe and Nicholas confessed to hiding him."

"Right? Otherwise it would have been a rather incriminating discussion."

I flipped the page to the second transcript, which was of the closed conversation between Christopher and Nicholas with the judge and the court reporter present.

Nicholas: I don't want Mommy to go away.

Christopher: Why would she have to go away?

Nicholas: They're going to send her away for hurting that man.

Christopher: Who did she hurt?

Nicholas: The bad man who was going to take Lucas away. But it wasn't her fault.

Judge Simmons: Can you tell us more about the man who was going to take Lucas?

Nicholas: The one with the beard.

The judge produced Exhibit A, a mug shot of Lee Chambers.

Judge Simmons: Is the man you're speaking about in one of these photos?

Nicholas: That's him. He came to our house with another man.

Judge Simmons: For the record, Nicholas has identified Lee Chambers.

Christopher: Who was the other man?

Nicholas: The one I told you about. He had a snake on his arm.

The judge produces Exhibit B, a mug shot of Wes Creed.

Judge Simmons: Is the man with the snake on his arm in one of these photos?

Nicholas: Yeah. That's him.

Judge Simmons: For the record, Nicholas has identified Wes Creed, who has a tattoo of a serpent on his right arm.

Christopher: Tell us what happened when they came to your house.

Nicholas: The guy with the beard and my mom were yelling so loud the twins started crying.

Judge Simmons: Did the man with the beard come into your house?

Nicholas nods.

Judge Simmons: You must speak your answer, Nicholas.

Nicholas: Yes.

Christopher: Where was the guy with the snake on his arm?

Nicholas: Out on the porch.

Christopher: What happened next?

Nicholas: The man with the beard said he was going to tell on mommy to daddy.

Judge Simmons: Did the man visit you before that night?

Nicholas nods.

Judge Simmons: Don't forget to speak your answer.

Nicholas: Yes.

Judge Simmons: Do you remember how many times he visited?

Nicholas: No.

Judge Simmons: Did he visit more than twice?

Nicholas: Yes.

Christopher: What happened when he visited?

Nicholas: Mommy made us all go watch TV.

Christopher: What happened the last time he came to the house that was different?

Nicholas: He made Mommy cry and they both went outside. I saw him grab Mommy, so I followed and started yelling at him to leave her alone. She told me to go back inside.

Christopher: Did you?

Nicholas: No. (Nicholas has started to cry now.)

Judge Simmons: Can you tell us what happened next?

Nicholas: Mommy was trying to stop him from leaving, but he kept walking and dragging her and hurting her. I ran at him and pushed him away, and that's when he fell down the steps. Mommy didn't hurt him. I did. But she said I should never tell anyone what happened. You won't send her away will you?

Judge Simmons: Let's take a break.

*   *   *

Judge Simmons: Nicholas, do you know what an accident is?

Nicholas: Yes.

Judge Simmons: It sounds to me like it was an accident that caused the man to get hurt. Did you mean the man any harm?

Nicholas: I just wanted him to leave us alone.

Christopher: You were protecting your mom.

Nicholas: That's what we do, right?

Christopher: Yep. That's what we do. You were very brave, Nicholas.

Judge Simmons: What did the man with the snake on his arm do after the other man fell down the steps?

Nicholas: I don't know. Mommy took me inside.

Judge Simmons: Is that why you decided to hide Lucas on the boat?

Nicholas: I put him there because they said he was worth a lot of money. (Nicholas is crying again) But when I went to rescue him, the boat was gone.

Christopher: But he's okay now. You were being a good brother.

"Wow," I said, my fingers shaking as I pushed the transcripts back across the table. "That is one heck of a lot for a child to have to deal with."

"No kidding." Laura tucked the file into her backpack.

"Has this been verified?"

"According to the Kleisters's attorney, Helene confirmed his statement. The attorney was laying the groundwork for mitigating circumstances by claiming the reason for her reluctance to cooperate with the police was because she was protecting Nicholas."

"No matter how misguided her thinking was, she was trying to protect her child."

"Among other things." She raised her eyebrows.

"And hide her drug use?"

"Yep."

"Why then was Matthew Kleister arrested?"

"He confessed." Laura shook her head. "Not knowing what Nicholas had said in the closed conference with the judge, he felt it was the only thing he could do to protect his son. Turns out, he wasn't even in Whale Rock that night."

"I guess he's the true hero in this story," I said. "But now that Lee Chambers's death has been declared accidental, what's next?"

"Well, his death may have been accidental, but he didn't put himself in that dumpster. I guess they'll have to figure out what exactly took place after Nicholas pushed him, including how everyone's DNA ended up on the rug used to dispose of his body. That includes Christopher Savage's."

* * *

When I got back to The Bluffs, I found my laptop opened to my documents as the room filled with a distinctive and familiar aroma.

"Now what are you trying to tell me?" I said to the mischievous spirits who seemed to enjoy communicating with me through more modern means. "Which one would you have me open?" I asked aloud of my spirit guides. Voila! Highlighted was Zoe's most recent email about Dr. Zane.

"You're right!" I slapped my forehead. "I never called her."

I picked up the phone and was put through to the doctor's voicemail. While I waited for a callback, I decided to fold some laundry and found that I'd never actually returned the socks and underwear and shorts that had all been soiled when Wes Creed scared Nicholas. Looking at those small socks prompted me to recall how Lucas's bloody shoe had been found at Christopher's cottage. I thought back to the conversation in which Christopher was telling Daniel and me what had happened. Could I have just uncovered the answer to Christopher Savage's DNA dilemma?

*   *   *

"Up for company again?" Daniel asked, a bit chagrinned, when he arrived home.

"Who?"

"Jason stopped by the harbor and asked if he and Laura could stop by."

"For dinner?" I opened the refrigerator, pondering what we could whip up on short notice.

"They're bringing takeout. Giuseppe's has reopened for business."

I let out a nearly orgasmic groan. "I've been dying for a Margherita pie."

"Now you can live." Daniel headed for the stairs. When Laura and Jason showed up with sparkling grape juice, I had more than a hint of the reason for the spontaneous dinner.

"We have some exciting news," Jason announced, barely through the door. He was the happiest I'd seen him in weeks. Even Gypsy had emerged from her hiding place under the table to wag a greeting.

"Don't keep us in suspense," I said, sending a surreptitious wink in Laura's direction as Daniel took the pizza boxes from Jason's grasp.

"We're pregnant!" Laura and Jason shouted in unison.

"That's great news." Daniel hugged Laura, then patted Jason's back, saying. "I'm pretty sure I have some porch cigars for later."

"When are you due?" I asked, pretending this was all news to me.

"Late February."

"A winter baby?" Daniel feigned freezing and made a face. "Brrr!"

"I'll have you know," Laura said, wagging a finger at him in response, "I just read a report yesterday that babies born in the winter are smarter and more easygoing than babies born in the summer."

"That's what they study these days?" Daniel scrunched his face in bewilderment, then asked as he opened a pizza box, "What about babies born to mothers who eat anchovies?"

"That one's for me." Jason grabbed the box away. "Margherita for Cassie and my girl, and sausage and peppers for you."

"Are you going to find out the sex?" I asked.

"We're divided on that one. Still working through it." Laura smiled up at Jason as he popped the cork on the sparkling grape juice.

"Cheers!" Daniel rejoiced, though not once did he look at me. I wondered if he was also thinking about our earlier talk.

My phone chimed while the pizza was being divvied up.

"Be right back." I held up the phone and walked into the library, Gypsy following at my heels. "Hey, Christopher. Thanks for calling me back."

"Is Gypsy okay?"

"She's fine, though missing you." I reached down to pet her head. "How's your father?"

"Better than expected." That was all he offered. "What did you call about?"

"I need to know if you remember something."

"Okay, what?"

"When we first met, you had a bandage on your hand. How did you get hurt?"

"I cut it chopping vegetables with one of Land's End's kitchen knives."

"Did that happen before or after you bandaged up Lucas's foot the day he cut it?"

"Before, I think." A few seconds later he said, "Actually, I'm certain it was before."

"Try to remember exactly what you did before and after you bandaged Lucas's foot."

"I don't understand what you're getting at here." His frustration was palpable.

"Humor me, please? Step by step."

There was a long pause before he began to recount what he recalled about the incident.

"Lucas slipped while climbing on the rocks and cut his foot on a shell. I was sitting on the cottage deck when Nicholas brought him to me. Lucas was crying. I walked over to the clothesline and grabbed a towel to wipe away the sand and wrap up his foot. I had Nicholas hold it tight while I went inside for some bandages. I came back and put some ointment on the cut and bandaged it up."

"What color was the towel?"

"Blue. Every towel in Land's End is blue. It must be Robyn's favorite color."

"Then what? And try to be as specific as possible."

"Let's see. I put his socks back on. I then went to get the beach cart to give them a ride back up to their house."

"Did you take the towel with you?"

"Take it where?"

"To get the cart."

"Um, yeah. I threw it over the outdoor shower door."

"Do you remember what you did with that towel later? Maybe you washed it?"

He paused to consider the question. "I'm sorry, I don't remember."

"Where's the outdoor shower located?"

"Between the carport and the storage room."

"Then what did you do?"

"I took the beach cart down from its hook and brought it back to the boys and lifted Lucas into the cart."

"Where were his shoes?"

"I thought Nicholas was carrying them, but obviously not. Or they fell off. I wasn't paying that much attention. I was just trying to get two small kids back home."

"Okay, thanks. This has been helpful."

"Helpful how?"

"I can't say yet."

"You must have a theory."

"It's such a long shot, Christopher. I'd rather wait until I'm on firmer ground with this."

"A long shot, huh?" His tone was wary.

"Yes, but one I still believe is worth betting on."

* * *

I was distracted as the four of us munched on pizza, chatting idly about Laura and Jason's plans to look for a different place to live.

The conversation eventually drifted to the Lee Chambers case.

"Brooks told me after the hearing today that the death was ruled an accident," Laura said, casting a furtive look in my direction.

"We still have some details to work out." Jason's tone was cautious.

I worried Laura would try to steer the discussion toward the subject of the transcripts. Sliding my plate aside and leaning my elbows on the table, I said, "I can't help but wonder what will happen to that family."

"I doubt that marriage will survive," Jason said, finishing off one last slice of pizza. "It seemed to be on shaky ground to begin with."

"Not all couples are meant to be together," Daniel said. I couldn't argue as both Daniel and I had one failed marriage each under our belts. He pushed back from the table and began collecting the dishes. "Jason and I will clean up."

When the kitchen was as sparkling as two men can leave it, they retired to the porch with their stinky cigars. I had to smile as Jason started coughing.

"Your husband is not broken in on cigars."

"And I don't want him to be," Laura said, holding her nose. "Definitely not with a baby around."

"I don't think you need worry." I peeked out the window to the porch. "He's looking kind of green."

"Is something bothering you?" Laura asked and then lowered her voice. "I'm not prying, it's just, there seemed to be a little tension between you and Daniel tonight."

"We're both really tired." I smiled. "Don't worry about me. You've got other things to think about now."

"It doesn't mean I can't be available if you need a friend."

"I'll keep it in mind, but truly, everything's fine." Though I couldn't ignore the calling-card scent of Percy and Celeste, as the room suddenly filled with the acrid scent of burnt sugar.

* * *

Laura and Jason departed, taking their aura of happiness with them. Daniel claimed exhaustion and went to bed while I took Gypsy for a moonlight stroll. I punched in Brooks's number and waited. After the seventh ring, he finally answered.

"Is it too late to call?" I asked.

"No, but your timing isn't great." He kept his voice low, leaving me guessing whether he was working a case.

"This will be quick."

"What have you got?"

"Was a blue towel found with Lee Chambers's body?"

39

Cassandra

The Bluffs ~ Present day

I t had been two weeks since the storm hit Whale Rock, and Laura's article was being published in the weekend edition of the *Cape Cod Times*. We'd invited her and Jason over to celebrate, but once again my cupboard was bare. Daniel had promised to cook if I did the shopping, so I made a mad dash to Orleans for some special ingredients. Now that people were starting to return after the storm, the grocery store shelves were emptying faster than they could be restocked. But I managed to purchase what I needed.

After the marketing was finished, I navigated a shortcut, to avoid Route 6, which took me past Wizards, the dive bar where I'd met Teddy last year. Lo and behold, there was his gray Jeep. I slowed, considering I might pop in and join him in a nice cold beer. That's when I spied the WRPD cruiser at the other end of the parking lot, where Teddy and Brooks were engaged in what appeared to be a serious discussion. Both men had their arms folded, standing with the same *don't screw with me* posture. What I wouldn't give to be listening to that conversation. Teddy brushed aside his dark blonde hair in that very familiar way, and that's when it hit me. *Oh my God! How had I missed it for so long?*

I drove home in a distracted fog as images passed through my mind of all the similarities between the two men. For as long as I've known Teddy, I've been trying to figure out who he reminded me of.

I did a quick approximation of Teddy's age and calculated the timing of a potential love connection between Brooks and Theo Howell. Now at least Zoe's reactions to the woman made sense. My dilemma was figuring out just who I should ask about this epiphany of mine. Certainly not Zoe. Lu had already shut me down once. Probably not good timing to ask Brooks either. Would he have confided in Daniel? Doubtful. I had no time to ponder this revelation further as I had offered to be Daniel's sous chef.

*　*　*

"Here's to your first byline on a big story." I raised my glass of sparkling water.

"I must admit, it is exciting." Laura was glowing, but who knew if it was more from her pregnancy or this milestone in her career. "I couldn't have done it without Brooks."

"Nice of you to give credit where it's due," Jason deadpanned.

"Well, I certainly never got a peep from you."

"It's part of our deal." He gave her a serious look. "We don't talk about work."

"At least you have plenty of other equally important topics to discuss these days. Baby names, which type of jogging stroller to buy . . ."

"Where to live," Daniel added.

Laura and Jason looked at each other.

"We can tell them," Laura nudged.

"I suppose we can trust you guys not to outbid us," Jason said with mock reluctance. "We've put an offer on the Parker place."

"That's one of my favorites!" The home was located just on the outskirts of town. Private but still walkable. "Convenient to the station."

"That might be as much a curse as a blessing." He dipped his head in dramatic fashion before adding knowingly, "But my bride fell in love with it, so what's a man to do?"

"It will be great," Laura said, dismissing her husband's worries. "You'll be able to pop home for lunch, visit me and the baby. You'll see."

"After all the hours I've put in during these past two weeks, I'll be taking Brooks up on his promise of paternity leave."

"You deserve it," Daniel said.

"Is the case almost wrapped up?" I asked.

"The plea deal for Helene Kleister is still being worked out, to her benefit with the strong-arming of her parents' law firm." Jason shook his head in dismay. "Brooks was hoping for reckless endangerment, but she'll probably go to rehab instead of serving any time."

"Her story is that she wanted to call nine-one-one to report the fall, but Wes Creed intervened and convinced her otherwise," Daniel said, indicating he was still in the loop.

"Courtesy of some blackmail, which Helene paid," Jason added with a smirk.

"What will happen to Wes?" I asked.

"Let's see: perjury, covering up a crime, blackmail, and interfering with the investigation?" Jason pretended to add up the list.

"Threatening a witness?" Laura added. Handwriting analysis indicated that Wes Creed had penned the menacing note to Zack Renner.

"Two witnesses," I said, reminding them of the incident on our porch. "He had Nicholas petrified."

"Creed will do time," Daniel stated confidently. "He also continued to supply Helene with her Adderall after Lee Chambers was gone."

"What about the kidnapping charges?" Laura wanted to know.

"Creed adamantly claimed no involvement but admitted that Chambers talked about it. Though he says they ultimately decided kidnapping was too risky. So instead they went with blackmail, threatening to reveal Helene's drug problem."

"A deadly move as it turned out." I shivered, picturing the scene in my mind.

Forensics had been able to reconstruct the scene. Lee Chambers had been standing at the top of the stairs and lost his balance when Nicholas shoved him away from his mother. Damage to the railing, which had previously been blamed on the storm, was now determined to have happened during the fall. Miraculously, a tuft of hair had become tangled in the railing and had not been blown free by high winds. Even after the storm, there remained latent blood-stains on the revetment wall near the bottom of the stairs, where Lee Chambers's head had landed.

"Poor Nicholas," I said. "Not only did he feel responsible for a man's death, but there he was trying to save his little brother; I can't imagine his terror when he went to retrieve Lucas only to find the ship had sailed."

"Then to hold on to the secret about Lee Chambers's death." Laura lifted her hands dramatically. "What was his mother thinking?"

I paused a moment to reflect on how badly that might have ended.

"Not to defend her drug use, but four kids under six are a lot to handle."

Laura looked down at her belly. "I'm worried about adjusting to one."

"You'll be a natural." I had no doubt Laura would breeze through all the challenges from teething to potty training, with Jason right at her side.

"Nicholas will be starting counseling soon," Daniel assured us.

"He'll need it," I said.

"Those poor children." Laura held a protective hand over her belly.

"Not everyone is cut out for raising children," Jason said.

Daniel raised his eyebrows in a knowing way, causing me to tense. Had he confided in Jason his reluctance to start a family?

"The senior Kleisters are going to move in with Matthew and the kids for a while. They seem like steady, sensible folks."

"I have a feeling Christopher will play a role as well," I said.

"You've been in touch?" Daniel asked, narrowing his eyes, in what? A hint of jealousy perhaps?

"Only when he called to see if Gypsy could stay on a few more days." The dog nudged my hand at the sound of her name. "He's very grateful for how things concluded on his behalf."

"No kidding he's grateful. To you," Jason said to me. "Good job with the towel."

"A long shot and a lucky guess."

"Lucky for Savage, for sure," Daniel added.

As I'd suspected, a blue towel had indeed been found when Lee Chambers's body was discovered, a detail Brooks had kept very quiet. Fortunately for Christopher, the towel had been the sole source of his DNA, which had been easily explained by his actions and corroborated by Wes Creed, who admitted he'd taken the rug from the storage closet at Land's End. He'd grabbed the blue towel from the outdoor shower to wipe away Lee's blood from his hands and later wrapped it around the dead man's head before rolling up the body in the rug.

"Was it ever determined how all the Kleisters's DNA came to be on the rug?" Laura leaned in, drooling for details.

"They presented as human hair strands, none of which had originated from the rug itself," Daniel explained, having been involved in that aspect of the case. "Helene's hairs could have transferred at any point of her physical interaction with Chambers, whereas strands of Nicholas's hair became snagged by one of Chambers's buttons when he pushed him. According to his mother, he had slammed the man head first."

"What I want to know," I said, "is how Wes Creed managed to get the rug from that storage closet without being noticed by Christopher."

"Luck played a hand in that," Jason answered. "He arrived just as Christopher was leaving to walk his dog. The door to the cottage was left unlocked, which allowed him to sneak in for the spare key and take the rug without being noticed."

"The key that was found by the dumpster," I said, feeling the eyes of both Daniel and Laura on me.

"Yep. He admitted that he'd lost it but had no idea where," Jason continued. "He looked everywhere, but when it was never reported, he thought he was in the clear."

"He's a sloppy criminal," Laura observed.

"Not a very bright one either," Daniel said, shaking his head. "How could he imagine it wouldn't be discovered that the rug came from Robyn's house?"

"I guess he thought the dumpster would carry the body away and get lost in some landfill," Jason said. "Heartless creep."

"Did Robyn report the rug missing?" Laura asked.

I tensed at this question, wondering how much Jason knew about my involvement.

"According to Brooks, a set of keys went missing when Robyn's boat was dry-docked during the storm. She went back to the cottage to look for her spare keys and found that some others were missing as well. After confronting Wes, she had a funny feeling, so she came forward and reported it."

My heart melted a little. Brooks had managed to keep me out of it while not compromising his principles or the investigation.

"If I were Robyn Landers, I'd have been freaking out." Laura mock-shivered.

"She was nervous about being implicated and offered to do whatever she could to help us."

"Good thing you spotted that key ring near the dumpster," Laura said.

"It was the key"—I flashed a grin—"to solving the mystery."

"Pun intended?" Daniel asked, rolling his eyes.

"Always."

40
Cassandra

"Cassandra?" I'd nearly walked past Lu Ketchner, dressed to kill as usual.

"Just who I was hoping to run into," I told her.

She arched her perfectly tweezed brows. "You have something to exhibit?"

"You have a one-track mind, Lu." I shook my head. "No, that's not what I wanted to see you about."

She narrowed her eyes in a practiced way to prevent the formation of crow's feet while waiting for me to gather my courage. "Well then, what is it?"

"Did everyone but me know that Brooks is Teddy's father?" I blurted out.

"I don't know what you're talking about." Her usually smooth forehead crinkled convincingly, making me question my presumption.

"Yeah, right."

"Why do you think that?"

"Just take a look at them."

She shrugged. "I've seen Teddy *maybe* twice since I met him at your exhibit last year."

"He's Theo Howell's son. Zoe told me Theo and Brooks had a fling back in the day."

Lu blinked quickly, as if images of the past were clicking through her head. But all she said was, "Ahh."

"I just can't believe nobody ever told me."

"This could be a figment of that overactive imagination of yours, which I love by the way when it's coming through a brush and onto a canvas. But you're being dramatic, Cassie."

"That's rich! If there's drama here, it lies in Zoe's quick disappearance all those years ago." That silenced Lu, so I continued my mini-rant. "Not to mention it would have explained a lot about her reasons for leaving Whale Rock."

"Trust me, it would only have explained a small part of your sister's history." Lu placed her hands on her hips. "Look, I don't enjoy turbulence when I'm flying, and I certainly don't expect it when I'm on terra firma. But for some reason, when it comes to you and your sister, it's always a bumpy ride."

With that, she bid adieu, leaving me even more curious about Zoe's Whale Rock past.

I was itching to find out the truth about Brooks and Teddy and decided my best bet was to pry it out of Evelyn. When I arrived at Hilliard House, I found the inn eerily quiet, making the old-fashioned counter bell sound even more startling. Evelyn came scurrying out, wiping her hands on the tattered apron she wore when baking.

"Morning, Cassie." She motioned me to follow. "I've got some muffins in the oven."

"Where is everyone?" I asked, trailing her into the kitchen.

"George is at Costco, restocking supplies." She opened the oven door to test one of the muffins with a toothpick before sliding the rack back in and resetting the timer. "We'd donated just about everything we had: toilet paper, paper towels, all our canned goods."

"Where are all your guests?"

"The AC went on the fritz during the storm, and with this heat?" She made a fanning gesture. "We needed to make sure it was up and running before we welcomed anyone back."

"Feels cool in here today."

"It's finally working. Hallelujah!" She cracked open the oven door for another peek, then removed two large trays of muffins, filling the room with a most intoxicating aroma. "We'll be full again tomorrow."

"Those smell yum."

"Cranberry walnut. We'll each have one when they cool." She pointed her chin toward the small table in a quiet kitchen corner reserved for her and George and filled two cups with coffee. "I am so ready for Whale Rock to return to normal."

"Were you able to see the Kleisters before they left?" I asked as she set one cup in front of me.

"Briefly." She shook her head. "What a long road they have in front of them."

I nodded.

"And that other mess?" She took the chair across from me. "Homicides aren't good for business."

"The Lee Chambers case is almost all tied up I'm told." I then segued to my primary subject of interest. "Brooks needs a vacation."

"No kidding. I can't recall the last time he took any time off."

"He also needs a love interest. Do you know if he's dating anyone?" I asked casually.

"I'm not sure." Evelyn slowly stirred cream into her coffee. "Brooks has always kept that part of his life private. It's touchy considering his history with Zoe."

"He's not seeing Theo Howell again, is he?"

Evelyn's shocked expression was telling.

"Look, I know Teddy Howell is Brooks's son." Might as well cut to the chase.

"Who told you?" she asked. "Surely not Zoe?"

"No, but why *would* she keep such a secret from me?"

Evelyn peered at me suspiciously. "If it wasn't Zoe who told you, then how did you find out?"

"I figured it out. I'm only embarrassed that it took me so long. Anybody with eyes can see how much Teddy looks like Brooks. They even have similar mannerisms. If Teddy had inherited the famous

Kincaid chuckle, there'd be no denying it." I took a sip of coffee before delving deeper. "What about Teddy? Does he know?"

She nodded, then stood and walked to the oven and brought back two muffins.

"Zoe tells me Theo never married." I peeled off the paper lining of my still warm muffin and took a bite. "Mmm."

"You have spoken to her about this?" In a reflexive gesture, Evelyn placed her hand on her heart.

"Teddy came up in conversation a couple of times. Zoe made a few comments of the green-eyed monster variety, which piqued my curiosity. She left the rest for me to figure out on my own. I think she wanted me to know but didn't want to be the one to tell me."

"You could be right." She tilted her head thoughtfully, popping a bite of muffin into her mouth.

"Did Mama and Papa know?"

"Are you kidding?" Evelyn's eyes widened. "Only the inner circle knew. And Brooks and Theo, it goes without saying."

"So how did this all happen?"

"You need to promise you'll keep this between us." She was in damage control mode.

"I won't say anything." Though I thought it would inevitably come out. That it had remained a secret this long in such a small town was just short of impossible. I gave a nudge to keep her talking. "If I understood Zoe's past better, I think it would help our relationship."

Evelyn's forehead puckered. Finally, she said, "You have a point. We've always thought of you as Baby Cass. You were so much younger, and we felt a responsibility to protect you."

"Look at me, Ev." I pointed dramatically at my face. "I'm a grown woman. I deserve to know what happened."

"I suppose you do." She was gazing into her coffee cup. "But where do I start?"

"The beginning?" I suggested.

"It was the beginning of the end. The end of our own age of inno-cence." She sighed, her expression mingled resignation and regret. "It was so long ago, and yet I remember it like yesterday." She took in a deep, resigned breath and began. "Zoe and Brooks broke up right before our senior year of college. I don't even remember what the fight had been about, but it had lasting ramifications."

"Is that when Theo entered the picture?"

She sighed sadly. "It was the briefest of flings."

Apparently not brief enough.

"Anyhow, Brooks and Zoe made up during Thanksgiving break, and we were all relieved and preparing for their happily-ever-after. Brooks had dropped hints of a proposal on New Year's Eve."

"But it wasn't to be."

"No. By the time Zoe came back home for Christmas, Brooks had learned of Theo's pregnancy and that he was the father."

It was the confirmation I'd been seeking, but hearing it made it a wrenching reality.

"Poor Zoe. She must have been devastated."

"I think it was even worse for Brooks."

"Why didn't he marry Theo?" It surprised me Brooks wouldn't choose the honorable path.

"He offered, but Theo refused. Brooks never confided in us about the arrangements he and Theo made, but we assumed he'd agreed to step aside since he was never involved in Teddy's life while he was growing up. I'm sure he must have had mixed emotions. Not wanting to abandon his son and yet free to return to Zoe."

"But he didn't."

"It was too late. Too much irreparable damage." Evelyn was looking at me intently, probably assessing how much more she should say. I sent her a pleading look. "You must *never* give Zoe an inkling that you know. It would kill her."

"Promise." I crossed my heart. "Our relationship is complex, and I find her incredibly annoying at times, but I would never do anything to intentionally hurt my sister."

"Not a word to anyone." She pointed a finger at me, accentuating each name with a jab in the air. "Not Brooks. Not Teddy. Not Lu. Not even Daniel. Nobody."

"I will never repeat what you tell me to another living soul."

She hesitated for a long time, making me wonder if she was reconsidering, and then finally said, "In the midst of all this, Zoe found out she too was pregnant."

Was my gasp audible?

"It had happened when they got back together at Thanksgiving. Your parents didn't know. She never even told Brooks."

"My God. How horrible for her." My eyes were stinging, but I blinked back the tears. I had only been a kid myself then, but I felt awful that I'd had no idea.

"It was," she agreed. "As you can work out, your sister chose to terminate the pregnancy. I went with her to a clinic in Boston. It was New Year's Eve. The night Zoe should have been sporting a sparkling engagement ring, she was lying on a cold sterile examination table in an abortion clinic, sad and frightened."

I couldn't get my head around Zoe's decision to have an abortion. Zoe, who had always dreamed of a house full of children, who had tried but never became pregnant with Oliver.

"I was the only other person who knew." Evelyn spun her coffee cup absently. "I always suspected your Granny Fi found out, but I couldn't be sure."

I knew Zoe had held some type of grudge against our grandmother; it wouldn't be surprising if this drama was at the root of the animosity. It would also explain why Granny Fi had been so quick to escort me to the Planned Parenthood clinic for birth control when she learned of my own early sexual antics.

"Do you think the abortion did some damage? Could it have been the cause of her infertility?" I asked, wanting and not wanting to know the answer.

Evelyn rubbed her forehead pensively. "I doubt the fertility docs would have suggested IVF if there'd been some damage."

"Zoe went through in vitro fertilization?"

"She never told you?"

"Another of the many secrets my sister kept from me through the years." I did not say anything about Zoe's miscarriages, in case it was another secret my sister held onto. "The Mitchell Family Curse strikes again," I said, only half-sarcastically. "So when did Teddy and Brooks connect?"

Evelyn sipped her coffee. "Several years ago, Teddy became involved with an unsavory crowd. Theo asked Brooks to get involved. She thought he'd be a helpful influence."

"It's funny." I shook my head. "Ever since I met Teddy, I've been trying to figure out who he reminded me of. There's so much of Brooks in him, now I can't believe it took so long to make the connection."

"They both inherited the handsome gene for sure."

"Does Lu know that Teddy is Brooks's son?" I was curious if she'd been genuinely surprised when I asked her, or a very good actress.

"She knew about the fling and the breakup, but she was studying art history in Europe at the time." Evelyn tipped her head from side to side. "She may not know everything."

I found this difficult to fathom. Lu, Zoe, Brooks, Evelyn, and her husband George had always been such a tight-knit group of friends.

"I can tell by your face that you're skeptical." She tapped fingernails on the side of her coffee mug, chewing thoughtfully on her lower lip. "Look, Zoe made it a taboo subject, and George and I have always tried to honor her need to forget and move on. We never spoke of it again."

"Until now," I said.

"That's right."

"At least Brooks is finally a part of Teddy's life."

"I don't think it's a walk in the park quite yet for either of them. More of a work in progress."

A quick replay of the interactions I'd witnessed between the two men brought to mind Teddy's hostility toward Brooks. I felt a sudden ache in my heart. Chalk up one more tragic tale of woe for Whale Rock.

Evelyn reached across the table for my hands, and I gave hers a squeeze.

"As hard as the truth can be to know, sometimes it's the only way to heal."

"Now you sound like your Granny Fi." Evelyn winked, lightening the mood a bit.

"Really, thank you for telling me."

"Back to your original question about Brooks's dating life . . ." Evelyn made a sour face. "I *have* heard that he's been spending an unusual amount of time with Theo."

"I know he's been helping Teddy convince his mother about a career choice," I told her. "Maybe it's as simple as that. At least I hope. I'd love to see Brooks and Zoe back together one day."

"With everything that's been going on these past two weeks"— Evelyn lifted her shoulders—"I haven't had an opportunity to talk with your sister. Is she going ahead with the divorce?"

"I really don't know what's going on with that," I lied.

We heard the sound of George coming back from his Costco adventure. Having just learned the tragic story of Zoe and Brooks's past, I wasn't up for idle chitchat, so I slipped out the front door.

It truly was a gift Evelyn had given me. I felt I now understood how there had been more to Zoe's fleeing Whale Rock than the curse against our family. It broke my heart to think of all she had dealt with alone: the fear, the betrayal, the loss.

At home, I took some time with Mama's journals. Gypsy curled up at my feet on the porch as I caressed the pages of my mother's writings. She wrote of the devastation resulting from each of her many miscarriages, about her own obsession with the Mitchell family curse, and of the terrible smells in the house that nearly drove her mad. But I was more convinced than ever that the stench had been Percy and Celeste's deep expression of grief. First, all those lost Mitchell baby boys through Mama's miscarriages. Then Zoe's baby taken by an abortion. In their deep distress, I suspected Percy and Celeste had emitted an egregious odor to match their own misery.

I wiped away the wetness from the tear that had spilled onto the final page. There was much more to learn, but not from the journal I held on my lap, which ended abruptly. There must be another journal, or journals, but I wouldn't push for it just yet. Knowing all the heartache my sister had experienced, I vowed to be more patient and understanding.

I was jarred from my deep fog of contemplation by the vibration of my phone against my hip. Perhaps psychic abilities were also in our genes.

"Good morning, Zo-Zo. I was just thinking of you. You'll be happy to know I have an appointment with Dr. Zane."

"I'm glad I don't have to nag you anymore."

I updated her on everything that had happened in the aftermath of the storm, at least all that I was privileged to tell.

"I need to tell you something, Zoe. Something that may be hard for you to talk about."

She hesitated before saying, "Okay."

"I'm sorry that I've bugged you about Brooks. I didn't understand just how delicate the subject was until recently." I took in a deep breath. "When you brought up Theo Howell and my friend Teddy being her son, it made me very curious. It took me a while, but I eventually figured out that Brooks is his father."

"Zo-Zo?" I said after an awkward silence.

"I'm still here." She cleared her throat before asking, "How did you manage to find out?"

"Lots of little hints since you mentioned it. Mostly, Teddy has inherited Brooks's good looks. I can send you a photo."

"No! I don't need to see a photograph of his . . . love child," she spit out the words.

"Zoe, it's ancient history now."

A cynical laugh followed. "You say that as if Brooks and Theo's association is in the past."

"They do share a child, so I imagine there's been the need for them to communicate over the years," I said to placate her. "I do know he's been going to bat for Teddy with Theo on some issues."

"What's this Teddy like?"

The question surprised me, but I told her, "He's an awfully nice kid, Zoe."

This was met with more quiet.

"This wouldn't bother you if you didn't still have feelings for Brooks, and I have no doubt he still pines for you. Otherwise, he'd have moved on by now, and he certainly wouldn't be calling you."

She gave a little huff. "Might I remind you I'm still married."

"A marriage that's about to end," I shot back. "Regardless, if you let go of the disappointments of the past, maybe you can be open to the possibilities of a future with Brooks."

"You're sounding more and more like Granny Fi every day." I hoped that was a smile I heard in her tone.

"I will take that as a compliment."

41

Cassandra

"Y ou'll hate saying goodbye to Gypsy," Laura said, a few days later as we walked along the beach behind Whistler and Gypsy.

"I know. I've grown attached to her." The two dogs ran playfully ahead; it was a shame it had taken them so long to make peace, especially now that Christopher was coming back for Gypsy. He was meeting later today with Edgar and Laura, in keeping his promise to help them with the book, and had been kind to include me.

"What was the business that kept Christopher in New York?" Laura asked.

"Remember those sealed documents from his early years of teaching? There's a hearing."

She frowned. "But the Whale Rock cases have been resolved."

"Yes, however, the dean of Bridgewater Academy had been questioned, and that apparently brought Christopher's past under scrutiny. The school's administration put in a request to see the records."

Fortunately, Tyler Stendall had finally been persuaded to give his permission to unseal the documents. Christopher told me that it had been Zach Renner who'd pushed Tyler to finally come out and admit the truth. As Granny Fi used to say, *"You'll be happier being yourself instead of pretending to be someone else."*

"I hope it works out."

"Me too. He's a good guy."

"Hey, isn't that Robyn?" Laura pointed to where Gypsy and Whistler were greeting another beach walker.

"What gave her away? Those legs?" I waved as we got closer.

She was giving the dogs her full attention and they were loving it. "I think I'll miss Whistler more than anyone," she told us.

"Are you going somewhere?" Laura asked.

"I'm selling Land's End. The realtor said it will sell quickly."

"No doubt. It's a great location." I gazed out toward the bay and then back to Robyn. "Whale Rock will hate to see you go."

"No offense, but after everything that's happened?" She wrinkled her freckled nose in a habit. "I think it's time to start fresh somewhere else."

"You know Christopher is coming back today?" I said.

She nodded. "I'm letting him stay through Labor Day. I'll wait until he leaves to put it on the market."

"You've been a great neighbor," Laura told her. "Keep in touch. Let us know where you land."

"We'll have to plan our girls' night before you leave."

"I could use a good stiff drink." She laughed, then promised to call soon, but I had my doubts I'd hear from her again.

*　*　*

When Christopher arrived later that morning, Gypsy leaped up into his arms, licking his face with as much love and devotion as any creature could show for another.

"It's okay," he told her over and over again while Sister Bernadetta watched the lovefest. After Gypsy finally settled, the threesome walked over to where I'd been waiting on the porch.

"Welcome back to The Bluffs," I told them.

"Do you mind if I take Gypsy for a walk to your family graveyard?" Christopher asked. I suspected a visit would be more meaningful now that he knew that Barnacle Boy was the Antonio his mother had been trying to tell him about near the end of her life.

"Of course," I said, then sent a questioning look to Sister Bernadetta.

She gave a subtle shake to her head and asked, "Mind if I sit here with you while Christopher goes?"

"Not at all. I'll get us something cold to drink," I said after she took a rocker and began fanning herself with an issue of *Ocean Navigator.*

"They say this heat wave will break soon." I set a tall glass of lemonade on the side table.

"Christopher needs time alone with Antonio." She pointed westward. "Looks like storm clouds out there."

We sat in a respectful silence until she said, "It was another storm that brought great sadness to our family."

I unfolded the copy of the fifty-year-old article about the shipwreck that happened in Cape Cod Bay a few weeks before Barnacle Boy washed up on our shores. I handed it to her and asked, "Was it this storm?"

She quickly perused the words and passed it back to me and nodded.

"Were you there?" Laura, Edgar, and I had only been able to piece together small fragments of the story.

"No. I had secretly entered the novitiate and had begun a period of seclusion. What I know I have learned from my brother and a friend of his. The two men who are mentioned in that article." She lifted the glass, carefully wiping the condensation with her napkin before taking a drink. "My sister came to Whale Rock last year, trying to find the grave."

"Seriously?"

"It was right before her treatment began, and she'd been visiting me in Boston. It was only later that I learned she'd hired one of those Uber drivers." She gave a sad little shake to her head. "But they never found your home."

"It's a little out of the way," I said.

"One of the articles mentioned Kinsey Cove as the location where Antonio's body had been found." She turned to look at me. "Your father was the one to find him?"

I nodded.

"She had the driver take her there. That's where she finally said goodbye to her son. Christopher's brother. My sister told me this the last time I saw her. That's when she asked me to find his grave."

"The wildflowers were from you?"

"Yes."

"The article didn't mention that a little boy had been on the boat. No distress signal had been sent. No child reported overboard. No child reported missing at all." I knew it wasn't fair to be asking these questions, but I couldn't help myself. "I'm sorry if you think I'm prying, but it's hard to explain what"—I stopped myself from saying Barnacle Boy—"that lost little boy means to me. My grandmother used to tell me stories about him when I was little, and it's almost as if he's been a part of my family all these years."

"Your family had been so gracious to make sure a lost soul had a final home." She offered that kindly smile of hers. "I shall tell you what I know, as much as I can before Christopher returns."

She took in a deep breath and began. At the end of the concise recounting, I knew the condensed version of Renata's early life and how she later became Renée. I'd learned about the relationship she'd had with the wealthy Phillip Welles and the resulting pregnancy. It had been threats from the Welles family that had frightened her into hastily forming a plan to keep Antonio safe.

"My brother, Vito, came up with a plan of escape." Sister Bernadetta wiped at the wetness on her cheeks. "It ended badly."

"How did you find out?"

"My brother's friend—Thomas was his name—finally persuaded Mother Superior to let him see me. As soon as I saw his face, I knew the news was bad." She rubbed her temples. "Not only had we lost Antonio, but my brother was gravely ill. Vito had searched for hours that first day and for many days afterward. He wouldn't even leave to tell our sister. He sent Thomas, who told me Renata had been hysterical—understandably so—her horrific screams sending passersby scurrying away. And then Vito had become too ill to go see her, a serious lung infection. When I finally made it to his bedside, he was delirious."

"How terrible for both of them."

"My sister told me later that she couldn't have borne seeing our brother. It had become unthinkable to face anyone who knew what had happened to her son. Then one day she simply slipped away."

"To New York," I said. "The perfect place to lose oneself in the anonymity of crowds."

"Yes, and where she could hide from her most haunting regret: not allowing the Welles family to have Antonio, because then her son at least would have lived."

"I can't imagine living with such a burden."

"As hard as it was to lose her, I understood that leaving had been her salvation."

I felt a kinship with Sister Bernadetta. Hadn't my sister done the same—left our home and family to save herself?

She pulled from her simple pocketbook a folded piece of paper and handed it to me.

"A copy of Vito's letter?" I asked after reading the first line, now translated to English.

She held her hand over mine and nodded toward the ridge where Christopher and Gypsy were approaching. Sister Bernadetta walked toward her nephew, leaving me alone with the translated version of the letter I'd found when first snooping in Christopher's things.

My dear sister,

I am dying inside to write you this letter. If I wasn't so ill myself, I would come to you and offer whatever comfort I could. I can barely face each day without Antonio, and cannot imagine how difficult it has been for you without your beautiful boy.

You must believe me, had I known there was a chance of a storm so fierce, I would never have risked taking Tonio out on that boat. Thomas and I did everything we could to save our sweet boy, but we got caught by the devil and we lost. I should have come to you right away, but I was determined not to stop searching for Tonio until I could bring him to you alive and well.

Every morning, I wake wishing I could have a second chance to relive the day we lost him and make different choices. But God will not allow it. He is punishing me for my pride and my foolishness. Why he has punished you and Antonio, I cannot answer.

Some days I wish for death to take me as it almost did as I searched and searched for our Tonio. Death would relieve me of facing the awful truth. The priest Isabella has brought to me tells me it's the coward's way out. I have confessed the entire story, and he has absolved me of my sins. But I don't care what the priest says or even what God thinks. I only care that you know the truth and can find a place in your heart for me again.

Though I don't deserve your forgiveness, I beg you for it. I would give up my own life to bring Antonio back to you.

I love you,

Vito

How does one find the courage to face a tragedy as terrible as what befell Vito and Renée? The scent that surrounded me was light and sweet and comforting. I hoped my spirit guides would always be there to help protect me from such misfortune and heartbreak.

42

Cassandra

The book Edgar was writing would no longer be a work of fiction. Now that one of Whale Rock's enduring mysteries had been solved, it would instead be a true account of *The Lost Boy of Whale Rock*. He'd selected the title after I told him that's what Granny Fi and I used to call Barnacle Boy.

"There was a lot of piecing together of facts from letters and old articles. Thank goodness Isabella has been able to bridge most of the gaps." Christopher turned to where his aunt was seated beside him. "It nearly remained a mystery."

"God would have eventually brought me to you," the nun said, fingering the simple gold cross necklace she wore. His slight frown may have been a sign that he didn't share her confidence. Or perhaps it was her faith he doubted.

Over crab cakes and rocket salad, courtesy of Jimmy, Isabella told us Antonio's story, beginning with the orphaned siblings' immigration from Italy and their time in Boston. Edgar interrupted occasionally for a question or clarification, but when it came time for the dramatic ending of the story, we all remained silently rapt.

"When did Ma finally open the envelope Uncle Vito gave her in Italy?" Christopher eased his chair back.

"Not until after her cancer diagnosis. She understood it then," Sister Bernadetta told us. "It wasn't until her condition deteriorated that she became more confused. Especially about that article with the Welles family."

"I can't even imagine how your mother must have felt, learning all those years later that Antonio's body had washed ashore?" Laura had wrapped her arms around her belly, as she did more and more these days. Did all pregnant women do the same thing? A subliminal means of protecting the little beings growing within?

"I know you were against exhuming the body." Edgar hesitated a second, and before he could finish, Christopher held up both hands to stop him.

"I'm not changing my mind." His tone was defiant, but then he caught himself and softened as he went on to explain, "I feel I must honor my uncle's wishes."

Isabella pulled out another letter from her pocketbook and reverently placed it on the table. "My brother's friend Thomas sent Vito a clipping of an article about a young boy's body being washed ashore in your town. This is my brother's response."

Christopher unfolded it and read, *"Renata is gone from us as much as Antonio is. Let the boy rest in peace anonymously,"* He handed the letter back to his aunt and said, "Now that he is no longer anonymous, I'd like to leave him where he's been well taken care of over the decades."

"You misunderstand. I'm not trying to persuade you otherwise. I merely wish to explain that I've realized we needn't exhume the body to prove it's Antonio." Edgar pulled out a sheet of paper and slid it over for Christopher to see.

"What is this?" he asked before perusing the document.

"I was finally able to track down the medical examiner's report." Edgar pointed to a section. "When the boy was discovered, there was a medallion on a chain found still clinging to the body. I've spoken with some experts in the field and they've seen this before. What probably occurred was the chain became imbedded into bone, securing it."

"Was it a Saint Christopher's medal?" Sister Bernadetta asked.

Edgar nodded.

"I placed a medal around my nephew Antonio's neck the morning before they sailed." This time in the telling the sister was less emotional. "It had a distinguishing mark?"

"Yes." Edgar adjusted his glasses and scooted his chair closer to show them. "See here? They took a photo."

He showed it to Isabella, and she nodded. "The mark of the medal worker in our town."

Christopher squinted at the photo while caressing his own medal, the one given to him by his mother before she died. He showed Edgar the back of his medal. "It's the same mark."

Laura shuffled through some papers and then said, "We did some research on your mother's maiden name."

"D'Esposti?" Sister Bernadetta said.

"We learned that D'Esposti is a variation of the name Esposito, which in Italy, many years ago, was the surname given to abandoned children or those relinquished to orphanages. Probably why it's a popular Italian surname."

Christopher washed his hands over his face, evidently hit hard by the uncanny coincidence. He then checked the reaction of his aunt.

"My siblings and I were orphaned, but we were not abandoned. The people in our town kept us together." She paused, bringing her fingertips to the corner of her eyes. "Antonio is another matter."

"I once knew a boy named Jerry Esposito," Jimmy started, probably thinking it a good time for lightening the mood, but Edgar sent him a warning look, forcing him to mumble, "Never mind. It was a long time ago."

"It's a little-known bit of history." Edgar removed his glasses to rub the bridge of his nose before assuring them, "We don't have to include it in the book."

We all sat quietly for a moment while Jimmy cleared the dishes. He gave Christopher's shoulder a squeeze and said, "I just have to say, Jerry Esposito was a real peach."

What could we do but laugh? Edgar smiled fondly at his husband and asked, "Speaking of peaches, where's that cobbler you've been bragging about all morning?"

"Coming right up." Jimmy dashed over to the sideboard to dish up dessert, Gypsy at his heels.

As we all dug in, there was a chorus of "This is great!" "Yum!" "The best!" "Delish!"

Jimmy waved away the compliments, but the twinkle in his smiling eyes told how warmed he was by them.

"You're a lucky man," Christopher told Edgar. "Gypsy's quite taken with Jimmy, and she's an excellent barometer of character."

"He bribes her with treats," Edgar whispered.

"I know," Christopher whispered back, his eyes crinkling in amusement. It was amazing how the once aloof stranger had evolved into having a natural ease with us. He became serious again when he asked, "Did I mention my plans to replace the gravestone? Well, not exactly replace it, but add a new one." He turned to me and said, "As long as you're okay with it."

"You'll leave the unknown boy marker?" Edgar asked before I had a chance to give it thought.

"I don't see why it should be removed. There's a special history to it that reminds us of how the people of Whale Rock looked after him." Christopher went on to tell us his plans. "I'd like to have a stone made with Antonio's real name and dates of birth and death."

"I understand you not wanting to disturb his grave," Edgar said. "But after all these years of his being alone, I'm surprised you don't want to move him closer to your family."

"As it turns out, I may be the one moving closer to him. I'm considering buying my own little piece of Whale Rock heaven," Christopher told us. "Assuming I can find something."

"I've been real estate shopping recently, and I can tell you that beach cottages in Whale Rock are a rare find," Laura said between bites of cobbler. "They usually get handed down from generation to generation."

"You'd leave your school?" I asked, worried that the hearing hadn't gone as well as he hoped.

"Not permanently. I love my teaching position at Bridgewater Academy, but I'm thinking of buying a small cottage here."

Christopher offered a sad smile. "A refuge for my father and Aunt Isabella to heal. A place to invite my Italian cousins someday."

"In that case," I told him, "I hear Robyn Landers has decided to sell Land's End—assuming you don't feel too superstitious about going back there after what happened."

Edgar winked at me. "The Mitchell family knows all about those types of rumors."

"Hey, that's how my father was able to buy back The Bluffs." I held up my hands at Christopher's questioning look. "I'll tell you the story another time. Today is for remembering Antonio."

"And making plans for your future," Edgar added.

Christopher fingered the medal on the chain he'd replaced around his neck. "My mother may have been superstitious, but I'm not."

Jimmy raised his glass. "Then let me be the first to welcome you to Whale Rock."

43

Cassandra

The next morning, I ventured into town, the streets back to being filled with their usual summer crowds. Fortunately, the parking space behind Coastal Vintage Wares was free, though a shiver passed through me as I gazed over to where the dumpster once stood. My mission today wasn't to see Archie, but I decided to stop by to tell him what we'd learned about the St. Christopher's medal.

"You could knock me over with a feather," he said after I told him.

"It is an incredible story," I agreed.

"Thank you for telling me. Who knows which version I would've gotten first? Evelyn Hilliard's or Stella Kruk's?"

I smiled inwardly, knowing that the name Archie Stanfield was also fairly high on the list of town gossips.

"I will admit, I'm glad that Barnacle Boy is no longer unknown. All lost children deserve to be discovered."

"Such a sweet sentiment, Archie," I said. "You're the one who told us about the medal in the first place. You deserved to know."

The bell tinkled and a group of older ladies swarmed into the storm.

"Back to normal." I gave him the thumbs-up and then skirted around the group to exit the store. My next stop was Uncommon Grounds, to pick up donuts for the Whale Rock police force. Even though I knew they sometimes found me to be an annoyance, what better way to make amends?

After delivering the goodies to the break room and placing a little note by the box, I took a donut and a large coffee in to Brooks.

"Light and sweet, just like you like it." As I said the words, it jolted a memory. Teddy ordered his coffee the same. Chalk another one up for similarities between father and son!

"You have a minute for an old friend?" I asked.

"Sure thing, Cassie. Especially one who was *key* in helping to solve some recent cases." He closed up the file he'd been working on and leaned back in his chair.

"That pun is really getting old."

"So what's up?"

"You know Zoe's getting divorced, right?"

He nodded, looking suddenly wary.

"She's going to need someone to lean on."

Brooks rubbed his chin, and I could tell he wasn't comfortable with where this was heading.

"I know you have a history, but I sense there's still something there between the two of you."

He cleared his throat and leaned his arms on the desk. "My history with your sister is complicated."

"If you want a future with my sister, you're going to have to deal with some trust issue baggage from her marriage to Oliver."

"Her trust issues go back further than that."

"I know," I said. "I also know that Teddy Howell is your son," I admitted. This was met with piercing silence as he narrowed his eyes at me. I could almost see the workings of his brain as he tried to gauge what I already knew about the private areas of his life.

"Who told you?" he finally asked, sounding more wounded than angry.

"Mostly I figured it out, and others innocently filled in the small gaps."

"I can pretty much guess who those *innocents* are."

"Don't be too hard on your friends. They always have your back."

Brooks harrumphed. "No doubt, soon it'll be out there for public consumption. It would have been nice for Ted and me to share it ourselves when we were ready."

I understood exactly how he felt. But living in Whale Rock made it very hard to have a private life, especially as a prominent resident.

"Teddy's a good kid," I segued.

"He's getting there." His words belied the pride that swept across his face.

"From the moment I met him, he reminded me of someone." I was still amazed at how long it took me to make the connection. "He's a handsome guy, Chuckles."

"He is that." He raised his eyebrows. "Don't forget, his mother was Miss Massachusetts."

"That's not what I meant." He ignored the compliment, so I went on to say, "Teddy's lucky to have you in his life."

"He doesn't always see it that way," he said, returning his attention to a stack of files.

"Do any of us see things the way they truly are?" I then quoted something my Granny Fi always said: *"Mirrors don't lie, but they don't show your insides either."*

Brooks looked at me over his glasses. "When did you become such a philosopher?"

"Don't forget, I have Fiona Patrick's genes."

"She was a character, that one." He gazed thoughtfully toward the ceiling before finally adding, "My favorite was *"Don't throw the baby out with the dish water."*

"You mean bath water."

"Oh yeah." He let loose his famous chuckle, which was a joy to my ears.

"It was nice of you to give Teddy one of my paintings."

"More psychic abilities?"

"I saw it at his house. I remember at my last exhibit you purchased two of my paintings. I always wondered where the second one ended up."

"He loves it," he said while removing the lid to his coffee and blowing at the rising steam. It deeply pleased me to know both father and son had given my work a prominent place in their homes. It would please me even more if Brooks could build a world with Teddy in which Zoe might also fit comfortably. But knowing my sister, that would be a challenging proposition.

44

Cassandra

The Bluffs ~ One month after the storm

I'd returned to The Bluffs following an appointment with the genetic specialist and was greeted by the sweet burning scent of Percy and Celeste.

"Yes, I know you're pleased." For the past few weeks their signals had been all over the place, but there'd been much going on in my little world. Even once the messes—literal and figurative—left in the storm's wake had been tidied up as well as could be expected, the spirits still hovered closely. Today, I'd at last discovered why.

The ship's bell ring announced the call I was expecting. Zoe would be eager to know all the details from the appointment.

"What were the test results?" she asked immediately.

"I did test positive for a genetic abnormality," I told her while putting on the teakettle. "Your thinking was on the right track, Zo-Zo. I'm so glad you discovered the research and pushed me to be tested."

"Was there any explanation as to why Mama was able to carry you and me to term but none of the baby boys?"

"When reviewing the history, Dr. Zane said that you and I are lucky to be here. But there's no research to indicate the abnormality affects only one sex. Just a fluke of nature, I guess."

"I don't know," Zoe hedged. "We don't know whether Mama's genetic disorder was part of the curse."

I found it odd that my sister didn't want to believe in the existence of the spirits of our great-grandparents, yet she was willing to hold on to the possibility that an oath uttered a century ago still had power against our family.

"Well, we do know that Mama's many miscarriages were rooted in science," I countered. "And we shouldn't assume it was Mama who carried this defective gene. There's research that indicates the father can also be a carrier."

"Well then, if these miscarriages were caused by Papa, that strengthens the argument for the curse."

I kicked myself for not keeping that bit of scientific data to myself. "The fact is, we don't know whether this originated with Mama or Papa's family." Though I imagined one day scientists would uncover this mystery as well. "But either way, it no longer matters, Zoe. Medical advances have offered a way to beat it."

"There's a treatment?" she asked eagerly.

"Yes, and I've started the protocol."

We were both quiet for a minute. I was thinking about what Dr. Zane had told me about the somewhat experimental nature of the protocol I was on, a detail I would not share with my worrywart sister.

"Will there be side effects?"

"Fortunately, no." I left out the part about needing to be closely monitored. Especially now.

"How long will you need to be on this treatment?"

"I'm not sure," I fibbed. By my calculations, another six months.

After ending the call with my sister, I took my cup of tea into the study, where I basked in the delightful, sweet burning sugar aroma that surrounded me. Percy and Celeste were indeed happy.

"We aren't out of the woods yet," I told them. I'd need to tell Daniel first, a prospect that had me as excited as I was petrified.

"Out of what woods?" Daniel asked, startling me so that I nearly dropped my teacup.

"When did you get home?" I hadn't heard a thing.

"Just now." He came and sat next to me on the leather loveseat. "You seemed far away. Sorry to interrupt your daydreams."

"I'm always glad to see you." I reached up and placed a palm on his cheek. "Taking the afternoon off?"

"I'm worried about you." He kissed my palm and then kept hold of my hand. "I snooped in your calendar and saw that you had a doctor's appointment today."

My face flushed hot.

"Is everything okay?"

"I hope so." *It's a fact that's not going to change. Just rip off that bandage,* Granny Fi whispered in my ear, as the bolstering sweet burning scent intensified, giving me the strength to tell him, "We're pregnant."

*   *   *

After telling Daniel about the genetic disorder and how miraculous it was that our baby had survived the first precarious months before I even began the treatment, he quickly came around to the idea of a life with children.

"It appears this little person we created has a destiny to fulfill," he said after we left the next doctor's visit together, following an important ultrasound. All signs were indicating a normal pregnancy.

The relief had been joyous and staggering. I would be able to keep both the men in my life. Yes, we were going to have a boy. Daniel Mitchell Benjamin was due in March.

There'd been so many signs that I'd missed, the first being my unexpected bout of seasickness, which never before had I experienced. Now I could attribute the episode to erratic hormones and low blood sugar, both known causes of morning sickness. Clothes were getting snug, and my phoenix tattoo was comically distorted due to my expanding tummy. I could no long blame the Twizzlers; in fact, they were high on the list of my pregnancy craving foods, second only to peanut butter. The pleasant scent of burning sugar had also been inescapable—especially when Laura visited. It appeared that Percy and Celeste were as excited as we all are that our babies will arrive within a couple months of each other.

One late Sunday afternoon, I was in my studio, painting a picture for the nursery, when I received a text from Daniel: *Meet me down at Percy's Bluffs.*

Be there in five, I replied after cleaning the paint from my hands. I stood back and assessed the work in progress on my easel. The image was of a gleeful little boy being carried over the waves by two dolphins. It was my tribute to the lost boy of Whale Rock.

When I got close to the cliffs, I noticed Daniel was sitting next to a large box. As I approached, the box seemed to wobble.

"An early wedding present," he said, lifting aside the loose lid of the box to reveal the most adorable bundle of black fur.

"A puppy?" I squealed, as he placed it in my arms. "For me?"

"For us. And for little Danny Junior."

"Oh my goodness, you are the cutest thing." I nuzzled my little friend. "Where did you find him?"

"Johnny's dog had a litter of puppies right after the storm. All of them black as coal. I picked this little guy out because he was the only one with any kind of distinguishing marking." He pointed to the puppy's chin. "See the ghost of white there?"

That's when I noticed the little velvet bag tied to the puppy's collar. "What's this?"

"Your second early wedding present."

I sent him a puzzling look as I pulled at the ties of the bag.

"It was your mother's engagement ring," he told me as I peeked inside.

"Here let me," he said and then slid it onto my left ring finger.

I held out my hand to admire Mama's ring as the sun caught the glimmering diamond. I couldn't put into words the thrill it gave me to have this connection to my parents. Papa had given it to Zoe after Mama died, perhaps in hopes of bridging the divide that had formed between my sister and The Bluffs. But Zoe had never worn it.

"Your sister sent it to me. Said you should have it."

When Daniel proposed the first time, I'd insisted I didn't want an engagement ring. But this was different. I would cherish Mama's ring—for many reasons—not the least of which was that Zoe understood how much it would mean to me.

"Zoe's planning to come for the wedding," he told me.

"Really?" I remained skeptical.

"That's what she said in her note when she sent the ring."

I was overwhelmed by happiness and the scent of burning sugar.

"Does this mean you still want to marry me?" Daniel pulled me to him.

"More than anything." I was still holding the puppy when I leaned in to kiss Daniel, and we both received tickling tongue licks.

"What are we going to call him?"

"Ghost, of course."

"You're going to call a black dog Ghost?" He laughed as he scratched the puppy's chin.

"Isn't that ghost of white on his chin why you picked him?"

I smiled up at the man with whom I'd be sharing my life, thinking that maybe someday I'd tell him the real reason I chose the name. Meanwhile, I sent a wink to the mischievous spirits who always hovered closely. They knew.

ACKNOWLEDGEMENTS

A novel doesn't make it to the shelves without the thoughtful input, expert contribution, and caring touch of many other people aside from the author.

My fabulous agent tops the list. Jill Grosjean continues to be a stalwart champion, and I will be eternally grateful for her tireless effort and dedication on behalf of my writing. Over the past decade she has also become my friend.

The early readers are the bravest and more helpful than they can imagine. Cia Marion's eyes are always the first on the pages, often reading many iterations, and her suggestions are typically on target. A special thank you to *all* those who read early versions of *Storm of Secrets* and offered important feedback and encouragement.

I am fortunate to have a generous critique partner in Rosemary Dibattista, whom I met during the infancy stage of my writing journey. She is a treasure and a friend.

Shannon Jamieson Vazquez is a talented editor who skillfully opened my mind to a different vision while always respecting my ownership of the story. Thank you to all the folks at Crooked Lane Books who brought this series to life.

My friends inspire me as much as they encourage me, not to mention they are *the best* book publicists. This journey would not have been possible without their support, nor would it have been as much fun. *I love you all.* Thank you to those who graciously opened their homes to host author talks and book signing events and for introducing me to their communities.

I'm grateful to all the readers, many of whom I've met on book tours. If you are holding this book right now, thank you for taking a chance on me. Many thanks also to the book clubs who have selected my novels. For those who invited me to join them in group discussions—you have all been a delight!

To the libraries and the bookshops who've added my novels to your shelves and literally placed my books in readers' hands, none of this can happen without your help.

My mother's spirit remains with me, and her essence can be found in the pages of every book I write.

Most importantly, all my love and gratitude to you, Geoffrey. You are the best person for bouncing off ideas, especially when I stumble on plot snags and legal questions. I would never have been able to do this without your patience and tolerance of the countless hours spent with my laptop in our home's *theater of creativity.*

To learn more about Loretta Marion's books please visit:
www.lorettamarion.com